# CLOUDBURST

# Virginia Andrews® Books

**The Dollanganger Family Series**
Flowers in the Attic
Petals on the Wind
If There Be Thorns
Seeds of Yesterday
Garden of Shadows

**The Casteel Family Series**
Heaven
Dark Angel
Fallen Hearts
Gates of Paradise
Web of Dreams

**The Cutler Family Series**
Dawn
Secrets of the Morning
Twilight's Child
Midnight Whispers
Darkest Hour

**The Landry Family Series**
Ruby
Pearl in the Mist
All That Glitters
Hidden Jewel
Tarnished Gold

**The Logan Family Series**
Melody
Heart Song
Unfinished Symphony
Music of the Night
Olivia

**The Orphans Miniseries**
Butterfly
Crystal
Brooke
Raven
Runaways (full-length novel)

**The Wildflowers Miniseries**
Misty
Star
Jade
Cat
Into the Garden (full-length novel)

My Sweet Audrina
(does not belong to a series)

**The Hudson Family Series**
Rain
Lightning Strikes
Eye of the Storm
The End of the Rainbow

**The Shooting Stars Series**
Cinnamon
Ice
Rose
Honey
Falling Stars

**The De Beers Family Series**
Willow
Wicked Forest
Twisted Roots
Into the Woods
Hidden Leaves

**The Broken Wings Series**
Broken Wings
Midnight Flight

**The Gemini Series**
Celeste
Black Cat
Child of Darkness

**The Shadows Series**
April Shadows
Girl in the Shadows

**The Early Spring Series**
Broken Flower
Scattered Leaves

**The Secrets Series**
Secrets in the Attic
Secrets in the Shadows

**The Delia Series**
Delia's Crossing
Delia's Heart
Delia's Gift

**The Heavenstone Series**
The Heavenstone Secrets
Secret Whispers

**The March Family Series**
Family Storms
Cloudburst

Daughter of Darkness

# Virginia ANDREWS

# CLOUDBURST

**SIMON &
SCHUSTER**

London · New York · Sydney · Toronto · New Delhi

A CBS COMPANY

First published in the US by Gallery, 2011
A division of Simon & Schuster, Inc.
First published in Great Britain by Simon & Schuster UK Ltd, 2012
A CBS COMPANY

1 3 5 7 9 10 8 6 4 2

Simon & Schuster UK Ltd
1st Floor
222 Gray's Inn Road
London WC1X 8HB

www.simonandschuster.co.uk

Simon & Schuster Australia
Sydney

A CIP catalogue record for this book is available from the British Library

Trade paperback ISBN: 978-0-85720-789-0
Hardback ISBN: 978-0-85720-788-3
Ebook ISBN: 978-0-85720-791-3

Printed and bound by CPI Group (UK) Ltd, Croydon, CR0 4YY

# CLOUDBURST

# ❧ *Prologue* ❧

*J*ust like there are all kinds of noise in our lives, there are all kinds of silence as well.

Mrs. Caro, my foster parents' cook, is from Ballyvaughan, a small coastal village in County Clare, Ireland, and she says, "When the sea is calm, it's like the world is holdin' its breath, darlin'. It's so peaceful your heart seems to go into a slumber, and you feel so content. To me, that's the sweetest silence."

I knew that silence, too. When my mother and I were sleeping on the beach or when we sat quietly and just stared out at the ocean, I heard the same silence, and Mrs. Caro is right. It is sweet because it brings a feeling of peace and even hope to your heart.

Another silence is the silence just before sleep, when you put the lights out. Even in the Marches', my foster parents', home, this enormous mansion in Pacific Palisades, California, with all of the servants moving about and the army of workers on the property, it can get quiet enough at night to hear your own thoughts or hear the door in your mind begin to open to permit your dreams and nightmares to tiptoe into your head.

In this deep silence before I do fall asleep, my memories of my mother and me living homelessly in Santa Monica often come rushing back into my mind. They are very unpleasant memories, but try as hard as I may, I cannot forget them or keep them out. It's like trying to stop the rain with a single umbrella.

Years after my father deserted us and depression and defeat had driven my mother into alcoholism, we literally slept in a very large carton on the beach and sold my mother's calligraphy and my handmade lanyards to tourists on the boardwalk. That little money kept us barely alive until the fateful rainy night when the girl who is my foster parents' daughter, Kiera March, high on Ecstasy, drove through a red light and struck my mother and me crossing the Pacific Coast Highway. Mama was killed instantly, and I was injured seriously enough to spend weeks in the hospital recuperating from a serious femur fracture.

Oh, how silent the world was for me then.

There was the silence of tragedy but also the silence that comes with great anger and rage, when you hate the sound of your own voice and especially the sound of other voices, none of which can really make you feel any better and many of which are empty, mechanical voices without sincere compassion, voices with no particular interest in you or your welfare. You become just part of their routine, another daily statistic to be included in some report.

There is probably no deeper silence than the silence

that follows the loss of someone you love. I had suffered this silence, so I understood Jordan March's desperate search for someone new to love after she had lost her younger daughter, Alena, to acute leukemia. From what I could see, because she and her husband, Donald, had favored Alena so much, their older daughter Kiera's resentment and jealousy fueled her rebellious and practically suicidal behavior, whether it took the shape of drugs, sex, and alcohol or simply driving fast and recklessly.

Partly out of a sense of guilt and partly out of a desire to have me take Alena's place in her heart, Jordan March surprised me with an idea one day at the hospital. She offered to take me into her home and give me all the things a wealthy family could give me. I, of course, hesitated. How could I go and live beside Kiera March, the girl whose wild and thoughtless behavior was responsible for my mother's death? Wouldn't that be the gravest insult against my own mother? Not that I cared about it then, but what would other people think of me?

My private-duty nurse, Jackie Knee, a nurse Jordan March personally arranged for and paid for, told me to accept Jordan March's offer and take everything I could from the wealthy Marches. Maybe that was my initial reason for entering their home and assuming many of Alena's things, besides living in her bedroom suite. Gradually, though, I found myself feeling sorry for Mr. and Mrs. March and, eventually, even feeling sorry for Kiera.

Did I forgive her, or deep down inside did I always harbor hate and a desire for vengeance? It took me a very long time to find that answer. Goodness knows that I had many more reasons to hate her after I was brought to her home. Naturally, she resented my presence. In the beginning, even her father did. I understood why. After all, I was a constant reminder to him about what a terrible thing Kiera had done, and a parent, especially one as proud and egotistical as Donald March, couldn't help but hate feeling responsible and hate everyone and everything that made him do so.

Gradually, as Jordan March tried harder and harder to turn me into her lost daughter, Alena, Kiera had another reason to despise me. Once again, it seemed as though she was becoming second best, at least as far as her mother was concerned, and I wasn't even blood-related. I should have known she wouldn't stand by to let this happen to her again, that she would do anything and everything she could to drive me from her home.

Despite how poor her school grades were, Kiera was far from unintelligent. She was clever and conniving. Eventually, she succeeded in having me believe she not only had accepted me in her life but also wanted to be the big sister to me that she wasn't able to be for Alena. Her regret seemed so sincere that I bought into it. I was flattered that she included me with her friends, all seniors. It helped me to feel important at a time when I was feeling very sorry for myself.

Later, she succeeded in getting me seduced by one of her boyfriends and then got me into serious trouble with her parents by making it seem as though it had been entirely my fault. She convinced them that I had never really left the tough, gritty street life behind. As incredible as it was, she had them believing I was corrupting her and her friends and not vice versa.

But in the end, I thought that her conscience about the way she had treated and thought of her sister, Alena, and what she had done to me drove her to be reckless again, and she nearly died of a drug overdose. All of the mean things that she and her friends had done to me were revealed when her friends, overwhelmed by her near demise, confessed to being part of Kiera's schemes.

Now imprisoned in a silence of her own making, she did seem to begin to change. However, I had suffered too much because of her simply to accept the things she said and the way she behaved toward me after all of this. I didn't come right out and say so. I just took longer to believe in anything.

My mother used to say that a little skepticism is a blessing. "It's like a safety valve," she told me. "It will keep you from falling too far too fast." She was bitter by then. My father had not only left us without a word but had also taken all of our money and anything else we had of any value. Forced to accept whatever employment she could get, my mother was often exploited. She grew more and more depressed, let herself go physically and mentally, and began to drink heavily. Eventually, we were evicted from our home.

"Remember this, Sasha," she told me during one of her more sober moments while we sat on the beach and stared at the ocean. "The world is divided into two kinds of people, the gullible and the deceptive. It's only good and sensible self-defense to be distrusting and be a little deceptive yourself. This isn't paradise yet. We're always in one danger or another no matter where we are."

I didn't understand all she was telling me back then, but I could feel her pain and agony. It washed away her beautiful smile and smothered to death the softness in her soul. I know she drank anything alcoholic because she hated herself, hated what she had become, even more than she hated my father. She was choking on her own venom. I cried for her often then, cried more for her than I cried for myself.

Ironically, her death had brought me to the lap of luxury. Not only did I now have far, far more than I had then or even could imagine having, but I also had more than probably ninety-nine percent of girls my age. After having once been a pitiful creature on the streets, I found myself now being envied by girls and boys who I had thought were princes and princesses themselves.

I challenge you to try to do what I have trouble doing even today. Try to imagine a nearly fourteen-year-old girl having to sleep with her mother on the beach in a large carton, a girl with nearly no clothes, old shoes, who couldn't go to school, a girl who had to wash herself in public toilets, a girl for whom finding a quarter or even a dime on the sidewalk or the beach was like finding gold.

Then try to imagine this girl being taken out of a hospital room full of welfare patients and brought to a private room where she was given a private-duty nurse, treated by the biggest specialists, and then brought flowers and gifts she had only dreamed about while walking past store windows.

Imagine this girl taken to live in a mansion that could only be approached on a private road, a uniquely styled house with a tower that made it look like a castle. Not only did it have tennis courts and an indoor pool and an outdoor Olympic-size pool, but there was also a man-made lake big enough for rowboats. Imagine her being given a room that was larger than the house in which she had once lived, a suite with a closet that looked half the length of a basketball court, filled with clothes and shoes, many of which had never been worn more than once and some of which still had the price tags attached to them.

Imagine her having her own private physical therapist to get her strong and well again by exercising in the indoor pool in that same mansion. She was also provided with her own private tutor to get her ready to go to school again—not just any school, but a beautiful private school with only the children of the very rich attending and with classes small enough for each and every student to get personal attention.

If you can imagine all of that, you can see me now, years later, a high school senior bedecked in only the most fashionable styles and trends, a girl who is constantly told she is exotically beautiful, something her mother was and she always dreamed she would be. You can see me as an honor student, popular, who on her seventeenth birthday was presented with her own red BMW hardtop convertible.

How often I have sat by the window in my suite and looked out at the well-manicured grounds, the Olympic-size pool and tennis courts, and closed my eyes, feeling sure that when I opened them again, I'd be back on the beach, sitting beside my ragtag mother, staring out at the sea, both of us left dumbfounded by how quickly hardship and misery had grasped and tightly held the two of us.

But when I opened my eyes, I was still here, still the ward of a very wealthy foster family, gliding through life without a worry in the world.

Kiera was off at her charm-school college now. Her parents had yet to learn it, but she had told me she thought she was close to becoming engaged to an English boy, Richard Nandi Chenik, whose famous architect father had been knighted. She e-mailed me almost daily, describing her social life and sharing her most intimate love secrets. I knew how hard she had been working at making me feel like her sister again. I imagined she was doing it because she needed my forgiveness and because, despite what a brave and often arrogant façade she had, she was basically a very lonely person, lonely and especially afraid that I would replace her in her father's heart. I thought that was something she would never have to fear.

Even though my foster mother desperately tried to make me feel as loved as her lost daughter had felt, I knew I was still a guest, an orphan in her husband's eyes. Eventually, he was kind, full of praise for me, and certainly generous, but there was always that look of restraint, that realization that I was not his real daughter. He could only care for me just so much the way a father would before that look came into his eyes, and he would pull back and become more distant and formal.

Mrs. March was aware of it as well. She tried so hard

to regain a daughter, to hold on to her idea of a family. Her new goal now, her method of overcoming this last hurdle, was to have her and Mr. March legally adopt me. From time to time, I couldn't help but hear them discussing it. Up until now, he was reluctant. To justify his hesitancy, he pointed out the complicated legal and financial considerations. He also emphasized that they had established a trust fund of a quarter of a million dollars for my college education.

"It's not that we're not looking after her future," he said.

Another one of his excuses was the emotional and psychological impact it would have on Kiera.

"Let's wait until she is more settled, more adult. Even though she is doing well—better, in fact, than I ever expected—she is still quite fragile, Jordan. You know what her therapist, Dr. Ralston, told us about sibling rivalry and how that diminished her self-esteem. Go slowly, or you'll destroy all the progress she has made," he warned, and my foster mother stepped back again and again.

It would be a little longer before I would understand the real reasons he was hesitant. Some of them did have to do with what he was saying, but the biggest reason lay in wait, as patient as a confident tiger who knew his prey was coming closer. He would pounce when the time was right.

And the poor lamb, innocent and trusting—I, Sasha Porter—could fall victim.

My mother's words never were forgotten. They lingered now in the shadows of this exquisite mansion. Often, even on one of my happier days here, I would hear them as if her ghost dressed in shadows stood in some corner waiting for me to walk by.

*It's only good self-defense to be distrusting.*
*Remember the safety valve.*
*Always be skeptical.*
I heard her, but would I listen?

And even if I did, could I stop any of it from happening?

My mother came to believe everything was decided for us even before we were born. It was futile to fight destiny. Why try? Why bother? She had been that discouraged and defeated.

I couldn't blame her for feeling that way. I hoped she was wrong.

But deep in my heart, I was afraid she was right.

I was afraid that someday, I would be as stunned and lost as she was the day she died.

And that there would be a new silence.

# 1

## *Rise and Shine*

"What are you doing still in bed?" Mrs. Duval cried in that sharp but overly dramatic attempt at anger, with her hands on her waist and her shoulders stiffly back in the posture of a drill sergeant. She always kept her dark brown hair in a tight bun, with what Mrs. Caro said was "nary a strand free to wander on its own." Both of them were live-in servants. Mrs. Duval and her husband, Alberto, lived in a four-room apartment over the garage that housed six cars, one of them being mine now. Mrs. Caro had a bedroom at the rear of the mansion. Other part-time maids came and went, mostly because they didn't live up to Mrs. Duval's standards.

She pressed the button that drew apart the curtains on my windows, and a tide of bright Southern California morning sun rushed in and over the room. When I was four, my mother told me the sun was made of rich, luscious butter. I used to dream of capturing a ray and smearing it over a slice of toast.

When I told my mother the dream, she laughed and said, "If anyone could do that, Sasha, you can, but you'll burn your tongue on it."

All of those sweeter moments, delicious and bright, hung like stars in the dark sky of my past life. I could pluck them as someone would pluck fruit and savor the wonderful memory. My greatest fear was that with time, they would fade and eventually disappear, leaving me in total darkness.

"Well? Why are you still sleeping, Sasha?" Mrs. Duval asked with as much of a scowl as she could muster. "Did you stay up too late again talking on that phone?"

My foster parents' head housekeeper long ago had dropped what little formality had existed between us since the day I came to live with the Marches. I doubted she had expected I would last so long in this home, but as the years went by and the reality of it settled in, she softened and became more like one of the grandmothers I had never known.

I had suspected she liked me from the start, anyway. She knew what had brought me here. From time to time, she risked asking me about my mother in little ways but never ventured so far as to ask me about the night of the horrible accident. Like everyone else—except Kiera, who caused it, of course—it was something unspoken but something that never seemed to go away. It loomed like a stubborn, bruised cloud in the sky, no matter how bright the day. The three years that had passed hadn't diminished it. They had hardened it, had made it muscular and angry, until it resembled a tightly closed fist, always ready to come crashing down on any moment of happiness I dared enjoy.

"I didn't stay up that late, but I forgot to set my alarm," I said, still clutching the soft, lavender-scented comforter about me. Only my face was uncovered.

"I thought so," she said. "Mrs. Caro looked at the eggs she was about to break, looked at me and then up at the ceiling, and said, 'That girl hasn't stirred. You better go see why, Mrs. Duval.' How she can see through walls and ceilings never ceases to amaze me."

It amused me how the two of them always addressed each other as Mrs. Duval and Mrs. Caro. I wondered if they were that formal when they were alone. I suspected they were.

I didn't move when she told me what Mrs. Caro had said, but I nodded in agreement. Without hearing a weather report, Mrs. Caro could predict when it would rain even days before it started. I thought she had senses not yet discovered.

"I swear, Sasha, one of these nights, you're going to smother, wrapping yourself so tightly in that comforter," Mrs. Duval continued as she came in to scoop up my socks and the jeans I had left over the side chair. I wasn't sloppy, but she was always picking up after someone in this house, especially Kiera, who dropped her things disdainfully everywhere.

"It's too comfy," I moaned. "I hate getting out of bed."

She paused and nodded.

"I remember when you first could get out of bed easily after your months of therapy, you didn't hesitate to do so. You were usually up before anyone else in this house.

It didn't take long for you to pick up someone else's bad habits, I'm afraid," she muttered. "I can only imagine what else would go on if she wasn't off in that college." She paused with a suspicious expression on her face and stared at me. Did she think I had done something else that would meet with her disapproval, that there was some other way Kiera had infected me?

"What?"

"I always wonder. It is a real college, isn't it?" she asked, and I laughed with relief.

I threw off my comforter and sat up.

"Yes, it's a real college, Mrs. Duval. She has homework and lectures to attend and has to pass tests. It's just a very expensive, exclusive school with students from all over, including Asia, as well as Europe."

"Well," she said, tightening her lips, "I don't care how rich you are. Money can buy you right up to the steps of heaven, but after that, you'd better have something else to offer to get those gates to open."

"Kiera's not thinking about heaven," I said.

She grunted in agreement, and I rose, stretched, and looked at the clock. I did have to get moving.

Two weeks ago, my foster parents surprised me on my seventeenth birthday with a red BMW hardtop convertible. The sight of it took my breath away. Jordan had arranged for my private driving lessons, and Donald had let me drive his Bentley three different times. I thought that was to see if I was ready to drive my foster mother's Jaguar sedan occasionally. Never did I dream they were planning such a gift. From what I heard them say to each other about it, I assumed it was mostly Jordan's idea.

Anyway, having my own car meant I could take a little longer to get ready for school. I didn't have to get up earlier for Donald to drive me on his way to work, and Jordan didn't have to change any of her plans or get up earlier herself. Often, they had Mrs. Duval's husband, Alberto, drive me or pick me up, but I knew that took him away from his work.

The private school I attended had no buses. The students were all from families rich enough to have drivers or had parents with the time to cart them to and fro. Many were often brought in taxicabs or in chauffeured limousines. It was quite a sight to see four or five of them lined up at the end of a school day. Someone who didn't know would think the school was having a black-tie affair for some very important government official.

I quickly pinned up my long black hair, which I kept at the length my mother had kept hers, just below her wing bones, and hurried to my bathroom to shower. If I let her, Mrs. Duval would put out my clothes, but she always chose something more conservative than I would have chosen to wear. Today I was excited about wearing the outfit Jordan had bought me over the past weekend at Mademoiselle Boutique in Beverly Hills. The teenagers who went there for clothes didn't have to break piggy banks. That was for sure.

I had a pair of low-rise skinny jeans with sequins down both legs in quarter-moon shapes and a fancy ruffle tee top.

Jordan had bought me a new Zsa Zsa Zebra cross-body bag to go with it and a pair of platform pumps. I also had the Ed Hardy Showgirl Geisha watch still in its box. Donald had brought it back for me when he had gone to Tokyo last month. He said he thought it was amusing to find something made in America at the airport there.

"Whenever I see anything cute that's Oriental, I think of you," he told me.

I was surprised to hear it. Even Jordan looked surprised to hear that I was on his mind when he traveled.

"He certainly doesn't think of me that often," she muttered. She was always complaining about how he wasn't in touch with her enough on these trips lately.

After I dressed and brushed my hair, I hovered over the twenty or so necklaces I had. I had been favoring the recycled African green glass, but I also liked the chunky marbled bead necklace. There were so many other good choices that would go well with what I was going to wear. I paused to look at the opulence.

Was Mrs. Duval right? Was I getting to be just as spoiled as Kiera? Mrs. Caro would always look at Mrs. Duval if she made any comment suggesting that and say, "After what she has been through, that girl deserves to be a little spoiled." Mrs. Duval didn't disagree, but she wasn't one to countenance waste or laziness, not that I wanted to be wasteful or lazy, either.

"The clock's ticking," Mrs. Duval called from the hallway as she passed my room, carrying some fresh linen to Jordan and Donald's bedroom.

I scooped up the marbled bead necklace, slipped it over

my head, and started for the doorway, but I paused when I saw there was an e-mail from Kiera on my computer. Lately, she was writing to me late at night, long after I had gone to sleep. Too often, she would call very late, too. Despite what I told Mrs. Duval about Kiera's school, I couldn't help but wonder what sort of work she was doing there these days, especially now that she was claiming she was having a hot new romance. Maybe Mrs. Duval wasn't so off with her suspicions. Maybe the students at Kiera's school paid so much to be there that their teachers bent rules and grades to make sure they passed, after all.

*Hey,* she began as if we were right next to each other. *Richard just left. That's right, I smuggled him into my room last night through the window. Lucky I'm on the first floor of the dorm. I didn't think he would do it, no matter how much I promised him. When I first met him, he was so English. You know what I mean, correct and perfect, wiping his lips after every bite at lunch and leaning over to wipe mine if the smallest crumb was stuck on my lip. I never had a boyfriend who pulled the chair out for me, opened every door, including rushing around to open the car door like some chauffeur, and then hold out his arm. He hates walking side-by-side without my taking his arm.*

*As you know, at first I found him annoyingly proper. I hated having to remember all the rules of good etiquette. I especially hated those charm-school lessons my mother ordered both Alena and me to take from that woman who squeaked when she walked, Mrs.*

*Catherine Emmerline Turner. Even Alena hated her coming around, although she would never complain. Alena never complained about anything, even when she was sick, but you know I'm a professional complainer, so I had no problem.*

*Anyway, Richard proved to be so sweet, and he's so obviously head over heels in love with me, I couldn't keep ignoring him. I'm slowly changing him, anyway, showing him how to relax and have fun, which is what he did last night in my bed. I'm so glad I bought the Kama Sutra book I was telling you about a few weeks ago. I promised him something different every time, and he was practically screaming with pleasure. In fact, I had to put my hand in his mouth and—.*

"Sasha," I heard, and looked up from the computer. "Everyone's worried you're going to be late for school," Jordan said. She was in my doorway and wearing her light green velvet robe. Her hair wasn't brushed, and she wore no makeup, which was something she would never do when I first arrived. I wasn't the only one who was changing in little ways. "You know I don't want you speeding in your new car. Donald says the police favor red cars, especially expensive ones."

"Okay, coming," I sang.

I quickly clicked off the e-mail and shut off the computer. I didn't like leaving it on when I wasn't in the room. I had no doubt Jordan would have a hemorrhage or something if she read any of my e-mails from Kiera lately. It was very important to Kiera that I keep secret what we wrote to each other, anyway, and at this point, I wanted her to trust me. I still relied on her for some advice when it came to boys at our school—or boys anywhere, for that matter.

"Sorry," I said, joining Jordan in the doorway.

She nodded at my computer. "What was that you were reading?"

"Oh, you know my friends. They have to send me every new bit of gossip."

"What did we do without computers?" she asked herself as we walked to the stairway.

Unless I ran all the way, it took nearly thirty seconds to get there. The mansion, something built in a style the Marches called Richardsonian Romanesque, had three floors. We slept on the second level. There were guest rooms on the third floor and a storage room with family artifacts that neither Jordan nor Donald knew what to do with or where to place, even in this huge house. All of it waited like refugees hoping for a visa to another home. I realized that no matter how rich people were, most still hoarded really useless things. I'd probably be the same way. I had nothing when I came here, but if I could have brought even the smallest, most insignificant thing, I would have brought it and cherished it.

Donald and Jordan's bedroom was right down the hall from mine. Kiera's was closer to the stairway. When I first arrived, nothing was changed in my room. It was, as I understood it, exactly as it had been the day Alena died. She had loved giraffes, so there were pictures and paintings of them, lamps shaped like giraffes, and giraffes on most of the linen and pillowcases, as well as on the wallpaper. They were all still there, but over the course of three years, the suite had come a little closer to suiting who I was. The wallpaper had been changed only in the bathroom, but some of the things I liked were hung on the suite walls, including many of the works of calligraphy I did both in art class at school and at home. Donald had one in his office here, and Jordan had put one up in the entertainment room.

It had always been a delicate thing to change or replace anything that had been Alena's. First, I didn't want anyone to think I'd rather that they forget her and think only of me now. For a long time after I first arrived, I had felt her presence in the room and even had secret talks with her. Second, despite the time that had passed since her death, Jordan and Donald never seemed to be past it. I often caught one or the other looking at Alena's picture or something of hers and then growing teary-eyed. Their sighs were deep and pained.

Inevitably, my identity eventually had to take hold in this room, however. More than once when I first arrived, I offered to move to another room. There were so many guest suites that were just as large and comfortable, but Jordan wouldn't hear of it. She wanted me close, and she told me it did her heart good to know that someone like me was living in Alena's room. Even to this day, she referred to it that way, despite all that was mine in it now. Despite how long I had been here, it was still and probably always would be Alena's room.

"Donald left already," Jordan told me as we started to descend the curved stairway. "He's going to Boston for four days," she added.

I didn't sense sadness in her voice as much as a note of defeat and acceptance. Donald had been traveling more and more and had been away from home for longer and longer periods of time. For as long as I'd been here, he always took business trips, but they did seem more spaced out back then and never for as many days. Jordan had begun to complain about it often at dinner, but he either didn't respond or said it couldn't be helped. He told her that they were busier than ever and it would be foolish to pass up big opportunities.

"Besides," he said once, "you always knew what it would be like for us when we were married. You knew how I was about the things that I did. There should be no real surprises."

I remember looking at her and wondering if she really had known. My mother hadn't known what it would eventually be like when she got married to my father. I was sure that, like Jordan, she had had other dreams and visions for their marriage. It wasn't fair for Donald to say that to Jordan, I thought. It made it sound as though she were partly to blame and should not complain. After all, didn't he know who she was? Didn't he realize how alone and lost she might feel?

"I'm going to a dinner tonight," Jordan added as we continued down the stairway. "I'm sorry you have to eat alone. If you want, you can invite one of your friends over, but be sure you get your homework done, okay? Not that I have to remind you," she said. "It's just a habit I got into whenever I spoke to Kiera."

I nodded but immediately began to think about whom I

would choose. I knew it was very immodest of me to say it, but whomever I chose would be the object of envy for the other girls in my class with whom I was friendly. It wasn't only because they would be coming to this extraordinary house with its game room and theater, its indoor and outdoor pools and tennis courts. I was far from oblivious when it came to how popular I had become at school for other reasons. In the beginning, it surprised me and even made me feel a little uncomfortable, but over time, I grew used to other girls vying for the seat next to mine or winning my friendship and approval. My phone was ringing too often, not only for Mrs. Duval and Jordan but for me as well. I hated gossip and backstabbing, especially when it came to girl bullying, but I would be a liar if I denied that being so important to them made me feel good.

Of course, I wasn't receiving phone calls and attention only from girls, but until now, I hadn't settled on any one boy. Nothing seemed to annoy them more than my dating someone one weekend and then another the following one. I hadn't dated anyone for weeks now. Despite what Kiera and her friends had ended up doing to me, I was impressed with how they all avoided long-term relationships. Long-term for them was two weeks. "Playing the field," Kiera used to say, "is a lot more fun. Besides, our parents are right. We're too young to get so serious."

Maybe it was just my imagination, but I thought I saw looks of envy and regret on the faces of the girls who were going steady. Their time was so dominated by their boyfriends they didn't spend much of it with us.

"Girls who go steady so young are insecure," Kiera told me. "They don't have confidence in themselves. They're terrified that no one will ask them out." She laughed and added, "Like Mrs. Caro is fond of saying, 'A bird in hand is grand.' But that's not for me. I'd probably squeeze it to death."

How stupid it would sound to anyone if I told them that Kiera's words were still important to me. "Look at what she did to you, getting you to believe in a club called Virgins Anonymous and literally having you raped on that boat ride to Catalina Island. Why would you think anything someone like that had said was important or significant?" he or she would surely ask.

Because despite all that, I would tell them, I was still in her world, and no one knew better what rules to play by in that world than Kiera March. You have to give the devil her due. Besides, don't forget, coming here from where I had been and what I had gone through was like landing on another planet for me.

In the beginning, I was terrified that the other students would learn the truth about me, discover that I had been homeless and lived on the streets. I thought their parents surely would warn them to stay away from me. They would tell them that I could be diseased or something. Despite living in the Marches' home, I would be like a leper.

Ironically, at least in the beginning, Kiera was afraid that her friends would learn the truth about me, too, but of course, not for the same reasons. More students would know what she had done, and then she would be tainted not only by that crime but also by living beside a girl like me. To her, that was akin to some subtle punishment. So she went along with the story that I was her cousin who had moved in with her and her parents because my parents had been killed in a car accident. That was why I limped when I first arrived, why I had been injured, too.

When everything was eventually revealed, thanks to Kiera's nearly killing herself with a drug known on the street as G, the truth about me emerged. By then, everyone had accepted me in the school. I was doing very well in my classes and had become a lead clarinet player in the orchestra. To my surprise, after all was known, I became something of a heroine. Instead of the truth chasing my classmates away from me, it drew them to me. Everyone wanted to know more about me. Suddenly, being poor and downtrodden was romantic.

Did I exploit all of this? Probably, but whom did I hurt? It felt good to take advantage of other girls and boys who had enjoyed so much, anyway. They weren't born with a silver spoon in their mouths. They were born with a gold one. If it was all reversed and they could, they wouldn't hesitate to take advantage of me, I thought.

Did I lead the other girls to believe that I was far more sophisticated and worldly when it came to sex and boys than I really was? Yes, but I enjoyed the way they looked up to me, spoke to me, competed for my attention. After all, I had not only survived what had been done to me here, but I had also survived the streets. I had been to hell and back. Who could claim the same or similar experiences? They made me feel like a local celebrity, a sort of Pygmalion, Audrey Hepburn in *My Fair Lady,* educated and washed until she could no longer be distinguished from the blue bloods.

All of that reverence and respect never ended. In fact, it was happening more than ever, and I couldn't help but smile at the irony. I sat where Kiera had sat, walked where she had walked, and held court just the way she had. I was the queen now, and I wasn't about to give up my throne over a pang of conscience. I told myself there wasn't anything I could do to any of them in this school, anyway, that she or he couldn't survive, not with their support systems.

*Enjoy yourself, Sasha,* I told myself. As Mrs. Caro had said many times, "She deserves to be a little spoiled."

Mrs. Caro had my breakfast ready seconds after I sat at the table in what the Marches called their breakfast nook. Rarely did we have breakfast in the dining room since Kiera had gone off to college. The nook had bay windows that looked out on the beautiful gardens, the rolling lawn where the Marches had some statuary and stone benches. It looked like a private park. There was so much to maintain that they had more than a dozen employees for Alberto to supervise. For me, it was still too much to believe that one family had all this. What they spent on maintenance could probably feed all of the homeless people I had met and known. Kiera always took it all for granted. No matter what my response to something wonderful here was, she always said, "What's the big deal? If we didn't have it, someone else would, and why should they have it and not us?"

*Live where I have lived, be who I have been, and you'll understand why it is a big deal,* I thought, and then I thought, *Well, maybe not you.*

"Just coffee for me and a piece of toast," Jordan told

Mrs. Caro. "I'm having a big lunch out today," she added before Mrs. Caro could ask after her health.

*She's going out to lunch and dinner,* I thought. Lately, both she and Donald seemed to want to get away from their beautiful house and estate. Perhaps the memories of Alena were haunting them even more than ever with Kiera away. I was sure I didn't fill the caverns in their hearts. Jordan had tried by having me wear Alena's things, sleep in her room, and learn to play the clarinet. I was even using her clarinet. Even though it all distracted her from her sorrow for a while, it didn't end it. Nothing would, just as nothing would end my mourning my mother's terrible death.

"Has Kiera been writing to you? I haven't heard from her for more than two weeks," Jordan said. I knew she suspected I had been reading something from Kiera on the computer.

Although it was painful to tell her that yes, Kiera was communicating with me far more than she was with her, I didn't want to lie to her again.

"Yes," I said.

"Well, has she said any more about this young man from England? Donald asked me last night, and I could tell him nothing."

"She's still seeing him. She sounds happy about it, too."

"Um. I feel sorry for him," she said. Mrs. Caro served her some coffee. She glanced at me, raised her eyebrows, and returned to the kitchen to get Jordan her toast.

"She tells me he's a proper Englishman," I said.

"Yes, I heard about that. She said his father was knighted. It's hard to believe she would be with anyone proper," she replied, and sipped her coffee. "I don't enjoy speaking about her like this, but I am not one of those mothers who refuses to see her child's flaws, especially this child."

I looked down and continued to eat my eggs.

"I'm not saying I'm not happy that you and she have developed a friendlier relationship. If anything, I think that's wonderful of you. The way you treated her with so much kindness after she did that stupid drug thing and all the other things to you impressed both Donald and me, but always be careful. You're too sweet and trusting, just the way Alena was and would be today. You both have too much angel in you."

"I'll be careful," I promised. Lately, I wasn't feeling anything angelic about myself. I was feeling more guilt because of the way Jordan often compared me to Alena.

Mrs. Caro brought her the toast. She nibbled on it like a small rabbit and stared ahead.

When I was in the hospital after the accident and Jackie Knee urged me to accept Jordan's offer and take what I could from her and her family, she was surely envisioning what she thought was a pretty close to perfect world, a world in which everything you wanted was at your fingertips. She was right about it to a certain extent. What could I ask for now that I didn't have materially?

But as I looked at Jordan lost in her own sad thoughts for a moment, I thought this was far from a perfect world. Sadness was a permanent guest here. It crawled about through the shadows, walked freely during the night, visiting both Jordan and Donald and even me. Outside, the grass couldn't be greener, the flowers brighter, the fountains more luscious and crystal clear, but despite the pleasures I was enjoying and the comfort I experienced, in the back of my mind, I knew it was wrong to begin here by standing in a dead girl's shoes. I could feel the dread. Something sometime in the near future would make me regret the Marches' generosity in ways I couldn't imagine. It was coming. Like Mrs. Caro, I could sense things others could not, and deep down, I was afraid.

"Oh, you'd better get a move on," Jordan said. "Remember, no speeding. I don't know what I would do if something happened to you, too."

"I'm okay. I have plenty of time," I said, but wiped my mouth and rose. I was going to bring the plates into the kitchen, but Mrs. Caro, as usual, was right on the mark, as if she had been hovering behind the door listening and waiting for her cue, as if we were all in a play.

I thanked her again, gave Jordan a kiss on the cheek as I had started doing recently, and headed out. My schoolbag was in the entryway on the eighteenth-century wood bench Jordan had bought at an auction in France. I had gotten into the habit of putting it there after I had done my homework. If there was anything the teachers at my school hated, it was a student forgetting his or her books. On more than one occasion, my classmates would call home for something they had forgotten, and their parents would either bring it or send it along in a taxicab or limousine. It wasn't so strange to see a uniformed chauffeur bring something into the school.

I stepped out into another very warm late October morning with a sky as blue as a summer sky. Mrs. Caro always talked about the weather. Donald didn't believe there was a man-made climate change, but she would always shake her head and mutter, "Somethin's not right, and it's not nature's fault."

I walked to the garage. It wasn't far, but lately it was practically the only walking outside of the school that I was doing. When we were homeless, Mama and I seemed to walk forever some days. Even when I had a new pair of sneakers, my feet would blister, and hers began to look like the feet of someone who walked on a bed of nails.

Just before I reached the garage, my cell phone vibrated, and I paused to answer.

"Hi," I heard. "Have you left for school yet?"

"Who's this?" I asked, even though I knew full well who it was.

Shayne Peters was a starting guard on the basketball team, six feet two, with a shock of rich golden brown hair. His father was a famous criminal attorney who had recently defended a congressman accused of murdering his wife. He had gotten him acquitted.

Shayne had been going with Sydney Woods, but they recently had broken up. The rumor mill blamed it on me. The story was that he had a big crush on me, and Sydney, finally disgusted with him, gave his class ring back to him. I don't know how that had all started. I had done little to encourage him.

"It's Shayne!" he cried, obviously upset that I didn't recognize his voice.

"How can I help you?" I asked in the most formal tone of voice I could muster.

"Huh? Look, my car won't start. Can you pick me up on the way to school?"

"No. I'm late," I said. "Take a taxi."

"Wait!" he cried, anticipating my hanging up. "Are you going to the game Friday? It's a home game, and I thought that after the game we—"

"I'm not sure. I have an opportunity to see *Madame Butterfly*. Box seats."

"What?"

"See you in school," I said, and hung up.

I had no opportunity to see *Madame Butterfly*, but the idea had just popped into my head. I smiled to myself as I got into my car. I could just imagine the look of surprise on his face, but I remembered the advice Kiera had given me about the boys in our school. "They like to take you for granted because they take everything else for granted. Make them work for every smile you give them, and don't give them many."

*I'll e-mail her about it later,* I thought. She loved hearing about my romantic exploits, especially when I appeared to be following her lead.

Alberto waved to me as I drove out and waited for the gate to open. From the outside, it looked like a solid orange wall twelve feet high. There were security cameras everywhere. One of my friends who came here, Jessica Taylor, said, "The only thing missing here is a moat and crocodiles."

When I arrived at school, I parked in the student lot where all of us who had cars had reserved places. As I headed for the front door, I saw Shayne pull in, driving his own car and parking in his spot.

His own car? Deception, I thought. So much for him needing me to pick him up. I wouldn't ever go out with him, since the only way he could get my attention was to try to deceive me. If it's there at the start, it will certainly be there throughout your relationship and at the end for sure.

Mama taught me that.

I felt confident that I could and would recognize it every time I saw it.

But I was still young and idealistic.

I had no idea what deception awaited me or the direction from which it would come—and certainly no idea about how close it was.

## ❧ 2 ❧

# New Student

When I first entered this school, I was nervous and self-conscious for many reasons, not the least of which was my limping. The injury I had suffered could have healed improperly because of how quickly and carelessly I was initially treated. I could have been limping all my life. One leg might not have grown as fast or as long as the other, but Jordan March brought in Dr. Milan, a top specialist who reset my cast, and after nearly a year, my limp grew less and less obvious, until eventually it was completely gone. Probably no other girl in the school took as much pride in her walk now as I did after that, although many interpreted it as my being snobby and absorbed with myself. I was simply grateful and more conscious of my posture and my gait.

I don't know how many girls can actually envision themselves when they walk or sit and talk, but I can. Maybe I'm thinking more about my mother than I am about myself, but I see a picture of a girl with a rich, unblemished complexion and silky black hair to go with her black onyx eyes, small nose, and perfectly shaped slightly raised lips. She is lithe, with a figure other girls envy and boys dream of when they fantasize. I always focus ahead when I walk, no matter where I am, and so I seemed undistracted and unconcerned, an exotic statue of self-confidence. Kiera was the first one to mention this to me. She called it my "wow factor."

"Every girl needs one," she said. "Mine is the way I shift my eyes and turn my shoulders. I radiate sex. I can see it in their faces, women as well as men."

I thought she was simply jealous of something else about me, but under the note of envy in her voice, I did hear an appreciation and respect for something I did on my own. Because of her, even though people couldn't tell, I was even more self-conscious about the way I walked and sat. Besides, in this school, I didn't lack reminders.

"You walk through the halls of this school as if you own it," Ray Stowe told me earlier this year. I had stopped at my hall locker. He was one of the senior boys who were upset with my attitude toward them. Maybe they thought I should kowtow like some obedient Asian woman. "I know Donald March was one of the principal builders of it, but that doesn't mean you own it."

Ray's father was a builder, too. I imagined there was some friendly and maybe not-so-friendly competition.

I looked first at my girlfriends who were standing by their lockers. They had overheard him.

"Don't slouch so much, and you can look as if you own it, too, instead of looking as if you're ashamed to be here or don't think you're good enough," I told him. Everyone around us laughed. Unable to come up with a good enough counter, he straightened his posture, looked at the smiling faces around us, and walked away.

Some of the girls who hung with me repeated the things I said all day, especially when I took down one of the boys who was so full of himself. The school had only three hundred students from grades seven to twelve, so having the whole student body hear something someone else said or something someone else did was not difficult. That was especially true for the senior high. We had only sixty-two students in the senior class. Our class sizes were a quarter of what they were in many public schools. It was difficult, even for some of the more modest students, not to feel extra special and not to have their voices drip with pride about being a student at Pacifica.

My memories of my public grade-school days were so vague now. It wasn't all that long after my father deserted us that it became more and more difficult to attend the school I was at. However, like most children that age, I was still excited about going there every school day. After the initial days, older students seemed to be generally blasé about it, but not me. I was still as excited as ever about going to school.

Attending Pacifica was special for so many reasons. Few schools glittered and sparkled as much. Dr. Steiner, the principal, was obsessive about cleanliness. Our desks were actually washed down nightly with antiseptic soaps to prevent the spread of colds and flu. Vandalism here was equivalent to a capital crime. There were little signs warning about it everywhere, especially outside. A student could be expelled for it, and his or her parents would forfeit the tuition, an amount that would surely keep some families in food and shelter for two years. We also had a security service to monitor visitors and protect the property at night.

I suspect that I would have done as well in my academics at a public school as I did here, but being in this environment was so safe and pleasant that I looked forward to schoolwork and assignments every day, just the way I had when I was six and seven. Our teachers were happy, too. They could maintain discipline easily and were paid better than public-school teachers. My music teacher, Mr. Denacio, was the only teacher I had who growled and looked dissatisfied at times, but I knew from the start that his bark was worse than his bite. I also knew he bragged about me and how quickly I had become one of his best clarinet players ever.

Despite the families and the wealth these students came from, the chatter in homeroom and in the hallways between classes was no different from the chatter that occurred at most public schools that were populated instead by mostly low- and middle-income students. All of my girlfriends were anxious to talk about themselves and about boys they liked or wished liked them. One other thing I had learned from Kiera was to let them all blabber first and then, almost as an afterthought, give my opinions and talk about myself. It always worked. It gave me that authenticity, that demeanor of an experienced observer. In their eyes, I had the patience and the wisdom. Sometimes I felt they were more attentive to me than they were to their teachers and parents and would do whatever I suggested, even though their parents and teachers were dead set against it and the consequences could be severe.

After this particular school day began, I noticed that Shayne Peters not only avoided talking to me all morning but avoided looking at me as well. I didn't think anyone else noticed, but at lunch, Sydney Woods looked as if she had won *American Idol* or something when she came charging into the cafeteria. She was that ecstatic. She rushed over to my table and held up her right thumb. All of us stopped talking to look.

"You're da bomb!" she told me, while it was she who looked as if she might explode.

"Who set you on fire?" Jessica asked.

"Never mind. Sasha, what did you do to Shayne?" Sydney asked. Everyone turned to me.

"Nothing. Why?"

"He's telling his friends you treated him like . . . how did he put it? Like a nobody," she said with glee. "You acted as if you didn't know who he was when he called you? Perfect. When did he call you, anyway?" she asked, obviously wondering if he had called while they were still technically a couple.

"Well, nobody called this morning," I said.

"So, when did he call?"

"I just told you. Nobody called this morning," I said. She stared a moment, and then she broke into a hysterical laugh, and so did everyone else. That, I knew, was going to be the quote of the day. *Nobody called this morning.* Sydney, who was a good student, especially in English, walked around reciting Emily Dickinson's poem, especially when she was in Shayne's hearing range. *I'm nobody! Who are you? Are you nobody, too?*

It was turning out to be another fun day for me. Any of the girls who hadn't heard the story caught up with me in the hallways between classes to find out what was going on. As casually as I could, I described Shayne calling me to pick him up and my refusal. I made it sound like nothing, which in my mind it was, but often the most trivial things became important at Pacifica. Maybe that was because most everybody had a father or a mother to solve serious problems for them.

In any case, it felt good to be the center of everyone's attention, the subject of all the busy-bee buzzing. I couldn't wait to get home and to my computer to describe it all in an e-mail to Kiera. I knew how much she would appreciate my actions and the results. I didn't know why it had become so important to me to please her. If there was anyone in the world I should enjoy displeasing, it was Kiera. Perhaps I was still trying to prove myself to be as exciting and as popular as she was. I suspected she didn't enjoy that. This was just another way to demonstrate it.

And then something happened that replaced the headlines about Shayne and me before the day had ended. That afternoon, there was a new buzz about two new students who were entering the school. Cora Hatch, who helped Mrs. Knox, Dr. Steiner's secretary, during her free period, was rushing around with the breaking news. It reached me at the start of chemistry class. Cora came right to me as I was taking my seat.

"Guess what? Bradley Garfield's kids are transferring into Pacifica," she said, nearly out of breath. "One is in the eighth grade—his daughter, Summer. And his son, Ryder, is in our class, a senior."

"Did you say Bradley Garfield?" Lily Albert, who sat behind me, asked. She had big eyes as it was, but at this moment, they looked as if they would pop and ooze all over her face like broken egg yolks.

"Yes."

"*The* Bradley Garfield?"

Cora nodded.

I wasn't into soap operas the way most of the girls in my class were, but I knew Bradley Garfield was a lead on *Endless Days*, the top new soap opera. During his television acting hiatus, he starred in a big movie with Julie Thomas, who had been nominated for an Academy Award last year. The movie was a blockbuster love story, *Reflections of a Broken Heart*. There was already chatter about a possible Academy Award nomination for him, too.

"Don't these two have a mother, too?" I asked Cora. "Or did he give birth to them, as well?"

"Oh, yes. She's an actress, or was. Don't you know who she is?"

"I forgot to renew my subscription to *Hollywood Gossip Girls*."

"Very funny. She works on and off, but she still models and does commercials. Beverly Ransome. She's beautiful. She was in *People* last month. She's the one who brought them here today. I said hello to her. She's even more beautiful in person, but I was too shocked to ask for her autograph."

"I'm sure Mrs. Knox wouldn't have liked it if you had," I said.

There were other children of people in the entertainment business attending our school. Making them self-conscious about their fame was an unwritten no-no, but I did really know that Bradley Garfield was the flavor of the month. His picture was on billboards throughout the city, and he was on the covers of dozens of magazines. I couldn't help but wonder what it was like to be the son or daughter of someone like that. Would it make them arrogant? If there was one thing this school didn't need more of, it was arrogance. It was practically seeping out the doors and windows.

I didn't have long to wait to find out. Just after our class began, Dr. Steiner escorted Ryder Garfield to our room. Our teacher, Mr. Malamud, stopped his introduction to the day's lesson instantly, and all eyes turned to the doorway. I could almost hear the chorus of heart throbs beginning. Even my own heart felt as if it shuddered and skipped a beat.

Ryder Garfield had inherited most of his father's good looks. He was easily six feet tall, with a tennis player's firm-looking but lean body. He wore his light brown, almost amber-colored hair long but swept back neatly on the sides. He was dressed in a leather jacket with a black T-shirt and straight-leg jeans and a pair of black cowboy boots. He didn't look timid or nervous to me. He looked bored, even a little disgusted, as if he entered a new school on a weekly basis or something.

"Excuse me, Mr. Malamud," Dr. Steiner began. "I'd like your class to welcome a new student, Ryder Garfield."

"Sure," Mr. Malamud said. "Welcome to Pacifica, Ryder. Were you taking chemistry in the school you had attended?"

"Of course," Ryder said.

Mr. Malamud nodded and quickly looked around the classroom. He reached behind himself to pluck a textbook off the shelf and then walked down my aisle. There were two empty desks in the classroom, one to my right and one in the rear on the left. He put the textbook on the desk to my right and smiled at Ryder, who lowered his head a little and slipped onto the seat. He was carrying a briefcase and opened it immediately to take out a notebook.

"That's what I like. Someone who comes prepared to get right to work," Mr. Malamud told the class. Ryder didn't move a muscle or lift his head. "Does the textbook look familiar?" Mr. Malamud asked him.

Ryder looked it over as if he were considering buying it and nodded. He didn't smile or look up at Mr. Malamud. He clicked a pen open and then sat back. He didn't look at anyone else, either, but I could see the tightness in his jaw. It radiated through his shoulders and into the stiff way he held his upper body. He looked like someone readying himself for a head-on crash.

"Ryder has a sister entering the eighth grade," Dr. Steiner said. "Her name is Summer. I hope you will all give them both a warm welcome. Please don't hesitate to come see me if you have any problems or questions, Ryder," she added.

He didn't turn to her or respond. Dr. Steiner nodded at Mr. Malamud, and he returned to the front of the classroom.

"We were just about to begin the chapter titled 'The Mole,'" he began. "Can anyone tell me what a mole is?"

A dozen hands went up, mostly girls who were eager to show off for our new celebrity student.

I saw Ryder begin to thumb through the text, so I leaned over and said, "It's under the heading Chemical Reactions."

He glanced at me.

"No kidding, Dick Tracy," he said.

I recoiled like someone slapped. Many of the boys in this school could be unpleasant, especially if they were with their friends and wanted to show off by belittling someone. Normally, I would send it right back to them threefold. I had a reputation for the quick comeback. Since they knew of my former life, they were always a bit wary of me, anyway. Ray Stowe was the latest victim who could testify about it. Who knew how rough I could be considering the world from which I came?

But for a brand-new student to be this way to me immediately took even me by surprise. From the way he sat there staring at the text, I thought he might be very angry that he had been enrolled at Pacifica and just wanted to take it out on anyone who made himself or herself available. Right now, he looked more like someone sulking, someone ready to jump down anyone's throat.

"Well, pardon me," I muttered, "for caring enough to offer you some help."

He acted as if he hadn't heard me. He never looked at me again, nor did he look at anyone else, for that matter, during the entire class. Mr. Malamud didn't call on him or ask him to read anything. I had the feeling that if he had, Ryder would have ignored him anyway. Even though he had acted as if he would, I saw that he didn't take a single note during class. When the bell rang, he got up quickly and started out, still avoiding looking at me. He spoke to no one. Some of the girls sped up to walk beside him in the hallway. I saw Jessica speak to him. He looked at her, shook his head, and kept walking, even a little faster. She stopped dead in her tracks, looking after him.

"What did you ask him?" I asked when I caught up to her.

"What class he had next and if he needed any help to find it," she told me. "He just shook his head, but did you see his eyes? Did you ever see eyes so blue?"

"Maybe they're tinted contacts," I told her, and headed for English class.

He was in my English class, too, which meant that he would also be in my math class, the last class of the day. By the time I entered the room, Mr. Madeo already had given him the anthology of English literature and was showing him to the last desk in the first row, which, again, was just across from mine. I took my seat without looking at him.

"Another class with Dick Tracy," he said, just loudly enough for me to hear, but still not looking at me.

I turned to him slowly. "Are you addressing me?"

He jerked his head around. "Sure. I thought you'd tell me what page to turn to," he said, turning to the correct page, Act II, Scene 1, of *Hamlet*. Obviously, Mr. Madeo had already told him where we were.

"Looks like you already asked Sherlock Holmes and don't need the help of poor Dick Tracy," I said. Out of the corner of my eye, I saw him nearly smile. It was nearly, because as soon as his lips began to relax, he seemed to catch himself and return to his deadpan look.

Mr. Madeo always had a little twinkle in his eye when he called on students in his class. He knew whom he would catch unawares and who would probably have the answer. There were some students in the class who hadn't been introduced to Ryder, but most knew who he was by now and had already whispered about him to others. Some gaped at him without any pretense. They had gaped at me, too, on my first day but not like this, I thought. I was sure he wished he was somewhere else. However, I wasn't surprised to see Mr. Madeo call on him about halfway through the class discussion.

"Let's hear from a new voice," he said. "Ryder, what do you make of this line, 'for there is nothing either good or bad, but thinking makes it so'?"

"It's pretty obvious," Ryder said.

"Not to everyone. Enlighten us."

"What's good to someone might be bad to someone else, depending on what they bring to the situation. Hamlet's depressed about his father's death and his mother marrying his uncle, so the world of Denmark looks like a prison to him but not to his friends."

"Sasha, how do you rate that answer?"

I glanced at Ryder. "It's good to me but maybe bad to you," I said. "Thinking makes it so."

Mr. Madeo laughed.

Ryder looked at me and, this time, couldn't stop his smile.

He didn't say anything to me when the bell rang, but on the way to math, he walked by and said, "Neat answer."

He kept going, not waiting for my response. We were on completely opposite sides of the classroom in math. He was closer to the door. When the bell rang to end the class and the day, he practically shot out the door like someone already late for an appointment.

At the end of lunch, I had decided to invite Jessica over, and she had called her mother to tell her she was going home with me. She was waiting at the exit to the parking lot.

"Did you speak to him yet?" she asked. "If anyone can get him into a conversation, I bet it's you."

"Speak to whom?"

"Ryder. What other boy could I have meant?" she cried, bouncing on her feet.

"There are about thirty other boys in the senior class, Jessica."

"Oh, come on," she said. She smiled. "I saw him say something to you in the hallway, but I couldn't see if you said anything back."

"What were you doing, following his every move?"

"Are you kidding? Like a moth to a candle," she said unashamedly. I laughed, and we stepped out to the parking lot.

Both of us stopped instantly. Just ahead of us, Ryder was talking excitedly and obviously angrily at his sister. His arms were flailing about, his hands clenched into fists. His sister stood there with her head down and then looked up at him undaunted.

I thought she was a very pretty girl with diminutive facial features. She had hair the same shade as his, neatly styled with bangs. I remembered she was in the eighth grade and thought she was quite tall for her age. She was developing a very nice figure, too. She turned away from him, and then he pushed her toward his car, a classic-style Ford Mustang. We could see she said something nasty to him and then got in quickly.

"What was that all about?" Jessica muttered.

He got in and backed out of his space, almost hitting Yesenia Romero. Her father was the weatherman for one of the more popular Latino television stations. She screamed after him and waved her fist as he drove out, but he was still yelling at his sister and jerking his right hand in the air between them and surely didn't notice or hear Yesenia.

"What was that shouting all about?" Jessica asked Yesenia before I could. She had been closer to them than us before they got into his car.

She looked at us and calmed down. "That's that new boy."

"We know who he is," Jessica said. "What was going on between him and his sister?"

"He was bawling her out for taking off her bra."

"What?" I said, smiling.

"That's what he was angry about. He said he was going to tell their mother. He called her some names, too. She must have gone into the bathroom between classes to do it,

I guess. He said with the blouse she had on and no bra, she might as well have started the new school topless."

Jessica and I looked at each other and laughed.

"Did you see him back out? He didn't even notice he almost hit me," Yesenia said, growing angry again. "I might just report him. You saw it!"

"Oh, give him a break," Jessica told her. "It's his first day. He's just nervous."

Yesenia raised her eyebrows. "As nervous as a rattlesnake and probably just as dangerous," she said, and headed for her car.

"So what do you think? He's some kind of prude, someone who has a sex hang-up or something?" Jessica asked me as we got into my car.

"Maybe he was just being her big brother," I suggested.

"My brother wouldn't waste his breath telling me what to do and not to do, especially when it came to what I wore, and he certainly wouldn't bawl me out in a parking lot loud enough for others to hear."

Her brother was a sophomore at Michigan State and on the football team.

"Of course he wouldn't. You're a lost cause," I told her, and started out of the parking lot.

"Okay. Out with it. Everything has gotten more interesting now. So let's hear what he said to you in the hallway."

"He commented in two words on an answer I gave in English class."

"That was it?" she said with obvious disappointment.

"Maybe he's restricted to only a dozen words an hour," I muttered.

"What was the two-word comment?" she asked.

" 'Neat answer.' "

"That was it? Weren't you disappointed?"

"Jessica, I wasn't devastated by his mere presence. Stop making it into a thing."

She nodded, but I could see she wasn't satisfied. "Maybe he's the strong, silent type," she said, looking for a positive explanation.

"Maybe just silent."

"I'd like to be the one who finds out."

"Then practice sign language," I said, and she laughed.

"I still love the way you treated Shayne Peters."

I smiled, remembering again how much I wanted to e-mail Kiera about it—and this new student, I guessed.

Jordan was home when we arrived. She was happy I had chosen Jessica. She was very friendly with Jessica's mother, who was part of what Mr. March called her "clutch lunch gang."

"How was school?" she asked us.

"Certainly not very boring today," Jessica said.

"Oh? What happened?"

"Among other things, a famous actor's children were admitted," Jessica replied before I could.

"What actor?"

"Bradley Garfield. You know who he is married to?" Jessica asked Jordan.

"Beverly Ransome. Isn't that nice?"

I wasn't surprised that Jordan knew. She had at least two dozen magazine subscriptions, and from the way she described some of her "clutch lunch gang" lunches, celebrities were often the chief topic of discussion. The celebrities set the fashions they all followed.

"How old are the children?" she asked me.

"One is in eighth grade."

"Her name is Summer," Jessica said, "but I knew both their names before they came to our school."

"And the other child?"

"Not a child," Jessica said. "He's in our class. Ryder. He's soooo it," she added.

Jordan raised her eyebrows, smiled, and looked to me. "Oh?"

"Yes," I added, "the drooling began immediately. Our custodian, Mr. Hull, is going to have to work hard at cleaning up the mess."

Jordan laughed. "Well, I don't see how he couldn't be good-looking with those two as parents. Is their daughter pretty?"

"We only saw a little of her, but she's pretty," I said.

"And apparently a handful," Jessica added.

"Oh? Why?"

"Let's not start spreading rumors so soon, Jessica. Give them twenty-four hours."

"I'm not spreading rumors. I—"

"Does Mrs. Caro know I have a guest?" I asked Jordan quickly to change the subject.

"Yes," Jordan said.

"Okay. Let's get on to our homework," I told Jessica.

"I'll see you before I leave," Jordan said, and Jessica and I went up to my room.

While she chose music for us, I began an e-mail to

Kiera. I didn't want to finish reading her e-mail to me from last night while Jessica was there. She also knew that I didn't like anyone looking over my shoulder when I wrote to Kiera.

I described the episode with Shayne Peters in detail and even included my little joke about Nobody at lunch. Then I mentioned Ryder Garfield, but I didn't go into any detail, and I certainly didn't describe any of my feelings about him.

What were my feelings, anyway? I wondered. I'd be the last to say he wasn't very good-looking, and I had to confess that I was looking at him whenever I had the chance to do so. I just made more of an effort not to be as obvious about it as most of the other girls. His initial nasty attitude had turned me off, but his reaction to my response in English class not only turned me back on to him but, despite the way I spoke to Jessica, made me even more intrigued. I did want to get to know him and looked forward to tomorrow.

Jessica had chosen music for us to listen to, but she was already on my phone talking to Claire Simpson about Ryder Garfield. Claire had graduated last year and was at UCLA. Jessica was friendly with her because their parents were very close. Claire's father worked for the *Hollywood Reporter,* so if anyone at our school would have some nitty-gritty for us, it was she. I finished my e-mail just as Jessica finished her phone call.

"Okay, I got it," she began as if I had asked her to do it. "The Garfields bought a new house near the school, but Claire made a phone call while I was on hold and thinks there were some problems at their old school, which was also a private school, of course."

"What kind of problems?"

"She's not sure, but she thinks it involved Summer. She's digging into it for me."

"So maybe that was why he was so angry at her in the parking lot."

"Exactly. Claire is confident she can find out."

"I'm sure she can. She probably works for the CIA. What difference is it going to make, anyway?" I asked, and went to my book bag.

"You're not really going to start on our homework, are you?"

"I'm not going to sit here and talk about Ryder and Summer Garfield. You wanted to watch that new Blu-ray movie we have, I thought."

"Whatever," she said, disappointed. "I guess I need some help in math anyway."

Jordan stopped by before she left. She hadn't told me where she was going to dinner or with whom, but I didn't think much of that. There were many other times when she left for something and didn't speak of it until the next day or even days later. However, although she looked very nice and as well put together as ever, I had been here long enough and with her long enough to know that wherever she was going and whomever she was seeing were not just to pass the time or fill the gap Mr. March left by being away. I thought she looked worried, in fact, and wished I had no one with me so I could have asked her about it.

I had gotten so I knew her moods almost as well as her natural children would. When someone is your own flesh and blood, you have that special sense, that connection that gives you a real sixth sense about each other. Jordan had tried so hard to make me feel more like her real daughter. I knew she lived for the day when I would call her Mother, but I couldn't get myself to do that yet and probably never would. In the beginning, it was difficult even to refer to her as Jordan and not Mrs. March.

Despite that, a part of me wanted to feel closer to her. At times, I thought I needed her almost as much as she needed me to help fill the great hole in her heart that Alena's death had caused. I was always reluctant to show her any affection. It was easy to sound appreciative and grateful, but to throw my arms around her, to kiss her lovingly, to reach for her hand when we walked in the street or in shopping centers, or even to smile warmly and bathe in the sunshine of her affection was still, after three years, very difficult, if not impossible, to do. Besides the danger of riling up Kiera's jealousy, I felt as though every soft word, every mechanical kiss on the cheek, every embrace was a small betrayal of my mother.

Would or could I ever get past all that and really feel as if I was part of the March family?

I wished I had Mrs. Caro's clairvoyance, her prescience and wisdom, so that one morning I could throw open a window, look out at this beautiful world I was in, and see where it would all take me. I knew if I asked her, she would avoid answering, even though she knew. She would say something like, "You need to make your own discoveries."

But I was here because I had not been able to foresee what would happen if I didn't stop my mother from crossing a street. What could I prevent or do about my own future?

"Stop thinking so much," Jessica told me before we went down to dinner. I had finished my work and helping her with her math and was just staring at nothing. "You make me nervous." I started to protest, but then she added, "Unless you're thinking about Ryder Garfield."

I smiled.

Maybe she was right.

Maybe I should be doing nothing else but that.

"I lied about his eyes," I said. "They were definitely not tinted contacts."

She widened her smile.

"And I could think of nothing else but filling them only with me."

It was like magic. Our laughter was like music. It was going to be a fun night after all.

All dark thoughts fell helplessly away. We couldn't get enough of each other's intimate dreams and wishes.

And all because of Ryder Garfield.

But I also sensed a note of caution in the air. This might not make every day Christmas.

*Be careful,* I told my heart. *You have seen enough disappointment and tragedy to fill the life of someone four times your age.*

But I knew that hearts are never cautious. It's not their job to be cautious.

# 3
## Gossip

*U*nfortunately, as she often did, Kiera called me after midnight. I was more upset than usual because she broke into a dream I was having about Ryder Garfield. In it, he revealed that he knew everything about my past. He was whispering to me in class without looking in my direction.

"My father is talking about having a movie made about you and your mother. You have to tell me everything in great detail," he said. "We'll have to spend lots of time talking . . . alone."

Then, as he turned to me in my dream, the phone rang, and I was snatched out of my deep sleep. I hated the sound of the phone at that moment and glared at it, but I didn't want it to keep ringing. It might wake Jordan.

She hadn't returned home until after Jessica's mother came to pick her up. Her mother was disappointed that Jordan wasn't there and was a little annoyed with me when she asked where she had gone and I had to tell her I really didn't know.

"Well, isn't Donald away? Did he come back earlier than expected?"

"No, he's still away," I said.

"Well, I wish she would have called me. I wasn't doing anything special tonight," she muttered.

Jessica's mother was a dark-haired woman at least fifteen or so pounds overweight for her five-foot-five frame. I had been to Jessica's house often enough to know that her mother was someone who was interested in everyone else's life more than she was interested in her own. Even Jessica admitted that her mother could write the Pacifica parents' gossip column.

"Tell me about this new student," Kiera said the moment I said hello. "Is he as good-looking as his father?"

"Kiera, it's nearly twelve-thirty! I'm half awake, if that. Do you have to call so late all the time?"

"You sleep too much anyway. Well? Tell me."

"Yes, he's just as good-looking, if not better-looking."

"Better? Maybe I graduated too soon."

"Why? I thought you were falling in love."

"Did you read my last e-mail?"

Despite how sleepy I was, I still managed to blush recalling the details of the lovemaking she had correctly described as gymnastic.

"Yes, I read it."

"Well?"

"What do you want me to say? I'm happy for you."

"You sound very jealous. Are you?"

"I'm too tired to be anything, Kiera."

"Um. I loved what you did to that Shayne Peters. His

older brother wasn't much different. He used to follow me around like a puppy. I finally had to tell him not to bother even speaking to me if he didn't get a face transplant. How's my mother?"

"She's upset that you don't call her more."

"Did you tell her anything more about Richard?"

"Just that you said he was a proper Englishman."

"And what did she say?"

I didn't want to tell her exactly what she had said. "She said she wished you'd call her to tell her more about him and you. Your father was asking."

"He was? He hasn't called to see how I am for weeks," she said, trying to sound angry but unable not to sound more disappointed and hurt.

"He seems very busy."

"Why do you say that?"

"He's traveling more and longer."

She was quiet for a moment and then said, "There are phones everywhere, and he has one of the world's best cell phones, doesn't he?"

I didn't know what to say. "Maybe you should call him."

"To do what? Remind him he should be calling me? He's the father; I'm the daughter. Forget about it. Let's talk about really important things. How's your car?"

"Still smells brand-new."

"We have a four-day weekend coming up, but I'm not sure I'm coming home. Richard has nowhere to go, and I don't want to leave him alone."

"Bring him here."

"Not yet," she said. "I'm afraid that once he meets my

parents, he'll make for the high road, as they say in England. Gotta go. I was supposed to write a summary of an essay for tomorrow's English class. It's so annoying to have to do any work," she added with a laugh. "Watch for my next sexual episode."

I let her hang up first, and then I did and fell back onto my pillow. What was it she saw about her parents now that made her afraid of introducing a new boyfriend to them? Or was it simply that she was afraid he'd be so overwhelmed by her home and wealth that he would be intimidated and leave her? She had told me he was the son of a knighted, successful architect. Surely that couldn't be it, and Kiera was never one to understate herself and her family's wealth. No, I didn't expect that there would be any surprises. Maybe she feared that her parents would not approve of Richard, and not vice versa. Of course, their approval of her friends or boyfriends never seemed to matter very much to her anyway. That made me even more curious about him.

I closed my eyes, but my thoughts wouldn't stop dancing. *Go back to dreaming about Ryder,* I told myself, *or you'll never get to sleep.* I was able to do just that, and my dreams and sleep became so deep that once again, Mrs. Duval had to waken me.

"I swear," she said, raising the curtains to let the sunshine slap me in the face. "I'm going to have to come in here at night and turn on your alarm clock myself."

My eyes were squeezed so tightly shut to avoid the light that I thought the skin would rip on my forehead. I groaned, took a breath, and sat up to face the day. She stood there looking at me with her hands on her hips again. This time, she really did look upset.

"Once is an accident. Twice is a mistake," she said. "Especially if it's in a row."

"I'm sorry. I got too involved in . . ."

"Yes?"

"Homework, and I forgot the clock."

She tucked the corners of her lips deep into her face and shook her head. Why couldn't I lie as well as Kiera, or was it just that I couldn't lie well to someone like Mrs. Duval?

"Mrs. Caro thinks you should have oatmeal today. She's at the stove," she added, and started out.

"Is Mrs. March up yet?"

She paused in the doorway. Although she tried to hide it, I saw worry in her face.

"No, and maybe you should not disturb her," she added, and left.

I rose like Lazarus from the grave, stunned and surprised that I could move, and headed for the shower. Under my breath, I mumbled curses at Kiera for waking me after midnight. That conversation seemed to be more like a dream anyway. Later, at breakfast, even though just the thought of swallowing anything was exhausting, I forced myself to eat most of the oatmeal and the piece of wheat toast with her homemade jam that Mrs. Caro insisted I have. She had my daily vitamins set out as well. I didn't have one foster mother, I thought—I had three now. It was as if all of my bad habits were under surveillance from the moment I awoke to the moment I fell asleep in this house.

By the time I was ready to leave for school, Jordan had still not come down. The only times this happened were when she was sick with a cold or the flu. Generally, though, her health was very good, as was Mr. March's. Mrs. Duval stepped into her shoes and took on the duty of seeing me off, warnings and all.

"You drive carefully," she said, "and no speeding," she added, just the way Jordan would.

"Is Mrs. March all right, Mrs. Duval?"

"She'll be just fine," she said, which was her way of telling me she didn't think so.

Whom had Jordan seen last night? What was troubling her? I wondered as I got into my car. Was it just her husband's intensity about his business now? It was true that there was no blood relationship to tie us together, and my status was still that of a foster child, but time, the hard experiences I had had with Kiera and her friends, the Marches' generosity, all of it, had drawn me closer and closer to the family I had every right to despise. I couldn't help myself. I cared about them all now at least as much as most of the girls at school cared about their families. I tried to put it all aside as I drove.

It was only about a fifteen-minute drive. On rainy days, it might take five or ten minutes more. Nevertheless, I was usually one of the first to pull into the parking lot, even when I rose later than Mrs. Duval and Mrs. Caro would like. They had their act together in such a way that they were able to move me through the morning and out the door at just about the same time.

I was surprised to see Ryder and his sister arrive only

moments after I had. He had looked so unhappy during the time he was here yesterday, and after finishing the day with an argument with his sister in the parking lot, he had seemed to me to be a good candidate for late arrival or perhaps no arrival at all. I had thought there was a real possibility that he had gone home and complained about Pacifica so much that his parents had given in and had let him transfer back to his old school or some other school. Wouldn't the girls be disappointed? Wouldn't I?

It wouldn't be impossible for Ryder to withdraw. Parents of the students at this school struck me as the sort of people who bought their way into happiness, no matter what. If they were annoyed with their cars, no matter how small the annoyance, they traded them in instantly. If they didn't like the decor in their homes, they brought in a decorator and paid top dollar to make changes quickly. If it was too cold for a week, they hopped on a plane and went to Hawaii. Inconveniences were stamped out like roaches. How many times had I heard the girls in my class moan and groan about the electricity being off for a few hours because of a storm or the batteries daring to die in their iPods and cell phones? Tragedy had a new definition here. It was defined by as little as a broken fingernail.

Surely a family as well known and as successful as Ryder Garfield's was no different. Rather than hear his complaints, his parents could surely just buy him into another school. Yet here he was, and early, too. I sat in my car and watched him in my rearview mirror as he emerged from his. From the way his sister glared at him and hurried off, I knew their argument hadn't ended. Perhaps he had complained about her to his parents and she had been punished in some way she thought cruel and unusual, such as the confiscation of her MP3 player. He stood there for a moment watching her saunter off.

When I got out of my car, he turned toward me. I wasn't sure what I would do. I was about to raise my hand and say hi, when he lowered his head, turned, and walked slowly toward the school entrance. Whatever friendly overture I had read into his two words to me after English class yesterday had obviously been misunderstood, I thought. He had no interest in being friendly. However, it occurred to me that he might be in my homeroom and perhaps the same morning classes as well. I couldn't wait to see how he would treat me then, if he bothered treating me any way at all.

More often than not, our school lives were like a teenage soap opera. Maybe that was why so many of us were addicted to them. Here, we were on a stage of our own making, and all of us, including me, walked and talked with one eye on our immediate audience but another on everyone around us to see who was looking at us, who was listening to us, who was waiting to see what we were doing.

*Me! Me! Me!*

I felt like screaming it after Ryder as he approached the door.

*Hey, Mr. Big Shot. Look at me!*

For a moment, I thought I might have done just that, because he turned at the door and looked back at me. It was just a glance. He wasn't waiting to hold the door or anything, but pathetic me, I was excited by it. I hurried on.

He was in my homeroom, but he was assigned to a seat in the rear. When I walked in, he was taking his seat and didn't care to look at anyone. Before I could say or do anything to get his attention, my girlfriends began arriving right behind me. I did see him glance my way while they talked excitedly about what they had seen or done last night. I thought he smiled, but maybe it was a sneer. With him, it looked as if it would always be difficult to tell the difference.

We did have some morning classes together, but in all of them, we were too far apart to talk, and before lunch, I had instrumental music. As more of my girlfriends found him distant and disinterested, their overall opinions were beginning to cement with the most obvious conclusion taking the headline quickly: "He's very stuck-up. He's in love with himself."

Those thoughts were logical here. Very few of my friends could envision any boy being so aloof and indifferent to them for any other reason. His parents were really famous, so he didn't want to lower himself enough to have any sort of conversation with anyone here, least of all a relationship.

"He's just out-and-out boring," Joey Marcus decided. That pleased them even more. Jessica was the last to fall in line, but not before she looked at me to see if I was going to be in agreement. I said nothing, so she chanced it, and then, looking for confirmation, asked me if I agreed. We were all gathered outside the library. Some of us had study hall there. We still had another minute until the bell rang for class.

"It's too easy," I said.

For a moment, it looked as if they had all been put on pause. They stood there staring at me.

"What's that mean? What's too easy?" Sydney Woods asked first.

"It's too convenient to say he's conceited. You don't have to think about him at all after that."

"Maybe we don't want to," Barbara Feld said. They all started to nod.

"I don't believe that. You probably had an orgasm thinking about him last night," I replied. It was vintage Kiera, for sure. Their mouths fell open. "Better get to class," I added, and hurried away. Some of them would be late. They were that stunned.

Ryder was only two desks behind me in the next row in social studies class. He was already seated when I entered the room and started for my desk. Just as I passed him, I heard him say, "Queen bee."

I stopped. "Excuse me?"

"From the way they gather around you, you look like the queen bee."

"Be careful you don't get stung."

"Queen bees only use their stingers to dispose of other queens," he replied. "Each of them should be careful, not me."

The bell rang, so I slipped into my seat. I wanted to look back at him, but I didn't do it once during the whole class period. When the bell rang to end it, he was up but talking with Gary Stevens, who I thought was one of the nicer boys in our class. He was slim, with curly red hair and freckles that looked like drops of pure honey on his cheeks. His father was an accountant whose clients included many of the parents in Pacifica, but Gary seemed the most unassuming of the boys in our class. He had a great sense of humor, was bright and maybe a little immature, but I did find him the easiest to talk with, maybe because he was so meek at times. The girls couldn't understand why I bothered.

"His idea of a good time is playing with his Wii," Mona Kirland said.

"Not his wee-wee?" Lily Albert added, and everyone around us laughed. Everyone, that is, but me.

"Sometimes," I told them, "it's nice to talk to someone who's not trying to upstage you all the time. You don't have to guard every word you say or worry he'll go making up stories about you afterward. Try it. You might like it."

Some of them actually did, and I laughed to myself, thinking how the other boys were wondering why Gary was suddenly so popular.

I think Ryder felt comfortable with him as well, and when I went to lunch after instrumental class, I saw them sitting together at a table outside the cafeteria. I sat with my girlfriends and watched him out of the corner of my eye. Our lunch conversation had returned to more ordinary subjects such as soap opera stories, clothes, and makeup. Halfway through lunch, Jessica came out of the building. I had been wondering where she was. I could see the excitement in her face. She obviously had something to tell me.

I deliberately stayed back when the warning bell sounded and everyone started back into the building.

"Where were you?" I asked her.

"Claire found out about Summer," she said, sotto voce.

"You heard about this just now?"

"I called her. She told me to try reaching her about now."

"You're not supposed to have your cell phone on in school. You could have been suspended."

"I went into the bathroom. No one heard me."

"Why risk it?"

"Are you kidding?"

"Yes, I guess so. There should be a motto over the front entrance," I said. "'Gossip, the lifeblood of Pacifica.' Let's go in."

"Don't you want to know what she found out?"

I watched Ryder walk into the building with Gary and then looked at her. "Well, obviously if I don't let you tell me, I'll be responsible for the first human being to really burst from scandalous information. Go on."

"Summer was caught in the athletic storage room making love to her boyfriend, who happened to be a junior. She was to be quietly expelled, but the Garfields were given the option of just having her and Ryder transferred."

"Why him, too?"

"Isn't it obvious? I figure he's supposed to be keeping an eye on her. That explains the outburst in the parking lot yesterday about her going braless. Well?" she asked, as if she had climbed Mount Everest or something.

I gave her my best stern glare. "If you spread this stuff around, you'll make it really hard for both of them here," I said. "And if one other person tells me this stuff, I'll know you did."

"What are you so upset about? I thought you wanted to know."

"Never mind. You just remember what I said," I warned, and started in ahead of her.

When I was at my hall locker, I saw Ryder talking to his sister. She stood with her arms embracing her books and listened. Then, without speaking, she turned and walked away from him. He watched her a moment and headed in my direction. I deliberately walked a little slower, but he didn't stop to walk with me. He passed me, but I heard him mumble, "Shouldn't you be in your hive?"

"Very funny!" I shouted after him.

I glared at him across the aisle when I took my seat.

"Why are you so nasty?" I asked before Mr. Malamud began the class.

"Just comes to me naturally, I guess," he said.

"Maybe we all need to be inoculated before we catch it," I said.

He looked at me wryly and then gave me a much warmer smile.

I held my breath, expecting some sort of sarcastic comment to follow, but it didn't come. He actually looked friendly for a few moments in English class. Throughout the day, I had noticed that aside from Gary, he rarely spoke to anyone. It wasn't that the other boys had a lack of interest in him. I did see attempts being made to strike up conversations in the hallways and at lunch, but he either shrugged, shook his head, simply nodded, or replied in some monosyllabic way. His responses were quickly turning them all off.

In some ways, he reminded me of myself when I first entered the school. I was always afraid of getting into too many conversations, or long ones. The obvious fear was that I would reveal too many details about myself and damage the fiction Jordan had created about me, both for my benefit and for Kiera's. I was somewhat shy as well, having not had any friends my age for some time and also being quite intimidated by these well-off students who probably wasted in one day what my mother and I had lived off for a week.

I couldn't imagine why Ryder Garfield would be shy. Surely, because of his famous parents, he had been introduced to and often saw big movie stars. He was at fancy celebrations and award events. There was certainly nothing shy about his sister. What reminded me of myself was the way he seemed to be afraid that someone would discover who he really was, too.

Mr. Madeo gave us what he called a writing challenge midway through the period. He had different quotes from the remainder of *Hamlet* written on slips of paper and handed them out. Based on what we had done and learned so far, we were to interpret the quote and relate it to the rest of the play. I noticed it took Ryder only ten minutes to read his and write his answer. He glanced at me, and I looked up. As soon as I did so, he shifted his glance away.

"Too late," I said.

He turned back. "Excuse me?"

"You were caught looking."

He stared a moment, and then he shook his head and raised his hand.

"Yes, Ryder," Mr. Madeo said.

"I'm done here. Can I hand it in and go to the restroom?"

"Done? You sure?"

"Yes."

Mr. Madeo shrugged and picked up his paper. He glanced at it. "Man of few words?"

"I'll say," Shayne Peters quipped from the back of the classroom. Everyone laughed. Ryder's face turned a shade of crimson.

"Okay," Mr. Madeo said.

Ryder rose, scooped his book into his bag, and started out.

"Save me a seat!" Shayne shouted after him. Again, the class laughed.

I quickly finished the point I was making about my quote and raised my hand, too.

"Don't tell me you need to go to the restroom, too," Mr. Madeo said with a smile.

I nodded. He picked up my paper, glanced at it, and just nodded. I got up quickly.

"Don't go to the same restroom," Shayne shouted after me. The class started to titter again, but I stopped and looked at him.

"At least I know the difference," I said.

There was a loud cheer, mostly from the other boys. Mr. Madeo called for silence, and I left.

As I was heading toward the girls' room, I looked out the side door that opened to the ballfields and saw Ryder sitting on a railing and looking down. I hesitated and then headed for the door. He looked up when I stepped out.

"Class over? I didn't hear the bell," he said, looking as if I had caught him doing something illegal.

"No, I was finished and asked to go to the girls' room."

"Is it out here?"

"Very funny. I thought you were going to the boys' room."

"That *is* out here," he said, and I laughed. He looked away.

"You hate it here, don't you?" I asked.

"Not any more than I hated where I was," he said, turning back. "You look pretty content. How come you're so popular?"

"Who said I was?"

"Didn't take me long to see that. What are you, disabled? That's what someone with modesty would be here."

"Is that why you seem to be having trouble making many friends?"

"Friends? People don't make friends here. They make contacts. They use each other. It's in the air."

"Didn't you have any real friends in your previous school?"

"No, and I didn't have any in grade school, either." He glared at me, his eyes narrowing. "What's your idea of a friend, anyway? Someone to share lipstick with?"

"No. My God, you're so bitter."

The bell rang, and he slipped off the railing.

"So," he said, reaching for the door. "Next time you want to talk to me, bring some sugar."

"I thought I had!" I shouted after him. He didn't look

back. I stamped the ground, hating myself for even making an effort. Maybe the girls were right about him, I thought, and vowed to do my best to ignore him.

I certainly wouldn't dream about him, I told myself, and opened the door.

I didn't calm down fast, either. Jessica and Joey came rushing toward me when they saw me.

"Was that a plan you made with him?" Jessica asked.

"What?"

"Getting out of class together like that. Did you and Ryder plan that?"

"Get real," I said, starting away. My rage felt like fire around my face.

"We saw you come in the door soon after he did," Joey called after me. "You were out there with him, weren't you?"

I turned around and smiled. "I was out there with Nobody," I said, and continued walking away.

# 4

## Jordan's Secret

"Whenever you get angry, you lose control of yourself in so many ways," my mother told me almost every time she got angry at my father. "No matter what, in the end, you're always the one who loses. Remember that."

The immediate result of my rage took place in my next class. I was fuming so much I wasn't paying any attention, and when I was called on to answer a question, I didn't even realize I had been called upon, much less answer the question. The resounding sound of my name being repeated snapped me out of it. I saw everyone was looking my way—everyone but Ryder, who kept his face fixed forward as though he couldn't care less.

"I'm sorry, Mr. Leshner," I said.

"Rein in your thoughts, Sasha," he said.

I nodded. He didn't repeat the question for me. He went on to someone else. After class, I hurried up front to apologize to him.

"It's not like you to be daydreaming. Anything wrong?" he asked.

"No. It was just my being stupid," I said.

"Don't make it a new habit, and we'll be fine," he said. His forgiveness only made me feel worse.

I avoided Ryder for the remainder of the day. My friends sensed that I was in a bad mood, and everyone kept her distance—everyone, that is, except Jessica, who always looked like someone on the verge of a nervous breakdown when there was something she didn't know about someone in school. She practically followed me to my car after school, waiting for me to tell her what really happened between me and Ryder Garfield. Finally, I spun on her so abruptly she stepped back like someone who thought she might be slapped.

"Look, Jessica, I'm really not interested in talking about him. I've had enough darkness and disappointment in my life to fill the Grand Canyon, and your pestering me about it doesn't help."

"I'm sorry. I just—"

"Just stop," I said, and got into my car. Before I started the engine, I saw him walking out with his sister beside him, her head down. I had the feeling he had been critical of her again. I thought the look on his face would stop a clock.

*How can anyone go through life so unhappy?* I wondered, but shook the thought out of my head and backed out. Whether it was reflexive or whether despite my determination something inside me continually drew me to look at him, I don't know. But I looked into my rearview mirror to see him walking to his car, and I did see him turn to look my way.

Why was he interested in seeing me leave?

It was exactly this confusion about him that fanned the flames of my interest, no matter how I tried to smother them. I was comfortable with most of the boys in this school, because they were, as Kiera might say, "as easy to see through as a new plate-glass window." I hadn't met anyone who was clever and subtle enough to catch me off guard—anyone before Ryder Garfield, that is. Was I thinking about him because I was genuinely interested in him, or was I simply annoyed that I couldn't figure him out and pigeonhole him along with the other boys? Even the expert, Kiera March, would have trouble this time.

When I drove up to the house, I saw Jordan sitting out by the tennis courts. She was alone and looked as if she was so deep in thought she hadn't heard me drive up. As soon as I parked, I hurried over to her. I knew she was deep in thought because she didn't realize I was coming over to her until I was practically on top of her. She turned and smiled.

"Oh, you're home," she said, and looked at her watch. "I had no idea how late it was."

"Are you all right?"

"Yes, yes," she said. "Once in a while, I like to stop to smell the roses, something Donald hasn't learned to do, apparently. Come, sit beside me," she said, starting to move over on the bench, and then she stopped. "No, better yet, drop your schoolbag here, and let's walk to the lake. We had some geese on it last night, you know. They're flying south."

I put my bag on the bench and walked beside her over the stone-tiled path.

"Did you hear the geese this morning?"

"No." I didn't want to tell her I had gotten up late again. "I wasn't outside very long before I got into my car. They must have gone by then."

"Oh, I bet you're the cat's meow with that car. My father loved that expression, *the cat's meow*. Ever hear anyone say it?"

I shook my head.

"My father said it a lot, especially if I was feeling a bit down. He'd boom, 'What's the matter now?' and then, lowering the tone of his voice, he'd add, 'You have nothing to worry about, Jordan. You're the cat's meow.' My brother, Gerald, always made fun of me when my father said that. He'd start meowing or hissing. Sometimes he does it even now. Can you imagine a man that age meowing on the phone? Imagine if his secretary overheard him doing that."

She laughed.

"My brother, the big, important Washington lawyer."

"Why doesn't he come here more often?" I asked. Since I had been at the Marches' home, Jordan's brother, Gerald Wilson, had been here only twice, and one time was to help with Kiera's legal troubles. He brought his wife, Danielle, only once. From what I could see, she rarely called Jordan. Their three boys had little contact with Jordan and Donald March.

"He's like Donald, too busy to breathe," she muttered, not disguising her bitterness.

"Maybe you two should go on a holiday."

She paused and looked out at the lake. "Yes, to re-charge our love batteries," she said. "It's what the doctor is ordering."

"A real doctor?"

"No," she said, smiling. "A therapist we see who special-izes in marriage counseling."

"Oh." I hadn't realized she and her husband were seeing a marriage counselor, but it didn't completely surprise me. I heard her suck in air the way someone who was in pain would. She wiped her eyes before any tear could emerge.

"What's wrong?" I asked.

"Oh, just silly stuff, I'm sure."

There was a bench at the lake so people could sit and look out at the water. She sat, and I sat beside her. It was very quiet, the only sound being the gentle lapping of the water against the rowboats as the breeze combed the top of the lake and sent ripples across its surface. The sky was spotted here and there with small puffs of clouds. They looked dabbed on a blue velvet canvas.

"Donald might be having an affair or affairs," she revealed, still staring at the water. "I was with someone last night who is convinced of it and couldn't wait to let me know. People can be like that, you know, especially your so-called good friends, so be aware of it."

"Be like what?" I asked. Her words had nearly stolen away my breath.

"Eager to give you bad news and watch you wallow in it."

"Why would friends be like that if they're your friends?"

She smiled. "You'll find out soon enough, if you haven't

already, that there are friends and there are friends. What you have most of the time are acquaintances. A real friend is so rare that if you have three during your entire lifetime, you're a very fortunate person, and that applies to relatives as well. Most will be envious or think themselves superior. A real friend would have avoided giving me any bad news for as long as possible and not jumped at the opportunity to tell me there was a possibility of it."

"Don't have anything to do with her anymore," I said.

She smiled again. "I won't go out of my way to spend private time with her, but if I peeled off all the, quote, friends I have who are like her, I'd be a pretty lonely person, especially with a husband who is off so much."

"Don't you have any real friends?"

"Not lately," she said. "I did when I was at school." Her face warmed at the memories. "Our destinies took us in different directions, but I would bet anything that if we were together again, we'd be like two people who never left each other. I'm sure you'll have friends like that, too, when you go to college." She sighed deeply and then looked at me as if she had just realized she had been saying these things to me.

"I hope so."

She smiled for a few seconds and then shut it off as she would a flashlight. "Please promise you will never mention any of this to Kiera. I don't want to add to her personal difficulties," she said.

"I wouldn't."

"You know better than anyone how clever she can be with her questions."

"I won't say anything. I promise, but are you sure your husband is doing these things?"

"No. Nowadays, especially here, people just assume everyone will. It's as if infidelity is part of the air we breathe or something. Of course, many couples who experience the loss Donald and I have experienced often do drift apart. That was one of the reasons we began with a therapist. Ironically, Kiera's problems have kept Donald and me closer, although we do get into arguments about her. He was always making excuses for her, and you know firsthand what that led to. I think, however, that after it all came to a head with her nearly killing herself, his eyes lost that rose-colored haze, and he finally began to see the truth. Maybe that is what drives him to work harder and stay away longer," she added, almost as a hope.

I was listening to her and for the most part thought she might be right, but what I was thinking about under it all was how easily she could reveal these things to me and not worry about how it would affect me. Why wasn't she afraid of disturbing me as much as she was afraid of disturbing Kiera? Why did we have to be sure Kiera didn't know there were any storms brewing in her family and home?

The answer was that no matter how much she did for me, how much she wanted me to feel like her daughter, she couldn't make that leap to a place reserved for only a naturally born child, one who carried the blood of her own family. We shared no ancestry unless we went back to Adam and Eve.

"Oh!" She suddenly gasped. "I'm so sorry to be burdening you with any of this. Look at me, feeling sorry for myself with you, of all people, after all you have suffered. You must think me as selfish as Kiera."

"No," I said. "I'm happy you feel comfortable enough with me to talk about it," I added, not wanting to give her any other reason for sorrow.

"Are you? How grown up of you to say it. I must confess, you are much more mature than I was at your age, but I grew up in a home where being mature wasn't as necessary. Someone was always there to mop up, if you know what I mean."

"Like Kiera," I said. Maybe I said it too quickly. I saw her wince.

"Yes, like Kiera. You would think I would have known better, but Donald . . ."

"I understand," I said.

She nodded and patted me on my hand. "You do, don't you? I'm so grateful to have you here. You're becoming my true friend, and I hope I'm becoming yours."

"You are," I said.

She gave me a big hug. "Okay, now, let's stop talking about me. Tell me about school today. I'm sure it was another exciting day, and I'm sure Ryder Garfield noticed you."

I shook my head.

"Don't be shy, Sasha. No one is very shy in this house or in your school, I bet."

"I'm not shy, Jordan. Ryder Garfield is a very unhappy person."

"Really? You can tell that already?"

"You have to be deaf and blind not to see it, but I'm afraid most of my . . . acquaintances are just that. They think he's super-conceited. In Pacifica, being conceited is normal, so the only way for them to interpret his indifference to them is to describe him as super-conceited."

She laughed and then turned serious. "You've been through so much darkness and despair, Sasha. Don't go looking for it in other people. Everything I've done for you is designed to bring light and happiness into your life. Don't waste it on someone who won't appreciate it or care. You just avoid him, then."

"I'll see," I said. I was just as surprised as she was to hear me say it.

She leaned to the left and looked at me with a smile on her lips. "You're not smitten that quickly, are you?"

I felt myself blush, the heat coming into my neck first and then spilling into my cheeks. "No," I said, even too emphatically for my own satisfaction. "I just don't like to judge people too quickly or unfairly. It happened to me."

She nodded. "Well, you're right. That's a good quality to possess. Just be careful with your relationships, and don't hesitate to come to me for anything."

She looked out at the lake again. The afternoon sun at this time of the fall was low enough to have its rays filtered by the treetops. It turned half of the lake into a kaleidoscope of shapes and colors. One lone tern wandering inland swooped down with curiosity and seemed to glide over the water before rising over the trees.

"I'd better let you get to your homework and tend to some of my phone calls. I'm on the board of directors of the MS Foundation, and we're setting up another gala to raise funds."

She rose and reached for my hand as we walked back to where I had left my schoolbag.

"Mrs. Caro is preparing one of your favorite dishes tonight, her vegetarian lasagna."

"She's a wonderful cook. Where did you get her? I never asked her or you, and Kiera never told me."

"Donald stole her away from another family. They were getting into a bad divorce, anyway, and she was unhappy there. She's been unhappy here, too, but not since you arrived. You've brought sunshine into this house."

She kissed me on the cheek and went off to her office to continue her charity work. Although I saw that she enjoyed helping people—after all, look what she had done for me—I knew as well that she did the work to distract herself and keep her sanity. She had lost a daughter, had a daughter who was almost as good as lost, and now possibly had a husband who was drifting away.

Why couldn't Kiera see all of this and care more for her own mother? As soon as I was in my room, I checked my computer, and sure enough, there was another e-mail from her:

> Well, it happened.
>
> Richard went and did it.
>
> He bought me an engagement ring with an enormous diamond, but I didn't take it yet. His face almost slipped off his skull. Gruesome thought, but that's how disappointed he looked.
>
> Oh, I didn't turn him down. I just told him to keep it in his pocket, and I would think about it. I like him enough. Maybe I even love him.

*Can you tell me exactly what falling in love is supposed to mean and what exactly is supposed to happen inside you? Don't give me some romantic drivel, either, or quote some romance novel. I know you're not sure, either, because you've never been in love, but I'd like to know how you're going to know that you are and it's not just another crush. I read where someday people will try each other on like clothes. I suppose I've been doing that all my life. I can see you smiling and nodding.*

*Well, what's wrong with that, anyway? I can tell you this. I don't want to end up like my mother, and don't start firing back all the good things about her and my father or become like my therapist and try to get me to express why I feel that way. I just do, and that's that.*

*Anyway, back to Richard. I enjoy making love to him more than I've enjoyed it with any other boy. Sometimes it does feel like it's for the first time. I'm not always the wild daughter of the Kama Sutra. Often, I'm as tender as he is. Once recently when we made love, I actually began to cry. He thought I might be upset, but I was happy, contented. Is that love?*

*He still amuses me with his English expressions and his surprise at practically everything I say or do. I suppose that's fresh, and maybe that's part of being in love.*

*He's one of the most handsome men I've ever been with. None of the other men at this school is as well put together. He told me he had a valet taking care of him from the age of four. If there is something about me out of place, he gets right to fixing it. I'll never be unpresentable with him. Having someone look after you so attentively is important to love, I guess.*

*He'll never do anything to upset me, and if he somehow should, he immediately apologizes and practically throws himself at my feet, begging for forgiveness. My unhappiness, even for a moment, makes him unhappy. Is that love? I don't exactly feel that way toward him. If he looks unhappy, I don't work hard at getting him to be happy again, but I do feel bad about it. Is that enough for me to say I'm in love with him?*

*I hate the thought of having children. Actually, what I really hate is the thought of getting pregnant. Maybe I could hire a surrogate, but if I were going to have a child, I could see myself having it with Richard. There is no doubt that he would be a devoted father and would do everything he could to make a child less of a burden for me. That must be part of being in love.*

*I keep thinking about my father's reaction if I should accept the ring. Lately, I've been thinking he would be relieved to know someone else would have to take care of me, but I'd like to think he would be saddened by it, too, by feeling like he's losing his little girl. Do you think he would? I know my mother would probably have a big celebration and invite her garden party friends. She'd get drunk on champagne toasting Richard and saying, "I feel sorry for you."*

*Anyway, how many girls accept an engagement ring from a man their parents have yet to meet? That would surely ruffle their feathers. Do you think that's what's making me hesitate? There you go, smiling, maybe even laughing at the idea that I'd even consider that or care.*

*Would someone in love care?*

*I suppose it's sad that the only one I can talk to about any of this is you. I haven't a friend here I would trust with anything more than my mascara.*

*I'm tired of talking about myself. Let's talk about you. What do you think of me?*

*Just kidding.*

*Tell me the latest about Ryder Garfield. I'm sure he knows your name by now.*

*Kiera*

*P.S.: I just decided to tell Richard I'd wear the ring for a while to see if it fits not only my finger but my heart as well. Doesn't that sound romantic? Or does it sound idiotic? Sometimes I can't tell the difference.*

I sat thinking about what she had written. She was certainly right to say that I would not be any sort of expert on love. However, what she was describing made it sound as if Richard was surely in love with her. I didn't want to come right out and say it, but I couldn't imagine her being in love with anyone. She was just too selfish ever to be in love.

That was the answer, but I couldn't write it that way. Instead, I wrote back that you know you're in love when you care about someone more than you care about yourself. I was afraid that I would be ending their romance.

She might agree and then tell him she wasn't in love with him. She should add that she would never be because she wouldn't ever care more about someone else than she did about herself, but she wouldn't.

Reading her e-mail and thinking about a way to respond got me to think more about Ryder Garfield. If I truly believed he was a very unhappy person, suffering inside himself, and that was why he was so unpleasant, and I really wanted to care, I shouldn't be thinking of how upset he made me. Did I want to care? Why should I care about someone I had barely spoken to? Kiera would call me a bleeding heart and say something like, "You need a transfusion of selfishness."

My telephone rang and shook me out of these deep thoughts. It was Jessica. Like her mother, she just didn't give up when it came to gossipy drivel.

"It gets worse," she said as soon as I said hello.

"What does?"

"The story about Summer Garfield. She wasn't just caught making love in school. She got pregnant and had an abortion."

"Claire told you all this? How would she know this? C'mon, Jessica."

"Reliable sources. That's all they ever say in her father's business, but they're right more than they're wrong."

"I don't believe it," I said.

"It explains why Ryder's so serious and angry-looking all the time, don't you think? It must be like a house of horrors in that home."

"I don't know. I know one thing, though. If you spread this around—"

"I'm not! You're the only one I've told, but these things have a way of getting out eventually."

"So do rats."

"If he wasn't very nice to you, why do you care so much?" Jessica asked, obviously growing annoyed.

"Maybe because I remember a time when I wished people cared about me," I said.

"Oh," was all she could respond, but it did take her down a peg or two.

Although they knew of my previous life on the streets as a homeless person, most of the girls at the school avoided mentioning it or asking me about it. It was all too ugly and unpleasant for their delicate ears. I could tell them about rats, about the rats that came around my mother and me when we slept on the beach, and waking up feeling one run over my feet. I could tell them about having to bathe in a public toilet and having to hold my breath to avoid inhaling too much of the stench. I could tell them about the tar I would pick off my toes at the end of the day or the days I was so hungry I thought I would eat insects.

Whenever I was with any of my school friends in a mall or just walking in the streets and I saw someone homeless pleading for small change, I felt the skin cringe at the back of my neck. My girlfriends could look right at these people as if they weren't there, but I had to find something to give them. Only once or twice did someone else offer any change or dollars, and then only because I had done so. If anyone spoke about them, the others quickly shut her up with a look or a nudge and nod at me. Jessica said that when the girls spoke about me, most refused to believe I had really been that badly off. They were comforted by saying that it all had to be exaggerated.

How I wished it had been.

"Well," Jessica said. "I thought I should tell you what I found out. I can't imagine what it must have been like at Ryder's home when this all happened, how his parents took the news. Probably they were both afraid for their careers and still worry about it."

"Maybe they were afraid for their daughter, too," I said.

"Maybe," she said, but not with any enthusiasm. I thought that was cold, but later I would come to believe that she was probably right.

No matter what I did, I thought, I would never really fit into this world. The question was, would I get too deeply into it ever to get out?

I told her I would talk to her later and went to do my homework. Mrs. Caro did make a wonderful lasagna for me. Jordan enjoyed it as much as I did, and at dinner, she was more buoyant, concentrating on her gala and how big and elegant it was going to be. She was confident that they would get Tony Castle to entertain. He had been very popular at one time and in dozens of films and on Broadway.

"We need someone who can sing like Sinatra," she said. "It fits with a black-tie affair."

The way she said it reminded me of people who buy paintings not for their own beauty but for how they will fit in with their decor. The artist would certainly be unhappy to have been reduced to a decorator's coordination idea. I remember it being the same when my mother sold her calligraphy on the beach. Many of the people who bought one had talked about how it would fit this wall or that room and not about how beautiful and unique a work it was in and of itself. But still, we were grateful for every sale. It meant we'd eat.

After dinner, I went up to finish my homework and start a paper I had to do for English, even though it wasn't due for two weeks. It was on *Hamlet,* and rereading scenes to find the quotes I wanted reminded me of Ryder's sharp answer in class and his sort of backhanded compliment of mine. Maybe he wanted to be friendly, I thought. Maybe he was simply afraid. Maybe how he acted was the only way he knew.

Unable to concentrate, I rose and went to my closet to pick out what I would wear tomorrow. Although I wouldn't come right out and say it even to myself, I knew in my heart that I wanted to look special, more special than ever, if that was possible. I toyed with my hair and thought about my makeup. While I was at my vanity table, Jordan came to the door, tapped gently, and entered.

"Donald called," she said. "He's coming home tomorrow. He said he was able to get everything done faster than he had first thought."

"Oh, great."

"Yes," she said. She looked so hopeful and pleased.

*She really does love him,* I thought. If only Kiera could speak to her the way a daughter should speak with her mother, she would get the best guidance regarding Richard. I would have had that sort of relationship with my mother, for sure. Also, I felt a little guilty knowing what was going on around that engagement ring with Jordan not knowing. It would be a shock to both her and her husband if Kiera showed up wearing the ring.

Were they destined to be forever disappointed with her?

If Jessica's stories were true, were Ryder's parents destined to be forever disappointed with their daughter, Summer?

*I'm back to my mother's belief,* I thought, *back to the question about our futures.*

Did we have any control, after all?

I wondered what Ryder Garfield thought. Did he feel helpless trying to influence and control his sister? Did he hate having to do it or hate more that he would not succeed?

Jordan was great and wonderful to me. How could I ask for any more out of anyone right now?

But how I missed my mother. Even homeless, sitting lost and desperate together on a beach, she would hear more than my words, my questions. She would hear my heart, and she would know, the way anyone's mother would know, what was best for me.

I had lost so much that night in the rain.

It was not possible for anyone to tell which drops on my cheek were tears and which were raindrops.

I couldn't even tell myself.

Only a mother could do that, and not having her or anyone else who could do it left me so alone.

Jordan kissed me good night and went to sleep feeling hopeful.

I went to sleep listening for the voice I would never hear again.

But when I closed my eyes, I saw Ryder Garfield's face when I had first approached him outside. He looked as if he was listening for the same voice, as desperately as I was.

*When he realizes that,* I thought, *he won't be afraid of me.*

## 5

## *Getting to Know You*

ary says you were a homeless person," I heard, and turned around in the hallway on my way to our first class. Ryder Garfield was walking right behind me. When I left homeroom, I didn't look back, so I didn't know he was that close. I glanced at him, saw nothing warm and friendly in his face, and kept walking. He drew closer until his lips were practically touching my earlobe. "I guess that life-in-the-street stuff was a little bit of an exaggeration, huh?"

I stopped so quickly he almost walked into me.

"Whoa," he said. "Can't you signal?"

"Can't you watch where you're going?"

"Well?" he said, stepping up beside me now. "What's the living-in-the-streets story?"

"Why should you care?"

"I can't help it. I have a built-in fantasy detector and have to attack them whenever I hear or see them."

I looked at him. He was so positive about me, so smug in his assumptions. "My mother and I were evicted from our home when my father deserted us. We couldn't keep up the cost of a hotel and eventually ended up living in the streets and on the beach in Santa Monica. You can't even begin to imagine how much I would rather you were right and it was all exaggerated. This is one time your built-in fantasy detector malfunctioned. Add it to your list of things wrong with yourself," I added, and continued walking, but a little faster. This time, he didn't catch up, but when we sat in the classroom, he looked at me instead of looking forward. He was staring at me so long that I finally said, "What?"

"You don't look like someone who lived on the streets."

"Oh, you would know? You really look at them?"

"Enough to know you don't."

"Well, I don't live there now, and I haven't for three years. I don't have any visible scars from it, if that's what you mean. The scars I carry are inside."

He nodded.

"Nothing else nasty to say?"

"I'll think of something," he replied, and then he gave me a real smile. I felt the rage dissipate in my body and laughed, but I turned serious quickly when the bell rang. I wasn't going to be caught not paying attention in any class today, and especially not because of him again.

As the class began, he looked somewhat more involved in the work as well and did take notes this time. When he was called on, he answered the question quickly. After the bell to end class rang, he didn't jump up to rush out. He took his time, obviously waiting for me to get started, and then he joined me before anyone else could.

"I'd like to hear about all that," he said.

"Hear about all what?"

"Your life in the streets. What else? Certainly not chemistry."

"Why is it so important to you?"

"Something tells me it's head and shoulders over the droll garbage most of the other girls in this place would spew if I lent an ear to it. You know, Mark Antony's speech in *Julius Caesar:* 'Friends, Romans, countrymen. Lend me your ears.' Only here it's 'I want to talk about myself and make myself sound so wonderful you'll be grateful for five minutes of my attention.' "

That made me laugh. He was so right on about that. "That's not quite Shakespeare," I said.

"You get the drift. Well?"

"I don't like talking about that time in my my life."

"You don't have to be ashamed with me," he said.

I stopped walking and turned on him sharply. "I'm not ashamed. Even though we were very poor and these people here are very rich, they were never and are not now any better than me. I'm just not happy about bringing back some of the ugliest memories of my life."

He nodded. He didn't say anything else for a moment, so I thought that was it. He was finished with me. He'd spin off and be gone. But he stood there, shrugged indifferently, and said, "Okay, when you're ready to talk, I'm ready to listen."

"What makes you think I'd want you to listen or it would matter to me if you did?"

He smiled confidently. My indignation caught fire again. I could feel my blood start to boil.

"You don't appear to be deaf, and you don't look stupid," I said. "So I guess it's that, like everyone else here, you're just used to getting what you want."

Before he could respond with any smart reply, I joined the Hassler twins, Vera and Mary. They were the sweetest, most unassuming girls in our class and without a doubt the most unattractive because of their unfortunate heavy hips and plain faces, with mouths a little too small and eyes too beady. They wore their hair too short, making their chubbiness more pronounced. Their parents were divorced, and they lived with their mother in what the girls here called a really middle-class house. From the disparaging way the other girls described it, someone would think they lived in a slum. The story was that their mother made their father pay the high tuition for Pacifica as part of her revenge. I supposed all that was why they were the shiest in our class and usually spent most of their time together. I tried to bring them into anything I could, but it never translated into other girls being friendly to them or inviting them to any parties or outings.

Right now, I felt as if going to them was retreating to a safe haven. I was sure Ryder was surprised at how easily I could walk away from him. I couldn't help but be a bit like Kiera and make Ryder work hard now for any friendly smile or soft words from me, but as it turned out, even the Hassler twins were fascinated with Ryder Garfield. It was becoming almost impossible to go anywhere in this school to get away from him.

"We saw you talking to Ryder Garfield. He talks to you more than he talks to any other girl here," Vera said, watching him walk away from us.

"Most of the boys talk to Sasha more than the other girls," Mary pointed out. She was the sharper and sterner of the two. "Do you like him?" she asked me.

"I haven't formed an opinion of him, but I can tell you that he's not easy to like," I said.

"He would be easy for me," Vera said.

"Freddy Krueger would be easy for you," Mary told her.

"Shut up. He would not."

"Whether Ryder Garfield is easy or not, he's not worth you two arguing about," I said. "Did you get the paper done for Mr. Leshner's class?"

"It took us so long to find all those references," Vera said.

"Didn't you use your computer?"

"Mary said we shouldn't. Mr. Leshner might not like that."

"He never said you couldn't."

"She's not telling you the truth. We couldn't use our computer because there's something wrong with our computer, and my father hasn't sent anyone over to fix it, and my mother won't spend the money. She says it's his responsibility," Mary revealed. Vera looked embarrassed.

"Why don't you tell your mother to have it fixed and send him the bill?" I asked.

"That's a good idea," Vera said, but Mary shook her head.

"He'll procrastinate just to aggravate her, and all we'll hear from our mother is why did we tell her to do that."

Vera looked at me, perhaps hoping I could come up with some other solution.

"Then one of you call him yourself and complain."

"Yeah, right," Mary said. "That always works with my father. He has what are known as very holy ears."

"Holy ears? What's that?"

"Ears with holes in them for requests he doesn't like or care to fulfill," she said. "It's my mother's description, but it fits."

"I'm sorry," I said.

The more I talked with most of these girls in Pacifica and heard about their family lives, the more I wondered if any of them was ever any better off than I was.

We entered the classroom.

"I have a copy of *Flicks* magazines in my bag," Vera told me in a whisper, and nodded at Ryder. "His father is on the cover."

"Vera," I said, "unless he's a fireman, he puts his pants on one leg at a time, just like your father. Stop thinking of him as anything more."

I left both her and Mary looking a little stunned and took my seat.

"All right," Ryder Garfield said before the class began. I looked up at him. "You're right."

"Pardon me?"

"I'm sorry."

"Sorry? For what?"

"For being a nasty bastard," he said.

We stared at each other, and then I smiled. "Okay. Now that you have reached the point where you can admit it, you can join the NBA."

"The NBA? Basketball?"

"No, Nasty Bastards Anonymous. It works the same way Alcoholics Anonymous works. The first meeting is today at lunch."

He laughed. "Are you in it, too?"

"Sometimes. Especially around here," I said. "It is like an addiction."

His smile widened. "I'll be there," he said.

*Damn you, Kiera,* I thought, *your techniques with boys really are infallible.* Maybe I had taken on many of Kiera's traits, I thought, but what of it? They weren't bad so far and certainly weren't bad for me, someone who had once been too shy and embarrassed to look at herself in a mirror.

Later, when I walked outside with my lunch and stepped away from the girls, Jessica practically leaped out of her seat. "Where are you sitting?"

I nodded at the table where Ryder was sitting alone.

"Did he ask you to sit with him?"

Everyone paused to hear my response. "Since he joined the NBA, I thought I would give him another chance," I said.

"Huh?"

I laughed to myself as I headed for Ryder's table. He looked up, and then, to my surprise and I'm sure that of just about the rest of the student body who were watching, he stood up before I sat. *Won't Kiera be interested in that?* I thought. She thought Richard was the only proper gentleman.

"Is that all you eat for lunch?" he asked me, nodding at my salad.

"I could live on salad, cheese, and bread."

He sat and stared guiltily at his hamburger and fries. "My parents are neurotic when it comes to food, too."

"I'm far from neurotic, Ryder. I just think about what I eat. Why are your parents neurotic?"

"Are you kidding? My mother claims the camera puts anywhere from five to ten pounds on her, and my father, although he pretends not to, thinks the same way. It's not who you are and what you can do in this world. It's what you look like. Don't you know that?"

I shrugged. "Not to me. I must be from another planet."

He nodded and began to eat his hamburger. "So, am I permitted to ask how you came to be living here and attending one of the most expensive private high schools in California, if not the whole country?"

"Gary seems to have told you everything else. He didn't tell you that?"

"Maybe he thought I wasn't interested enough."

"Maybe you led him to believe you weren't."

"Maybe I wasn't," he replied sharply. "Maybe I am now, okay?"

"Why?"

"Why what?"

"Why are you interested now?"

He looked away. I could see the frustration in his face from the way his neck strained and tightened his cheeks and jaw.

"I don't want you to strain yourself thinking of a good answer, Ryder," I said. "Forget it."

"You are a tough nut to crack," he said, turning back to me.

"You're not exactly soft yogurt."

He laughed. "No, I guess I'm not."

He looked up, and then his eyes narrowed and the humor left his face. I saw that he was looking past me, and I turned to see his sister sitting between two boys. I kept eating and tried to ignore the new rage I could see building in his face.

"So, tell me," I said, "why are you interested in learning about me now?"

"You want the truth?" he asked, sounding and looking so upset that I thought he was going to start shouting or something. But I wasn't going to back down.

"Yes, I'd like that for a change. It's like taking a shower or a bath here."

"You're the first girl I've met in a while who is at least vaguely interesting to me."

"Vaguely? Well, I guess that's sort of a compliment," I said. "Maybe that's the best you can do."

"Maybe it is."

"Okay." I shrugged. "Next time I see you, I'll bring along a magnifying glass so I don't miss anything nice."

He stared at me a moment and then he sat back, smiling and shaking his head. "What is your name?"

"You don't know my name?"

"I heard our teachers call you Sasha, but what's your whole name?"

"Gary didn't tell you that, either?"

"I didn't really feel like talking about you with Gary," he admitted. "You show the slightest interest in someone, and the whole school has you practically married."

"Sasha Fawne Porter. What's yours?"

"Ryder Martin Garfield."

I put my fork down, wiped my hand with my napkin, and then extended it.

He looked at it and took it.

*"Enchantée,"* I said.

*"De la même manière."*

"You speak French?"

"A little. We lived in Paris for five months when my father was making a film there and my mother was doing some modeling for a French designer. What about you?"

"Just what I'm learning in class. How come you're not in French class? It would probably be easier for you."

"No, it wouldn't. I never had a formal class. I just learned on the streets," he said. "The streets, get it? So maybe we have something in common."

"Is that supposed to be funny?"

"To some people, I guess, but you want to know something?" he said, leaning toward me. "I'm convinced that what we learn on the streets lasts longer and has more meaning than what we learn here. Take it for what it's worth, and make whatever you want out of it," he added. "If you can't stand it, leave." He bit angrily into his food.

"You're pretty sensitive. Anyone ever tell you that?"

"Me? You practically had me assassinated for asking about your street life."

"That's different."

"Because it's you. Maybe you're not so interesting, after all. Maybe that's why you're so guarded."

"Maybe I'm not."

"I'll bring a magnifying glass to school tomorrow and tell you," he replied.

We stared at each other, neither wanting to give ground by relaxing a lip or even blinking, and then we both laughed.

I glanced slightly to my right and saw that my girl-friends—most of the school, in fact—were watching us intently. If they could hear our conversation, they would think they were watching a tennis match.

"Okay," I said. "I'll tell you about myself, but only if you do the same."

"I don't have much to tell," he said. "You'll be disappointed, even bored."

"I'll pretend not to be," I said, "and that will make you feel important."

He smiled again. "You are more than vaguely interesting."

"Ah, more than vaguely. I guess that's progress," I said. "You're slowly slipping into the body of a human being."

He laughed. "Okay," he said. "We'll play you show me yours and I'll show you mine."

"Careful," I said. "You could end up naked."

His jaw finally fell.

"Finish your hamburger," I said, "before it gets cold."

Obediently, he began to eat, not taking his eyes off me. I could almost feel the wall between us begin to crumble. The question was, did I really want it to crumble? Did I really want to relive my past, and from what he was telling me, did I really want to hear more family dysfunction?

"I've been to five different schools since grade school," he told me when the warning bell sounded.

"Five? Why?"

"Our traveling, mostly. For a little while, Summer and I had a tutor."

"I had one when I first came here. I hadn't been in school for nearly a year, so there was a lot of catching up to do."

"How come nobody checked on you? I thought you had to be in school. It's a law."

"Are you kidding? When you're homeless, you don't exist. Nobody even looks or cares, and that includes policemen. Believe me."

"Sometimes I feel like I don't exist. Maybe I'm homeless and don't realize it," he said as we entered the building. "I mean, a house doesn't automatically mean a home, and having parents doesn't mean you have a family."

I thought about Kiera. Maybe he had far more in common with her than he had with me. "I know what you mean."

"Do you?" he asked, as if he thought I was patronizing him.

"Yes. My stepsister would say the same thing, and for her, it would be very true."

"I'd like to hear about that."

"All you seem to want to hear is bad, ugly, or dark news."

"It's like flies attracted to garbage," he muttered.

I can't say I wasn't used to other students staring at me from time to time, but walking with Ryder, I felt the eyes of our classmates so glued to us I wanted to flick them off the way you might flick dandruff or dust. He either was oblivious or simply no longer cared.

"I think we're going to need more time to get to know each other," he declared at the classroom doorway. "These little intermissions between classes don't do it."

I was speechless a moment, recalling my first dream about him. He had used almost the exact same words in the dream. Neither of us moved or spoke for a moment. Other students brushed by us, all of them looking at us as we stared at each other.

"What do you suggest?" I asked.

"Well, you have your own car, so I can't offer to drive you home, and I have to take my sister home first, anyway."

"Let me think about it," I said.

"Yeah, do that," he snapped back, and entered the classroom.

Did I really want to have anything to do with anyone who had such a hair trigger, I wondered, no matter how good-looking or interesting he was?

I entered the class and took my seat. I could see the girls smiling at me and laughed to myself. If they only knew how hard to know Ryder Garfield was, they wouldn't be anywhere nearly as envious, I thought.

He grew calmer as the day came to a close, and before we left to go to the parking lot, he gave me his cell-phone number.

"Let me know whatever you decide," he said. He looked toward his sister approaching. "Unfortunately, my life isn't exactly my own right now."

"I'll call you," I promised.

My thought was to have him come over after school after he had dropped off his sister, but I wanted to get permission from Jordan first. I always got her permission before I invited anyone to the house, even though she had told me countless times to consider the March house my house, too, and not to stand on any ceremony. Despite the years and the many, many wonderful things they did for me, I couldn't take that final step she so wanted me to take and truly see myself as her and Donald's daughter. It didn't have to do with their not legally adopting me yet, either. Even if and when they did, I was sure I still wouldn't get to the place Jordan wanted me to get to. I doubted that I ever would or even should.

The moment Ryder left me, Charlotte Harris, Jessica, and Sydney pounced.

"Wow, what's going on with you and Ryder?" Charlotte asked.

"You two were pretty tight all day," Sydney said.

"C'mon, tell us," Jessica whined.

"Nothing's going on. We simply got to know each other a little more. And we weren't that tight, Sydney."

They stared at me, waiting for something delicious to add.

"I don't know if it's going anywhere yet, so don't go blabbering about us," I said.

"Did he invite you to his house? Are you going to meet his father and mother?" Charlotte asked.

"I don't know," I said, and started for my car.

"You don't know what?" Sydney asked. The three of them followed me like cans tied to the back of a newlywed couple's car.

"Stop making something of it. It's nothing." I paused. They waited, and with a smile I added, "Yet."

They all squealed as I got into my car.

"If there's anyone who could handle him, it's you," Sydney said before I closed my door.

"Why?" I asked her. I gave her an intent look, and she started to fumble for words.

"I just mean . . . I mean . . . with . . . what's happened to you . . . you just know what to do better than any of us."

"Not everyone and every situation is the same, Sydney. And I didn't grow up around kids whose families were rich and famous."

"I know. I just thought . . ." She looked at the other two for help.

It always bothered me that most of the girls in my class who knew what Kiera and her friends had done to me when I first came to this school treated it as a war wound or something similar. They practically had me wearing a Purple Heart. It was good for my ego to have them think I was so sophisticated, but the truth was, it didn't make me all that much wiser when it came to relationships with boys. If anything, it made me more frightened, and maybe that was really why I was so hesitant about being involved with one boy all this time.

I realized that this was partly my fault. Instead of telling them that I didn't know what was right or wrong for them to do when they came to me with their romantic problems, I offered suggestions. Sometimes I even tested some of the questions out with Kiera. *Give the devil her due,* I would think. *Let's see what she would tell them.* And most of the time, I thought her advice was good and gave it, but now I was sorry I had gone so far with this. It was enough to be responsible for myself, much less everyone else's teenage love life.

"It's nothing to spend any time over," I offered, but the three of them smiled at me as if I were the delusional one. "See you tomorrow," I said, and closed the door.

"You better call me tonight," Jessica called after me.

I waved at her and drove off, feeling strangely numb. It was as if I had left my body and was as light as air. I felt emotionally exhausted. The banter I had with Ryder was stressful at times but also exciting. I could see that he was sincere when he said he was interested in me. If he had been to five different schools, he surely had met many girls, girls who were like the girls here, excited about who he was and how good-looking he was. Some of the girls in this school might as well have waved a white flag at him, announcing their complete surrender to his every whim and wish, and there were many who were very attractive, some who I thought were far more beautiful than I was.

And yet he was drawn to me. Despite the Grand Canyon of differences between us, between the world into which he was born and the world into which I was, I felt we did share something very important. Both of us, despite how we might appear to others, were deeply wounded. I couldn't help sensing that he was as lonely as I was at times, and as lost. We came to the same place over different roads of pain and suffering, but we were like two people who had found each other on a deserted island, undecided about whether we even should try to get off it and return to the world.

Was it good for me to be close to someone like Ryder or even just around him? Could I fall back into deep depressions? Should I tell him my story and, in doing so, revive so much pain? Maybe once he learned the terrible details, he would avoid me anyway. If he was looking to me to cheer him up or give him some sort of hope, he might be terribly disappointed.

And what about me? I knew what it was to be poor and almost invisible. When I was that way, living with my mother in the streets, I would often stare in awe at the well-dressed, beautiful women who drove expensive cars. I was sure some of them were celebrities. We lived in a place where celebrities were often sighted. How I envied them. And if I should see someone like that with a little girl beside her or holding her hand, how much I envied her or wanted to be just like her. Surely they lived in a perfect world.

But here was Ryder Garfield and his sister, Summer, children of the beautiful people, wealthy and famous, and yet both of them seemed unhappy and lost. What did I hope to learn from being with him? That there was no good place to be? That whether you had parents who were wealthy and successful or parents who were failures, you still ended up on that same island? What did matter, then?

Jordan had warned me about having anything to do with someone who was dark and unhappy. Was she right? Why was I both excited and frightened by the prospect of getting to know Ryder more and maybe becoming his lover? Was I just destined for this sad part of life? Would I always dwell in the darkness and feel tears on my cheeks in the rain?

I drove onto the March estate, conflicted. A part of me was saying that I shouldn't even ask her for permission to invite him. *Forget him. This can lead to no good. Tell him your foster mother didn't approve or give you permission to invite him.* It might be easier that way to discourage him, to stop this before it became too late.

But another part of me was clamoring for the challenge and the excitement. Just as he told me that I was the most interesting girl in the school, I saw him as the most interesting boy yet. *So it's a challenge. So what? If you retreat now, you'll always retreat whenever a relationship shows the slightest difficulty. You'll end up either like Kiera, always skeptical and selfish, or like Jordan, afraid and alone.*

What would my mother tell me to do?

How I hated the silences I had heard and the silences I would hear.

How I longed for someone with not only wisdom to give me but true, real, and deep love.

Would I ever have that again?

# 6

# *Fighting*

 was surprised to find Jordan sitting alone in my room. My first thought—and fear—was that she had been into my computer, suspecting that Kiera and I were keeping an e-mail correspondence that I didn't share with her, and had read some of Kiera's outrageous e-mails, but I could see that the computer was not turned on, and Jordan wasn't very fond of computers. She had one, but she rarely used it. She told me, "I still like the feel and sound of someone's voice. E-mails are just too impersonal. I can tell what someone is really thinking when I hear him or her speak, and that is especially true for my own daughter."

She sat with her back to the door, looking out the window, and was in such deep thought that she didn't seem to hear me enter.

"Jordan?"

She turned, and for a moment, I thought she had taken one of those pills I knew she took to calm herself. Sometimes they made her look pretty spaced out. I know her husband hated it when she did that. Right now, she looked as if she didn't recognize me. I could see the confusion whirling about in her face.

"Jordan? Are you all right?" I said, approaching her.

"Oh," she said, snapping out of her look of bewilderment. "Yes, yes, Sasha. I'm sorry. I was in deep thought for a moment and was thinking back to when I would sometimes wait here for Alena to return from school. Before she became very sick, she would bounce up the stairs and burst through that doorway, exploding with excitement about something she had done in school or something that was going to be done. No matter how bad my day was, it all became warm and sunny again. Just embracing her and kissing her did that for me."

I nodded but couldn't help thinking that she was comparing me with Alena and was very disappointed. I wasn't coming home as buoyant and happy, perhaps, or at least excited enough to cheer her up and help her forget any dark thoughts, and I never rushed to have her embrace me. I was still haunted by dark thoughts of my own, and neither the size of this house nor all of its luxury could shut them out completely.

"I'm sorry," I said.

"What? Oh, yes, yes. Well, there's nothing more we can do about it, is there?" She shook her head and then smiled. "But do tell me about your day. Were you absolutely amazing in instrumental class again?"

"Any day Mr. Denacio doesn't slam his hand on the desk and rant about how little everyone is practicing is a good day for me, as well as the others. I like the music he's chosen for us to play at the next concert. I guess that shows when I play. He looked very pleased."

"Oh, that's wonderful," she said, and stood. "And guess what? My college daughter called finally to tell me she was growing more serious about this young man, Richard Nandi Chenik. I asked her what that meant, and she just laughed the way she does when she doesn't want to tell me something and said, 'Let's wait and see.' What am I waiting to see? I hope she's not getting herself into any serious trouble," she added, glancing at the computer. The implication was clear. If I knew something about it, I should tell her.

"I don't think so," I said.

"But you don't know?"

"When it comes to Kiera's love life, I don't think even Kiera knows," I said, and Jordan laughed.

"How true. And *your* love life?"

"Well, as a matter of fact, I was coming to see you to ask if I could invite someone over after school tomorrow," I said.

She tilted her head and looked at me with suspicion. "Not that dreary boy you and Jessica described, I hope."

"He's not really that dreary. I got to know him a little better," I said.

"You know, I do worry about you even more than I worry about Kiera these days, Sasha. Most girls wouldn't be able to contend with what you've experienced, but all that's happened damages you in ways that even you are not aware of. Believe me, you are still very fragile."

"I know. It's all right. I'll be fine," I said.

She hesitated and then nodded. "Okay. I'd like to meet him, actually, and Donald will be home tomorrow, remember, so he can meet him as well. I've always trusted Donald's impressions about people. It's part of what he does, his training and his success."

For a moment, I wanted to change my mind. The one thing that I was sure Ryder would hate would be to be put on display or obviously evaluated. I know I wouldn't like it, but I supposed it was only natural for parents to do that, especially today. Everyone was worried about the influence of other teenagers. It seemed that no one's son or daughter could ever be the originator of trouble. It was always because of someone else's child.

"What are you planning on doing with him? Playing tennis? Studying? It's not really warm enough to swim outside, but I suppose you could swim in the indoor pool. Would he like that?"

"I'm not sure what he likes and doesn't like to do," I said. "I'm not even sure he will want to come here."

"Really? Well, if anyone thinks he's too good for you, he's not good enough for me. Remember that," she said. She glanced around the room once more and started out.

After she left, I tried to concentrate on my homework, but my mind kept drifting back to Ryder. I took out his cell-phone number and put it on my desk. I was still very hesitant. Maybe Jordan was right. *Do you know what you're getting yourself into?* I asked myself once more. *You put on a good act, but Jordan is wrong when she says you are still very fragile.*

I returned to my homework, but from the way my mind

kept wandering, I knew I wouldn't get much done until I confronted this question. Finally, I made the call. My heart was thumping so hard in my ear while the phone rang that I wondered if I would hear him when he answered. If he was in the slightest way sarcastic or nasty, I was determined simply to hang up immediately.

"Central casting," I heard, and for a moment, I did think I had called the wrong number.

"Ryder?"

"Ah, and to whom might I be speaking this fine day?" he asked in a pretty good Irish brogue.

"Mademoiselle Sasha Porter," I said.

"Herself, is it?"

"In the flesh. Do you always answer your phone like that?"

"I don't usually answer my phone," he said.

"Then why have it?"

"You know why Linus in *Peanuts* had a blanket? Same reason."

"Oh, you're really funny."

"Believe me, it's my full intent to be."

I had to laugh. "Okay, I'm calling to ask if you would like to come over to the March residence after school tomorrow, after you drop off your sister, of course."

"Of course."

"Of course you'll come or of course after you drop off your sister?"

"To this foggy brain, they seem one and the same. In a word, the answer is yes. Do I need anything special to get onto the property—a passport, blood tests, FBI clearance?"

"Normally, all three, but tomorrow is a free day, so you're in luck."

"I'm truly grateful."

"You don't know where I live or anything, do you? Or did Gary describe it?"

"Now, let me think before I answer that. I don't want you to think I'm some sort of fortune hunter or anything."

"I have no worry about that. I have no legal ties to anything here, so it wouldn't do you any good, anyway."

"Oh."

It occurred to me that I might be assuming too much. How many of the students at Pacifica really understood that I was a ward and not an adopted child?

"Disappointed?"

"Actually, relieved," he said. "The parents of the last heiress I went out with had me fingerprinted and followed."

"That still might happen," I warned. Knowing Jordan, I was actually only half kidding.

"Now you do make it sound interesting. Shall we discuss the details at school tomorrow?"

"Every chance we can get," I said, and he laughed.

"I'm beginning to think that with you, I might not need a magnifying glass after all."

"The jury's still out for me as concerns you."

He laughed again. I heard some noise behind him.

"Where are you?"

"I'm in Santa Monica," he said. "On the beach."

For a moment, I couldn't speak, nor could I swallow. Did his going there have something to do with me? Was he trying to imagine what my life had been like?

"Why?" I asked.

"I just needed my dose of ocean. It calms me down. Did it do that for you?"

"Sometimes," I said. "I wasn't exactly a visitor, a tourist, and I didn't have the luxury of leaving or turning it off."

"Understood. I'm on my way home. To be continued," he added, and hung up before I could say another word.

Kiera would never stand for a boy hanging up before she had, I thought. She would let him know it, too, and maybe never see or speak with him again. I was trying to keep myself from getting too aggravated about it when my phone rang. It was Ryder.

"I forgot something," he said.

"What?"

"Good-bye."

He hung up, and I shook my head. Should I laugh or cry, encourage him or run from him? I went to my computer.

*Okay, Kiera,* I began. *Ryder Garfield knows my name now, and in fact, I've invited him over tomorrow after school. He's very complicated, maybe even too complicated for you. He seems—no, strike that—he obviously has a chip on his shoulder, and I almost got into some out-and-out fights with him when we first met and afterward, but somehow, don't ask me exactly how, we warmed to each other, and I guess I can say he's interesting. He thinks I am, too.*

*Yes, he's very good-looking, but there are a number of good-looking boys at Pacifica. I can't say exactly*

*what it is about Ryder that both attracts and discour-*
*ages me, but whatever it is, it's different.*

*He can be funny but very sarcastic—mean,*
*actually—and then suddenly, he'll say something so*
*sweet or complimentary, and I don't know how to*
*react. I know I stop fighting, but I'm not sure I'm doing*
*the right thing. You don't have to tell me how quickly*
*you would destroy him. I know, but for some reason, I*
*don't want to get the better of him, even though I do or,*
*rather, know I could.*

*It strikes me that we're both in some sort of compli-*
*cated situation with men. You are far more along than I*
*am or maybe ever will be, but still.*

*I'll tell you more after I spend tomorrow afternoon*
*with him.*

*In the meantime, Jordan tells me you called her and*
*told her about Richard. Have you made any decision*
*yet about the ring? Can I give you some advice? Don't*
*accept it before they meet him. You never listen to any-*
*thing I say, so I don't expect you will now, but I want to*
*be on record as giving you that advice.*

*Please don't call me after midnight tonight. Have*
*some mercy.*
*Sasha*

I sent the e-mail. I was feeling better, so I returned to
my homework. Later, after dinner, just before I started to
prepare for bed, Jessica called.

"Why didn't you call me?" she asked.

"For what?"

"Thanks a lot. I thought I was your best friend. What about Ryder?"

"I don't have anything significant to tell you about him yet. I'll tell you when I do."

"So, you are going to see him?" She pounced.

"I'm going to explore," I told her.

"Explore? Oh." She was silent for a moment and then asked, "What does that actually mean?"

"It means I'm going to see if we have anything to say to each other, share anything in common, even have the slightest possibility of having any sort of relationship."

"I don't know how to do that," she said. "Boys still confuse me."

"There's no specific way, Jessica. You spend some time with someone and see where it goes. Stop looking for recipes and formulas for everything, especially your relationships. It's never that simple."

"I don't, but you do make it sound easy."

I laughed. "It's far from that, believe me, especially for me."

"Sometimes I wish I'd had experiences like you had," she said.

Lately, this romanticizing of my hard time with my mother when we were homeless and the subsequent mean things that were done to me when I came to live with the Marches angered me. It was so typical of these rich and spoiled girls to try to see my life as they saw one of their soap operas. It was truly as if they believed someone could shout "Cut!" and all the nasty and unpleasant things would fade away with the stage lights.

"That's because you never did have those experiences, Jessica. I'm here because my mother was killed crossing the street on a rainy night, and I was almost killed as well. I was in great pain, both physically and emotionally, and although I don't show it, I still am. You have your mother and father. You have a family."

"I'm sorry. I'm sorry," she quickly recited. "I didn't mean anything."

"No, you didn't. That's the problem, really. Very few of you mean anything," I said, and hung up, still fuming.

I sat there with my hand over the phone. If she called right back crying, I'd probably say I was sorry, too, but apparently, I had been so sharp and biting that she was afraid to redial. When I reviewed my words and the way I must have sounded, I realized I resembled Ryder Garfield. Even after so little contact with him, was I taking on some of his bitterness? I didn't even know why he was so bitter. What was his pain?

After I calmed down some more, I did feel bad about the way I had spoken to Jessica. I shouldn't have taken it out on her. She wasn't the only one who treated me this way, and after all, I was partly responsible for the way they thought about me. From the way I lived now, it did seem to them as though none of what had happened was that devastating. I did well in school. I was attractive and witty. I didn't mope about, and I wasn't seeing a therapist, nor did I act out and get into trouble. I was popular and of course, I had so much in the way of material things, things they cherished. Why wouldn't they envy me?

Before I got myself ready for bed, I decided to call her

back and tell her I was sorry I had jumped down her throat. She was so happy I called that she couldn't stop apologizing herself. I thought I would make her night by telling her about my inviting Ryder to the March estate.

"And he's coming?"

"I think so," I said. "When I'm sure, I'll tell you."

"Thanks."

"Don't say anything about it, please. He's not comfortable at Pacifica yet."

"I won't. I promise."

"See you tomorrow."

"Great. I can't wait to hear how things go between you two."

One thing I was grateful for, I told myself when I went to bed, was that I didn't have to live my life vicariously through someone else, like Jessica was doing through me. It always amazed me, regardless of what I had and could do now. No matter how obvious and clear it was that I should be the one envious of Jessica and the others, they were envious of me.

*Whatever gifts you gave me, Mama*, I thought, *were surely wonderful, gifts most other girls my age apparently never have.* I fell asleep easily, wrapping myself snugly in the sound of my mother's voice, the scent of her beautiful freshly washed hair, and the softness of her lips on my cheek. As long as I could remember all of that, I would be safe, even here, I thought.

When Ryder drove into the school parking lot the next morning, I saw that he was alone. Once again, he arrived moments after I had. Actually, I had stalled getting out of the car in the hope that he would, and when he did, I got out, joining him.

"Where's your sister?" I asked.

"I forgot today was her inside-out day."

"Inside-out day? What's that?"

"She sees the therapist my mother arranged for her to see. He turns her inside out and looks for cracks and holes in her head."

"Oh."

"Don't you have a therapist? I thought it was like having a dentist around here," he said as we started for the entrance.

"No, but my foster sister, Kiera, has one. She was seeing him regularly and now sees him only when she's home."

"See? Like a dental checkup. He takes mental X-rays and looks for cavities."

I couldn't help but laugh.

"I have one, too," he revealed at the door. I paused. "He thinks I need a mental root canal."

He walked in ahead of me. I caught up, and we started for homeroom. Every one of my girlfriends lingered to say good morning, obviously looking for him to reply. He didn't.

"How long have you been seeing a therapist?" I asked.

"I can't remember when I wasn't," he said, and paused at the classroom door. "Why? Scare you? It's all right. You don't have to look for any excuses to avoid me. I won't come over to your palace today," he added, and went to his desk, again leaving me stunned.

Everyone was rushing in around me, trying to start

conversations, but I would be damned if I was going to put up with his tantrums. I marched across the room and stood by his desk. He looked up.

"I was only making conversation, Ryder. I am not afraid of you or put off by your seeing a therapist. As you say, it's equivalent to seeing a dentist, and from what I can see, you might need some root canal after all."

I turned and went to my desk, my rage so evident that all eyes were on me. I plopped into my seat and didn't look at anyone. I wasn't sure whom I was more angry at, him or myself for permitting him to get under my skin so quickly. Jessica and many of the girls were looking at me and then at him and then back to me. She made a gesture to indicate *What's up?* and I shook my head. The bell rang, and Mrs. Nelson called for everyone to take his or her seat and be quiet. Sometimes Dr. Steiner began the day with an announcement or two. I looked up, surprised, when I heard Mrs. Nelson say, "Yes, Ryder?"

I turned to look at him. He stood up.

"I'd like to apologize," he said.

"Apologize? To whom and for what?" Mrs. Nelson asked.

"To Sasha Fawne Porter," he said. "For my being a nasty bastard."

There was a little laughter, but everyone was more surprised and shocked than amused.

"I don't think that sort of language is called for, Mr. Garfield, and I don't think it is necessary for you to make your apology to another student a public thing in any case," Mrs. Nelson said.

"Seemed like a good idea at the time," he replied, and sat.

Everyone looked to see what she would do or say next, but Dr. Steiner came on the public-address system to talk about a change in the schedule. The faculty was going to have its meetings early next week instead of in two weeks, and students would not attend classes. There was a loud cheer from our homeroom and from all of the ones down the hallway in celebration of a day off.

Mrs. Nelson took attendance. Just before the bell rang to start the day, she asked Ryder to come up. I left the room with everyone else, and of course, Jessica and my other girlfriends wanted to know what that was all about.

"What did he say to you?" Sydney asked.

"Was it really nasty?" Keana Welles wanted to know. She was obviously hoping it was.

Jessica stood there waiting with the others for my answer. When I had a confrontation with any other boy, as I'd had with Shayne Peters recently, they were all eager to hear about it, and whenever any of them had any problems, they did come running to me for advice. I knew I shouldn't be annoyed at their interest now, but somehow, I did feel differently about Ryder Garfield. He wasn't just a big challenge. There was something deep down inside me that kept me attracted to him.

"Since he apologized, I don't think it's right for me to say," I told them.

There were audible groans of disappointment. I deliberately walked slowly.

"Are you very upset about it?" Jessica asked in a whisper.

"No," I said. "I'll tell you later," I promised, and she smiled so brightly she practically glowed.

Kiera was famous for doing this, I told myself, making one of her girlfriends feel special by promising to tell her something none of the others knew. She spoke to others the same way. Before she was finished, half a dozen of them would claim to be her best friend.

I glanced back and saw Ryder come out of homeroom.

"I'll catch up with you," I told Jessica, and turned to wait for him.

"She's scary," he said, nodding back toward homeroom. "I saw two long fangs start to grow while she was bawling me out."

"You're such an idiot. Why did you do that?"

He shrugged. "Seemed like a good idea to me. Public confession was supposed to be purifying, according to the Puritans."

"You won't find any Puritans here," I said, and he laughed.

"You haven't said whether or not you forgive me," he said when we reached our first classroom.

"You're on probation," I told him.

"How did you know?" he replied, his face deadly serious.

I stared at him, not knowing what to say. Was that why he was so standoffish? Then he laughed and entered the room.

"You creep!" I cried. He looked back, smiling.

Being with him was definitely like riding a roller coaster, I thought. Was he bipolar? Or was he just an angry, insecure young man? Once again, I had to question whether I wanted to get more involved with someone like him. There were a number of boys in our class, besides Shayne Peters, who were so much less complicated and probably would treat me like a little goddess.

To satisfy Jessica's curiosity, I blamed what had happened between Ryder and me on his concern about his sister. I imagined that everyone would learn about her seeing a therapist, anyway. No one would be all that shocked. Ryder wasn't too far off when he referred to it as being like seeing a dentist around here. At lunch, Ryder and I talked about after school. We again sat apart from everyone else.

"I don't have to go home first now," he said. "I can follow you if you want."

"Sure, that's great."

"So what are you planning? Studying together or arm wrestling?" he asked.

"No studying, unless that's something you want to do. Besides, I have a feeling we'd be terrible at it."

He laughed. "That's for sure. Okay, so? What does one do on a palatial estate?"

"There's a lake. We can go rowing, and although I'm not that good, we can play tennis. Do you like tennis?"

"I can take it or leave it. My mother hired a pro to give me lessons when we lived in Spain one summer. I was only twelve, and she was afraid I'd be bored."

"You've been so many places."

"Yeah. My passport is full. You been anywhere out of the country?"

"No," I said. "Unless you want to count this," I said, gazing around.

He looked at me for a moment and then smiled. "That's very good. I think I might get to like you," he said.

"Thanks. I'm so flattered."

He looked at the other students watching us and then leaned toward me. "You sure you're not one of those narc plants or something and you're not really about twenty-four?"

"I'll check my birth certificate," I said.

He nodded. "No, I'll check it."

We both laughed. I looked at the other students again. Aside from his conversations with Gary Stevens, who seemed disinterested in him now, Ryder had not made a single other male friend in the three days he was here. Whatever he had done or said had discouraged them.

"What extracurricular activities did you participate in at the other schools you attended?" I asked.

"Extracurricular? Don't you sound like a guidance counselor?"

"What would you call them?"

"I wasn't on any teams, if that's what you mean, and I didn't join any clubs. I'm with Groucho Marx."

"What?"

"I don't want to belong to any organization that would have me as a member."

"Don't you ever say anything serious?"

"If I answered that, I'd have to be serious, and you'd have your answer."

"Okay. I call a truce for now," I said as the bell rang for afternoon classes.

"Great. It will give me time to take my wounded off the battlefield," he said.

We followed everyone into the building.

"Hey," Shayne Peters said. He was right behind us. Ryder and I turned. "How much are you paying her?"

"Paying? For what?"

"Her time."

"Oh." Ryder smiled at him. "Actually, we're doing barter."

"Barter?"

"Yeah, you know, like the Indians, trading. She'll talk to me if I will talk to you, so I guess this equals what?" he asked me.

"You tell me," I said. "You're the one who decided on the rates and values."

Shayne stood there looking dumbfounded. "What?"

"Okay," Ryder said. "Let's see. I wasted twenty seconds on him. The current exchange rate is twenty minutes of quality time for every second of moronic, right?"

"Sounds good to me," I said, laughing.

"Huh?" Shayne said.

"See your local moron translator for a translation," Ryder told him.

We walked ahead.

"Assholes!" Shayne called after us.

We sped up, laughing harder, and for the first time, I felt I had made the right decision.

He was worth knowing.

And more important, he wouldn't hurt me.

The question lingering out there now was, would I hurt him?

## ❧ 7 ❧
## *Meeting the Marches*

*H*e followed me home. I glanced into my rearview mirror every ten or twenty seconds, half expecting that he would either turn off and disappear or just stop and watch me disappear around a turn, but he stayed right with me up to the gate. He smiled when the orange wall opened. I knew he would be surprised. Most people were, because Mr. March had designed it so you couldn't tell it opened. We drove in and up the long driveway to park. It was a particularly beautiful day. There wasn't a cloud in the sky. All around us, the grounds people were at work on bushes, lawns, and fountains.

"Are they preparing for some big event?" he asked me as soon as we were both out of our cars.

"No, this is just regular weekly maintenance, but there is something being done here daily."

"You could have some major event on this property. We've been at a few, but I don't think the properties were this large."

"They have charity events here."

He nodded and looked up at the house. "I saw something built in this style somewhere. It's radical."

"It's called Richardson Romanesque. The house took years to build. Jordan told me her husband wanted something very unique."

"He got it," Ryder said. "It looks like it should be a museum and not a home."

"It's very impressive inside as well," I said. "Beautifully decorated but too big to be exactly cozy. There's even an indoor pool."

"I heard."

"Oh, so you did ask about it?" I hoped that indicated more interest in me than in the Marches.

"You don't have to ask. People just start talking about it. In fact, my mother knows about this house."

"Oh?"

"Very little when it comes to the rich and beautiful gets by her," he said, sounding a little bitter about it. "Where's your room?"

"Up there," I said, pointing to my bedroom windows. "Second floor. Third floor is mostly guest rooms, and there's an attic full of things that will probably never be used, at least by the Marches."

He looked to the left at the tennis courts. "You're high enough to see over the tops of trees. I bet you see the ocean."

"Yes. One side of my bedroom looks out over the outside pool and cabana. It was Alena March's room," I added.

"The little girl who died?"

"Yes."

He nodded and looked up at the house again and then toward the tennis courts. "I've been in great European chateaus. We stayed in some very expensive hotels in Rome and Paris. One time, we were in Vienna for three days and stayed at a hotel that had its own little park . . . Im Palais Schwarzenberg. But I think this beats it all. It's the biggest private residence I've seen for someone who was not part of a royal family. I wonder if there's anything like it in the whole state."

"I wouldn't know," I said. "I haven't been farther than Disneyland. Jordan and Mr. March have been talking about taking me on a European holiday, but it hasn't happened yet."

He looked at me as if he was finally seeing me for who I was, the ward of a rich family. I was sure it was triggering dozens of questions, questions my girlfriends and any other boy I had been with had asked and were still asking. With most, I was reluctant to answer, but for reasons I had not quite yet understood, I felt like telling Ryder everything and anything he wanted to know.

"You call her Jordan, but you call him Mr. March?"

"Yes. I used to call them both Mr. and Mrs. March."

"I suppose that's progress. How long have you been living here?"

"Three years."

"I know it would sound crazy to most people for me to ask, but are you really happy here?"

"It's not crazy," I said.

"You didn't answer." He smiled at my silence. "You feel guilty when you're happy, is that it?"

"Let's go in," I said instead of replying. "I'll show you around, and you'll meet the Marches. Mr. March is supposed to be back," I added.

"Oh? Where did he go?"

"He's often away on business. He runs a major public relations firm and has clients all over the United States and in Europe."

I led him to the front door and took a deep breath before opening it.

"You act like you're going underwater," he said.

I glanced at him and nodded. "It does feel that way sometimes."

We entered.

As if she had been waiting anxiously just inside the door of her office-den, Jordan came hurrying down the hallway and calling to us. She was wearing one of her more expensive designer suits, a charcoal skirt and a jacket, and had her hair pinned up. She looked as if she had just stepped out of an executive office. I was sure Ryder was wondering if she was in any way involved in Donald March's business affairs. Sometimes I thought she dressed like a businesswoman just to pretend she did something more important. She did wear clothes like this whenever she went to a charity club or committee meeting and sometimes used Mr. March's secretarial services for her personal business.

"There you are," she said. "Donald arrived just over an

hour ago. Come in, please. I'm Jordan March," she said to Ryder.

"Ryder Garfield," he replied. He looked at her hand, and then he took it and gave her what I thought was a rather exaggerated smile, his eyes wide. He looked around. "You must have quite an electric bill."

Jordan laughed. "We have quite an everything bill. I know you two want to explore, but just come in for a few minutes," she urged, indicating one of the sitting rooms, as she called them. Ryder looked at me with a gleeful gleam in his eyes. It made my heart go pitter-patter to think what might come out of his mouth at any moment. We followed her.

I was interested in how Ryder would react to everything he saw here. Even though he was from a very well-to-do, famous family and apparently had seen many amazing things already in his life, I was curious to see what would impress him. Most of the girls I had brought here were so amazed that they couldn't help gushing compliments about the large paintings, the oversized chandeliers, and the rich European furniture, tables from Spain, settees and chairs from France, and wall mirrors from England. I don't think I ever stopped being overwhelmed, but perhaps because I saw so much unhappiness beneath the surface, I had become a little indifferent to it all.

Sometimes I wished we all lived in a modest little home that made it impossible for us to ignore each other or avoid confronting each other's worries and sadness. Here, anyone could find himself or herself on another planet, never having to confront anyone else's dark face all day if he didn't want to. I used to feel, and still did to an extent, that going down to dinner was like visiting strangers who lived miles away.

Ryder went directly to the piano and ran his hand over the top.

"It's a beaut," he said.

"That's an East Indian rosewood," Jordan said. "Do you play?"

"I did," Ryder said, which took me by surprise. "My mother had me take lessons for years. She always managed to have a piano for me wherever we went to live when she or my father was on location for extended periods. I stopped about two years ago."

"Why?"

He shrugged and then, smiling at me, said, "I ran out of notes."

"What?" Jordan held her smile. She looked at me.

"He's kidding," I said quickly. "You never mentioned you played the piano. Really, why did you stop, Ryder?" I asked pointedly. The expression on my face was clear. *Give her a serious answer, or else.*

"I just lost interest," he said. He shrugged. "I was never very good, and taking lessons wasn't going to change it."

"That's a mistake." We turned as Mr. March entered. He had changed into his black velvet smoking jacket and black slacks. His light brown hair looked as though he'd had it trimmed and styled an hour ago, but that was Mr. March, always looking impeccable. Sometimes I thought he saw himself as a modern-day prince living in a palace. I thought he looked quite tanned and rested for someone who had gone on another business trip.

"Oh, this is my husband, Donald March," Jordan said. "Donald, this is Ryder Garfield, the young man who just entered Sasha's school."

From the way she widened her eyes when she mentioned Ryder's name, I understood that she had already discussed Ryder with him to make sure he knew who he was and who his parents were. Mr. March nodded, glanced at me, and then extended his hand.

"Pleased to meet you, Ryder," he said when Ryder shook his hand. "But I couldn't help hearing your excuse for giving up piano. I find that most people give up on themselves before other people give up on them, especially young people today. Too often, your generation doesn't have the staying power necessary to find success. You've got to work on that," he said, wagging his right forefinger.

"Thanks for the free advice," Ryder said. "One thing your generation isn't stingy about," he added, and Mr. March's cheeks took on a slight crimson glow.

"Well, I wish I had listened more to my parents," Mr. March countered.

Ryder widened his smile as if he had won a point in a debate. "You mean you don't feel successful enough?"

Mr. March's spine seemed to petrify. For a moment, I thought he had turned to stone entirely, but then he smiled. It wasn't a smile with any warmth behind it.

"You can always improve. Once you stop thinking that, you might as well put yourself on a shelf. Perseverance, determination, ambition . . . those are the building blocks for a successful life. And you don't sit on your laurels and soak in your own sunshine," he continued, still in lecture mode. Even I was surprised at how insistent he was being. "You have to be like a man walking a tightrope."

"How's that?" Ryder asked, with more of a smirk than a smile.

"You don't look down to see how high up you are. Once you do that, you fall. You just keep going forward."

"It's got to end somewhere," Ryder insisted. They were acting like two stubborn little boys.

"It ends when you're willing to give up, and I say, for those who do, failure's meant to be. I'm sure both your parents had many obstacles and overcame them with perseverance, determination, and ambition."

Ryder was silent. Mentioning his parents was to him like someone hitting below the belt. I could see the conflict raging in his face. His eyes were like windows revealing the tension. Jordan might have sensed it, too, when she looked at the expression on my face.

"They're too young for such talk," she said, hoping to take the heaviness out of the conversation quickly.

"You're never too young for such talk," Mr. March insisted. "So what are your interests, if I may ask?" He sat and nodded toward the settee across from him. "Are you inclined toward some show-business career as well?"

Ryder looked at me with accusation in his eyes. Did he think I had led him into some sort of trap? Put him under a spotlight for a cross-examination and interrogation? I shook my head slightly.

"Doubt it. Right now, I'm into model planes and boats," Ryder said without sitting.

"Pardon?"

"I find them interesting and relaxing. What do you do for relaxation, Mr. March?"

"That's a good question," Jordan said. "What do you do, Donald? I'm afraid my husband is a workaholic," she added before Mr. March could attempt a response.

"People always accuse other people who strive continually for excellence of being workaholics. It never occurs to them that maybe these people enjoy what they do. If I may be permitted to give you some additional free advice, it's that you should find something you enjoy. That way, it will never seem to be work to you, and you won't be so concerned about relaxation. My work actually relaxes me. Isn't it the same for your parents?"

"If it is, they've kept it a big secret," Ryder said. Both Jordan and her husband looked taken aback. I couldn't help but smile. I'd known him long enough already to know that it was a typical Ryder Garfield reply.

"Ryder doesn't like talking about his famous parents very much," I offered. "People are always trying to get information out of him about them."

"Well, we're not exactly working for *Entertainment Tonight*," Mr. March said sharply.

"I understand what Sasha means," Jordan said, instantly coming to my defense. Mr. March shot a look at her that would have bowled over a bull. "Are you enjoying Pacifica?" she asked Ryder.

"It's all right," he said with a small shrug.

"Just all right?" Mr. March pursued. "It's rated the top private school in the state. You're lucky to be there. Take advantage of all the opportunities it offers. Are you in any sport? The band?"

"Just navigating the rapids is sport enough for me right now," Ryder said.

"What rapids?" Mr. March asked. He looked at me for help.

"Daily life among the rich and famous," Ryder replied.

Mr. March just stared, but when he was agitated, he had a habit of moving his tongue against one cheek and then the other, making it look as if a small animal was trying to find the way out.

"Well, Sasha, why don't you show Ryder around the house and property?" Jordan suggested, the way a referee might to ease tension. "Did you want Mrs. Caro to prepare a snack for you two?"

"Ryder?" I said.

"No, thank you, Mrs. March. In our family, eating between meals, unless it's taking coffee with a producer, director, or agent, is a capital offense."

Jordan looked to me to see if he was kidding. I knew he was and thought that Mr. March might at least smile, but he continued to glare at him and then looked at me before standing. His face was full of disapproval.

"Well, I have some matters to address. Enjoy yourselves, while you can," he added.

"I thought your work was your enjoyment," Ryder blurted before Mr. March could turn away and start out.

"Yes, but I still have to pay attention to it," Mr. March retorted in a sharp, poorly disguised tone of annoyance. "You can neglect and be irresponsible even with the things you enjoy."

He looked at Jordan and relaxed his shoulders. Then he offered a weak smile.

"You'll learn that the pleasure is in the journey. That's why practicing shouldn't seem like a burden, whether it's playing the piano or the clarinet, as Sasha plays, or something in sports, whatever."

He left. None of us spoke for a moment, and then Jordan said she had to speak with Mrs. Caro about tonight's dinner.

"Will you be staying for dinner, Ryder?" she asked.

"No, thank you, Mrs. March."

"Well, if you need anything, Sasha . . ."

"Thank you, Jordan," I said.

She started out. Ryder looked at me.

"I'm sorry," I said.

"I'm not really interested in seeing anything in the house at the moment. Let's get some fresh air," Ryder said, and we walked out, him moving ahead of me almost as if he wanted to escape. We paused on the steps. "Now I know why you took a deep breath before entering the house. Is he always like that?"

"Actually, I don't remember him ever being that direct and confrontational. I was as surprised as you were, believe me. He should have been that way more with Kiera's boyfriends, the ones she brought home when I was here. He never seemed to pay much attention to anyone I brought home."

"I was about to say I wasn't here to ask for your hand in marriage or something, but I didn't want to be that impolite, even though he would have deserved it. You don't know why he jumped down my throat like that? Was it something else that put him into that mood?"

I didn't want to get into the possible tension between Mr. March and his wife. I shrugged. "I'm really sorry, Ryder."

He nodded. "I'm not blaming you."

We started toward the tennis courts.

"Maybe he's just being overprotective," I suggested, and began to tell him about my first experiences with Kiera and her friends. I was sure that Gary had given him some of the highlights, but he seemed surprised to hear the nitty-gritty details concerning me and her boyfriends. I went into detail about the Virgins Anonymous club they had pretended to belong to and the initiation ceremony.

The expression on his face softened in sympathy. "You had to make love someplace where you might be discovered or seen?"

"The more chance of that, the bigger the respect the others gave you, supposedly. As I said, it was all a setup to hurt me."

"So on top of their daughter when she was high on something hitting you and your mother and killing your mother, they also accused you of being the bad one, the one who told these perfect girls all about the nasty stuff and suggested they do these things?"

"Yes."

"And they believed it?"

"Mr. March was especially gullible like that until Kiera overdosed on G and her house of cards came tumbling down."

"They owe you a helluva lot. No wonder they bought you that car."

"Nothing they can give me can make up for my mother," I said. "And remember, legally, I'm still an orphan, and they are just foster parents. They don't have to do anything more than provide food and shelter."

"They don't want to adopt you, or you don't want them to?"

"I suppose it's both. Jordan wants it."

"But Mr. Know-it-all doesn't?"

"He's resisting."

"Lucky for you. Right?"

"I don't know, Ryder. It's not easy dealing with all of this. Sometimes I feel like running away, and sometimes I think I'm very lucky "

"I'm the same way."

"Really?"

"Yes, but obviously for different reasons. Okay. You showed me enough of yours," he said.

We kept walking until we reached the lake. I watched as he looked at it all. Most of the kids my age whom I brought here weren't all that interested in sitting at the lake or rowing. They wanted to see the theater and watch some videos or just gossip.

"This is beautiful," he said. "If I lived here, I'd be here every day. Good place to get away from it all."

"Because?"

He was silent.

"So where's the quid pro quo?"

He smiled. "Excuse me?"

"You just said I showed you mine," I said.

"Okay, okay." He sat on the bench, and I sat beside him. Then he made a circle in the air. "We'll do this the way they pitch stories in Hollywood for directors, producers, and actors. Ryder Garfield's life story. Huck Finn meets *Rebel Without a Cause.*"

"Huh?"

"That's the pitch line. Hollywood people need it laid out simply in tags or slogans. First act. When Ryder Garfield was young," he began, "before Summer was born, his glamorous, world-renowned mother was working a lot. Ryder had a nanny from England, an au pair."

"That's why you have that slightly British accent?"

"Does he? Okay, we'll think about casting a young English actor. Please hold your questions until the end. Don't you know that most Hollywood producers have a five-minute attention span? Okay. Ryder's nanny was a bigger influence on him than his own mother, so he picks up some of her accent. He's a neat little boy, always well dressed and schooled in proper etiquette."

"Like standing up when a woman comes to his table," I said.

He shook his head. "If you're going to write this . . ."

"I'm listening, sorry."

"As I said, Ryder is with his nanny more than he is with

his mother. His nanny is still with them when his sister, Summer, is born. She's raising the baby, really, because the first chance their mother gets to return to work, she's out and into the celebrity scene full blast, like someone who has been suffocated because of her pregnancy. Their father, acting all the time, chasing parts, is out as well. Both of their parents, in fact, miss their birthdays occasionally. When someone is young, that hurts, hurts deeply. Back then, Ryder feels sorrier for Summer than for himself. Eventually, he and his sister are old enough to take care of themselves, and their nanny is dismissed. It's a sad day, because to them, it's like losing their mother."

He paused to look at my reaction. I just stared at him quietly, waiting.

"Act Two. Their mother vows to be more of a mother, of course, but things don't change all that much. There are maids taking up the slack. Even when they go on trips, there is always someone hired to care for both Summer and him, mostly Summer. Coming to their mother with a problem is usually like speaking to a translator. She sends them off to talk to their father or some therapist at the drop of a pin."

"And their father?"

"Ah. He's always intent on being a big movie star, you see. There are long periods of time when he isn't home, and even when he is, he's out and busy so much. For a joke once, Ryder takes one of his father's eight-by-twelve head shots and puts it on a piece of wood that he then attaches to a short pole. Using his camera that has a timer, he has

Summer and him take pictures with it, making it look as if their father is with them at restaurants or when they go shopping. Their mother thinks it is funny until Ryder puts it on a chair at the dinner table. His father finds out and gives him one of his he-should-feel-sorry-for-him lectures."

"Feel sorry for him? How did that work?"

"Simple . . . something like your Mr. March. Here he was working so hard to make a success so Ryder's family could enjoy all of these wonderful things, like big homes, servants, trips, expensive clothes, and here Ryder was being unappreciative. Ryder guesses it eased his father's conscience."

"So Ryder doesn't like his father?"

"Ryder doesn't know who he is. He thinks his father has treated the parent role as just another role. That leads to another thing he does that gets his father pretty hot."

"What?"

"He writes a scenario for him, gives his father lines to say. Of course, his father doesn't see the humor and never gets the point. In short, Ryder Garfield is just as much an orphan as you are. The big difference is that his parents expect him to pretend he's not. And they wonder why Summer gets into trouble."

"Is that part of your Act Two?"

"Exactly."

"What happens to her?"

He smiled. "You don't know?"

"I know only rumors, Ryder."

"Yeah, I'm sure. Rumors." He paused. I thought he wasn't going to speak about her, but then he started again.

"She gets pregnant, but she keeps it a secret so long it is almost too late to do anything about it. Their father is the sort of person who would rather ignore a problem, anyway. She takes after him. He thinks he literally expects some writer will come in and do a rewrite of what happens, and he can forget the old version. Anyway, he blames the whole thing on Ryder."

"Why?"

"He's her big brother. He should have been watching over her. Ryder's father forgets how many times Ryder has warned him and his mother about her. The whole thing causes a big embarrassment and cover-up, and they are shipped to another private school.

"At the start of Act Three, his mother and his father expect him to make sure she behaves at Pacifica. There's a big blow-up between them on the first day of school. I think you saw that in the trailer."

I put my hand on his arm. I could see how describing all of this as a movie was disturbing him.

"Your parents are so famous everyone at school thinks you have the perfect life," I said.

"Yeah, I know." He looked back at the mansion and the property. "I imagine they think the same about you now, the poor little rich girl. Cinderella herself."

"I'm not rich. I'm dependent on them, and they're rich. Besides, Cinderella lived happily ever after, and I'm not sure what my ending will be like."

"You and me both," he muttered. "I haven't written the third act completely yet."

"Pretty funny, the two of us feeling sorry for ourselves."

I shifted my gaze from him and then back to him. He looked at me without speaking. I thought I could see the pain behind his beautiful eyes, the same pain I often saw in my own when I looked in the mirror. In tiny increments, as if we had been captured by a slow-motion camera, we brought our lips to each other's and didn't kiss so much as touch. He pulled back quickly, as if he had made a mistake.

"It's all right," I said. "I wanted you to do that, but with more determination."

He smiled, and then he kissed me for real, his hands on my shoulders. When I lowered my head to his shoulder, he embraced me, and we sat there at the lake, just holding each other. I heard Alberto shouting something in Spanish to one of his grounds people, and I pulled back.

"I don't feel like going rowing just now. Let's go see your room," Ryder suggested. I nodded. "Next time I come, we'll have more time and maybe go rowing."

"I'd like that."

We started for the house. I kept my arms around myself, but after a few moments, I lowered them, and he took my hand. He paused as if he had forgotten something back at the lake.

"What?"

"I just realized that I told you more than I've told anyone else. Including my therapist," he said.

"You don't have to worry about my telling anyone else," I said, thinking that was what concerned him.

"No. That's not it."

"What, then?"

"I'm surprised at myself," he said. We started to walk again. "Or maybe . . ."

"What?"

"Maybe I'm surprised about you."

"A good surprise?"

"I'm still here, aren't I?"

I laughed, and we entered the house and ascended the stairway. Before we reached the top, I glanced down and saw Mr. March looking up at us. He looked very upset, his face awash in displeasure. Did he think it was wrong for me to bring Ryder to my room? It was the first time I would be alone with a boy there. I was never very comfortable inviting friends here, even though Jordan encouraged it. Regardless of the time that had gone by, I still couldn't help feeling I was bringing classmates to someone else's home. It was truly like a guest inviting her own guests.

"Impressive," Ryder said when we stepped into my suite. "Bigger than mine or Summer's, that's for sure. In fact, I think this is bigger than my parents' master bedroom."

"I still feel lost in it."

He began to look at everything. "You're into giraffes?"

"No, that was Alena's thing."

"Well, why is all of that still here? You said you've been here three years."

"I don't mind. In fact," I said, "it helps me feel closer to her."

"Why do you have to feel closer to her?"

"It's not easy to explain. It makes me feel less lonely," I offered.

He nodded and then paused to look at some of my calligraphy. "I know what this is," he said. "They call it . . . ca . . ."

"Calligraphy," I said.

"Yeah. Why are they here?"

"I did them."

"You did these? I'm impressed."

"My mother taught me. Her mother had taught her. When we were living in Santa Monica, she sold her work on the boardwalk."

"What did you do?"

"I did lanyards."

"You made enough to get by?"

"Some days. Some days not, and those days we ate very little."

"When I was at the beach yesterday, I saw some people selling stuff, but nothing like arts and crafts."

"Hungry and desperate people will sell anything they can for a day's food."

He nodded and then just threw himself onto my bed.

"Comfy," he said. "Like sleeping in marshmallow, I bet." He lay there with his hands behind his head, looking up at the ceiling. "So, you've had a few boyfriends?"

"No."

He raised his head. "No? Gary says you're practically a one-girl escort service."

"A little exaggeration. I have had dates with a half-dozen or so boys."

"Or so?"

"Stop. I haven't had any real boyfriends. Actually,

*escort* is a more accurate description of the boys I've been with."

"Did they come here to pick you up?"

"Yes."

"And Mr. March? How did he treat them?"

"Most of the time, he wasn't here, and I told you, if he was, he didn't show any particular interest."

"What did I do to deserve it? Stop playing the piano?"

I laughed. "I haven't dated anyone this year yet. Maybe since you're the first I've invited . . ."

"Really?"

"Yes, really. What about you? I bet you're the real escort service."

"You'd be surprised, too. Among other things, I'm allergic to airheads."

"There hasn't been a girl who wasn't one?"

He was silent.

"What about at the last school?"

He sat up. "Why is it so important to know what my past romantic experiences have been?"

"Why is it so important for you to know mine?"

"You're more interesting."

"Right. You're the one in the movie, not me."

He laughed. "Your story would make a better movie than mine. Did you have a boyfriend when you were living on the street?"

"Get serious."

He smiled, and then he did become serious. "I have a confession to make. I didn't go to Santa Monica just to look at the ocean. I went to imagine what it must have been like for you sleeping on the beach and everything."

"How did you do?"

He shook his head. "I've camped out when I was younger, but living out there like that must have been something else. I mean, where exactly did you and your mother sleep?"

"I told you before. I really don't want to talk about all that, Ryder."

He put up his hands. "Okay, sorry. Since you told me about the calligraphy and the lanyards, I thought maybe . . ."

"I don't want to dwell on it. I still get nightmares."

"I bet. Sorry."

He got off the bed and looked into my closet.

"Isn't it against some zoning ordinance to have a clothing store in your house here?"

"Very funny. Most of it was Alena's."

"Well, why is that stuff still in there? It can't be your size. They could give it to needy people."

"Jordan can't get herself to take it out. It's all too final."

He nodded and then looked at me with that sympathetic face he wore at the lake. "This has to be hard for you. I shouldn't be asking so many questions about your situation here. It's unfair. You can't do all that much about what goes on here, I imagine."

"I'll survive."

"I bet. I wish I could say the same."

"You will, too."

He stared at me a moment. I felt there was something more he wanted to say, something he truly had never said to anyone. My heart beat faster in anticipation, but I could see in his eyes that the moment had passed.

"I guess I should start for home. Summer's probably back and might set the house on fire or something. But I'm glad I came," he added quickly.

"I'm glad you came, too."

I walked to him, and we kissed, stepping back into the closet. This time, the kiss was very passionate. It wasn't only the excitement that came from the way he drew me closer. We were touching each other in ways that stirred the passion we had only begun to realize and explore inside us. I wanted it to last longer. His hands moved under and up my blouse. His breathing quickened. His lips glided gracefully off mine and down to my neck. I welcomed his fingers gently lifting away my bra and pressed myself against him. I lifted my head back and felt as if I was sinking into him.

And then we heard Mrs. Duval call my name. We parted instantly, and I fumbled with my clothes.

"Who's that?" he whispered. I put my fingers on his lips and stepped out of the closet.

"Hi, Mrs. Duval. What's wrong?"

"Mr. March sent me up to tell you he'd like to see you in his office before dinner," she said. She stood there, obviously aware that Ryder was in the closet.

"Thank you. Tell him I'll be there."

"Everything all right?"

"Yes, I'm just . . . yes," I said.

She nodded and then left.

"Who was that?"

"It was just Mrs. Duval. She's sort of the house manager."

"He had to send her up here? What's he want? Does he always do that, send someone to fetch you, or is he doing it just because of me?"

"No, he's done it before," I said.

"I guess he likes ordering everyone around. I'd better get going."

"I'll walk you out."

There was no one downstairs when we descended. I walked to his car with him.

"Call me later," I said.

"You sure you want me to?"

"Of course I do. I don't kiss just anyone in my closet," I said. I kissed him quickly and turned to head back into the house.

"Hey," he called.

"What?"

"Maybe we'll both run away one of these days. You already know how to survive out there. We'll do what Romeo and Juliet should have done."

"There's nothing to romanticize about it, Ryder. It's better to stay and face your demons here."

"You haven't met mine yet," he said, and got into his car. I stood there watching him drive off, and then I went inside and headed for Mr. March's office.

I didn't want to tell Ryder, but his sending for me through Mrs. Duval was exactly what he would do when he sent for Kiera to bawl her out or chastise her for something she had done. Maybe, like Jordan, he was going to question me about her, about what she might have told me. I didn't want to become their little spy, reporting on their daughter. I thought I had seen too much betrayal in my life already to see or be a part of any more.

Little did I know that I had just begun.

# 8

## *A Strange Interest*

Mr. March's office door was open, but he didn't hear me coming. He was bent over his oversized dark cherry-wood desk, his hands over his forehead and eyes. I immediately noticed that he had moved my calligraphy of the word *Mother* that I had made nearly three years ago. I had given it to the Marches, and he was very impressed with it. They had put it in their entertainment center, which annoyed Kiera at the time. Now he had taken it from the entertainment center to his office and hung it in a prominent place on the wall as well. I knocked on the door, and he sat up instantly.

"Come in, Sasha," he said, and got up to come around his desk and lean back on the front of it. He nodded at the black leather settee on his left, and I sat. "Your friend gone?"

"Yes."

He nodded slightly and kept his gaze so fixed on me that I felt a little uncomfortable. Usually, Mr. March didn't stare at me like this. Many times during the past years, I had felt he was looking through me or past me. He didn't seem to hear the things I said or the things Jordan said about me. Like Jordan, I always assumed he was too absorbed with his business.

"I don't know where the time goes," he said, relaxing his lips. His eyes became softer, gentler. "When you were first brought here, you were hardly any bigger than Alena, and now look at you. You've become a really beautiful young lady right under my nose."

His unexpected, enthusiastic compliment took me by surprise. I felt myself blush. He looked up at my calligraphy.

"I should have known that someone so young who could so something so beautiful had a well of beauty within her that would eventually be drawn out for all to see. Not me, however," he said, still looking at the work of art.

He turned back to me. "I can be so blind sometimes," he continued. "I was guilty of the same thing when it came to Kiera. One day, she was my little girl, content with her dolls and computer games, and the next day, it seemed, she was asking to go on dates."

"Maybe fathers don't want to see it."

"Pardon?"

"They don't want their daughters to grow up," I suggested softly.

"Why not?" he asked with a smile.

"They don't want them to lose their innocence, to stop being the sole object of their affection. I also imagine when parents see that their children are older, they feel older," I added.

"Very astute. You are a very intelligent young lady," he said. "That's another thing I haven't appreciated enough. Jordan is right. We're lucky to have you here, and I hope you feel lucky to be here as well."

I had no answer for that. The only reason I was here was that their daughter had accidentally killed my mother and Jordan had felt responsible. Ryder was very perceptive when he said I felt guilty admitting that I was in any way happy here. It just seemed sinful even to think I was lucky. My silence seemed to make Mr. March nervous.

"In any case," he continued, now pacing a little, "I am determined not to be oblivious anymore and to take a more direct and firm interest in your welfare and future. I guess we both know very well that I missed the boat when it came to Kiera. The things that happened as a result are just as much my fault as hers. I won't let that happen with you."

He stopped in front of me.

"Up to now, I've let Jordan take the lead when it comes to you, your needs, and your wishes. I'll admit I wasn't completely for getting you your own car. I know too well how that can be a terrible detriment, a dangerous distraction for someone as young as you are. But she thought it would help to make you feel more a part of this family and give you the independence you needed. I wasn't going to argue about it, and," he said before I could say a word, "I'm confident now that you have the maturity and responsibility for it. At least, I hope and pray you do."

"I didn't ask for a car," I said softly. "It was a big surprise."

"No, you haven't asked for much. Another girl in your

position would surely have asked for much, much more. I like the fact that you appreciate things when they're given to you. Again," he said, pulling in the corners of his mouth, "we both know someone who was never that way, unfortunately.

"We're not here to talk about her, however," he said quickly. I was glad to hear that and relaxed a bit. He wasn't trying to use me as a family spy. "We're here only to talk about you.

"First, I want to promise you that I will devote more time to you, be here more for you. I hope that before long, you will feel comfortable coming to me with any problems you might have, any decisions you have to make."

"Thank you," I said. "I will."

"So," he said, surprising me by sitting beside me on the settee, "I'd like to begin by giving you a little advice about this boy you brought here today. Jordan was a little concerned about him, too. That's why it was so important for her that I be home early enough to meet him.

"Too often, when Kiera brought a boy home, I wasn't around, and Jordan was never as forceful as she should have been when it came to Kiera's sexual explorations. I realize that girls are doing that at alarmingly younger and younger ages."

He kept his smile and then reached out to touch my hair, stroking it ever so gently with the tips of his fingers.

"Like Kiera, you are a very beautiful young woman, Sasha, perhaps even more beautiful. You've inherited some exquisite features from your mother, I'm sure, even though I've never seen a picture of her. Your father couldn't have been too bad-looking to have attracted your mother in the first place, and second because of some of your other stunning qualities. I'm an expert when it comes to judging all this. It's part of what I do for a living, so there's no point in your trying to be modest and deny it," he followed quickly.

"I'm not," I said, which took him aback a little. "I know my mother was very beautiful, and my father was a handsome man."

He laughed. "It doesn't always follow that the children of good-looking people will be as good-looking. I'm sure, for example, that Ryder Garfield, as good-looking as you might think he is, doesn't have the special qualities that have made his father a cinematic idol or his mother a world-famous model."

"I'm not the only one at Pacifica who thinks he does," I said.

The gentleness in his eyes seemed to go *poof* and disappear, like a coin in a magician's hand.

"Yes, well, as your guardian with a parent's responsibility, I want to tell you that we should not permit ourselves to be attracted to someone solely on the basis of his or her looks. I'd like to think that anyone you admire and who admires you has more significant qualities. Most important, perhaps, is the fact that Jordan is right when she says you are still somewhat fragile. We're proud of your accomplishments, but we know how easily you could be . . . damaged. Now, Ryder certainly comes from a respectable family, famous parents, money and all that goes with it, but anyone would have to be blind or stupid not to see that there are turbulent waters running under the surface of his handsome face. I don't want you to be drawn down into them, not now, not ever," he said.

"That won't happen," I said as confidently as I could manage, even though in my heart of hearts, I wasn't absolutely sure of that.

He smiled again. "Ah, but that's where I come in," he said. "All young people, me included when I was young, feel they're immortal, infallible, or if they do suffer setbacks, that they have so much time ahead of them that the setbacks are insignificant. Take Kiera, for example. I didn't realize what was happening, but by the time I did, she was too wild to be reined in. You have to consider the advice of older, wiser people, especially older, wiser people who care about you very much."

"I'm not Kiera," I said, perhaps a bit too sharply.

He winced. "Well, as much as it pains me to say it, I hope you're right, but I have, even in my obliviousness, seen some similarities between you and her. Some of the similarities I like, of course. Kiera, for all her faults, does have some good qualities. I'm not completely wasted here," he said, as if Jordan could not have given her any of those qualities. "In any case, not being careful about with whom you form these early relationships can move you closer to her shoes, or the shoes she wore too long, if you get my drift."

"That won't occur, Mr. March," I said. "I'm not going to say that you and Mrs. March are wrong about Ryder Garfield. He is a troubled person. I realized that almost immediately, but I think I can be a good friend to him and help him, as he said, navigate the rapids."

That sharp, angry look invaded Mr. March's face again. "Don't develop the sin of arrogance, Sasha. Don't take on more than you can handle. That will make you more like the Kiera we both knew too well."

"I won't," I said.

He calmed a bit. "I hope not. In any case, I wanted you to know that I do have a strong interest in your welfare and will be here more for you than I have been. I know Jordan would love for you to think of her as you would a mother, but I'll be satisfied if you simply think of me as a good friend, okay?"

"Yes, Mr. March," I said.

His eyes narrowed, and lines in his temples deepened. "You know what I would like very much, Sasha? I'd like you to call me Donald instead of Mr. March. You've been here long enough to stop being so formal. I meant to tell you that. Will that be all right?"

"Yes, if it's all right with you," I said.

"More than all right. It's what I would prefer. Makes you sound more grown up, too, don't you think?"

I nodded.

He smiled and touched my hair again, holding some strands between his fingers. "You do have extraordinarily beautiful hair, Sasha. I imagine it's because you take care of yourself."

"It was one thing my mother wouldn't forget to tell me to look after, no matter where we were," I said.

He smiled. "You've been through so much. I'm sure you're far more mature than most girls in your class, if not all of them. I want you to know that I don't think of you as being a little girl anymore, Sasha. You're a young woman in my mind."

"Thank you," I said. He was still fingering my hair.

"I should take you with me sometimes. I go to some very interesting places, and if I must say so myself, I do some very exciting things. There are so many important and beautiful things for a girl like you to see, but maybe it's more important for a girl like you to be seen. Would you like that?"

"I guess," I said, not really knowing what he meant by being seen. Seen by whom? And for what?

He nodded as if he was making up his mind right then and there. "We'll do more things together, things I should have been doing with Kiera. That's a promise. You really would be helping me, too," he said. "I'd like to feel I can make up for the mistakes I've made. What do you say?"

"Sure," I said. What else could I say?

He widened his smile. "We'll get to know each other a lot better. I promise."

He just stared at me, and then he leaned over and kissed me on my cheek, very close to my lips.

I was stunned. Donald March had never kissed me like that. He had never fondled my hair, either. I had been without a mother for years now, but I had been without a father for years longer. Maybe I had never really had one. He wasn't a good husband, so how could he have been a good father?

When I was younger and I went somewhere with Jordan on weekends, I would see young girls my age walking with their parents, sometimes holding their father's hand

and not their mother's, and I would wonder what that felt like, what they felt like. Surely having their fathers beside them, holding them, guiding them, gave them a wonderful sense of security. How great it must be to be loved and protected and have such a special place in their fathers' hearts.

They were the girls I envied, the girls who enjoyed all of that, whereas I felt more like someone floating, unattached, drifting through my life without the sunshine of a mother's or father's smile to light the day. My parents were darkness and silence. Who, then, could possibly blame me for being so pleased, even a little intoxicated, with Donald March's offer to become closer and be more of a father to me?

"I'm getting hungry," he said, sitting back. "I didn't have a single meal close to the quality of the meals Mrs. Caro makes for us." He clapped his hands together, rubbing his palms, and stood. "I'll just finish a few things here and join you in the dining room soon." He reached for my hand, and I stood up. "Thanks for listening."

"Thanks for caring," I replied.

"That's very sweet of you to say."

He smiled and hugged me, holding me a little tighter and a little longer than I would have expected. Then he kissed my forehead and went to his desk. I looked at him. He lifted his hand, and I walked out.

Thoughts were bouncing back and forth in my brain like ping-pong balls. I had so much to think about and to understand. Although I didn't like what he had said about Ryder, it seemed obvious that my bringing Ryder here had triggered Donald March to take a more serious interest in my welfare. How could I complain about that? I could have argued with him more about Ryder, explained how intelligent he was and how sensitive and sweet, but for now, I thought it was better to leave it as it was. What a day this had been, I thought, and hurried up to my room to shower and change for dinner.

Lately, we hadn't been having as many dinners together as we used to, and when we did, the Marches, mainly because of Jordan's unhappiness, were often arguing about something. Whenever that occurred, I felt even more out of place, more like an intruder. Once, after a particularly bitter conversation between them, Jordan took me aside afterward to tell me that it wasn't always like that.

"It started after Alena's death and gradually grew worse when we began to have these problems with Kiera. You've seen some of that. I'm sorry you're seeing it now."

I was sure that was part of the reason they had been seeing a therapist together.

Now, especially after she had told me about her suspicions concerning Donald, I began to wonder if this marriage would even last much longer. My memories of my parents' marital problems were still quite fresh and vivid in my mind, despite how young I was, or maybe because of how young I was. More than once, I had heard it said that we're most impressionable at younger ages, and those impressions are so indelibly written inside us that we never lose them or their influences. That was certainly true for me. There was much I had not forgotten.

To date, Donald and Jordan's conflicts were confined to sharp discussions, pouting, and temper tantrums that resulted in neither speaking much to the other. My parents were nearly physical about their fights, my mother tossing things at my father or flailing out and breaking something in the house. Doors were slammed, hands slapped on tables and even against walls. Sometimes it felt as if the walls were rocking like in an earthquake. Here, however, there was just a new and deeper silence that made the smallest movements—the clink of a teacup, the shifting of silverware, the closing of a drawer, or just footsteps—echo through what had become deeper and darker shadows.

From what Donald March had said to me about Ryder when we were in his office, I expected that he would bring it up again at dinner and, as at other times, attach some blame to Jordan. I was waiting for him to tell her that she should not have approved of my bringing Ryder here or should have at least talked more about him with me first. I made up my mind that I would come to her defense, but he didn't do any of that.

In fact, Donald was more cheerful than ever at dinner. He was eager to talk about his business and his experiences with some of what he called the "colorful people" with whom he dealt, whether it was in making commercials, creating print advertisements, or product development. Maybe this was his way of warning me again about Ryder, this time quite subtly.

"Creative people have to be a little off-center to do what they do," he said. He was eating almost ravenously, which brought a smile to Jordan's face. "I mean, it affects their temperaments. It's no wonder so many of them are unstable when it comes to their family lives. I'm beginning to think there should be a way of licensing people for marriage."

"But don't you have to get a marriage license in every state?" Jordan asked.

"Yes, but I don't mean that, exactly."

"What do you mean?"

I waited to hear, too.

"A test, maybe. We make people take tests to get a driving license, don't we?"

Jordan laughed.

"It's not funny," he said. "I think it's a good idea. There would be far fewer divorces and children living with single parents or being in the middle of bad marital spats."

"What would be the test, Donald?"

"I don't know. We should have psychologists and other experts come up with it. Maybe they should start with this state or this city," he added, now looking at me. "The problem is more prevalent in the entertainment industry. It's practically impossible, it seems, for these men and women to have decent families and still pursue their film and music careers."

"I don't think they're any more distracted or busy than you are," Jordan said, and I thought that would be the beginning of another one of their mean arguments, but Donald just smiled and sipped his wine.

"I agree," he finally said, still looking more at me. "I've given all of that more thought and have decided to spend more time with you two. For starters, I'm going to do my best to avoid any weekend work."

"Really? That's wonderful, Donald," Jordan said. She looked to me. I just smiled softly. I don't know what she read in my face, but she turned back to him and warned, "Now, don't just say these things to make us happy and do the exact opposite. That would make things far worse."

"No, I mean it," he said firmly. He leaned back and shouted, "Mrs. Caro!"

She came hurrying into the dining room, wiping her hands on her napkin and looking fearful.

"You have outdone yourself tonight. I have been through a dozen states and eaten in some of the best restaurants lately, and no one has made a better filet mignon. You marinated this perfectly."

"Thank you, Mr. March."

"I hope you saved some for yourself and Mrs. Duval," he added.

She smiled. "My mum would always say a good cook better check the food he or she makes first," she replied, and Donald roared.

Jordan looked at me. Like me, she had expected that his confrontational manner with Ryder Garfield would carry through the evening, but it was as though none of that had happened. I couldn't recall when he was last this cheerful, in fact. Was it all because of the conversation we had in his office?

"When is your next concert, Sasha?" he asked.

"A week from Sunday."

"She has a little solo," Jordan said.

"Has she? I'm not missing that," he said. He emptied his wine in a single gulp and poured himself another. "I think it's time she attended a professional classical concert.

The Los Angeles Philharmonic is performing Chopin and Shostakovich next month. I have a contact who'll get us great seats. Would you like that, Sasha?"

"Yes," I said.

"Then consider it done."

He drank his wine and kept his eyes on me. There was something different in the gleam, something so unexpected that I felt my heart beat faster. It was similar to looks I had seen in the eyes of some of the boys I had dated, looks that raised alarms. At a party, if I had sipped something alcoholic, I immediately stopped, and invitations to go somewhere private were always avoided or rejected. To see something in Donald March that resembled this was even more alarming, because as far as I knew, this was the first time someone as old as he was looked at me with what I could call nothing but lust.

Perhaps I was overreacting, I thought. I hoped so. Perhaps the wine had clouded his thinking a little. I glanced at Jordan to see if she sensed anything similar in his attention to me, but she was so happy about the change in his mood at dinner and the promises he was making that she wouldn't see anything like that anyway.

"Well, we'll need to shop for a proper new dress for you, Sasha," she said.

"Exactly," Donald agreed. "Get her something that is more adult, something that brings out her maturity, and none of this faddy teenage stuff."

Finally, he was treading on Jordan's hallowed ground and doing something to rile her.

"I think I know where to take her and what to buy her for such an occasion, Donald."

"Oh, right, right," he said. "If anyone does, you do, Jordan. You can trust her judgment when it comes to things like this," he told me to emphasize the point. He reached out and patted Jordan's hand. She smiled again, but I thought he was merely placating her and, in fact, treating her the way he might treat Kiera.

She didn't see it that way. She brightened. "This is wonderful," she said. "We'll feel more like a family. Maybe Kiera will come home for this concert," she suggested.

"She has never shown interest in anything like this before," Donald said sharply. Then he smiled. "In any case, you had better call her immediately. These are impossible tickets to get. I'm not even sure I can get us three yet."

"I thought you just said . . ."

"I meant I would try to call in a favor."

She looked confused. "But . . . you just agreed that I should get Sasha a new dress and—"

"She would need it anyway," he said. "There'll be many other occasions like the concert, I'm sure." He rose. "I have a couple of things to do before I can relax for the evening. Ladies," he added with a smile, "please excuse me."

He walked out of the dining room. Jordan looked after him and then shrugged.

"Men," she said.

Later, after I went up to my room to start my homework, the phone rang. I was hoping it was Ryder, but it was Kiera.

"What's this about a concert? I couldn't understand my mother. My father was never big on classical music. He wants me to come home for it?"

I didn't want to say it wasn't his idea, it was her mother's.

"That's what was said at dinner."

"Maybe he's going through some midlife crisis. Men can have them at any age. I can tell you this. I'm not going to run home to go to hear a classical symphony concert. They're buying you a new dress for it?" she asked after a short pause.

"Yes."

"Whose idea was that?" she questioned sharply.

"Well, your father thought I didn't have anything appropriate."

"He never cared if I had anything appropriate."

I was silent.

"He probably is going through some sort of man's change of life. Has he seemed very different lately?"

"I haven't seen him all that much lately. He's been so busy."

"Um. Well, I certainly wouldn't leave Richard on a weekend and go sit in a stuffy concert hall. Besides, I'd have to go buy a new dress, and I don't have the time for it like you do."

"Well, I am in the school orchestra and . . ."

"Oh, let's stop talking about it. Tell me about Ryder. What did he think of where you live?"

"He was impressed, but he's been to many impressive places."

"I bet. So . . . did you get him up in your room?"

"Yes."

"And? C'mon. Out with the details. This is like pulling teeth."

"We're just getting to know each other, Kiera," I said. I didn't want to describe our passionate kissing in my closet. She'd only want more and more detail, and unlike her, I wasn't comfortable talking about it.

"That's how you get to know each other best," she said, followed by her little evil laugh. "I described my first date with Richard, remember? I thought he might think less of me at first, but the truth was, I excited him in ways he never expected. And still do!"

"Why don't you send me a picture of him?"

"Yes. I'll do that. Maybe a picture with his clothes off."

"Don't you dare."

She laughed. "I'll see. I'll expect a picture of Ryder in return."

I heard a beep on my phone. "I think that's him calling. You want to hold on while I check?"

"No. Send me an e-mail, a delicious one," she said, and hung up.

I flashed the line and said, "Hello."

"Did you get a lecture about me?"

I knew all I had to do was say yes and I'd never get him back or have him have any more to do with me.

"Talk about being arrogant," I said. "Why do you assume you were the topic of discussion?"

"Well, why did he want to see you in his office?"

"It's a long story," I said.

"Right. It was about me."

"No."

"Then start your long story," he said.

Beginning any relationship with deceit was certainly not a way to give it any lasting meaning, I thought, but in this case, stretching the truth a little would be better.

"The Marches are having a hard time with Kiera."

"Still?"

"She's seeing someone seriously at college, and she won't tell them how serious it is. Donald and Jordan know I exchange e-mails with her. They wanted me to tell them what I know."

"Donald? It's Donald now?"

"Yes, he asked me to call him Donald instead of Mr. March."

"More progress. Maybe he will agree to adopt you. Okay, I want some quid pro quo, too."

"What?"

"I came to your house, or your palace, today and saw your calligraphy. You have to come to my house and see my model planes and cars."

"You were serious? You do that?"

"Yes, and don't make fun of it."

"I'm not."

"Good. Get permission," he said. "If you can and if you want to, that is," he added.

"Yes, I would like that. Don't worry. I can."

"Okay. And I've made another decision," he added.

"What?"

"I like you," he said.

And then, like last time, he hung up before I could say anything else.

I waited for him to call back and tell me good night or something, but he didn't. He left his words hanging in the air, echoing in my ears instead.

"I like you."

Somehow I understood that something so easy for any other boy to say to me took a great deal of effort and trust for Ryder to say.

I knew I should be feeling happy about it, maybe even a little proud of myself.

But Donald March's warnings about my being arrogant were ringing in my ears as well.

What would I hear last before I fell asleep?

## 9

## *A Star Family*

rs. Duval didn't have to come to wake me the next
morning. I beat my alarm clock, too, and hopped
out of bed. I had forgotten to wash my hair the night before
and went directly to it. I was blow-drying it at my vanity
table when Mrs. Duval stopped by.

"Well," she said when I finished and rushed to put on
my panties and bra and the outfit I had chosen to wear, "I
wonder what's gotten us up and ready so early today."

I saw from the impish look on her face that she and
Mrs. Caro had surely been discussing me and Ryder.
Neither of them was obtrusive or obvious, but it always
amazed me how little went on here at the March estate
without their knowing. It was as if they had their ears to the
walls. I was sure, however, that Alberto had told Mrs. Duval
about Ryder and me walking to the lake. He might even
have seen us kiss.

"I'm not up any earlier than usual," I said.

"Yes, but we haven't been getting up as usual lately, have we?" she asked, hiding a smile, and left.

I stepped into the closet to finish dressing and had just pulled up my jeans when I sensed that someone was there. I thought Mrs. Duval had returned to tell me something, but when I turned, I saw Donald standing in the doorway. I had yet to put on my blouse.

"Oh," he said. "I wasn't sure you were still in the room. Just thought I would check before I left the house. I have a breakfast meeting this morning."

I pressed my blouse over my bra and looked at him. I could probably count on the fingers of my two hands how many times he had been in my room since I had come to live here. I used to think it was just as sad for him to see Alena's things as it was for Jordan to see them, maybe even more difficult for him, and that was why he avoided it.

"Sorry," he said, and started to turn away.

"What did you want?" I asked.

He turned back. "I wanted to tell you that your car plates arrived in the mail with your registration. I had Alberto put the plates on, but I also wanted you to know I had put the registration in the glove compartment if and when you need to show it. Not that I expect you to be in any accidents or get pulled over for tickets," he added. "You're driving safely. Just keep that up."

"I will. Thank you," I said, but I wondered how he knew I was driving safely. Was he having me watched, followed?

He stood there looking at me a moment and then nodded, started to turn away again, and stopped. I started putting on my blouse but stopped as well.

"Oh, what do you have after school today?"

Ryder had asked me to go to his house after school. I was sure I would do that today. If I came up with Donald's request as a reason not to, Ryder would surely take it personally.

"Today? I might have something," I said. "Why?"

"I thought if you weren't busy, you might come over to the office. I wanted to show you this new campaign we're doing for the High Rollers. I'm sure you know the rock group."

"I do, but I'm not crazy about them. They're too heavy metal for me."

"I hate them," he said, "but they're a very nice account. I'm trying to help them do a little more crossover, soften their image, and I thought someone like you might have some good insights."

"Can I come tomorrow?" I asked.

"Sure. Maybe that would be better. Now that I think of it, I have a lunch that might go late. Well, enjoy the day," he said, and left.

I stood there looking after him for a moment and then quickly finished dressing. Jordan, dressed and all made up, came down a few minutes after I had. She was as bright and buoyant as she was at dinner. Gone was that depressed air that had been hovering about her lately.

"You look very nice this morning," she said.

"Thank you. So do you. Are you going anywhere special?"

"Oh, I've got a lot to do today. But I've set aside Saturday for us," she added. "We'll spend the day picking out your dress for the concert and seeing to whatever alterations are necessary."

"Saturday?"

"Yes. Donald insisted we get it done. He said again that if for some reason he can't get the tickets, he'll get tickets to something just as good. He really is taking more interest in us," she added. Her happiness had improved her appetite. She asked for her favorite omelette with toast and some of Mrs. Caro's homemade jam.

"Is he?" I said. I didn't mean it to sound cynical, but I knew it did, or at least not enthusiastic enough for her.

"Oh, yes, yes. He made a big point of my shopping for your dress. He said it was time you had some really elegant clothing. He told me he thought you were quite a mature young lady now, and you should have a wardrobe to complement that. I must say, he didn't take this much interest in Kiera's wardrobe when she was your age, except to criticize it. That girl seemed to enjoy wearing things that would annoy us.

"Anyway, it was refreshing to see him really interested in us. Oh, I almost forgot. He said neither of us should make any plans for Friday night. He's taking us to Castles. You know, the very hot new Beverly Hills restaurant. Usually, it takes months to get a reservation for a Friday night. Stars like your sad friend's parents are seen there all the time."

I thought that gave me an opportunity to talk about Ryder. "I might get to meet them today," I said.

"Oh? How?"

"I might go to his house after school. He came here, so I thought it was only fair to go there."

"I see. Well, please let me know if you do go. I hope you'll be careful, Sasha. It's so easy to get swept along with all this Hollywood stuff," she said.

I thought that was almost funny. She had just finished telling me that Castles was a hot reservation because Hollywood celebrities were seen there often.

"Ryder is about as non-Hollywood as anyone could be."

"You hardly know him, dear."

"Sometimes it doesn't take all that long to get to know what someone's really like. If there's any mystery to most of the students at Pacifica, it's only who their plastic surgeon is or will be."

She froze for a moment. "Don't you like being there?"

"I appreciate all of the advantages it offers, Jordan, but I really don't want to be like most of the other girls. When someone came up with the slogan that beauty was only skin deep, he or she was surely talking about the Pacifica student body."

Her eyelids narrowed, and the softness fled from her face. "I don't remember you talking like this before, Sasha," she said. "I hope Ryder Garfield is not putting ideas into your head already."

"He hasn't said anything to me that I haven't said to myself," I replied. I glanced at my watch and wiped my lips.

"Don't get cynical on me," she warned as I started to rise. "You sound a little too much like Kiera."

I paused. Did I? I realized it was something Kiera might have said, but she would laugh about it, whereas I meant it.

"I'm really very happy to see Donald suddenly taking a greater interest in your welfare," she continued. "He's a great deal wiser than I am and will be a valuable adviser for you. We saw a little of that yesterday when he met Ryder. Donald has a wonderful eye for trouble and for avoiding it," she added with a tone of caution intended for me.

*Donald has a wonderful eye for trouble and avoiding it?* How quickly she had turned from criticizing him, I thought. The cruel voice inside me was clamoring for me to say, *If that is true, how do you explain Kiera? What about all the times you blamed him for letting her run wild, making excuses for her, getting her out of trouble?* If I did ask these questions, I was sure she would burst into tears. Ironically, even though she was keen to point out frequently how fragile I still was, she didn't see how fragile she was.

When I looked at her now, I wondered, was I looking at myself in years to come? Would I eventually choose to blind myself to all of the dark and negative things in my life and see everything through those famous rose-colored glasses? Would that be for me what it was for her, a way to survive, maybe the only way to survive? She had never looked as pathetic and lost to me as she did at this moment, and the irony was, she thought she was happy again.

"I don't want to seem ungrateful," I said. "I do appreciate his interest in my welfare, but he can't say he believes I'm more mature for my age and not trust in my judgment, too."

She nodded. "You're right. We're just so worried all the time. I don't have to tell you why."

"I'll be all right," I told her, and gave her a kiss on the cheek and started out.

"Don't drive fast," she called. "And let me know if you're not coming right home after school."

"Okay," I said.

When I stepped out of the house, I felt a sense of relief and wondered, was this what Kiera always felt when she finally was able to get away from her parents? Was this what made her even more rebellious? Everyone knew the best way to get someone, especially a teenager, to do something was to tell him or her not to do it. It wasn't something true only now; it was true always, and if Jordan and Donald looked back at their own youth and how they had behaved, they would admit it, too.

But I wasn't interested in Ryder just to be defiant or prove I was master of my own fate and captain of my own soul. I was drawn to him for so many better reasons, the most important of which was kinship. I sensed we were alike. We did have similar pain and were haunted by some of the same demons. My curiosity about his parents didn't come from the glamour and entertainment magazines. I wasn't thinking of them as being celebrities. I was thinking of them as being his parents, and failed parents at that.

Maybe he was as excited about school today as I was and for the same reasons. When I pulled into the parking lot, I saw that he was already there. His sister had gone in before him. He was waiting for me. There was something about the way he had dressed and brushed his hair that looked different, too. He simply looked sharper and, dare I think it, happier.

"Hey," he said.

"Hey."

He reached for my hand, and we started toward the entrance. Other students driving in glanced our way. Some gaped. Mona Kirland nearly drove into another car.

"So, can you come over to my house after school, or is that going to create a March earthquake?"

"No problem," I said. "It's educational."

"Educational?"

"An arts-and-crafts exhibit."

"Huh?"

"Your model planes, ships, and cars."

"Oh." He laughed as we entered the school and went to our lockers.

"I can't believe there are no locks on these lockers," he said.

"You didn't read your contract when you entered."

"No," he said, laughing. "I don't think I did. Why?"

"First, you should know that no one steals from anyone here. If anyone wants something someone else has, he or she just tells his or her parents, and they get it."

He laughed.

"But more important, the school wants the students to know that the staff can go into your locker at any time and search for drugs or cigarettes. Cigarettes are not permitted on campus."

"I guess I'll leave my porn magazines at home, too, then."

Our laughter drew even more attention, but neither of us cared.

Because of the rules about cell phones, I couldn't use

mine until lunch. I called Jordan then, but she was already at lunch with some of her friends. When I confirmed that I'd be going to Ryder's house, I thought she said a strange thing.

"I'll have to tell Donald," she said.

She hadn't ever said that to me before, whether I asked if I could go or told her I was going to a party or to another friend's house. I wanted to ask her why, but I didn't.

"Be careful" was the only other thing she said.

I guess my deep thinking about it was written on my face. When I joined Ryder at the table, he immediately asked me what was wrong. Of course, he followed that with, "What, they don't want you to go to my house now?"

"No, chill," I said. "Everything's not about you."

"Well, it should be," he said, trying to joke about his hair trigger. "So what's the problem?"

"Look, here's the problem I live with," I began. "Because their older daughter was equivalent to a time bomb, they measure everything I do now against what she did. They look for resemblances."

"Are there any?"

"I hope nothing like the things they're looking for," I said.

"You don't sound so sure."

"I'm sure, Ryder. Damn."

He stared at me. I thought his lips actually trembled. Now I was the one with the hair trigger. We were really alike, and maybe because he saw something more of himself in me, it bothered him. He already knew what he was capable of doing and not doing.

"Okay. Let's drop it. I've got to warn you, my parents will probably be home."

"Why do you have to warn me?"

"You'll see for yourself," he said.

After he said that, I couldn't help being nervous the remainder of the school day. When I looked at him in class, I thought he looked nervous, too. Now that the shoe was on the other foot, I realized how much he had been worried about what the Marches thought of him. Maybe that was why he had been antagonistic with Donald almost immediately. I was sure Ryder had brought other girls home. Perhaps none of them was good enough for him in his parents' eyes, or maybe his parents were just too protective of their own celebrity reputations. Whatever, I was concerned about what they would think of me. Had he told them anything about me? Did his sister know he was bringing me to their home today? Did she learn anything about me, and was she telling her parents things? I worked myself into such a mental knot about it all that I almost decided to cancel.

His house was in Beverly Hills, off Sunset Boulevard. He gave me the address to put in my GPS in case we were separated by traffic, but the plan was simply for me to follow him. As we walked out of our last class, I asked him if he had told his sister he was bringing me to their house.

"Tell her? Why?"

"I just wondered."

Instead of saying any more about it, he simply grimaced. If he hadn't told her, I assumed he would after we had left the parking lot. Fortunately, I was able to follow him closely and not lose him. If I had, I might have used it as an excuse to avoid going. I was that nervous.

Fifteen minutes later, we turned off Sunset and then turned into the driveway of a palatial Beverly Hills home. It wasn't an estate, but it was an impressive-looking Italian villa, a Tuscan residence, also gated. It was then, I imagined, that Summer realized I had been following them. She turned back to look at me waiting right behind them for the gate to open, and then she asked Ryder something. Whatever he said made her turn back to look at me again, and then she turned away. Even from where I was, I could see from her posture that she was upset. I imagined that any boyfriends were off-limits to her for now, and she was jealous of him.

We approached the house over a cobblestone motor court. There was a black Mercedes sedan parked beside a Lexus convertible with the top down. Ryder pulled up alongside the convertible, and I pulled up beside him. Summer practically leaped out of his car and headed toward the front entrance before I could say hello. He got out slowly.

"Your sister looks upset," I said when I got out and looked after her.

"She was born upset. Forget about her. Well, here it is. Home sweet home," he said.

"It's beautiful."

"A famous Hollywood producer was the original owner. The previous owner was from Saudi Arabia. My mother had the place totally redone. She might have it redone again in two weeks. She has ADD when it comes to decor, fashions, and cars. As far as I know, not men, though. Now, as for my father, I won't swear the same," he added as we walked slowly toward the front door.

I didn't say anything. He glanced at me, I think to see if I was spooked by the things he said. I already knew that he could say something just to get a reaction out of me.

He opened the door and stepped back. I entered a very large foyer. The house had vaulted ceilings with wood beams.

"These are Brazilian cherry-wood floors," he said. "We're ordered to tell anyone we bring here that immediately."

"It's beautiful, Ryder. How big is this house?"

The house had a wide-open look, so I could see into the kitchen as well.

"Ten thousand, with seven bedrooms and ten bathrooms. Everything is in the rear—the tennis court, the pool, an outdoor grill. There's even a small putting green. Neither of my parents swims very much. My mother doesn't play tennis at all. We never grilled at any of our other homes, and my father plays golf maybe twice a year, but usually only at celebrity events when he is invited and all expenses are paid. But we have to have it all!" Ryder said, his eyes exaggeratedly wide.

"Have all of what?" we heard. "What tall tales are you telling now, Ryder?"

A woman who was obviously Ryder's mother, Beverly Ransome, stepped out of the very large living room. She looked as if she had just this moment finished a modeling shoot. I wondered if she spent her whole day this put together. Like most models, she was tall, probably between five foot ten and five foot eleven. Her facial features were exquisite. The features of her face were so perfect, in fact, that I wondered if she could possibly have been born that way. Again, like most very successful models, her eyes captured attention first. They were cobalt blue and just almond-shaped enough to give her something of an unusual, alluring look. It wasn't hard to imagine why she was photogenic. She could probably make an amateur head-shot photographer look like some of the most famous professionals.

When she stepped more into the light that streamed through a skylight above us, her light brown hair meticulously styled into a basic French twist seemed to take on a slightly copper shade. She wore an A-line, V-neck chiffon lace dress that reminded me of something Jordan would wear to one of her elegant charity events, but it wasn't even three-thirty in the afternoon. My gaze went from her face to the heart-shaped diamond pendant on a necklace of white gold.

"Well, this is a surprise, Ryder," she said. "Why didn't you warn us that you were bringing someone home today?"

"Warn you?" he replied.

She glanced at him, but her eyes were all over me. "You know what I mean," she said. "We might have prepared something special."

"There's something special here every day," he said, both to her and to me.

"Aren't you going to introduce us?"

"If you give me a chance," he said. "Mother, this is Sasha Fawne Porter. She lives in that shack the Marches own, the one that made *Architectural Digest* a while back, the one you ooh'ed and ah'ed over."

"Oh. I'm happy to meet you, Sasha. Your home looks truly magnificent." I was about to tell her it wasn't really my home, when she added, "What I meant by something special is we would have planned to be here. My husband and I agreed to attend a publicity event for a new Warner Brothers film."

"That explains the uniform," Ryder said.

"Uniform?" both his mother and I said simultaneously.

She laughed. "I take it you attend Pacifica, Sasha."

"We didn't meet on the street," Ryder said. When he looked at me, I could see he was sorrier for me that he had blurted that than he was for his response to his mother.

The moment we had entered and she had appeared, I could feel the tension in the air.

"I'm not being critical, Ryder. All I'm saying is it would have been nicer if you had told us you were having a guest so I wouldn't have had to hear it from your sister as she ran by." She smiled at me. "My son has a ways to go when it comes to social etiquette. You're more than welcome," she continued. "I just hate meeting someone for the first time and then having to run out."

"Be fashionably late," Ryder suggested.

"We already will be that," she said, and laughed. She looked at her watch. "Your father takes longer than I do to get ready, which would shock most people."

"No one who knows him," Ryder said.

Her lips tightened.

"What a beautiful watch," I said, hoping to break the tension.

"Yes, it was a gift from a European count. It's a Harry Winston."

"I thought it was a watch," Ryder said.

"Ha, ha. My son is determined to give me some stress wrinkles."

"That way, whenever you look into a mirror, you'll think of me, Mother," Ryder said. He smiled and turned to me. "She'll be thinking of me almost all day."

"Ryder, you're not funny," she snapped. She turned sharply to me. "You must have quite the thick skin to be friends with him," she said, and then smiled the smile that surely put her in the top ten. "I love your hair."

"Thank you."

We heard footsteps from the left. I took a deep breath. If there was such tension between Ryder and his mother, what would there be between him and his father?

"*Bonjour, bonjour,*" he cried, walking with a spry step. As Jessica would say if she were beside me, Bradley Garfield was "drop-dead gorgeous." I had seen a number of movie stars from a distance and a few close up, but never in one's own home. I had always thought Donald was a handsome man, but he was right when he told me that Bradley Garfield had an indescribable cinematic quality. It was like watching an actor walk off the screen.

He wore a white sport jacket and black slacks with a turquoise shirt, the collar slightly up and the shirt's top two buttons unfastened. Except for a wedding ring and a gold and diamond pinkie ring, he wore no other jewelry. His watch looked just as expensive as hers. Maybe the count had given them both presents.

"So, who do we have here?" he asked.

"Whom," Ryder corrected.

I saw a flash of anger in Bradley Garfield's eyes before he smiled and corrected himself. "My son the scholar. And you are?"

"I'm Sasha," I said, stepping forward. He smiled the smile that sent thousands of girls pressing their thighs together and hyperventilating. He took my hand and looked at Ryder.

"Well, this is the top of a skyscraper up from the last few girls you brought home for us to meet."

Ryder looked away.

"We didn't know he was having company today," he told me. "Or we would have—"

"Baked a cake," Ryder finished for him. "*Ma mère* has already told her."

"Oh. Okay. I do hope we'll see you again, Sasha, when we can spend a little more time with you."

"Thank you," I said.

"Shall we go, my dear?" he asked his wife.

"I don't want Summer leaving the house, Ryder," she told him.

"We're not leaving the house, Mother. Sasha came to spend some time here."

"Good. Martha's preparing one of your favorite dinners, lobster fra diavolo. I wish we could stay."

"You could," Ryder said.

"Yes, well, it's not that easy. We'll be back before eleven," she said. "So long, Sasha. See if you can civilize my son a little for us."

"Call me if there's any problem," his mother told him.

Ryder kept his gaze on the floor. I could feel the agitation in his body. The tightness in his neck and his mouth and the way he clenched his fists actually frightened me. His mother brushed his cheek with what was more like an air kiss, and then she and his father walked out. It was as if air returned. Ryder relaxed and shrugged.

"Good ol' Mom and Dad," he said. "C'mon, I'll show you my room first, and then we can look at the rest of it."

"Where's Summer?"

"Locked in her closet by now. She usually comes home and goes right on the phone or the computer. When we came here, my parents assigned her the bedroom closest to theirs. It was a symbolic move to impress her with how much more they'll care about her, but the truth is, nothing much has changed, except I've been given more responsibility. It's like I'm the one being punished for the things she did."

"She is your sister."

"That's what they tell me," he said. "I've demanded DNA confirmation."

We walked down the tile hallway. There was beautiful statuary in niches all along the way. His bedroom was the first on the left. He was right. It was barely a third of the size of mine but by any measure still quite large. His bed was a beautiful hardwood headboard and frame, an Italian style with a pecan veneer. It had matching dressers and an armoire. Even his desk matched. The other side of the suite was cluttered with model planes and cars.

"Wow. You weren't kidding," I said, looking at them.

"My mother hates that I have it all in my bedroom. She wanted me to take over another bedroom for it, but I refused. It's practically the only thing in this house that's mine, really mine. She picked out everything else I have, including most of my clothes. It's the same for Summer. I suppose I should call this Beverly's room, just like yours is called Alena's."

I walked over to look at his model planes and cars, and some ships in bottles. The work was very intricate. I looked at the one he was currently doing.

"That's actually a replica of Columbus's *Santa Maria*," he said.

"How do you get the ship into a bottle?"

"Pure magic."

"No, really."

"There are a few different ways. The secret is the masts. You turn them down and use a thread to pull them back up. They have hinges. Then you cut away the thread."

"It must take a great deal of patience and concentration."

"Which is why I do it. I escape into the bottle with the ship," he said.

I thought he was only half kidding, if that much. I looked at the other models, and whenever I touched one, he would identify it, rattling off its history.

"You can learn a great deal from this hobby," I said.

"It's more than a hobby. It really is therapy," he said.

I dropped my pretense. I couldn't keep ignoring what was gnawing at me. "Why is there such tension between you and your parents, Ryder? I can understand the strain between them and Summer after what happened, but why between you and them? It can't be that they blame you completely for what she did."

He fingered one of his model cars. I thought he was just going to ignore me and go on to talk about another, but he pulled his fingers away from the one he was handling and turned to me with such pain in his eyes I thought I would lose my breath.

"They blame me for my mother's miscarriage with their third child," he said.

# 10

## *Passion*

$\mathcal{I}$ left that little detail out of the movie I was describing at
your lake. My parents base everything they do around
their careers," Ryder continued.

We were sitting on his bed. He leaned back on a pillow
and put his hands behind his head as he looked up at the
ceiling and began to talk as if he were in his therapist's
office. I had yet to say anything. My silence spoke for itself.
I could see it in the way he glanced at me before he lay back.
He was waiting for a sign of disapproval, something in my
face that told him I was uncomfortable. I wasn't judging
him, but at the moment, I regretted asking him anything
personal.

"I'm not saying other couples don't plan, but most
other prospective mothers don't have to agonize over their
looks and figures if they get pregnant like my mother did.
She's always accusing the camera of putting five or ten
pounds on her as it is."

He turned to me.

"It's just not comforting to know that if your mother had gotten that part or that modeling job, you might not have been born."

"You would have been born sometime, Ryder. They obviously wanted children."

"Yeah, but it would have been a different sperm. I might have come out nicer."

"You're nice. Stop it."

"Right. Anyway," he continued, looking back up at the ceiling, "we were all in Italy at the time. My father had been cast in a lead role in one of those cheaply made westerns. You know, the ones that made Clint Eastwood famous? I guess he was thinking he would become the next Clint Eastwood, so we went to Italy. I was only nine, and Summer was four at the time. I guess it's an understatement to say I was a mischievous brat. I hated being told what I could and couldn't do, especially by some nanny.

"My mother used to threaten me with 'I won't love you anymore.' I remember wondering if that was possible. Could your mother or your father turn off their love for you that easily? Even when I was that young, I would think that if they could, it couldn't be real love.

"Anyway, I ran away from home a few times while we were there. One time," he said, smiling, "I was hiding just outside the villa and watching everyone frantically searching and calling for me. I was spotted eventually, and they were really angry that I would let them agonize so much."

"Why did you do that?"

"My therapist says it was my call for attention. The way

I saw it, it was the kindest way he could come up with to tell my parents they were too into themselves. They didn't see it that way, of course. There had to be something wrong with me. I was punished, practically locked away until almost the end of my father's shoot.

"My mother was nearly six months pregnant at the time. She was always good about not showing her pregnancy until about the seventh month so fans didn't know, and they had been successful keeping it out of the entertainment press.

"When I was finally permitted to rejoin the human race, my mother, Summer, our nanny, and I went to a place called Positano in Italy. My mother wanted to do some shopping, and we were going to be permitted to go swimming in the ocean. Most of the shops are along this steep hill, at least the shops my mother wanted to visit. I thought we were taking too long to reach the beach at the bottom, so I decided to take off myself. Our nanny realized I was gone, which threw my mother into a panic. She left Summer with our nanny and began looking for me. I wasn't that far down the hill. She saw me, and called after me, and I started to run and was nearly hit by a man on a motorcycle. She screamed, ran after me, tripped, and took a nasty fall."

"And that was when she miscarried?"

"Yep. She had to be taken to the hospital. She was also pretty scraped up. The story about her pregnancy and miscarriage leaked out. Afterward, my father wouldn't talk to me except to bark an order here and there, and a dark silence fell over us all. Summer wasn't that upset, even at four. She was already jealous of the new baby that might come. I couldn't blame her. We shared so little in terms of parental love and concern that the prospect of dividing what little we had into thirds disturbed her."

"You were just a little boy. They can't be holding that against you now."

"Oh, my therapist has an answer for that, too. He says I'm holding it against myself but making it easier for myself to live with it by transferring my self-blame to them. He says as long as I can believe they hold a grudge, I'm comfortable with it."

"Maybe that's true, Ryder."

"Maybe it is; maybe it isn't," he said, the anger seeping into his voice. "You felt the tension just now. Was it all my imagination?"

I knew I was walking on thin ice. It was on the tip of my tongue to say he might be the one who was mainly bringing on the tension. From what I had seen, he wasn't exactly nice to them, either. But I was hesitant, as cautious as a soldier trying to disarm a bomb.

"Very few people know this stuff about us—about me, I should say," he said. "No one at Pacifica does, obviously."

"I'm not going to be the one to talk about it, if that's what you're thinking."

He was, but he didn't want to admit it. "I've never trusted anyone with the story, except, of course, my therapist," he said after a moment. "Somehow, maybe because of the hard life you had, I felt I could trust you."

"You can, so shut up about it," I said, and he smiled.

"This is all too depressing. We need the California fix," he said, sitting up.

"California fix? What's that? I hope not something to do with drugs."

"Not unless you consider golden sunshine, sparkling pools and fountains, pristine tennis courts, and a putting green drugs. C'mon. Let me show you our Disneyland."

He reached for my hand as he slipped off the bed, and we walked out, through the living room to some patio doors and out to the rear of the property. For a moment, we stood there looking at it all. Their property had a better view to the west than the Marches' estate had. There was more ocean to see in the distance.

"Well? Not too shabby, huh?"

"It's all very beautiful. You could spend time quietly here, too."

"Somehow, because it's my house, I can't," he said. "Of course, the pool is half the size of the one at the Marches', and they have two tennis courts and a lake."

"They have, not me," I reminded him. "Think of it this way. You're at home. I'm at a hotel."

He laughed. "You ever golf?"

"No. Donald belongs to an expensive golf club, and Jordan goes at least once a week with some of her friends, but I've never gone."

"They never offered to take you?"

"No. They used to take Kiera when she was younger, but she was so disruptive that they stopped."

"Let's putt around. I'm pretty good. I'm better than my father, in fact," he said, and led me to the shed where the equipment was kept. He gave me one of his mother's clubs to use and gathered up dozens of balls.

"I thought your mother didn't golf. How come she has all this?"

"As I tried to tell you before, you will see that we have lots of things we don't use very much. That's called being successful."

I laughed and followed him to the putting green. He set us up four feet from the hole.

"I was given professional lessons, of course," he said. "So was Summer, but she was so bored that she began deliberately to hit the ball in the opposite direction. Okay, so here's how I was taught to putt. You have to practice hitting the ball straight at the hole so you can focus on your stroke and not on what they call the break. If you get the stroke down but miss the break, it's just a matter of speed."

He got behind me, put his hands on my arms, and began to show me the putting stroke. His lips were grazing my cheeks.

"We've got to make sure this putter is straight back and straight to your line," he said, his voice softening. Gently, he moved me into the proper stance, his body against mine. I did try to concentrate, but his breathing and the feel of his thighs and his waist against me began to quicken my own breath.

"You smell so good," he whispered.

I tried a few strokes, and he tried to correct me, but we both sensed that this was going to be futile. His excitement was building. I didn't acknowledge it or move away. I wanted to turn in his arms and bring my lips to his. I might have done just that if we hadn't heard, *"That's disgusting!"*

Ryder's arms dropped instantly to his sides, and we

both looked back at the patio. Summer was standing there with her hands on her hips.

"I saw what you were doing to her," she said, whining and wagging her head. "What a way to pretend you're not doing it. So don't be complaining about me."

"Shut your dirty mouth!" he shouted.

"That's what you should be doing!" she screamed, and went back into the house.

He glared after her and then took a deep breath and turned back to me. "Sorry about that."

"Maybe she's just feeling miserable, Ryder. I could try to talk to her."

"Talk to her? I ask only people I don't like to do that," he said, and shook his head the way a dog might to throw off water. "Forget about her. Take some more putts. The object is to sink fifty in a row."

This time, he stood back to watch. I saw him glaring back at the house periodically. I tried to swing the way he had shown me, but I couldn't concentrate. It was like navigating through a minefield around here. Where was the softness? Where was the kindness and love that made them into a family?

I kept hitting the balls, but I made only one in ten attempts.

"I'm terrible at it," I said.

"I guess this is stupid," he said, taking the club from me. He practically ripped it from my hands. "It's the blind leading the blind, anyway. I don't play enough to justify teaching someone else."

"I thought you were telling me to do the right things."

"How would you know?"

He marched back to the shed to put everything away.

"You've got to have more confidence in yourself," I said when he slammed the shed door shut.

"Exactly. Do you know where I can get that? Is there a bank or something where I can withdraw some self-confidence? Or maybe someplace on the Internet. With one click, I can download the self-confidence I need, huh?"

"I simply meant that you should give yourself a chance, Ryder."

"For what?" he said, starting for the house.

"Maybe just for me right now," I told him, and he stopped and considered.

I held my breath. Was he going to come up with something so nasty that I would want to charge right out of there, get into my car, and drive off? I felt as if I was tottering on a cliff of emotion.

He smiled. "So, what am I, a challenge for you?"

"Seems to me it's the other way around," I replied.

His smile widened. "Okay," he said. "I'm sorry again for being a nasty bastard. In fact, if it continues, I might have that tattooed on my forehead soon."

"That's better than what I had tattooed once on me."

His eyebrows rose. "Really? You didn't tell me about that."

"I never tell on the first date, and we really haven't had a first date yet."

He laughed and reached for my hand again. On our way back to his room, he introduced me to their maid and cook, Martha Cooper. She was an African American woman in her fifties from Louisiana who had been trained at the Culinary Institute of America in Texas. I gathered that she had been working for the Garfields for the last two years. Ryder told me she had always worked for celebrities. He said the world of the rich and famous was like a closed little club in which the members shared not only servants but also beauty and health references.

"This sharing is another thing that makes them all feel special," he said as we headed back to his room. "Not that they need much more to do that."

"You sound prejudiced," I said, only half kidding.

"Huh? Prejudiced?"

"Don't hold their fame against them. They're not inferior just because they're well known."

That brought another smile to his face. I was beginning to think that if I could accumulate smile after smile, I might be able to make a difference with Ryder Garfield. The worry was that I would try too hard and lose him that way, too.

"That's my sister's room," he said, nodding at a closed door.

He paused and looked as if he might go charging at it to pound on it and start yelling at her again. Then he looked at me and thought better of it. We went into his room and he closed the door.

"Tell me about this tattoo," he said, and threw himself onto his bed. I hesitated. Neither Jordan nor Donald had mentioned it to me ever since. Occasionally, I looked at myself in a full-length mirror, but I was more comfortable pretending that it didn't exist. It was all just a nightmare.

"C'mon," he said. "You let the cat out of the bag."

I began to describe the club Kiera and her friends had created, Virgins Anonymous, in more detail and how they had shown me their tattoos, which I was later to discover were removable, temporary.

"Why would you do it, anyway?"

"They convinced me it was sort of an initiation rite, only they convinced me to do a real one."

I described how they had taken me to a tattoo parlor and voted on what I should have put on me. He sat listening intently. I was worried that he might think less of me when he learned how I had been so easily duped. I even told him that was the reason I didn't like describing what had happened to me.

"The few people I did tell always looked as if they thought it was as much my fault as Kiera's and her friends' fault."

"If they did, they're stupid," he said. "You were pretty vulnerable then, considering all you had suffered and how alone you felt."

"True, but I couldn't help feeling stupid."

"Where was this tattoo?"

"Here," I said, turning to place my hand over the spot that was just above my rear end.

"What happened to it? Is it still there?"

"No. It was removed, but there's a scar."

He stared.

"You want to see it?"

"Yes, but not because I don't believe you," he said.

I thought a moment, and then I began to unfasten my belt. I turned my back to him and slowly began to lower my jeans. He said nothing, but before I could raise them again, I felt his lips on my scar. They felt hot, and when I felt the tip of his tongue, my heart began to thump. I closed my eyes as his hands moved around my hips and gently held on to mine. Ever so slowly, he guided my jeans farther down, hooking my panties, too. He kept kissing me softly. When my jeans and my panties were down to my ankles, he turned me and kissed me on the lips.

Gently, he pulled me onto the bed, and we kissed again. He lifted his face from mine and stared.

"You're so beautiful," he said, stroking my hair. "From the moment I saw you, I couldn't get you out of my head."

"You certainly didn't show it."

He smiled. "I figured any girl who could take it and give it back like you did had to like me."

"Weird logic."

"I know."

We kissed again, his lips moving over my chin and onto my neck. A voice inside me was clamoring, *This is too fast. Calm down.* Yet I didn't push him away. I held him tighter and searched for his lips again and again. His breathing was outracing mine.

"Ryder," I said softly.

"I dreamed of you in my bed just like this," he whispered.

He worked my blouse over my head, unfastened my bra, and gently dropped my clothes over the side of the bed. Then, with his kisses, he carved a trail between my breasts, over them, and down my stomach.

There was a shouting match going on inside me now,

caution against passion. I made small attempts to stop, but they grew weaker and weaker. I felt as though I were chained, handcuffed by my own overwhelming desire.

He stood up and fumbled with his own clothing, throwing it off as if it was his clothes that were on fire and not him. When he started to bring himself back to me, I put up my hand.

"Ryder, I don't want to end up like your sister did."

He smiled and opened the drawer on the nightstand beside his bed to pluck out a contraceptive. I think the sight of it so handy had what most would think was an unexpected reaction in me. I knew Kiera and her friends would think the boy they were with was sophisticated enough for them to be with him. From the way they talked, they wanted nothing to do with innocent young men. But the thought that threw cold water over me was the possibility that Ryder had brought other girls here, right to this very place, and was always prepared.

"Wait," I said, moving to get my panties and jeans on.

His smile slowly fell away like a leaf descending. Confusion and disappointment rushed into his lips and his eyes. Before he could ask anything, my cell phone rang. I fumbled with my jeans, scooped up my blouse and bra, and snatched the phone out of my bag. It was Jordan.

"Where are you?" she asked, as if she could see for miles and through house walls.

"I'm still at Ryder Garfield's home. I've been invited to dinner here. They're having lobster fra diavolo."

I turned my back to Ryder. He started to dress.

"I remember you love it, but Donald would like you home for dinner," she said.

"Why?"

"I don't know his reason, Sasha, but he was very adamant about my calling you to tell you. Please do as he wishes."

I looked at Ryder. He had his pants on but was sitting on the bed, holding his shirt and glaring down at the floor. His face was still quite flushed, as I imagined was mine.

"Okay," I said.

"Is everything all right?"

"Yes," I snapped.

She had never heard that tone in my voice. It gave her pause. "Drive carefully," she said, and hung up. I held the phone for a moment and then flipped it closed and finished dressing. Ryder didn't speak. He just sat there staring at the floor.

"I'm sorry," I said.

He looked up at me, his eyes narrowing. Then he held up the contraceptive between his thumb and forefinger. "This spooked you?"

I didn't answer. I kept dressing.

"What, would you rather I didn't use it?"

"No, of course not," I said.

"So? I don't get it. You were into it even more than I was until I opened that drawer."

"It just felt . . ."

"What?"

"Too organized," I said.

He stared dumbfounded for a moment, and then suddenly, he laughed.

"It's not funny, Ryder."

"Of course it is." He began to finish dressing. "You think this is all a setup? This is my love nest? I parade girls in and out of here?"

"I don't know what to think."

"This is some irony. Probably most guys you were with didn't care."

"I haven't been with any guys who didn't care."

"Yes, you have. Weren't you seduced?"

"I mean, deliberately been with any," I corrected. The conversation was getting me upset. "I've got to go home. My foster parents want me at dinner there tonight."

"I'm sure," he said. He opened the drawer of the nightstand and threw the contraceptive into it.

"Look, Ryder, I like you. I'm sorry, but you're not the only one who has some issues to resolve," I said.

He looked up at me and nodded. "You're right. Hey, you have to understand that it's harder for a guy to put on the brakes than it is for a girl. I'm still skidding," he said, and smiled.

"This might help," I said, and leaned over to kiss him.

"How does that help?" he asked when I straightened up.

"Figure it out." I started for the door. "I have to go."

He shook his head and stood up. "You're missing some great food."

"I hope there'll be another time," I said. "I'm sorry. I'm still not my own person, if you know what I mean."

"Yeah, if anyone does, I do."

He followed me out and then took my hand at my car.

"You really don't believe I'm that much of a ladies' man, do you?"

"I guess not. It was just so fast and . . . convenient."

He laughed. "Women. You can't live without them, and you can't live with them."

"You could always become a monk," I said, and opened my car door.

"I think I'd rather take my chances with you."

I thought a moment. "Let's plan on next Tuesday. That day, the school's closed for teacher conferences."

"Plan on what?" he asked.

"Going rowing at the March lake. What else?"

He laughed, and I got into my car. "Hey," he said after I started the engine. He leaned into the passenger-side window. "Thanks for the quid pro quo."

"See you tomorrow," I said. "There's more to come."

He stood back and watched me drive out. I waved just before turning. He didn't wave back. He stood there staring after me as if I would be gone forever. I didn't know whether I felt sorrier for him than I did for myself.

Since the time when I was raped, I was always worried that I would never be able to have a real and loving relationship. It had been my fear ever since that I would always pull back whenever any young man got this close to me. I would be unable to trust anyone enough, no matter how much in love with me he seemed to be or even how much in love with him I seemed to be. The wound was too deep, the scar was too thick, and the memory, even as foggy as it was because of the drugs, was persistent, stubborn, indelible. It bubbled up in hot nightmares. It flashed its ugly face every time I felt sexually aroused, whether it was from something I read or something I saw.

I should hate more and forgive less, I thought. Perhaps through the power of hate, I could overcome the ghosts that haunted me at my most private and intimate moments. Rage gave strength, and strength was something I desperately needed.

Yes, I was good at witty dueling. I could inflict pain on the arrogant young men who teased me with their good looks, and I enjoyed the adulation I won from the girls who envied me and looked up to me, but I was in pain that they'd most likely never know and couldn't ever see. I didn't want their sympathy anyway.

I wanted someday to be able to throw off this weight that kept my chance for happiness and satisfaction underwater. As I drove away from Ryder, I did realize that if somehow I could help him to help me, we'd both be reborn.

We'd both rise out of the thick darkness into the light of wonderful days when we would truly be able to cherish who we really were. My name would be on his lips and his on mine. Just saying them would be like kissing. We would find the warmth and the sanctuary in each other's arms that would keep us protected, and all that had once made us lonely and lost would fall behind us as we rose toward the sun.

Why couldn't that be?

What was out there waiting to stop us?

## ❧ 11 ❧

# A Present

Jordan was so eager to hear about the Garfields that I wondered for a few moments if she hadn't exaggerated Donald's concern for my being home for dinner just so she could find out more about the Garfields. She practically pounced on me when I entered the house.

"Did you meet them?" she asked, almost before I had closed the door behind me.

"Yes."

"Well? What were they like?"

"She's very beautiful, and he's very handsome," I said.

Jordan grimaced. "I know that, Sasha. The whole world knows that. I mean, what were they like? Were they hospitable? Arrogant? Were they pleased you were invited to their home? Did they do anything with you? Oh, and what was their house like? Come in, come in," she urged, leading me into the living room on the right.

"I didn't spend that much time with them, Jordan," I

said, following her. "They were on their way to a publicity event for a new film."

"Publicity event? What film?"

"I forgot."

"What? You forgot? Your generation is so oblivious sometimes. So," she said, sitting on the settee to my right. "Go on. Tell me about the house."

"It's a beautiful Italian-style house. It's very big, open, with high ceilings, fancy floors. They have a pool, a tennis court, and a putting green."

"Putting green? I wonder why Donald never thought of having that. We could have our own golf course here. Back to the Garfields. Were they nice to talk to, at least? I mean, the little you did speak to them."

"Yes," I said. If I even gave her a hint of the tensions in that home, she would be pressuring me to stop seeing Ryder. "But, as I said, they were on their way out."

"Well, then what did you do?" she asked with obvious frustration.

"We talked, and then Ryder gave me some instructions about golf putting."

"Really?" She perked up. "You never said you were interested in golf. I could take you to my club for some professional instruction. It was a waste of money with Kiera."

"I'm not really interested in it. I was just being polite," I said.

"Oh. Were his parents going to be there for dinner?"

"I don't think so."

"I see. Well, Donald really wanted you here for dinner. He was adamant about it."

"Why?"

"I don't know. He'll be home soon." She thought a moment and then said, "I'm surprised you didn't ask for an autographed picture or something, or did you?"

"No, but maybe I will next time I see them, if you want one."

"Me? No, I thought you would want one. Bradley Garfield is almost everywhere you look these days. Why, last night on *Entertainment Tonight,* they did a good ten minutes on his growing career."

I didn't want to say it because I could see she would take it wrong, but I thought that the more I made of his parents' fame, the more annoyed Ryder would be with me. Probably all of his former friends, including prospective girlfriends, were gaga over them, which I'm sure made him uncomfortable. Anyone in his place would have to wonder if his friends were friends with him solely because of who his parents were.

Instead of saying all of that, I said, "Whenever we saw movie stars in the street, my mother would say they put their underwear on one leg at a time, just like us."

Lately, I hadn't been mentioning my mother or our lives in the street, but it just seemed to fit.

"Oh, she was right. Of course. We're too celebrity-crazy in this country."

I glanced at the miniature grandfather clock on the fireplace mantel.

"I'd better get a start on my homework," I said.

"You didn't do any schoolwork there? I thought you shared classes."

"I wasn't there that long. Maybe we would have if I had stayed for dinner."

"Are you going to see him again?" she asked before I could turn to leave. "I mean, like on a date or something?"

"I think so. We didn't have a chance to talk about doing anything this weekend. I know we're going to dinner Friday night."

"That's right."

"I might invite him here next Tuesday. We have a day off because of teacher conferences. As long as it's all right with you, I mean."

"Oh. Yes. Fine, fine. I'd rather know whom you were seeing and when than see you sneaking off like Kiera used to do. However, I do hope he has a more pleasant demeanor next time," she added, and rose.

I didn't respond. I headed out and up to my room really to start my homework. A little more than an hour later, Mrs. Duval told me that Mr. March was home and dinner would be served in about an hour. He sent her up also to tell me that I should wear something more formal than my regular school outfits. That request puzzled me. Unless we had guests, he never asked me to dress for dinner these days.

Immediately, I went to the closet to find something. While I was looking, my phone rang. I was hoping it might be Ryder, but it was Kiera.

"I followed your advice," she said, "and called my father today."

"Oh, good."

"It wasn't good. He barely spoke to me. He said he was in the middle of a meeting."

"Oh, I'm sorry."

"He was supposed to call me back after the meeting, but he hasn't."

"Maybe he will now?"

"Why? Is he home?"

"Just got home. I know he's going to be here for dinner."

She was quiet. "He told me he was going to a dinner meeting."

"Maybe it was canceled. I'll make sure he calls you."

"Don't do me any favors," she shot back. "If he has to be reminded to call me, I don't want him to bother. Besides, I'm going out with Richard in a little while, and I'm turning off my cell phone."

"I'm sure he'll call you tomorrow, then," I said.

"Are you? You're so sure of what my father will and won't do these days?"

I was silent a moment. Her tone was annoying, but then I had to consider that Donald was not being very nice to her. *Now he decides to try tough love?* I thought. *Where was he when it could have made a difference in her life?*

"Actually, no," I said. "He's been somewhat unpredictable. There is one thing that I can tell you about him for sure, however."

"Oh, and what's that?"

"He's not very fond of Ryder Garfield."

"Really? Tell me about that."

I described their first meeting and their verbal fencing. "Your father seemed quite irritated almost from the start. Your mother says he was like that with some of your boyfriends when you brought them home," I added.

"Most of the time, he seemed not to have any interest in them at all. Anyway, he was never critical of anyone to the extent you're describing. I wouldn't have let him," she said.

"There wasn't much I could do about it."

"I would have raised hell."

"I'm not you."

She was quiet a moment and then said something that really took me aback. "Maybe that's something you should tell my father. I'll talk to you later," she said, and hung up before I could respond.

I changed my clothes, fixed my hair, put on a little lipstick, and went down to the dining room. I was surprised to see Jordan sitting there alone. She was staring out the window and looked lost in thought. She didn't hear me enter until I pulled my chair back.

"Oh, how beautiful you look tonight, Sasha. What a good idea to dress for dinner."

"It wasn't my idea. Mr. March asked Mrs. Duval to tell me to," I said.

"Oh? He didn't say anything about that to me, but I've hardly spoken to him since he returned. He's been shut up in his office because of some problem with an account."

I saw from the way she was folding and unfolding her linen napkin that something else was bothering her. Donald's obsessing about his work was nothing terribly new, even if he had promised to spend more time with us. She stopped playing with her napkin and looked up at me.

"I just found out that Kiera had an extended weekend holiday recently because of her school's schedule, and she didn't mention it or think of coming home. I didn't want to say anything about it to Donald, but I suspect she went somewhere with this new boyfriend." She waited for my reaction, hoping I would tell her something either to confirm or to deny it.

"I don't know anything about that," I said. I wasn't going to get put in the middle here, I thought. It was like trying to put out a fire on both sides of you at once. "She hasn't mentioned it in her e-mails and phone calls. I never knew she had time off, either."

"Just like her, and Donald thinks she might have changed, become more responsible. He's back to deluding himself when it comes to her, I'm afraid."

"Who's back to deluding himself?" Donald asked, entering the dining room. He was in one of his velvet sports jackets, a dark blue, with a slightly lighter tie. I saw he had a small gift-wrapped box in his hand.

For a moment, Jordan was speechless. Then she looked from him to me and back to him. "Why didn't you tell me we were all getting dressed up for dinner tonight?"

"Well, you always do, Jordan. Sasha and I are the ones who usually look like poor relatives at dinner."

"I hardly think so, Donald. What's special about this evening, anyway?"

"Aha. That's the real surprise. I happened to run into Dr. Steiner, the principal of Pacifica, after my lunch today," he said as he sat. "She told me our Sasha has moved into a commanding lead for class valedictorian."

Jordan turned to me. "Is that true? Why didn't you say anything, Sasha?"

"It's far too early for the school to determine that," I said.

"Not according to Dr. Steiner. The boy running second isn't even close, and they decide on the basis of only two more grading periods. Wouldn't that be something?" he asked Jordan. "She'll be making the speech at graduation. Won't you be very proud?"

"Of course."

"What a publicity campaign I could run for this school, taking a girl with her background and bringing her to the top of her class." He paused and said, "If I were so inclined to do so. However, this is all too personal for us," he quickly added. "Nevertheless, we are very proud of you, Sasha, and to show our pride, I bought you a little gift. It's time you had some of your own jewelry, anyway, and stopped being dependent on Jordan or Kiera."

He handed me the box. I looked at Jordan.

She was as surprised as I was, only she didn't look happily surprised. She looked a little angry, in fact. "Why didn't you tell me you were going to do something like this, Donald?" she asked. "I think I might have helped choose something appropriate."

"Oh, I think this will be appropriate."

"And when did you have time to shop for such a thing, or did you assign it to one of your secretaries?"

"No, no, I did this myself. I told you I was going to devote more time to my girls, didn't I? Now you can think about the dress you're going to buy her this Saturday and how it would go with what's in the box. Of course, she can wear it at dinner tomorrow night as well."

"Really? Well, what's in the box?" Jordan asked, and nodded at me to open it.

I looked toward the kitchen door. Either Donald had told Mrs. Duval and Mrs. Caro to hold dinner, or they were listening and waiting to give the three of us time alone. I began to tear away the gift wrapping. I opened the box and took out a beautiful black pearl necklace in a setting of diamonds with a white gold chain. It glittered in the light of the chandelier. Donald leaped out of his seat and came around behind me. Jordan had yet to speak.

"Let's just see how it looks on her now, huh?" Donald said, taking the necklace from my fingers and undoing the clasp. He put it around my neck and fastened it. It fell softly a few inches below the base of my throat. "Well?"

"That's the most beautiful piece of costume jewelry I've seen lately," Jordan said. "I'll have to compliment you, Donald. Very nice."

"It's not costume jewelry," Donald replied.

"It's not?"

"She's doing real things. Why not give her real things?"

Jordan was speechless again. She rose out of her chair slowly and came over to look more closely at the necklace. Then she looked at Donald. "You never bought anything this expensive for Kiera."

"Kiera barely graduated, Jordan, and have you forgotten those diamond earrings of yours she lost? What were they, five thousand dollars?"

"You didn't make a big thing of it then, Donald. You claimed it on insurance."

"Why make a point of it now?" he said sharply. "Doesn't this look beautiful on her? Make sure you get a dress for her that shows the necklace well," he added. "Do you like it, Sasha?"

"How could anyone not like it? It's very beautiful," I said. "Thank you."

"You're welcome. As I said, we're proud of your accomplishments and very impressed with all of the top schools that have accepted you, some offering scholarships. You know they want you very much, and why shouldn't they? It adds to their prestige to have students like you."

He returned to his seat. Jordan stared at the necklace for a moment more and then returned to her seat. I looked at the necklace again. The first thought I had was, what was Kiera going to say when she heard about this? Her father didn't have time to talk to her, but he had time to go shopping for a necklace for me? Her last remark on the phone echoed. Any other girl in my position would probably be ecstatic to be given such a piece of jewelry, but I felt as numb as someone seeing an impending storm charging in from the horizon.

"Mrs. Duval," Donald called, and the kitchen door opened. Mrs. Duval and Mrs. Caro paraded in carrying the dinner. All that was missing was a drumroll. Mrs. Caro had a dish with a silver cover, and Mrs. Duval had our salads and bread. Mrs. Caro placed the silver-covered dish in front of Donald.

"What are we having?" Jordan asked, which surprised me. She was always in charge of the dinners.

"Another surprise," Donald said. He nodded at Mrs. Duval, who moved forward to lift off the silver cover. "Lobster fra diavolo," he announced.

I looked at Jordan to see if she was as shocked as I was.

I had told her that was what the Garfields were having tonight. Had she told Donald, or was this all an amazing coincidence?

"It looks absolutely delicious, Mrs. Caro," Donald said. "I'm sure it matches any other lobster fra diavolo anywhere," he added, directing himself more to me than to her. "Mrs. Duval, let's pour the wine, and tonight, be sure to give our future class valedictorian a glass."

Mrs. Duval looked surprised but did what he asked. Jordan squinted and stared at Donald. I was glad to see it wasn't only I who thought he was behaving strangely. When I first came here, he made a big show over my calligraphy, but his reactions to anything I did after that were always even-tempered, restrained. I thought he was as sensitive to Kiera's being jealous as I was.

He did most of the talking during dinner, describing this new account that he emphasized he wanted me to evaluate. I promised I would stop at his office tomorrow after school. I was hoping he had forgotten the comment Jordan had made just before he entered the dining room, but as if it had lingered there in midair, he suddenly turned to her and asked what she had meant when she said he had been deluding himself.

"Now, let's get back to what you said before I walked into the dining room, Jordan. Deluding myself about what?"

"Your daughter."

"Kiera?" He shook his head, looked at me and then back at her. "Now what has she done?"

"Apparently, she had an extended weekend and could

have come home but didn't. I have no idea where she went, but I suspect neither of us will be pleased when and if we ever find out."

"Maybe she never left the school," he said. "Anyway, that's hardly a reason to say I'm deluding myself, Jordan. You're still thinking only the worst possible things about her."

"Me? You're the one who just pointed out how she had lost my expensive earrings."

"That was a few years ago."

"Oh. Fine. I guess I should make nothing of the fact that she's avoiding us."

"When I was in college, I wasn't crazy about rushing home all the time, either."

"All the time? She hasn't been home once since she went this year. She wasn't home very much the year before, and she spent most of the summer with rich friends traveling through Europe. The girl is drifting farther and farther away from both of us, you included, Donald. I know it's easier to ignore it all, but I think it's time you had a good talk with her."

"She did say she would like to hear from you," I said, seeing the opportunity.

"She did hear from me," Donald replied, and finished another glass of wine. "I called her today."

"You called her?"

"Exactly. Why? She said I didn't?"

I shook my head. "I'm not sure. I might have gotten it wrong."

"I doubt it," Jordan said. "She's still exaggerating, distorting, and lying outright."

"What? She isn't failing any subject, and she hasn't had any problems at school, or we would have heard. Why would you say such a damning thing?" Donald demanded, his mood changing instantly. Usually, when he was this upset, Jordan backed down, but I could she wasn't going to this time. She was still smarting about not being included in picking out my gift.

"I don't believe this boy she's seeing is the son of some English aristocrat. I told her to bring him home if she liked, but she hasn't. She says more about him to Sasha than she does to me or you, for that matter."

"That's a girlie thing," Donald said, waving it off. "Hardly anything to get upset about."

"I've heard that before, Donald. And we both lived to regret it."

"All right, all right, I'll call her again," he said, relenting. "Maybe we'll all take a ride to her school one weekend."

Jordan was silent. She had said as much as she wanted to say. Her eyes fell on me, focused on my new necklace. For the first time since I had come here, I felt Jordan March was actually jealous of me, jealous of something I had besides my youth.

As soon as dinner ended, I went up to my room to ponder what all of this meant. Why did Kiera lie about her father not calling her? Or could it possibly be that he was lying to cover up for his neglect?

Family life was so complicated, and being rich or

famous didn't seem to provide any sort of relief from that. In fact, it might make it more complicated. If anyone should know how wonderful having a family could be, it was I. Most of my young life, I had been envious of other kids my age who had parents and brothers and sisters. As far as I could see, a family gave you a safety net. No matter what you did or what happened to you, they were there for you, supporting you, comforting you. Who took more pride in you and your accomplishments than your parents? Yes, sisters and brothers could be jealous of each other, but they couldn't help being proud of each other as well. Your success did bring something wonderful to them, too.

And yet I also knew how devastating the rupture of a family could be. Losing friendships, losing your job, and failing in your career were difficult to take, but there was always the prospect of new friends, new jobs, and even new careers. No girlfriend could really replace a mother, and for a boy, no friend could replace his father. Deep in my heart, I knew that Jordan March had hoped the opposite might be true for me, that one day I'd wake up and see her as my mother. Perhaps she had even hoped she'd wake up and see me as Alena.

No one could blame her, I supposed. Who wouldn't want to end the pain? But it was one thing to lose a mother or a daughter because of an illness or an accident and a far different thing to lose either one because of a family disagreement. People who loved each other deeply were obviously capable of hating each other just as deeply.

At the end of your life, at some dark moment when your whole life streamed through your mind like an all-day movie, all of the happiest moments highlighted, all of the smiles and laughter seen and heard once more, you surely couldn't help but feel the cold regret that would join the pallbearers who brought you to your final rest.

Surely you would wonder if there wasn't some way, some magical phrase you could have used, some words you had never thought of or had thought of but never spoken that could have mended and begun the healing of these wounds. Wasn't there something more, one thing more you could have done to change the downward movement of your family? Could you have pushed regret away with a simple "I'm sorry" or perhaps just by saying "I love you"?

I felt like calling Kiera up and saying only one thing to her. *The day will come when it will be too late for apologies and expressions of love. There'll be no one to hear them, and the empty echo of your own voice will haunt you until the day you die and maybe even within the grave in which you sleep. Don't let that happen.*

I practically lunged at my telephone when it rang. It jolted me out of my deep and troubled thoughts.

"Hey," I heard Ryder say.

His voice felt like cool rain on a hot, muggy day. My body softened and relaxed. "Hey."

"How was your dinner?"

Should I tell him that Donald had ordered the same exact meal for us? It was too weird for me; it would surely be too weird for him.

"My foster father found out about my grade-average standing in the class."

"Really? What is it?"

"I could be, I mean, I probably will be valedictorian if I just maintain my grade average. He wanted me home for dinner so he could give me a gift to show how proud of me they are."

"It wasn't a new pen, was it?"

I laughed. "Hardly." I still had the necklace on, and I touched it. "I have a feeling what it cost would have kept my mother and me safe and sound for years."

"What is it?"

"A pearl and diamond necklace. My foster mother is taking me for a new dress Saturday to wear to the concert my foster father is getting tickets for next month, and he wanted me to have it before she went shopping. At least, that's the story he gave."

"Why do you say that? You think there are other reasons?"

"Nothing is simple here," I said. I knew it sounded very cryptic, even dark and dangerous, but it came to mind.

"Sounds like we could easily exchange homes and families. Any chance of doing something this weekend? I didn't get the opportunity to ask."

"The Marches are taking me to dinner Friday night at a hot restaurant."

"Which one?"

"Castles."

"Boring," he sang. "Each table has a full-length mirror for the guests to look at themselves."

I laughed. "Saturday is free," I said.

"All right. I know a cheap, small, unimportant sushi joint in Venice Beach. Unless you want to stay clear of the ocean."

"I don't hate the ocean or the beach, Ryder. As long as I don't have to sleep on it."

He laughed. "Seven?"

"Yes, and Tuesday is fine for us here."

"Maybe after the real date, you won't want me coming over."

"Maybe I won't," I said a little too seriously, but I wasn't in the mood for anyone's self-pity. "But I doubt it," I added, "so shut up."

He laughed, and I said I had to get to my homework.

"You'd better, especially after accepting that gift," he told me.

*That gift,* I thought, and went to my vanity mirror to look at it again.

I made a decision when I took it off and put it back into its box.

I wouldn't be the one to tell Kiera about it. Later, she might be even angrier that I didn't, but it wasn't a lie, and it wasn't deceitful if the reason you did it was to keep someone else from being unhappy. That way, it wasn't bad, was it?

I smiled, remembering my little battle of quips in English class when Ryder had first entered school.

*Nothing either good or bad, but thinking makes it so.*

I chose to think it was good.

*Thank you, Shakespeare,* I thought, and put the necklace in a drawer.

If only we could put all of our troubles in a box and close it in a drawer, how well we would sleep and how easily we could turn from nightmares to sweet dreams.

## 12

## *Rumors*

My mother thinks you have potential," Ryder told me when we met in the parking lot the next morning.

"Potential? What's that mean? Potential for what? She hardly talked to me."

"As a model or something. What else? She certainly doesn't see you as a doctor or a lawyer. Not that you couldn't be," he quickly added. "It's the way she looks at all girls and other women. My father calls it feminine envy. All women, he says, think someone else is prettier and never think they're pretty enough. When he starts complaining about that, they really go at it. I sit back and watch. It's better than the soap opera he's in."

I laughed, but I thought he really did see his parents as people cast in roles. Every day of his life was simply another episode. He even talked about his sister as if she were playing a part she had been given at birth. I wondered if he saw himself the same way. Maybe he just didn't feel real.

"By the way, Summer wasn't too happy about the way my mother went on about you this morning."

"Why? Doesn't your mother compliment her?"

He looked at me as if I had asked the dumbest question. "With the way Summer dresses, what she does with the clothes my mother buys her, what she did recently, and that Gothic makeup she loves? I thought they'd break out into a fistfight over piercing. Dear old Mom, as you saw, hates stress, so she just shakes her head and walks away."

"Well, maybe Summer would behave better and have a better image of herself if your parents paid more attention to her, spent time talking to her and trying to reason with her."

"Dr. Sasha!" he cried. "Can I make an appointment for my parents with you today?"

I punched him in the shoulder, and he pretended it hurt. I pretended to be shocked and sorry, and he stopped and threw his arm around me.

"Hey, I'm just kidding."

"So am I," I said, and he laughed.

"I think I've finally met my match," he said as we entered the building. He still had his arm around my shoulders.

There wasn't a single senior high student who wasn't looking at us. I was always afraid of being too proud, too arrogant about my looks and achievements. Because of where I had come from and where I was now in my life, I told myself I could easily be a little egotistical and not have people criticize me for it, but I was still afraid of it. Look at how pride and vanity had practically destroyed Kiera.

We had been studying classic tragedy in English class, and I knew the famous statement about pride coming before a fall. When you were too big for yourself, you always made serious mistakes.

But being with Ryder and knowing who his parents were made it very difficult to act nonchalantly. The way the other students were looking at me now, the girls so full of envy, the boys so impressed, made me feel as if the Garfields' celebrity had somehow spread to me. What girl here didn't dream about being on the covers of magazines or a star in movies and television? Especially in this school, it was almost a natural part of being a teenager. You weren't normal if you didn't dream of these things. The stream of conversation in the hallways, in the cafeteria, in the bathrooms, everywhere, was fed from a pool of currently famous teenagers who were idolized. Almost everyone bragged about some experience that had brought him or her close to one of these much-publicized people.

"My parents know so-and-so."

"My father got me backstage tickets to this one's concert or that one's, and I got to shake his hand. He hugged me!"

"We actually ate dinner at the table next to so-and-so."

On and on it went, everyone trying to outdo everyone else with his or her celebrity experience. It was easy, at least for me, to see how much of it was exaggerated.

But there was no way to doubt me, to accuse me of exaggeration. I was seeing Ryder Garfield. I was at his home. I had to have had real contact with his parents. I was touched with the golden fingers. I already commanded their envy for other reasons. Now I was almost untouchable myself. Why, any day now, I might get photographed in the presence of one of Ryder's parents, and my picture could be in magazines or even on television. I could see all of these thoughts in the faces of other girls.

I tried to look away, shifting my gaze quickly from one face to another, and then caught Summer Garfield standing at the corner of the junior high corridor. She stood with a few of the other girls who were looking at Ryder and me, but her face wasn't awash with admiration. Her face was brilliant with red rage almost washing out her black lipstick and mascara. For a moment, her hateful stare took my breath away, and then Ryder turned us toward homeroom, and she was out of sight, but not out of mind, at least not out of my mind.

Even so, our day started out smoothly. Ryder was talkative in all of our morning classes and was even a little friendlier toward most of the other guys in our class. Between classes, we walked together, either holding hands or with his arm around my shoulders. I could see we were the focus of everyone's attention, especially again at lunch. I thought things were going very well. Bobby Jenkins even paused to tell me everyone was giving me credit for turning Ryder Garfield into a human being. But it was toward the end of the lunch hour when I realized things were not going to remain so picture-perfect. I could see it in the way other students were now looking at us. Something had occurred that had radically changed things.

As Ryder and I were heading for our first afternoon class, Jessica tapped me on the shoulder and asked if she could speak to me. I could see from the expression on her face that she was bringing me some unpleasant news. Jessica was one of those girls who seemed to feed like vampires on someone else's misery. Whose was it going to be this time?

"Go on. I'll catch up," I told Ryder, and hung back. "What?" I asked, impatient. I was getting intolerant of the immature behavior and planned to say something about it, even though it might lose me friends.

"Summer Garfield is spreading very nasty rumors about you," she said.

"What do you mean? What rumors?"

"She's been telling girls in her class that you did every-thing with Ryder at their house yesterday. You did go there."

"Did everything?"

"Everything!" she emphasized. "She claims she saw you. She says you're just like all the other girls Ryder brought home, star-struck and easy. She's going into disgusting detail." She smirked. "Are you sorry you told me to keep my mouth shut about her now?"

"No. Don't say anything about that."

"Sydney told me she heard something. I didn't tell her," she quickly added with her right hand up, palm out. "You're more important. His sister is telling these stories to everyone she can. People are believing her, Sasha. They've come up to me, because they know we're best friends, to get it all confirmed. It doesn't matter what I tell them or how I defend you. They just smile and say, 'Sure, sure.'"

"Okay. I'll take care of it. Thanks."

"You're welcome," she said, obviously happy that she

was doing me a favor and it wasn't vice versa. "I'll keep trying to do what I can to stop it."

"No! Don't do anything. Don't say anything, Jessica. The more you talk about it, the longer it lives," I said. "Just ignore it."

I hurried to catch up to Ryder, not sure what I should do. If I told him what Jessica had just told me, I knew he would go absolutely ballistic on Summer and maybe even cause a big scene here at Pacifica. On the other hand, if I didn't tell him and he found out what was being said very soon, which was quite possible, he might be angry with me for not warning him. Once the stories Summer was spreading reached all the boys in our class, especially a boy like Shayne Peters, they would be magnified and exaggerated. They would surely embarrass Ryder, I thought. I had no choice. *I'll have to tell him,* I thought. The question was when was the most opportune time.

He smiled as I entered class. We hadn't known each other that long, but I saw that he could see something was bothering me. Why couldn't I be a hard read like Kiera? Why wasn't I blessed more with the powers of deception? Why was I so honest inside, especially after the things I had been through? One would think I had been trained by experts when Kiera and her friends abused me. Why was everyone else around here but me so comfortable behind a mask? Ryder's eyebrows dipped toward each other as he raised his palms.

"What's up?" he asked just as the bell rang.

"I'll tell you after class," I whispered.

Since Jessica had told me what the topic of discussion

had been during lunch, I looked around and saw from the expressions on the other students' faces when they looked our way that Jessica was right. It was already all heard, digested, and believed by most. Of course, it made sense. Why wouldn't they think the son of a very famous Hollywood star and a world-famous mother could get a girl to do anything? Suddenly, I was the one who was feeling abused by their fame, not Ryder.

The moment the bell rang to end class, he was at me. All during class, I couldn't concentrate. Jessica's words echoed.

"Well? What got you so upset?"

"Your sister is spreading rumors about us," I said.

"What sort of rumors? Rumors about what?"

My own anger had boiled over, and try as I might, I couldn't restrain myself.

"About yesterday, when I was at your house," I said. I had to lower my voice because everyone was making a point of walking close to us in hopes of overhearing something they could spread.

Ryder's face reddened. "Tell me."

"All I heard was she's been saying I did everything with you. She claims she saw us."

"Everything?"

"Sexually, Ryder. Saying it that way leaves a lot to the imagination, and around here, imaginations have no limits or restrictions. According to Jessica, she's telling everyone that I'm just another in a long line of girls you were able to take advantage of."

The blood rushed into his face. "I'll take care of it," he said.

"Don't make a scene in the school. Please wait until you get home. You'll be falling right into her trap. She's unhappy, so she wants you to be unhappy, Ryder. Maybe you should just make your parents sit down and talk to her, tell them what—"

"I said I'll take care of it. And I mean now!" he said, and charged ahead of me toward the classroom door.

"Ryder!"

Why didn't I wait until the end of the day at least? I was sure he was heading for the junior high wing of the building. I hesitated just outside the classroom doorway and looked for him, hoping to call him back, but he didn't even get to make the turn in the hallway. Apparently, Shayne Peters and Kory Taylor had stopped him and made some sort of dirty comment. Even from where I was standing, I could see Ryder was steaming. I started in his direction, hoping still to prevent any problems, but I didn't get there in time.

Ryder turned and then swung back with his books clutched between his hands, slapping Shayne so hard on the left side of his face that he spun and then fell forward. Without a pause, Ryder continued turning and hit Kory on the jaw. He didn't fall, but he looked stunned. I shouted, *"No!"* but Ryder delivered a third blow, clubbing Kory just above his forehead. His legs gave out, and he sank to the hall floor.

Mr. Huntington, one of the high school math teachers, was in his doorway. At first, he was too shocked to move, but then he shot out and threw his arms around Ryder, pulling him away from the other two. Shayne had gotten to his feet. He was a little unsteady, but he was determined to throw a punch and did. Mr. Huntington, who stood a good six foot three himself, turned his body so that the punch was deflected off his shoulder.

By then, there was a big commotion in the hallway. Mr. Denacio came running from his classroom to help, and some of the other boys charged in to keep Shayne and Kory from going back at Ryder. All three were then directed to Dr. Steiner's office. I stood there holding my breath. Jessica, Sydney, and Charlotte rushed to my side. There was still a lot of shouting going on, and other teachers were ordering the students to get to their classes.

"What happened?" Jessica asked.

I looked at her, the numbness in me receding and pure rage washing through my body.

"Figure it out," I said, then turned and headed toward my next class. I held my books tightly against my chest. My body was still trembling, and oddly, what I feared was that my limp would return.

Practically everyone was late for class. After it settled down, I could feel that everyone's eyes were on me. I didn't look at anyone, but I didn't hear much, either. It was as if a meteor had hit the building. It all had happened that quickly. I didn't volunteer to answer any questions, and I didn't take a single note. Occasionally, I glanced at the doorway, hoping Ryder would appear, but he never did. When the bell rang to end the period, my girlfriends were around me again, this time all trying to be comforting.

I didn't see Ryder at all for the remainder of the day. I didn't see Shayne or Kory, either, for that matter, but by the end of the last period, word had spread that all three of them had been suspended and told to leave the building. This meant that none of them could return without his parents or a parent coming in to meet with Dr. Steiner. I headed for the parking lot, still bewildered.

Jessica made a point of telling me that she had not said anything to anyone, especially Shayne and Kory.

"I swear," she said. "They heard it all from someone else."

"Okay, Jessica."

At the moment, I didn't want to speak to any of them. They sensed it and kept their distance. When I stepped outside, I saw Summer standing with some other girls who were usually picked up by taxis or limousines. I realized that she had to be picked up that way since Ryder had been sent home, driven off the school grounds. It was probably for the best. I could just imagine him trying to drive and losing his temper at her at the same time.

Maybe I was a little crazy by now. I knew it would shock my friends, but I walked over to Summer Garfield and asked her if she wanted a ride home.

"What?" she asked, unsure that she had heard what she had heard.

"I can bring you home."

"I'd never get into a car with you now."

"Why? Are you afraid of me?" I asked.

She looked at the other girls, who were almost as shocked as she was. "I'm not afraid of you."

"So?"

"I don't want to be in the same car with you," she said, taking a step back.

"I know what it's like to hate yourself," I told her. "You don't know it yet, but I'm the best friend you have."

She was unable to think of anything to say. I smiled and walked away. When I got into my car, I turned on my cell phone and called Ryder. I thought he wasn't going to pick up, but he did just before the message system clicked on.

"Where are you?" I asked.

"You don't want to know."

"I wouldn't have asked if I didn't want to know, Ryder. Where are you?"

"I'm on the beach at Santa Monica," he said. "Just to the left of the pier."

"You didn't go home yet?"

"No. I don't want to ever go home."

"I'll be right there."

"Are you sure you want to be seen with me?"

"I said I'll be right there." I hung up before he could utter another word.

The pier was always busy because of the restaurants, the merry-go-round, and the Ferris wheel. On weekends, it could be wall-to-wall with people, mostly tourists. I remembered how my mother and I would try to sell her calligraphy and my lanyards there because there were so many people in one small area, but the police usually moved us away. Sometimes we were just there to get something to eat ourselves. I recalled one time when my mother insisted we go on the Ferris wheel and I go on the merry-go-round.

To me, even at that young age, it seemed to be a terrible waste of the little money we had at the time, but she was adamant. She so wanted us, especially me, to feel as though we had a normal life, even if it was only for twenty minutes. On that Ferris wheel and with me on the merry-go-round and her smiling and watching, we had put our misery on pause. Smiles and laughter were rare birds that flew in, alighted on our faces and in our hearts, and then left us longing for the whisper of their wings, the sound of their songs.

I remember when we walked away from the pier, leaving the music and the chatter, the lights and the aromas of food behind and entering the darkness again. The pier was one place I had avoided all this time. I was afraid of the memory, like someone who was afraid that where she was now was really all a dream. The moment I was near or on the pier, I feared I would wake up and be homeless and lost again.

However, it did seem to be a fitting place to meet Ryder now, considering how dark and unhappy we both were. After I parked, I walked slowly toward the pier and then turned left. The sun was still quite strong and bright, even though it was sinking into the western horizon. Back when Mama and I were homeless, the sunsets weren't romantic. They were beautiful, of course. The clouds would sometimes take on a pink-grapefruit shade, and then the turquoise would deepen around the puffs. Other times, they just looked as if they were embarrassed and blushing. To me, they would brighten more as the sun dipped. It was like a last shout and cry.

The reason we sat quietly as the sun set was that we knew darkness would soon follow. As if they had been sleeping under the sand, other homeless people would come out. We'd see people wandering without any particular destination in mind. It was simply important to keep moving, even if it was in a large circle. Mama used to say that they were all hoping for a train or a car that would stop to take them away. Some, the ones who were recently homeless, still had that spark of hope lighting their eyes, and some had already fallen through disbelief into a mindless oblivion, where they didn't have to keep questioning and complaining or even hoping. They could drift like one of those lost clouds.

Being here now, walking where I had once walked timidly, often terrified, tightened every muscle in my body the way someone would tighten up before the dentist put a drill in her mouth. The dryness in my mouth made my tongue feel like slate. For a moment, I couldn't swallow. It was as if the air had disappeared around me. All sound dulled. My heart began to race. I could hear it beating in my ears. I felt light. Any moment, I might just get swept up in the breeze and drift out over the ocean like some human kite. I glanced quickly at some of the homeless people, the women with greasy, dirty hair, their cheeks red or smudged, and the men shuffling along in shoes too large or too tight. No one seemed to look at me. Perhaps instead of them becoming invisible, I had become invisible.

I stepped onto the sand, slipped off my shoes to walk more easily, and searched the beach for a sign of Ryder. I didn't have to go far. He was almost directly in front of me, sitting with his back to me, his arms around his pulled-up knees, his head down. I hurried toward him.

"Hey," I said.

He turned, looked at me, and then looked out at the ocean. I sat beside him.

"It's my fault. I shouldn't have told you so fast," I began.

"What? You think those guys wouldn't have started teasing me if you hadn't told me what Summer had done? You had nothing to do with it."

"What did they say?"

"You don't want to hear it," he said, and threw a handful of sand at the water.

"What's going to happen now?"

"My parents will find a way to blame it mainly on me."

"But why? They've already had problems with your sister. It won't be a surprise."

"They've had problems with both of us. My sister is an idiot. They said that if things didn't work out here, they'd send us both to more military-style schools. I'm not going to any place like that."

"What will you do?"

"Disappear," he said. "Like you did out here."

"You don't want to do that," I said.

He stared at the sand and then looked at me. "I don't know what I want to do."

"Then I'll tell you what to do. Go home. Yes, apologize for losing your temper, but also explain how hard Summer made it for you today."

"My father will say what he always says. 'You should

have known better.' No matter what, it's always that. Like I have this committee of advisers with me all the time, and I would always know the best way to handle anything, but I don't listen. Look, even though I've told you some of it, you really don't know. No one knows how we live, what my family life is like, if you want to call it a family life. You saw some inkling of it yesterday, but in case it didn't sink in, I'll tell you. My parents are totally into themselves. End of story," he said, and stood. "I guess I'll go home and let them play their parts."

I started to rise, and he took my arm to guide me up and into his arms.

For a moment, he just held me, and then he kissed me. I don't think I'll ever forget that kiss, that moment. Yes, it was like some very romantic movie scene, the two of us on the beach, the ocean in the background, the breeze lifting strands of my hair, the terns circling as if they were part of it.

But the truth was, it wasn't one of those "I love you so much" kisses. He was kissing me and holding me as if he would never see me again. It felt more like a kiss good-bye than a kiss of love.

"You're something special," he whispered, still pressing me to him. "I wouldn't even bother to put up a fight if it weren't for you."

"Then put up a big fight," I told him.

He finally smiled.

Hand in hand, we walked back up the beach toward the pier. Neither of us spoke until we arrived at where we had to part to go to our cars.

"Will you call me later and let me know how it went?" I asked.

"Why ruin your night?"

"If you don't call, my night will be ruined."

"Okay," he said. He kissed me again. "I'll keep my temper under control, take the verbal whipping, say whatever I need to say, and keep my fingers crossed behind my back."

"Fingers crossed behind your back?"

"Don't you know that when you say something, make a promise, but keep your fingers crossed, it doesn't matter if you're lying? I wouldn't have known that, either. I don't think it's a big thing now, but it used to be. I saw it in a television movie my father was in. He had a son who did that."

To illustrate, Ryder held his right hand up with his middle finger crossing his index finger.

"I read that it dates back to a belief that it would ward off witches or other evil spirits. Maybe I'll do it every time I'm around my sister."

"Don't hate her," I said.

He pulled his head back. "Don't hate her? If anyone should, you should be the one who hates her today."

"I've seen what that kind of hatred does, and not to the person you hate but to yourself."

He shook his head. "You sure you're not an angel or something?"

"Hardly." I looked back at the boardwalk. "When we were living out there, there was this homeless woman who was a practicing psychic. I know that's kind of a trite character in movies, the vagabond person who utters some prophecy."

"Like the blind soothsayer in Shakespeare's *Julius Caesar*."

"Exactly. I saw lots of people give her money to get their fortunes told. Even other homeless people would do it. She would hold a person's hand, close her eyes, and make some very dramatic statement."

"What made her so special, especially if she was homeless?"

"There were many reasons people were homeless. There were stories about some of the people we saw, stories that they had enough money to rent a room but would rather live the way they were living. Maybe they were crazy. I don't know. She made enough money to survive. I did ask my mother why she could make predictions, and she told me to ask her, so one day, I did. The three of us were eating some sandwiches, sitting on a bench."

"What did she say?"

"She said she had the ability to feel either the love or the hate in people, and if there was more hate, she could predict unhappiness ahead, but if there was more love, she could feel pretty certain that they would eventually find happiness if they didn't have it. That was it. The whole thing."

He smiled and shook his head at me. "You sound like a New Age priestess or something."

"There's nothing new about that idea. Ever hear 'Love your neighbor'?"

"Okay. I'm convinced. I won't hate my sister. I'll thank her for being a bitch today."

"Don't thank her. Just try asking her why she did it."

"That's easy. She hates me because my parents made me her personal policeman."

"Find some common ground, Ryder. Make her see you don't relish the role your parents gave you to play."

"I should be afraid of you," he said after a long moment.

"Why?"

"You give me hope."

"So? That's good, isn't it?"

"Not if what's usually been true comes true again. It's a longer, harder fall when you raise yourself higher only to be disappointed."

"You won't be," I said.

He took my hand. "What do you feel? More hate or more love?"

I smiled. "I'm not a psychic because I lived out here, Ryder."

"Exactly," he said. He held me a moment and then walked off. I watched him. He never turned to look back at me.

I wanted to believe I had helped him, but he seemed to be walking into the darkness from which I had been rescued.

## 13

## *Bad News*

*I* remembered promising Donald that I would go to his office after school to see his advertisement campaign for the High Rollers, the rock group, but I was too upset to go. I thought I would simply say that I wasn't feeling well if he called the house. I should have known none of it would matter.

I knew my friend Jessica had a big mouth. Sometimes, when I asked her to keep something to herself, as I had done with the information she had dug up about Summer Garfield, I felt as if I was trying to plug up a leaky faucet with a piece of cotton. *Good luck,* I would tell myself. I already knew what her mother was like, and as Mr. Denacio was fond of saying every time a sister or brother did something wrong or right, "The apple doesn't fall far from the tree."

I suppose the Garfields were a big topic for discussion at the homes of most of the Pacifica students, anyway. It hadn't taken long for me to see that parents of students at

Pacifica took pride in whose children were sent to attend school alongside theirs. Their bragging rights were boosted with the news that a popular actor and model had entered their son and daughter at the same school. Maybe they thought this validated their own decision to choose Pacifica for their kids and pay the very high tuition.

Bad news always has a way of being sent special delivery, but bad news involving Ryder Garfield had e-mail speed. It arrived at the March home before I did, which probably shouldn't have astonished me, but what especially amazed me was how quickly the information had been shared with Donald. After I spoke with Jordan, I had the distinct impression that they had already had considerable discussion about my budding relationship with Ryder Garfield since I had brought him home with me. The intensity of this new concern about whom I associated with surprised me, especially because it seemed to originate more with Donald than with Jordan.

Jordan came hurrying down the corridor and called to me as I was opening the front door. I had the impression that she had been watching one of the video feeds of the gate, just sitting there and waiting for me, and therefore knew exactly when I had arrived.

"I heard about the terrible event at school," she began. "Apparently, the Peters boy had to be taken to the hospital to check for a concussion."

"No, probably to check for brains," I said. I even sounded like Kiera. My comeback startled Jordan, and for a moment, she stood there speechless. "I always thought I could look through one of his ears and out the other."

"This isn't at all funny, Sasha. Donald is very upset," she said. "He's very, very worried about you."

"Me? Why?"

"Why? Well, this boy . . . whom you're now seeing . . . he's the son of famous people, but obviously, he's unstable. We saw some of that when he was here, but this terrible event at the school makes it all so much worse."

"Don't say that. You don't even know what happened and why," I said.

"You don't condone such behavior, do you?" she snapped back at me. "You, of all people should know what violence can do to everyone involved."

"Yes, I do. That's why I feel sorrier for Ryder, Jordan. There are all sorts of violence. Saying and spreading hateful things can be just as devastating as a blow to the face. You, of all people, should know that," I countered.

It was a poorly veiled reference to the stories about Donald having affairs. Her face reddened, and she bristled. I had never been disrespectful or combative with either her or Donald, even when I had been accused of doing all sorts of things to Kiera. I was younger when that all happened, of course, and far more fragile than I was now, but I didn't feel I was defending myself as much as I was defending Ryder, who, despite what everyone thought about him and his rich and famous family, needed defending.

"Well, we'll talk about this later," she said.

"Good," I said. "We should."

I started up the stairway, trying to look strong and determined, even though my legs were trembling. Yes, the Marches owed me a lot, perhaps more than they could ever repay, but they had given me a great deal, too, and provided for me. I didn't need to be reminded that I was still technically a foster child, their ward, someone without any of my own family willing to claim me and provide for me. I was, for all practical purposes, an orphan. I didn't have to hear the threat of their giving up on me. They had almost done that when Kiera had them believing I was responsible for the bad things that were done when she was trying to destroy me. The echo of that threat lingered despite the revelations and my accomplishments. It hung out there like smog. The Marches could give up on me and turn me back to the state until I was eighteen.

It was a topic I was naturally interested in learning more about. At the moment, in America, there were an estimated half a million children in foster care. About half were in nonrelative homes. I was part of that statistic and felt like a second-class citizen even though I lived in a palatial home and had more than most girls from wealthy families had.

Sometimes, when I thought about my status in the world and compared myself with the other girls my age who were at Pacifica, I would think about my real father. My memories of him now were so vague. I had no pictures of him. Mama was so angry at him when he left us desolate that she destroyed any pictures of her and him that there were. There was never a letter from him since Mama's death. I wondered if he even knew about that. He never tried to contact me. Whenever I thought about him now, I had to rely more on my imagination than my memory.

Before Jordan brought me to the March home, she had a detective search for my father or for information about him. She was the one who had told me he had gone from Hawaii to Australia and had a new daughter. What greater rejection was there for any girl to experience than her father totally ignoring her very existence?

At first, especially when I was much younger, I used to think it was somehow my fault. It wasn't that I had done terrible things that he couldn't tolerate or understand; it was that he couldn't look at me and think of me as his daughter. It was one thing for him to have a love affair with an Asian woman and even marry her. For him, as for so many people, apparently, marriage wasn't that big a deal anymore. I often heard Jordan say that marriage today is like what young couples in high school and college did when they decided to go steady. For a while, it was hot and heavy, but there was always the expectation of a breakup. A wedding ring had become no more important than a class ring. Divorce, she said, was a new industry.

What I came to believe was that my father couldn't tolerate my Asian features. I was too different. I would look in the mirror and try to imagine what it was about me that disgusted him. Did he hate my eyes, my hair, the shape of my mouth? What? That was how I thought when I was so much younger. I couldn't think of any other reason he would be able to pick up and leave me forever without a good-bye or a phone call or a card. It had to have been my fault.

Even so, I couldn't help imagining him appearing one day. Of course, in my fantasy, he would be as young and as handsome as he had been when my mother first fell in love with him. He would be like someone who had awoken from a long sleep, my own Rip Van Winkle, who realized that he had left his daughter behind when he lost his mind and left us. He would have worked hard at tracking me down, and when he had, he would come here. I would see him drive up and see him out there looking up at my room. Somehow he would know exactly where I was in this great mansion. Mrs. Duval would call me down to meet someone, and I would descend the stairs wondering who this handsome person could be.

"Hi," he would say. "You're as beautiful as I imagined you would be. I'm so sorry I left you. I made a terrible mistake. I want you back. I know I can't make up for all the pain, but I want to try. I want to take care of you now. Please find it in your heart to forgive me."

Of course, I would be hesitant, even a little afraid, but his smile would wash that all away, and I would run to him, eager to have him embrace me. Now I would walk with my father and hold his hand, and I wouldn't feel that I was less than any other girl. He would tell me wonderful stories about his own youth and his own family.

"You'll never be an orphan again. You'll never be anyone's ward. You'll never be without family," he would promise.

Later I would take him to Mama's grave, and he would kneel in front of her headstone and beg her forgiveness. He would promise her that he would take good care of me, and we would both stand there and cry for her.

How many times I had dreamed this scenario. Right now, feeling more vulnerable than ever, I longed for such a dream to come true. Of course, it never happened.

His name was never mentioned, nor was there ever any reference to him and where he was now. I had a father made of smoke. A strong onshore breeze had washed him away.

I snapped out of my reverie and looked at the clock. The time drew closer to when I knew Donald would be arriving home. I tried to occupy myself with my homework but couldn't concentrate. Every time I heard a footstep or a door slam, I anticipated a knock on my bedroom door. Finally, Mrs. Duval came to tell me that Mr. and Mrs. March wanted to see me in Mr. March's office. I thanked her, put my books away, glanced at myself in the mirror to fix my hair, and started out.

We hadn't had one of these meetings in Donald March's office for a while. Most of the time, I had met just with Jordan in the living room or occasionally, as recently, with only Donald in his office. Our "family" conversations were usually held at the dinner table, but having one among the three of us like this in Donald's office made it seem much more serious and much more important.

Jordan was sitting on the settee looking meek and small, and Donald was behind his desk looking glum. Because of the long pause when I entered, I thought something even more terrible had occurred. Could it be that Shayne Peters really did have a concussion, perhaps something even worse? Had Ryder been arrested?

"Just sit on the settee," Donald said, spinning his chair so he could look directly at me.

I sat. Jordan dropped her gaze to her hands in her lap. She looked absolutely terrified for me.

"I'm sorry I didn't come to your office today," I began.

He put his hand up to stop me talking. Then he straightened up in his chair. "That's hardly important at the moment. We've been through quite a great deal together in the short time you have been with us. I suppose it has been like a roller-coaster ride for you, as well as for us. Last night, we were way high up because of your academic achievements, and today we're way down."

"Mr. March," I began, "before you start on what happened at school today, let me explain what . . ." His smile caused me to pause.

"You're not going to call me Donald anymore?"

Why was that so important right now? I wondered.

"Donald. What I wanted to say was that this whole thing was not Ryder Garfield's fault."

"Not his fault? Who hit those boys and sent one to the hospital?"

"They brought it on themselves. They went after him in the hallway first."

"Why?"

"They have been jealous of Ryder from the moment he entered the school."

"Jealous? Shayne Peters? He's the school's basketball star, isn't he? His father is a famous attorney, too. Maybe he's not on *Entertainment Tonight,* but everyone in this city knows who Austin Peters is. And they're quite well off financially. Why would Shayne Peters be jealous?"

"He's been trying to get me to go out with him. He doesn't take rejection well."

Donald paused. From the way his lips quivered, I thought he was fighting back a smile. He looked at Jordan and nodded. "Hear that? He doesn't take rejection well. Do you remember when Kiera said something very similar about the Myers boy when he acted out?"

She nodded obediently.

"She claimed he was practically haunting her," Donald explained. "I understood. Kiera was and is a very beautiful young lady. Eventually, he spray-painted our front gate with an obscenity. Some young men can't handle their hormones well. Now, this Ryder Garfield—"

"He can handle his hormones well," I said quickly. "It's his sister who can't. She's angry at Ryder because his parents have made him police her every action. They made him responsible for her behavior at Pacifica."

"Why?" Jordan asked. I looked at her. Could it possibly be that Jessica's mother hadn't told her?

"She got pregnant at the last school they were at."

"Pregnant?"

Donald nodded and smirked. "Star families."

"So, what did she do today?" Jordan asked.

"She spread terrible rumors about Ryder and me in school today, and Shayne and Kory Taylor said terrible things to him just at the moment Ryder learned what his sister was doing. He was angry. Anyone would be as angry and—"

"What sort of rumors?" Donald asked.

"Rumors about us . . . about what happened when I visited their home."

"What did happen?"

"Nothing," I said, probably too quickly.

I saw him wince and his eyes darken. "We've been

through something like this before with you, Sasha. Those stories . . ."

"Those were all untrue. You found that out," I said, looking to Jordan. She looked incapable of saying anything that would help me.

"Um," Donald said. "But let me tell you, accusations are on the front page. Acquittals are always on an inside page, sometimes buried away. People love to say where there's smoke, there's fire. You've done a terrific job of overcoming all that, Sasha. We don't want your efforts wasted."

"They won't be."

He looked away for a few moments. "As you know, I didn't have good vibes about this boy when he was here."

"He's a very sensitive, very intelligent person. It's not easy to grow up with famous parents."

"Maybe so, but that's not our concern. Our concern is you. We have taken on the responsibility for your welfare, Sasha. You know firsthand how difficult things have been for us with Kiera. We are determined not to make the same mistakes with you.

"For now," he continued, turning directly to me, "we would like you not to be seeing this boy socially. Let things die down, and maybe—"

"That's not fair!" I said. "This wasn't his fault!"

I knew I was shouting. My words thundered around me. Jordan stared at me, and Donald's face hardened.

He spoke very quietly, with obviously forced self-control. "We would like you to step back. You're not to bring him here again, and you're certainly not to go to his house."

"But he needs me," I said.

"Needs you?" Now Donald did smile. "You're barely seventeen, and I don't think you're experienced enough to provide therapy to an obviously troubled teenager, Sasha."

"That's not what I mean. I mean, yes, he needs a friend, and that would be like therapy, but—"

"We don't want you to see him socially," Donald hammered, pronouncing each word distinctly. "Is this clear? Do you understand? If you defy us, you'll be grounded, and I'll see to it that the car is taken away from you."

Tears actually burned my eyes. I looked to Jordan, but she looked down.

"Why don't you return to your room, calm down, and then come down to dinner?"

"I'm not hungry," I said defiantly. I stood up and started out.

"Be sure you come to dinner even if you just sit and stare at your food," Donald called after me. "We're not going to put up with tantrums."

*Not going to put up with tantrums? Where were you throughout Kiera's life?* I wanted to ask, but I hurried away to the stairway instead. I was to suffer not only because of the things their daughter had done to me but also because of the things she had done to them. The tears broke through as I went up. I flicked them off my cheeks and marched to my bedroom, closing the door behind me.

At first, I just stood there looking around the suite. Not since I had first come here had I felt more like a stranger. When I was younger, I had quickly embraced Alena's things. She was about my age when she died. The suite had a sacred feel to it, but now, perhaps because of how Donald was treating me, all of the business with the giraffes, the pictures, the wallpaper, and the replicas, looked babyish. Ryder was right. I should have insisted on being in one of the guest rooms. No matter what, that's what I was, after all, a guest.

I went to my desk and plopped into the chair. For a good minute or so, I just sat there sulking. Then I saw that I had another e-mail from Kiera. If ever I had wanted to talk to her, it was now, I thought. I should let her know that all of the bad things she had done were still rippling through my life. I was angry enough to get her and her parents into a bad argument. If they were going to be mean to me, I could be mean to them, the consequences be damned.

I opened her e-mail.

*Dear Sasha,*

> *Richard had to go back to England yesterday because his father is seriously ill. Believe it or not, I miss him already. He might be gone ten days.*
> *I heard you have a day off Tuesday. Why not drive up to my college Friday? You can skip one day of school on Monday and have a four-day weekend.*
> *Or can't you pull yourself away from Ryder Garfield?*
> *Tell you what.*
> *You know my college is near Santa Barbara. Why don't we all just meet there? I'll book us a room with*

*two double beds at the motel Richard and I go to on*
*weekends. Don't tell my parents. Tell them you're com-*
*ing here to spend the weekend with me at the dorm. I'll*
*have one of my roommates cover for us.*

    *Call me after you speak with my parents. Please try*
*to come. You know how much I hate to be bored.*

*Kiera*

I sat back and thought about it. What a wonderful solution. Ryder and I could have some private time together.
But after what had happened, could Ryder get his parents
to let him go? Then again, if he did join Kiera and me and
Donald and Jordan found out about it . . .

Was it worth the risk?

I began my return e-mail to Kiera describing all that had
happened.

Literally less than a minute after I sent it, my phone
rang.

"Wow!" I heard Kiera say after I said hello. I had
actually been afraid it was Ryder. I wasn't ready to tell
him what had gone on here. "And I thought I led a pretty
exciting life when I was at Pacifica."

"It's not exciting, Kiera. It's disgusting. I hate Pacifica."

"Don't get so dramatic. They'll start calling you Kiera."

"They practically have," I said.

"Really?"

I thought that would bother her, but she laughed.

"I guess I'm just too impressive, after all," she said.
"So? Are you going to come? I want to hear more, all the

nitty-gritty details. Have you slept with him? What do his parents think of you? Call me as soon as you speak to my parents."

"Don't have high hopes. Your father wants to put a ball and chain on me."

She laughed. "He tried that with me, too. You saw how far that got him. Cry to my mother. She'll be on your side more than she was on mine."

I wanted to tell her no, her mother was acting more timidly than I had ever seen her act, and I thought it was because she was afraid of losing Kiera's father. Was this a good time to mention the rumors? I had strong doubts that her mother ever mentioned any of it.

"I'll let you know," I said.

"Talk to them at dinner."

"I don't know if this is a good time for it, Kiera."

"Look, put on the remorseful face. That's what I used to do. Make it seem as if what he said to you sank in and you're really confused. You want to get away to think about it all and do the right things. He'll buy it, especially coming from you."

"I've been telling myself I'm not as good at that sort of thing as you were, or still are, Kiera."

"Don't sell yourself short. You're a woman now. It's built in."

I finally smiled. She was impossible. No one could turn a criticism of herself as quickly into a compliment.

"Listen, listen," she added. "Make it seem as if you're coming for me as much as for yourself. Tell them I sound lonely or something. They wouldn't believe such a thing normally, but coming from you, they might. Just find a way to get up here."

"I'll try."

"I'll wait by the phone. And work on Ryder, too. I can't wait to see him."

After I hung up, I sat there thinking. Maybe there was a darker part of myself that I had yet to explore. Maybe I could do what Kiera asked me to do. I wasn't bad at convincing the girls at Pacifica that I was far more sophisticated than I really was. Of course, in my mind, few of them had the perception or intelligence to see through my exaggerations. Fooling Jordan probably would be as easy, but fooling Donald was another thing. I had a deep suspicion that whatever skills Kiera had in that regard, she had inherited from him. I had seen him in action at work and with guests. The expression "He could sell ice to Eskimos" wasn't that far-fetched when it was applied to him.

I rose and went to change my clothes and wash away my tears and sadness. If I was going to do this act, I had better get on the makeup and costume, I thought. When I was ready, I went down to the dining room. As I descended the stairway, I tried to think only of what I might get to do. I could be with Ryder when he needed me the most. That built up my courage and my determination, helping me to overcome any remorse.

I just couldn't get myself to tell Ryder that I wouldn't be able to see him outside of school. My reluctance to do so wasn't simply because I really wanted to be with him. It was because of my fear for him. Something inside me, something I had captured when we lived on the streets, empowered me to see impending tragedies. In this case, though, with all of the obvious unhappiness in the Garfield family, it didn't exactly take the psychic on the beach to envision more heartache.

Jordan and Donald were already at the table. They didn't look much different from the way they had looked in Donald's office. Jordan still wore that face of trepidation. Perhaps in her mind and heart, she feared losing Alena again. Donald was stern, determined to drive out whatever of Kiera was in me. I took my seat.

Perhaps because they had both been working for the Marches so long, Mrs. Caro and Mrs. Duval sensed their mood. I suppose it permeated the mansion the way a strong, stale odor might. I could see it in the way they moved, their silence, and their avoidance of anyone's eyes, even mine. I waited for the food to be served, and after they went back into the kitchen, I said, "I'm sorry."

Both of them looked up.

"I have a built-in tendency to fall into troubled waters," I said.

"Oh, no. This is not your fault." Jordan was finally saying something to support me.

"You're simply young and finding your way. We want to help you do that, help you avoid as much trouble as possible. You've seen enough," Donald added.

I nodded and ate some of my salad. "My brain gets all fogged up when things like this happen."

"Understandable." Donald nodded and smiled.

*Here it comes,* I thought. *Will he see right through me?*

"I had a phone call from Kiera."

"Oh?" Jordan said.

"Don't tell me she already knows about this business at Pacifica. That kid should work for the *LA Times*," Donald told Jordan.

"No, she didn't know. She called because she was feeling a little lonely."

"Kiera?" Jordan said. "She has herself. How can she be lonely?"

"Stop that," Donald said sharply. "What about it?" he asked me.

"She knew that I'm off Tuesday and asked if I could come up there to spend a long weekend with her."

"Long weekend? Are you off Monday as well?" Donald asked.

"No, but I thought getting away might do both Kiera and me some good."

He paused and thought.

"I don't know if Kiera is the best influence on her at this moment," Jordan said.

Donald glared at her. "You don't want to give her a chance, do you?"

"Of course I do, but I just thought that—"

"You'd drive up?" Donald asked, interrupting.

"If you think I could."

"Of course you could. Why couldn't you?"

"I could leave Friday after school."

"But we're all going to Castles on Friday," Jordan said. It came out more like a whine.

"So, you and I will still go," Donald told her.

"And what about our shopping for her dress to wear to the concert, Donald? I made arrangements for this Saturday."

"The concert is a little less than a month away, Jordan. You'll have time when she's back."

"So you're giving her permission."

He looked at me so intently I thought I might just say that I had second thoughts. Jordan was right, but I pressed my lips together.

"I am, but I'd like you to leave by midafternoon," he said. "Traffic on Friday is hell in the late afternoon. I'll call Dr. Steiner myself. Under the circumstances, with your grades, I don't think there'll be a problem."

"Okay," I said quickly. "I'll call Kiera after dinner to tell her."

"No, I'll call her," Donald said. "I want to lay down some rules."

"No drinking or drugs, for one thing," Jordan said.

"I doubt you have to tell either of them that after what happened to Kiera, Jordan. I was referring to other things," he added, and left it cryptic.

I said nothing else. Kiera would surely call me after he had called her.

Jordan reached over to take my hand. "I suppose your getting away is a good idea, Sasha. Just be careful. By the time you return, I'm sure Ryder Garfield will have found another girlfriend and you won't feel so bad."

"If they let him return to Pacifica at all," Donald added. "I might have something to say about that as well."

I looked at him.

Why was he so adamant about Ryder and me, even to the point of doing something like this?

Something in his face frightened me.

He didn't look so much like a concerned parent.

He looked more like a jealous lover.

# 14

## Deception

You did it!" Kiera said when I said hello. "I just knew you could."

I was still feeling ambivalent about it. Now I was part of so much deception and lying that I felt as if I was standing on a ladder created out of cardboard. One more lie, and I would come tumbling down like Humpty Dumpty, and in both Donald's and Jordan's eyes, I wouldn't be able to be put together again.

"Did you call Ryder Garfield?"

"Not yet."

"What are you waiting for?"

"Your father said he was going to call you first. I wanted to be sure everything was still on. What did he say?"

"He was very tricky, or tried to be."

"What do you mean?"

"First, he was trying to see if I really invited you first or you invited yourself, and then he wanted to know what you had told me about Ryder Garfield. He sounded very suspicious. You were right. He has a particular dislike for him."

"Oh."

Maybe he had seen through me at dinner, I thought, but why would he still approve of my visiting Kiera? In this house, I could never believe things that were said the first time they were said. I had to think hard about why they were said and what they really meant. Here, the most difficult thing to find was the truth. Kiera lied constantly to her parents. Donald lied to Jordan, and Jordan lied constantly to herself. Now I was part of their world of falsehood. In a strange and eerie way, I had become a March, after all.

"Don't worry about it. I was very nonchalant," Kiera told me. "I said you told me he was a troubled but nice boy. You wanted advice on what to do, and I told you look for someone with no baggage. Who has time for other people's problems, especially boys'? He liked that and told me to encourage you not to get so serious with anyone while you were so young. He gave me a backhanded compliment. He said no one knows better than I do how to avoid being serious, and I could be a good influence on you for a change." She laughed. "Me? A good influence? I think when it comes to me, he really believes it's the other way around. No decent young man would get serious about me. Won't he be surprised when he finds out about Richard?

"Anyway," she continued, "I think that's why he approved your visiting me. I'm to give you a Kiera March pep talk. So, as Richard says, 'no worries.'"

"He says that? That's Australian, not English."

"He's brilliant. He can speak French, Italian, and

Australian," she said, and laughed again. "Are you calling Ryder, or aren't you?"

"Yes," I said.

"Okay. Let me know when that's settled. I've already made the reservation. I'll e-mail you the directions. We're going to have a great time. See you soon."

After we hung up, I sat thinking. Maybe it was all going too fast. Maybe I should have waited before asking permission to visit Kiera. I admitted to myself that I had acted out of anger, but now that Donald had called Kiera, it was too late to change my plans. Jordan and Donald would seriously question what had suddenly made me decide against going. Ironically, they would suspect some secret rendezvous between Ryder and me here instead of up there with Kiera.

Very nervous about it all, I called Ryder. I thought he wasn't going to pick up when it rang four times, but then I heard him say, "Just a minute." A good thirty seconds or so passed before he came on again.

"Hi."

"What happened? Why couldn't you talk?"

"I'm practically hiding in a closet," he said. "It's a little like Iraq or something here. IEDs everywhere I walk. Either my father or my mother has to cancel a shoot tomorrow to go with me to see Dr. Steiner, and that's equivalent to being diagnosed with a fatal illness in this family. They're arguing about it right now."

"I'm sorry, Ryder."

"Why are you sorry? You didn't do anything."

"I should have waited longer to tell you what was being said."

"It would have all happened anyway. So, has the news reached the March castle? Is your foster father or whatever you call him giving you a hard time about me?"

There didn't seem any way to postpone bad news when it came to Ryder Garfield. He knew too well how to look for it.

"Yes," I said. "He doesn't want me seeing you socially."

"Figures. It's my own fault. I provided the excuse. I certainly didn't want to make any trouble for you. I have enough to do making trouble for myself. If your psychic friend from the beach were here, she'd predict a long life of unhappiness."

"Don't think like that."

"No? Why shouldn't I? You were the first good thing to happen to me, and I blew it."

"No, you didn't. Listen, I was speaking to Kiera. She invited me to visit her this coming weekend, to take advantage of our Tuesday off. She suggested I ask you to meet us."

"Really? Where?"

"Not her dorm or college. She's renting a two-bed room at a motel she goes to with her English boyfriend. He had to return to England because of a serious family illness, so she asked me to visit, and then when she found out what happened with you, she suggested you come along, too."

"Will the Sheriff of Nottingham let you go?"

"Yes, but he thinks . . ."

"You're getting away from me?"

"Something like that."

"Hmm . . . that guy doesn't strike me as the naive type, Sasha."

"It's complicated. In an ironic way, he thinks I need advice from Kiera on how to conduct my romantic relationships."

"So we're in a romantic relationship?"

"I'm doing a calligraphy of love to give you. You'll figure it out after a while, say ten years."

He laughed. "When are you going?"

"I'm leaving early from school tomorrow."

"Just the three of us, then?"

"Yes." I paused. "I don't know what I'm saying or doing. You could get into more trouble. I could get into more trouble."

"But you still would like me to do it?"

"I just think this is all so unfair."

He was quiet. I was afraid I was pushing him into something he instinctively knew was bad, even dangerous.

"Don't do it, Ryder. Forget I even mentioned it. We'll only be sorrier."

"Not possible to be any sorrier than I am. I'm supposed to be grounded for a month, but I've ignored that before," he said. "You just tell me where and when. I'll be there."

"Are you sure?"

"Never more sure," he replied. "You don't want me just pouting at home like my sister, do you?"

"No, but what's going to happen when they realize you're gone?"

"They won't make a big scene. That would bring the

entertainment press to the doorstep. They'll tell the school I'm home sick or something and wait for me to return. As you know, I've run away before. Celebrities always lie about their real-life problems. It's practically expected. Don't worry about it."

"Okay."

"Then it's settled. I'll see you in school tomorrow after they cut off one of my fingers, and you can give me the details."

"Stop it," I said.

He didn't laugh. He just said good-bye and hung up.

The knock that followed on my door came so quickly after the call had ended that I suspected Donald had been standing out there listening. It gave me a burning chill when he entered. I was expecting the worst.

"Okay," he said. "I've had a talk with Kiera. She understands what I expect and don't expect. I've written a note for you to give to the office tomorrow, granting you permission to leave early." He put it on my desk. "I want you to call here to tell us when you have arrived. I assume you've gotten all the directions."

"Yes. Kiera's e-mailed them, but I remember when we all drove up there last year, anyway."

He nodded. "When you return, we'll talk again. I do want to spend more time with you, Sasha. I don't want you to see me as a prison guard or something."

He stepped closer to me and took my hand. The gesture surprised me.

"You're too precious to us now to have things go wrong just when you're on the threshold of doing great things. I won't let that happen. You'll have to learn to trust me more. Do you think you can do that?"

"Yes," I said.

He smiled. "I don't enjoy there being any tension between us, not a bit. I'd never admit this to anyone else," he added, "but I'm prouder of you than I am of my daughter."

He kissed me on the cheek and then brushed my hair before turning to leave. I stood there frozen. If he found out about the weekend and Ryder Garfield, he would surely feel deeply betrayed. I had no doubt he would want to get me out of his house and his life. It would seem so ridiculous to anyone who knew me now, but I feared finding myself back on the streets. It wasn't the first time such a fear had entered my mind, but it was usually in nightmares. In them, I saw myself, ragged and dirty, selling meaningless things or begging and suddenly seeing the girls of Pacifica come walking by, laughing at me, tossing pennies at me.

"To think she was once in our school and that we thought she was someone special," Jessica said in my dream.

*I must be crazy to take such a risk,* I thought. If my mother were here right now, she would surely be angry about it. She would tell me it was foolish to gamble anything on a boy who was so unstable.

Or would she see the kindness and love in my heart and tell me I was doing just what she would do if she were in my shoes? Was that wishful thinking? *Oh, I don't know what I should do,* I thought. It was agonizing.

The other girls in my school who were my age had

no idea what it was like to live without someone close enough to trust with your fears and concerns. They had real mothers, older sisters, and fathers. When I had troubled thoughts, I couldn't walk out of my room and knock softly on my parents' door to tell them and get their support and comfort. I had to speak to my mother's spirit and hope that somehow, some way, she would get the answers to me.

This was a loneliness they did not know and could not understand. Perhaps that was what drew me to Ryder Garfield more than anything. I saw the same sort of loneliness in him. We were two peas in a pod, all right, both orphans of sorts. Wasn't it harder for someone with a family to fall in love and want to be with someone who was an orphan? People are fond of saying you can choose your friends, but you can't choose your relatives. And yet marriages, good marriages, extend the family. Both the man and the woman feel more support, or they should. I knew there were conflicts, even out-and-out feuds between family members that broke up relationships, but who would prefer no family at the start?

Once I overheard a conversation between Jordan and two of her friends in the gold room, as they referred to one of the living rooms in this house. I wasn't eavesdropping, but as I was passing by, I heard my name mentioned, and then Mrs. Wayne said, "The disadvantage for any man marrying a girl like Sasha is he doesn't know enough about her background. From what you've told us, there's almost nothing known about her real father, and what is known isn't very complimentary."

"Yes, what will her children inherit?" Mrs. Becker

added. "What characteristics would be passed down? It's like getting a pig in a poke."

"I haven't heard that expression for ages," Jordan said, and they were off on another topic. I tiptoed past the door, but I couldn't help but think about what they had said. Was I a pig in a poke, more of a gamble for anyone to love because there was so little known about my background?

Although I had never met her, I knew my maternal grandmother was the one who taught Mama calligraphy. I also remembered that my grandparents had lived in Portland, Oregon, and that they had had my mother late in life, and my grandfather, who was a fisherman, had died in a fishing accident during a bad storm. Both of my paternal grandparents had died before I was born, so I had never met them, either. I remember my mother had old photographs of her parents, and I remember her parents had looked as if they could easily be her grandparents.

Now I couldn't tell anyone their first names or exactly where they had lived or anything about any of my mother's relatives. I was truly as anonymous as any orphan who was just dropped off at some orphanage as an infant. I hated thinking about these things. I knew it was bad to sit around feeling sorry for yourself.

I got busy and packed a travel bag since I would be leaving right from school tomorrow. When I checked my computer, I found Kiera's e-mail with the driving directions and the address of the motel. I printed out two copies, one for me and one for Ryder. After that, I dove into my schoolwork and did extra reading, hoping to make myself so tired I wouldn't be able to think so I would have no trouble falling right to sleep. It didn't work. I tossed and turned for hours, worrying that I had made the wrong decision. Finally, I passed out.

Even though I was still exhausted, I woke up just before the alarm went off. Mrs. Duval and Mrs. Caro knew about my long-weekend excursion. I didn't think either knew any reason to be worrying about it, but both looked worried when I saw them at breakfast. Jordan was there just after me. She told me that Donald had left for an early meeting in Las Vegas, but he had left money for me. She gave me five hundred dollars in twenty-dollar bills.

"Donald told me to tell you to buy something nice for yourself," she said.

"I have some money, and I have my credit card," I said.

"Yes, we know. Donald wanted you to have this," she emphasized. "And Kiera has her own money, so she shouldn't be asking you for any," she added.

Afterward, she followed me out to the car and watched me put my travel bag in the trunk.

"Keep your mind on your driving," she warned.

"I will. Thank you, Jordan."

She gave me a hug. "Tell my daughter . . ."

"Yes?"

"It would be nice if she spent some time with us, too," she said, and went back into the house.

Why couldn't she just say, *Tell her I love her*? I got into the car and headed to school.

Ryder's mother was the one who had had to move her schedule to take the meeting with Dr. Steiner. I saw that Ryder's car was already there when I pulled into the parking lot. Those students who had arrived were already chatting about his mother's appearance. I went directly to the office to give Mrs. Knox the permission letter for my early departure. While she read it, I looked at the closed door of Dr. Steiner's office. Mrs. Knox saw where my gaze went and cleared her throat.

"I'll give this to Dr. Steiner as soon as she's finished with this difficult meeting," she told me.

"Thank you," I said. I could see she that was dying to know what the reason was for my leaving school at lunchtime. I just smiled and left her.

Ryder didn't appear in any class until the period before lunch. Shayne and Kory were already in class. When Ryder entered, all conversations stopped, and, it seemed, so did all breathing. He ignored everyone, even me, and took his seat. He kept his eyes down. When the bell rang, I looked first at Shayne and Kory to see if they were going to start something again, but all they did was glare in his direction. I stood there, waiting for him to gather up his things.

"I'm on very strict probation," he said. "Can't look sideways at anyone, or it's the guillotine. Here's a good one," he continued as we started out. "My parents took a page from your foster father's book. They want me to avoid you. I had to promise to do so, or they threatened to go forward and put both Summer and me in a military-style school no matter what happens here at Pacifica."

"They blame me?" I asked.

"No. It's more like an 'I don't know how to handle a mature relationship yet' sort of thing."

"They believed the things your sister said?"

Since it was lunchtime, we didn't have to rush out. I, of course, was planning on leaving anyway.

"I'll walk you out to the parking lot," he replied instead of answering. "I'm not hungry, and I'm planning on slipping away shortly after you do."

"Oh, Ryder. This sounds so dangerous now."

"Danger is my middle name."

"No, really."

"What do you want me to do? Become a puppet here and not speak to you or see you again? Because that's the alternative to all of this, Sasha."

"Why did they believe those things about me?"

"It wasn't about you. It was about me. They're assuming I'll do something to ruin you, that I might already have done it. I'm poison, don't you see?"

"No, I don't," I said.

He paused and took a deep breath. "Summer's not the only mess in the family. I've been in trouble before, and I don't mean running away when I was little or stuff like that."

"You told me about your mother and the miscarriage."

"No. There was a girl at the last school. She was much younger than you."

"How much younger?"

"She looked much older than she was."

"How much younger?"

"She was thirteen."

"Oh, Ryder."

"She looked eighteen. Honest. One of those precocious puberty girls or something. I was stupid."

"What happened?"

"My father had to pay her parents off. Nothing terrible really happened, but . . ."

"But enough did?" I thought a moment. "Why did your parents want you to be your sister's watchdog, then? Why did they trust you?"

"A therapist told them that was the best way to deal with me, make me more responsible. This all happened the year before Summer's problem. I haven't been in any serious trouble since, so . . . it's all stupid and complicated, and I'm sick of it.

"I'm sick of living in a theater, walking and talking on a stage, playing a role every time we go anywhere or do anything, answering inane questions about my parents, fading into the background so as not to disturb their precious careers. I have to tiptoe through adolescence so as not to bring any untoward attention their way.

"How would you like to be lectured by a publicist when you were ten and eleven? Taught how to avoid the paparazzi, be schooled on how to answer questions and bawled out for telling too much about your family?

"How would you like to feel that your own parents regretted having you at all?"

The expression on my face angered him instead of giving him a sense of sympathy.

"Wish now that you didn't get involved with me at all? Sorry about it? Sorry you invited me to join you this weekend?"

"No, of course not."

"You have your own problems, I know. You don't need my baggage on top of yours."

"Stop it, Ryder. The only reason I agreed to meet Kiera was that it would give us an opportunity to be together without everyone watching us. I'm happy to take the risk, and don't delude yourself into thinking I'm not. When or if Donald March finds out I've defied him, he'll probably move to get me out of the March household."

Ryder was silent. Behind us, the student body was moving toward the cafeteria. The chatter was loud, as were the laughter and some students calling to others, but neither of us seemed to hear anything but the beating of our own hearts.

"I'm sorry," he said. "I guess I'm just angry about everything and taking it out on you, the one person I should cherish and protect."

"Let's not dwell on it anymore. Here are the directions and the motel's address," I said. "I'll be waiting for you."

He took the paper and put it between the pages of one of his books.

"I'm supposed to have lunch with my sister today. It's one of their brilliant solutions to seeing that we get along and make things hunky-dory. We both had to swear to try, so I'm in another performance for a while. As soon as the bell rings to end lunch, I'll pretend to be going in for class, but I'll go out to my car and follow you."

"I won't be angry at you if you change your mind at the last minute, Ryder."

"I'd be angry at myself," he said. He looked behind us, and then he stepped back into the corner and pulled me toward him so he could give me a kiss. "See you soon," he whispered, and walked quickly into the school to head for the cafeteria.

I glanced after him and then lowered my head and started into the parking lot and to my car. I hadn't told anyone that I was leaving early today, so it would come as a big surprise. I was sure it would be a topic of conversation for the rest of the day. I could envision Jessica pretending she knew something but was sworn to secrecy.

After I got into my car, I sat quietly for a few moments. My good and bad angels were screaming at each other. Not only was I being defiant and as deceptive as Kiera had ever been, but I was also getting Ryder into more trouble. All of this was so uncharacteristic of me. I couldn't deny that it was selfish. Was I behaving more like my father than my mother? Even though he had deserted me, I had his genes. He was biologically as much a part of me as my mother was. All these years, I had denied that because he had denied me, but it wasn't a realistic thing to do.

And yet I told myself that my defiance wasn't born only out of my selfishness. What was happening to Ryder and me was unfair. We needed this time together. Afterward, no matter what the consequences were, we would be stronger. I felt confident of that. Besides, if we did everything we were told to do now, the jealous and mean people around us would have won.

Strengthened with my resolve, I started the car and backed out of my parking spot.

I didn't look back.

It was time to look only ahead.

*We can change our destinies, Mama,* I thought.

I remembered taking her hand after we had sat on the beach for a long time watching the sun sink beneath the horizon. She had looked at me with surprise and then smiled.

"Time to go home?" she had asked.

"Yes, Mama," I had said, and we rose. She still held on to my hand as we plodded on down the beach. I had no idea where we would go that night or what home meant anymore, but we had walked on as if we both did.

That's the way I felt right now.

## 15

### Kiera's Return

*I* had never driven myself this long or this far. The weather, which looked at first as if it would bring rain, turned calm and partly cloudy as I went farther north. I was too nervous about what we were doing to worry about my driving, anyway. Following the directions Kiera had sent and using my GPS in the car brought me to the motel four hours later, which was very good driving time. Donald was right about the traffic. Leaving early made it possible. I called Kiera when I was close, and she was out in the motel parking area waiting for me when I pulled up.

Even when I hated the very sight of Kiera March, I had to admit to myself that she was beautiful. Almost as tall as Ryder's mother, with Jordan's light brown hair and azure eyes, high cheekbones, and full, feminine lips, she was stunning, and, of course, she knew it. When I had first come to the March residence and saw how attractive Kiera was, I wondered why. Shouldn't someone with an evil and selfish nature be uglier? Shouldn't the dark and ugly things such a person has within her show themselves, break out like pimples or grotesque birthmarks? She certainly shouldn't have the healthiest-looking hair and the richest-looking complexion.

That familiar line about beauty being only skin deep came to mind, but no matter how you tried to diminish the value and impact of physical beauty, it still won out. Men always treated attractive women better. Beauty inspired awe. A smile from Kiera March was more appreciated than a smile from someone as pure as a nun but who was average or homely. It was far easier for Kiera to get someone to do her bidding than it was for someone who could show logical reasons for it.

There she stood waiting for me and looking as radiant as ever with her hair obviously recently styled and her makeup perfect. She wore an expensive pair of designer jeans, high heels, and a turquoise light sweater that with her figure was as good as a spotlight. I saw the way men driving in or out or just walking turned their heads to look at her. She waved to me and pointed at a parking space. I pulled in, shut off the engine, and got out.

"You did well," she said, hugging me.

"Your father was right about how to avoid the heavy traffic."

"My father is always right about those sorts of things. How far behind you is Ryder Garfield? Did you leave about the same time?"

"No. He wasn't going to leave until after lunch, but he should be here soon," I said.

"You look great," she said, holding me at arm's length

the way some infrequently seen relative might. "Being in love brings out the beauty in you like sunshine brings out the color of a rose. That was a direct quote from Richard, something he told me just recently," she said, and brushed back her hair. She smiled at a passing driver who beeped his horn. A second did the same. "We're attracting so much attention we could cause an accident in the parking lot and get sued for being too beautiful."

"I didn't say I was in love," I told her. I wouldn't deny to myself that I was falling in love. I just didn't want her to be the first one who knew it.

"You are. You can't fool me."

"I thought you weren't sure what love was," I reminded her. She pulled the corners of her mouth in and shook her head.

"You always remember everything I say and throw it back at me," she complained, and then smiled. "Grab your bag. We have a little suite on the second floor. C'mon. I want to hear everything before he gets here. I have some fun plans for us. I know a dance club nearby, the better restaurants, everything. Of course," she said with a licentious smile, "I'll give you two plenty of time alone."

I took my bag out of the car and followed her to the stairway that led up to our room. It was a junior suite with a small sitting room that had two chairs, a table, and a sofa bed. There was a television there and in the bedroom, which had two queen-size beds. I saw she had a bottle of vodka in the sitting room on the coffee table.

"I wasn't sure what Ryder would like to drink, so I bought that. There's orange juice in the minibar."

"I don't know what he drinks or even if he does."

"Really? You two sound like real goody-goodies. I can't believe someone like Ryder Garfield with parents like his hasn't done lots of things."

She flopped onto the bed and threw herself back.

"Isn't this great? Away from all the gawking eyes and stuffy adults like my parents." She turned over to lean on her elbow. "My father's turned into a real stick-in-the-mud, huh?"

"He's just . . . very worried," I said.

"So worried he wants to invade your private life?"

"I guess he's just trying to be a good foster father."

"Good foster father? He's taking you to concerts, ordering a new dress be bought. I'd say he's going beyond the call of duty. What else has he done for you lately?"

Was this the time to mention the necklace?

"He was excited when he found out that I could be the class valedictorian."

"How did he do that? Don't tell me he's going to parent-teacher conferences. He was never around to do much of that for me."

"No, he bumped into Dr. Steiner."

"Really. How is old Dr. Steiner? Talk about a stick-in-the-mud. She has a stick up you know where."

"She's been nice to me," I said.

"I guess so, if she's bragging about you."

Something in her expression and tone of voice warned me against mentioning the necklace just yet. But she continued to stare hard at me, waiting for more.

"Don't you have something else to tell me about my father?" she asked. It suddenly occurred to me that Jordan might have told her.

"He bought me a present to celebrate my high school grades, if that's what you mean," I said, trying my best to make it sound like nothing. "I told him it was too soon. I could still not be the valedictorian."

"A present? My mother thought it was quite beautiful and expensive. How come you didn't tell me about it before this?" she asked, but before I could try to come up with an answer, she gave it. "You thought I would be jealous, upset?"

"Yes," I confessed.

"He's bought me plenty of expensive things. I'm not jealous as much as I'm surprised. When they bought you that car, I was amazed, but then I realized these things are so minor to my parents. We're so rich." She laughed. "I don't blame you for getting as much as you can."

"I'm not. I didn't ask for the car or for the necklace or anything."

"You're like me. You don't ask in so many words."

"I don't understand. How do we ask, then?"

"Forget about it," she said sharply. "None of that is important now. Cars, jewelry, expensive vacations are just taken for granted among the girls at this school. No one would be impressed if you drove up in that car and you were wearing the necklace."

"Where did all of your friends go for the weekend? I thought I might meet some of them."

"Oh, for what?" she said. "I just told you that they're a bunch of spoiled rich kids. You don't need to meet any more of them. You have me."

"What about the girls you went to Europe with?"

"What about them?"

"You hardly mention them anymore."

"They're all . . . jealous of me and Richard now. Isn't that the way with your plain-looking girlfriends, too, back in Pacifica? My girlfriends don't want to hear or know about my good times, so they deliberately avoid me."

"It's not that way back at Pacifica. They're constantly asking questions, but I try not to make them jealous," I said, and sat on the chair by the small desk.

"That's you, not me. You're more considerate. Oh, I don't want to talk about girls!" she cried, looking like someone with a mouthful of sour milk. "I want to talk about Ryder Garfield. What have you done with him? What sort of dates? Where have you gone? What kind of lover is he?"

"I told you, he was at your house, and then I went to his. That's all we've done together so far. He wasn't easy to get to know or like."

"And?"

"And what?"

"C'mon, Sasha. I've been sharing all of my intimate details concerning me and Richard with you. It's only fair that you describe all of yours."

"Quid pro quo," I muttered, thinking about Ryder.

"What? What's that?"

"Nothing. A Latin phrase that means an equal exchange."

"Huh? Stop with the dictionary, and get down to the sex," she said.

I looked at my watch. How far behind me was he? I hadn't been with Kiera five minutes, and already I was tense and nervous. I hoped she was telling the truth when she said she would give us plenty of time alone.

"Stop looking at your watch and worrying about the time and talk," she said.

"We haven't done the big I yet, if that's what you mean."

"Big I? What's that?"

"It. Done it."

She laughed and then turned serious again. "Well, what exactly did his sister make up about the two of you, or wasn't it all made up? There are other things to do beside the big I," she said.

Was this something I should feel comfortable doing? The girls at Pacifica seemed quite uninhibited when it came to discussing their love affairs. I remembered how embarrassed I was when Kiera first brought me to a meeting of that phony Virgins Anonymous club and the girls told their sex stories. Or made them up, I should say. Even though Kiera sent me her stories about her and Richard through the Internet, it was still embarrassing to know the details.

"Let's just say she might have read your Kama Sutra book."

"And?"

"I really don't know what she said, Kiera. All I was told in school was that she was telling her friends that she saw us do everything."

She nodded. "Very clever of her. That way, she leaves it up to their imaginations, and people always exaggerate when they imagine. I," she quickly added, "don't have to do that, of course. You want a drink?" she asked, getting up.

"No, not right now," I said.

"I hope you're not going to be the perfect little teenager or something up here."

"I'm far from perfect."

"Apparently, not according to Daddy Dearest," she said, and poured some vodka into a glass. I saw she had ice cubes in a pail. She opened the minibar and took out the orange juice. "Sure you won't have one? They're good, and they'll relax you. You're obviously a nervous wreck."

"Okay," I said, "but I'll pour my own," I added quickly.

"Suit yourself. We have a little balcony out here," she said, and opened the curtains and the sliding door. There was a table and two chairs on it.

I poured myself a quarter of what she had poured for herself and added more juice. The patio overlooked the parking lot but did afford a view of the mountains in the distance, too. I sat and sipped my drink.

I remembered that I had promised to let Jordan know when I arrived, so I made the call but got her answering machine. I left a message.

"Who are you calling already?"

"I promised your mother, but she's not home. I could call her cell phone."

"Will you relax? You left a message."

I put my phone away.

"Richard called me from London last night," she said. "He might be away longer than he thought. He's very dedicated to his family. There's no doubt that if I marry him, I'll have to live in England. I know that would just break my parents' hearts, especially my mother's."

"She's trying."

"Trying to what? Love me?" she snapped. And then she calmed and smiled. "I have someone who really loves me."

"Where's your engagement ring?"

"Oh." She smiled. "Why discourage any other boys in the meantime?"

"What do you mean?"

"I told you we're going to this fabulous dance club tonight. If I walk in wearing an engagement ring, I doubt I'd get the second look. I know I'll get the first."

"But . . . do you want to go out with other boys?"

"Do birds want to fly?"

"What if Richard finds out?"

"He's not having me followed, Sasha, and I'm sure he doesn't expect me to sit in my dorm room and do needlework."

"I do think being in love means being faithful, Kiera."

She tilted her head and smirked. "Please. Do you think my parents are faithful to each other?"

I felt my face redden. Had Jordan told her about her suspicions about Donald? Somehow, because of the strain in their relationship, I couldn't see Jordan confiding in her. Did this mean that Kiera knew something about her father that her mother didn't know?

"I thought they were," I said.

"Even after all I've taught you and all you've been through, you're still so naive."

"How do you know?"

"What? That you're naive?"

"No, that your parents aren't faithful to each other."

"I just know," she said, and turned away. Even so, I saw the look on her face. For a moment, I thought she was going to cry. Then she caught herself, took a deep breath, and turned back to me. "You didn't tell Ryder I was engaged or something, did you?"

"No."

She smiled. "Good. I don't need someone else making me feel guilty if I fancy someone later. That's the way Richard puts it . . . fancy. Isn't that cute? The first time we met, he said, 'I fancy you.' I didn't know what he meant. I said, 'Well, that's because I'm fancy,' and he laughed. We have such good times together. He has a wonderful sense of humor."

"He sounds so great. Did you bring a picture to show me?"

"Picture? Oh. No, I didn't think of it. I was in too much of a hurry to get out of there. The girls in my dorm were getting on my nerves with their trivial talk. They're always trying to find out what I do to keep looking beautiful. Like I have to do something. Is that him?"

"What?"

"The car that just drove in," she said, nodding toward the parking lot.

I stood up. "Yes," I said.

"He couldn't have been too far behind you, or else he was speeding. You know what that means?"

"What?"

"He expects a good time, not a goody-goody time," she said.

Ryder parked and stepped out of his car.

"We're up here!" Kiera shouted. He looked up and waved. "He is handsome," she said. "Better keep your eyes on him."

I went ahead of her to the door and stepped out to see him come up the stairway. As soon as he appeared, I ran to him, and he hugged me.

"Was it difficult getting away?" I asked him.

"I had to wait until Summer went to her class. I thought I could use the head start, so I went to class and then asked to go to the bathroom. I left my books on the desk. It probably took until the end of class before I was reported missing."

"Then you must have been speeding," Kiera said, coming up behind me.

"A little," Ryder said. "Hi."

"Hi. C'mon in. We started the party already," she said, holding up her glass of vodka and orange juice.

Ryder looked at me and then smiled. "Sure."

"I hope this is okay," Kiera said when we entered.

"It's fine," Ryder told her.

She went to the vodka and poured his drink, adding some ice cubes. "You want the orange juice?"

"Sure, thanks," he said after she handed it to him.

"Well, now," Kiera said, sitting in one of the chairs. We

sat on the sofa. "So, you're the famous couple who have been tearing up the floors of old Pacifica."

Ryder took a sip of his drink. "Not the floors. Just a few walls."

"Well, let's not worry about it for a few days," Kiera said. "There's a great dance club we can go to nearby. I know the guys at the door, so you two won't have any trouble getting in. Are you hungry?"

"A little," Ryder said, looking at me.

"I'm talking about food," Kiera said. She downed the rest of her drink. "Tell you what. You two need to catch your breath and stuff. Lots of stuff. I'll go pick up a couple of pizzas for now. I want to stop at the mall near here and get a few other things first, so I'll be gone about two hours."

She stood up.

"That way," she continued, "you can get a night's sleep, too."

"Night's sleep? Why would that be a problem?"

"I meant, when it comes time to sleep, you'll just go to sleep and won't need to think of or do anything else," she replied. She tossed her hair back and reached for her purse. "We'll have plenty of time later to get to know each other."

"Right," Ryder said. "Thanks for setting this up."

"I know it looks like it, but I didn't do it only for you two. I intend to have a fun night away from the dull dorm. Call me if you think of anything you need," she told me. "Although I think you have all you want for now," she added, nodding at Ryder.

We watched her leave.

"Wow," he said. "She doesn't beat around the bush."

"You can believe her when she says she did all this for herself as much as for us. She enjoys doing forbidden things or being part of them."

"I don't want to ever think of you as being forbidden, Sasha."

"I know. I feel the same way about you, but I can't deny that I'm afraid."

He put his glass down and turned to me. "Fear makes it all more exciting, not that I need anything to make me more excited about you," he said, and kissed me. "The whole time driving up here, I thought only of your eyes and your lips."

His words weren't just wonderful to hear. They were calming me, making me feel safe. This was right, I thought. What was being done to us was wrong. We kissed again, and then we both rose and walked slowly to the bedroom. I leaned against him, resting the side of my head on his shoulder. He kissed me again, softly and then more demandingly. I felt as if I was sinking into his arms, sinking into him. He pulled back the cover sheet on the bed, and we sat, still kissing and holding each other. His lips grazed my cheek, my neck. He lifted my light sweater off me. I raised my arms to help, and in moments, both moving in a delicious frenzy, we were naked, clinging to each other.

Before, when we were moving this quickly in his bedroom, I feared that I was being as gullible and as naive as I had been with Kiera's friends. It took me a long time to stop blaming myself as much as if not more than I blamed them for my being seduced. While most girls would be cautious and even reluctant for other reasons, I couldn't throw off the weight of my horrible memories that easily. Of course, I would question every kiss, every touch, every pronouncement of love and affection any boy made.

But I felt very close to Ryder now, despite how short our romance was to this point. In my heart, I felt the beat of his. In my mind, I heard his thoughts and fears. I had the same sense of desperation and the same great need to become closer, more intimate, more trusting. We found sanctuary in each other. In his smile and in his eyes, I saw not only the same sort of pain but also the way past it. It was difficult for either of us to believe in anyone or anything, for that matter, but we knew instinctively, even when we had fenced with each other verbally, that once we believed in each other, we would find the joy and salvation that love could bring.

He moved between my legs. He raised himself so he could look down at me, and then we began to make love, truly to become one with each other for a glorious time when all of the troubles we knew retreated, fled from our hunger for each other. *This can't be bad,* I thought. *We will know each other deeply, fully, and completely after this. I'll know his every whim and worry. He'll read every smile and silence in me. We'll sense each other's trepidations. We'll realize what really makes each of us happy. We will become knowledgeable about each other's moods and navigate safely to each other's hearts.*

My little cries of pleasure made him more graceful and gentle. When we were comfortably exhausted, we kissed to put a seal of satisfaction on each other's lips and then just lay there silently, holding hands and waiting for our hearts to calm, our blood to settle.

Suddenly, he laughed.

"What?"

"I was just imagining my father's face when my mother tells him I ran off. If he's with some actor friends, he'll moan and groan about how he's done everything he can for me. He'll become Othello or some other Shakespearean character crying out his frustration. He might even slip into a soliloquy or two."

"And your mother?"

"She'll rush out to get a facial. This could bring on a deep wrinkle."

"Oh, maybe we have gone too far, Ryder."

"They'll get over it."

"What will you tell them when you go back?"

"I went somewhere to think. They like that. I've used it a few times before. It makes me sound authentic. Worse comes to worst, I'll have to join Summer at the therapist's office. Let's not worry about it right now. I like Kiera's idea of having a good time. And I'm getting hungrier. I didn't eat much at lunch."

He sat up and looked at his watch.

"Maybe we should just meet her somewhere."

"I'll see where she is," I said, and got up, too. We both dressed, and I went to my cell phone. Hers rang and rang, but she didn't pick up. Her silly message came on.

"I know you're just dying because I didn't answer, but have hope and leave your name and number. I might call you back."

"Kiera. We were wondering if it wouldn't be better for us to meet you to eat. If you haven't ordered anything yet, call me and tell me where you are."

"She's probably in a place in that mall where cell phones don't pick up," Ryder said.

He went to the minibar to look for something to eat and found a package of peanuts and some cheese and crackers.

"Dinner!" he cried, and offered me some.

We both gobbled it all.

"This is the best meal I've had in a long time," he said. He checked his watch again. "I've got to get over to the mall, too, wherever it is, and buy a few things I'll need for the next day or so."

"You going to stay the whole time?"

"Maybe. What do you think?"

"Might look better if you leave earlier. I'll need to give Kiera some attention anyway."

"Right." He poured some juice for me and for himself. Then he sat back with a wide grin on his face.

"What's so funny?"

"How wonderful you are and how great this is," he said. "Yesterday at this time, I was about as depressed and down as I've ever been."

"Me, too."

"To us," he said, raising his glass.

"To us."

We had started to drink when we heard a knock on the door.

"Isn't she considerate?" Ryder said with a wide smile again.

"If anyone knows what goes on behind closed doors, she does," I said. "Coming," I called, and opened the door to face two California highway patrolmen. They looked past me at Ryder, who slowly rose.

"Ryder Garfield?" the one on my right asked.

"What's this?" Ryder asked.

"You've been reported as a missing person," the other patrolman said, moving in quickly.

"What? Who reported me?"

"Your parents," the first patrolman replied. "We'd like to make this easy. You're under eighteen. You're coming with us either voluntarily or otherwise. Considering who your parents are, we recommend it be voluntarily."

"This is bullshit. I'm not missing. I'll go home when I'm good and ready to."

"That's a bad choice, son," the second patrolman said, and moved in on Ryder.

"*DON'T!*" I cried.

Ryder tried to resist, but the second patrolman was on him as well, and in moments, they had his hands behind his back and his wrists cuffed. I pressed my fist against my mouth to contain another scream. Tears filled my eyes when Ryder looked at me with a desperate expression of helplessness.

"Let's go, son," the first patrolman said. They practically lifted him to move him forward.

I followed them out the door. When they reached the stairway, another motel guest was coming up. He moved quickly to get by them. Ryder looked back at me. He shook his head. Did he think this was somehow my fault?

"Ryder!" I called, but they moved him quickly down the stairs. I ran after them.

Their patrol car was just at the foot of the stairway. Ryder could see that there was no point in resisting. Before I could say another word to him, they stuffed him into the rear of the car. He seemed to collapse in there. I stood watching as they drove off. He never looked back.

I felt my legs soften beneath me and sat hard on the first step.

It was as if some invisible evil spirit had put his hands on my shoulders and pushed me down.

I felt as helpless as I had been walking behind my mother in the darkness on the beach, looking for the safety of a home.

# 16

## A Ruined Weekend

$\mathcal{J}$ was still sitting on the step when Kiera drove into the motel parking lot. She got out slowly and stopped when she saw me. I imagined she couldn't believe her eyes. I saw her look about with confusion. Ryder's car was still in the parking space he had taken. She raised her hands to ask what was happening. When I didn't respond, she started toward me.

"What's going on? Where's Ryder?"

"His parents called the police. They came to the suite and put him in handcuffs and dragged him off."

"Handcuffs?"

"They said he was considered a missing person, and because he was only seventeen, they could do it."

"Bummer," she said.

"It was horrible."

"Well, there's nothing you can do about it now. Let's go upstairs and get ready to go out. We can still have a good time."

"What? Didn't you hear what I said? They put him in a police car like some sort of criminal and dragged him away."

"I heard you, Sasha. So what are you going to do, mope in the room all weekend?"

I looked up at her. She turned away for a few moments and then turned back to me.

"They'll take him home. That's all. He's not going to jail or anything. Famous movie stars can get the police to do lots of things for them to cover up their family problems. It's the way it is. Maybe he'll run away again and call you from someplace else."

"You didn't see his face. He was devastated. I'm worried for him."

"So distract yourself, otherwise you'll go nuts," she said. She started up the stairs.

I stood up. Something occurred to me.

"How did they find him so fast?" I asked. She paused. "I mean, they came right to the door."

She started to turn away and then smiled. "You're the valedictorian, not me, but it seems quite simple."

"How?"

"The school most likely called his parents to tell him he was missing. They called my mother or my father, and they told them where you had gone. So they put two and two together, and *voilà*."

She started up again.

"But you didn't tell your parents we were staying here. You told me not to say anything and that your roommates would cover for us if they called," I reminded her.

She kept walking up the stairway. I sped up and caught

up to her in the hallway. I grabbed her arm and spun her around.

"Kiera!"

"Relax. One of my roommates obviously broke down and told," she said. "I'll find out who it was and break her neck. Although I probably can't blame her. I'm sure my mother was hysterical on the phone."

I thought for a moment and then hurried into the suite to get my cell phone. I saw there was a message on it. Kiera came in behind me. I held it up.

"I have a call from your mother."

"I'll talk to her and explain that it was my idea to come here."

"That's not the point," I said. "They thought I was listening to them and avoiding Ryder. Now they'll know I lied."

"Join the club."

"I don't belong in that club," I said, moving toward my things. "I think I'll just head back."

"What? Don't be stupid. I've been through many things like this with them. They'll get over it."

"Yes, but I won't," I said, gathering my things.

She stood there with her hands on her hips, her eyes widening with rage. "You're actually going to leave me here alone after I planned this whole thing out, went through all this trouble for you?"

"I won't be any fun to have with you, Kiera. I can't help it. Sorry."

"Great," she said, and went into the bedroom, slamming the door behind her.

"Kiera, don't be like that," I said. I waited, but she didn't respond.

Despite her tantrum, I couldn't change my mind. My body felt as if there were at least a half-dozen fuses all lit inside. If I was going to explode somewhere, I'd rather it be at home.

"I'll call you," I said, and headed out. Seeing Ryder's car still parked there brought tears to my eyes. How horrible it had to be for him to be driven all the way home in a police car and with his hands cuffed behind him like some common criminal. How could his parents do this to him?

I got into my car and started out of the parking lot. When I looked back and up, I saw Kiera on the small balcony. She had another glass of vodka and orange juice in one hand and a cigarette in the other. She wasn't looking at me. She was looking out at the mountains in the distance. I wondered if she would stay there or return to her dorm.

It took me much longer to get back into Los Angeles. I hit all sorts of traffic. At one point, there was a backup because of an accident. I wasn't really hungry despite eating little or nothing all day, but when I had a chance to turn off for gasoline, I bought myself a cereal bar and some water. I started to call Jordan again a number of times but thought it was better just to arrive. However, it was getting late, and when I was about an hour away, I did call.

"Where are you?" she asked immediately.

"Only an hour away."

"Donald is very upset. I'm very disappointed."

"I'm sorry. I'll explain when I get there. Did Kiera call you?"

"No. I think she called Donald," she said, "but I don't remember the time. Drive carefully," she added. Her voice was so small and distant that she sounded thousands of miles away. Before I could say anything else, she hung up.

It took me nearly an hour and a half to arrive at the front gate. I had been so tense the whole time that it was a wonder I didn't get into an accident. This wasn't going to be very pleasant for any of us.

I wasn't happy about defying their wishes, even though I felt justified. Since Kiera had left for college, I had done everything they asked of me. Although I wanted to succeed in school to please myself and for my mother's memory, I was also aware of how well it reflected on them. Until now, I had never done anything to displease either of them. I didn't violate the curfews they set for me. I avoided parties that could turn into Kiera-like parties. I took good care of everything they gave me and never took anything for granted.

I was aware of how hard Jordan tried to be more than a foster mother to me. I wouldn't deny that there were many times when the three of us went out to dinner or when they had guests for dinner and I was present that I felt almost like their natural child. I wanted to feel like family. I did the best I could to overcome all that made me hesitate or feel guilty about accepting them.

But I knew that this was going to make things different. Whether Donald was sincere about not wanting me to turn out like his daughter or whether it was just a matter of his ego, I expected that his disappointment was going to have dire consequences for me. It was very possible that he would carry through with a threat and throw me out of the

March house. If anything, he would now hammer home to Jordan how smart he was not to have legally adopted me.

I parked and went to the front door, pausing to catch my breath. It seemed like yesterday when I had stood there with Ryder and taken the same deep breath that made him say I looked as if I was about to go underwater. I certainly felt I was doing that right now.

No one was standing there when I entered. The house was ominously quiet and dimly lit. I waited for a moment to see if either Jordan or Donald would come charging out of a room, or even Mrs. Duval might appear, but no one did. Practically tiptoeing down the hallway, I stopped to glance into the sitting room on my right. At first, I saw no one, and I was about to turn to head for the stairway when I heard Donald say my name.

I looked again and saw him sitting under an unlit lamp. With only the reflection of another smaller light across the room illuminating him, he looked like a shadow shaped like a man. He reached up and turned on the lamp. I saw that he was sitting there with a drink in his hand. The sight of him so quiet and so dark frightened me. I didn't move.

"Please come in, Sasha," he said.

I entered slowly, looking to see if Jordan was sitting anywhere.

"Jordan's up in the bedroom," he said. "She's taking all this very hard. I had to get her to take her pills to sleep."

"I'm sorry," I said.

"Just sit," he replied in a very tired voice of defeat.

For a few long moments, he said nothing. I felt a great ache in my chest as I forced back my tears.

"It's very difficult, if not impossible, to predict how your children will turn out," he began. He sipped his drink. "As hard as it might be for you to believe, when Kiera was much younger, she was more like Alena. I don't know what changed her. Maybe it was the birth of her younger sister and the attention Alena needed and got, but there were times when I wondered if someone had substituted another young girl in our house." He smiled. "You know, like one of those *Twilight Zone* things or a horror movie.

"Anyway," he continued, "Jordan, especially, liked to believe, probably still likes to believe, that if Alena had made it to your age, she would have been just like you. I don't know how many times she's looked out the window at you doing something outside or commented about something you said or did at school and then said, 'just like Alena would.'"

"What was happening to Ryder Garfield and me just wasn't fair," I said. "If Alena was the way you and Jordan say she was, she would have felt the same way."

He lost his smile. "Alena was an angel. It wasn't in her to be able to betray anyone, much less anyone she loved."

"Then she wouldn't have betrayed Ryder Garfield," I insisted.

"Oh, please. How many times do you think you'll fall in love before you find someone you'll marry?"

"I don't know. How many times did you?"

He put his glass down hard on the side table. "I suggest you go up to your room and go to bed. Neither of us is in the right mood to discuss this intelligently or even calmly. Go on!" he ordered.

I flinched, and then I stood, picked up my travel bag, glanced at him, and hurried out of the room to the stairs. The hard, cold look on his face put speed in my steps. I practically ran up to my room. My heart was pounding so hard I thought I might faint. I stood there after I closed the door and hugged myself. I was actually too frightened to cry. My tears froze behind my eyes.

Still shaking, I put my things away, undressed, and got into bed. I thought I heard his footsteps in the hallway. It seemed that he stopped at my door. I held my breath, anticipating him entering, but he didn't. It grew deadly quiet again. The moon pushed away the clouds in front of it and sent beams of silvery light through the windows, lighting up Alena's wall of giraffes. For a moment, they looked as if they were all moving in a gallop, as if they had been frightened by a tiger or something. My imagination was running rampant.

I closed my eyes but immediately recalled Ryder's look of absolute pain as the police dragged him away. It was a haunting look. All I could think was that he somehow blamed me. Like me, he was surely wondering how they had come to the right motel and the right door so quickly. Did he think I had bragged to my girlfriends, telling them how we would have this rendezvous? Did he think it was all my fault? What was in his eyes?

I hoped and prayed that in the morning, I would some-how be able to speak to him and that somehow we would find our way back to each other. I thought that falling asleep would be practically impossible now, but I had underes-timated how much the driving and the emotional strain had battered me. I fell into such a deep sleep, in fact, that it seemed I had sunk into the bed. Even the morning sunlight streaming out of a cloudless sky and ripping away the darkness didn't wake me. If Mrs. Duval had come to see how I was, she surely had left quietly, hoping not to disturb me.

I would always remember hearing a shrill, piercing scream, even though no one in the March household had screamed. It woke me with the surprise of an electric shock. I shuddered for a moment like someone going into a convulsion, and then I sat up quickly and cried, "What?"

Silence greeted me. There was no one else in my suite. I glanced at the clock. I had slept until almost nine-fifteen. Feeling achy and groaning like a ninety-year-old woman, I struggled to get out of bed and into the bathroom. When I looked at myself in the mirror, I saw the face of someone who had not slept or, if she had, had tossed and turned through an avalanche of debilitating nightmares. Cold water did little to revive me. I had barely enough energy to run a brush through my hair twice. Then I went to throw something on and go face the music. There was no sense locking myself in my room to avoid it. What was done was done. I was prepared to accept whatever fate had in store for me.

Or at least, I thought I was. How would I ever know?

The silence in the house surprised me. No one was moving about on our floor. Where was Mrs. Duval, the other maids? Why hadn't Mrs. Caro sent for me? Surely, everyone knew I was home by now. I turned down the stairway slowly and paused. The silence below was just as deep. There was no one in sight. I was like the ghost of myself descending, not feeling my feet on the steps or my hand on the railing. Maybe I had died last night, and my body was still in my bed.

At the bottom of the stairway, I hesitated again to listen. I thought I heard someone sniffle and then the distinct sound of a cup and saucer. It was just Jordan at breakfast, I thought. She always woke late whenever she took something to help her sleep. I moved quickly to the dining room and stopped in the doorway. Jordan was there and so was Donald, but they were both looking down at their coffee. There was food on the table, but it all looked untouched—toast on plates, eggs looking more like displays in a restaurant storefront, and a full bowl of fruit.

Jordan looked up first. Her face appeared to shudder, as if the mere action of raising her head threw all of her features into a little earthquake. She brought her handkerchief to her mouth, and then Donald turned slowly and looked at me.

"What's wrong?" I asked.

"You had better sit down," Donald said.

I looked from his face to Jordan's. She still had the handkerchief pressed against her mouth. Now she looked unable to move, even to blink. I walked to my seat and sat.

"What?" I asked.

"If I've learned anything in this life so far, it's that you really don't know anyone."

*Oh, well,* I thought, *here comes another one of his long lectures.* I relaxed. I was mentally prepared for it, ready simply to sit and listen and try to look remorseful and attentive, as difficult as I expected it to be.

"No one knows what really goes on behind closed doors, within the walls of homes. How many times have we seen and heard neighbors claiming they would never have believed that their neighbor was a serial killer or something? Oh, I know this is the age of revelations, people spilling their most intimate secrets on talk shows. No one seems to have any self-respect anymore. Discretion is lost. At the drop of a hat, this one or that one admits he or she is a drug addict or was abused. You know what I mean?" he said, and looked at Jordan.

Her eyes moved to him but quickly came back to me, and that handkerchief still was over her mouth.

"Now, that's not to say we can't pick up some vibes ourselves, and obviously, the more experienced we are, the older we are, the better chance we have to do that, especially when we have gone through some hard experiences ourselves."

Jordan made a strange sound that seemed to catch in her throat like a scream she was holding down. My heartbeat quickened, and a slow but unrelenting warmth began to radiate out from under my breasts, climbing to the base of my throat. I looked at Donald.

"I'm definitely not one who likes to run about saying 'I told you so.' There's no satisfaction in being right when being right brings misery and sadness. In fact, if I had my druthers, as they say, I'd rather not have the wisdom and perception to foresee tragedy. Someone who has that suffers with it before, during, and after it happens."

"What are you talking about?" I finally asked.

"As I began to say, no one would expect a girl of your

age to know someone as well as, say, someone my age or Jordan's age might know someone. When you're young and innocent, there's no obstacle too difficult for you to overcome, no mountain too high to climb. No danger is forbidding enough. You're like these—what do they call them—young immortals who don't think they need health care or something. It's understandable. We've all been through that."

"I don't understand what you're trying to say, Donald. I'm sorry."

"Jordan received a phone call first thing this morning. That's the way it is with the women in her clutch lunch gang," he said, giving her a disapproving look. "Can't wait to get out bad news."

Now Jordan released a moan. It seemed to come from the very bottom of her soul and travel up her spine. I felt my heart stop.

"What?" I practically screamed.

"This troubled boy has apparently taken his own life," Donald said.

I heard the words, but they wouldn't navigate to that place in my brain where meaning dwelt. They seemed to go into my ears and then bounce off my skull and fall out again.

"What?" I thought I asked. I wasn't sure I was forming words, either.

"After he was brought home, he shut himself in his room. No one checked on him, we understand. Both his parents were at an affair. He had some sharp little tools he used for making his model planes and boats, apparently, and he bled to death. I'm afraid they won't be able to keep this out of the papers," he added. "It will be all over the news. You know how everything that happens to celebrities is Page One."

"The floor," I said.

"What?"

It felt as if it were sliding quickly to my right, and then the wall on the right started to slide into the ceiling, and the ceiling slid down into the wall on the left, and this kept going faster and faster until I was carried along and spun so fast I lost consciousness.

Later, Jordan told me that Donald had caught me and carried me up the stairs to my room and bed. I went in and out of consciousness for a while. A good friend of theirs, Dr. Battie, actually made a house call. He gave me a sedative, and I slept through most of the day.

Every time I did open my eyes, Jordan was sitting there offering words of comfort. I simply stared at her, telling myself that if I could force myself back to sleep, I could eventually bring the nightmare to an end. I'd wake up again. It would be morning. I'd shower, get dressed, and go down to breakfast to listen to Donald's lecture about how I had disappointed them. He would then talk about the future, admitting that perhaps they were a little too hard on me and that after things had settled down some, they'd permit me to invite Ryder to the house again, maybe to dinner, and we'd be more civilized about it all. Jordan would agree. I'd return to school, and we'd start where we had left off. Even Ryder's sister would behave. All I had to do was fall asleep and push the nightmare out.

But when I woke again, Jordan was still there. She was sorting through some clothes, separating garments. I watched her for a while because she didn't know I was awake.

"What are you doing?" I finally asked her.

"Oh, you're awake. Good. I've decided I have to give away some of these things that once belonged to Alena. They're too good to waste, and there are many young girls who could benefit. What good are they doing anyone hanging in this closet? Alena would be the first to agree."

I looked at the window and saw it was nearly twilight. "Didn't I get up this morning?"

"What's that? Oh. Yes, you were up."

She put one of the dresses down and came over to sit on my bed. She smiled and took my hand.

"You've had a terrible shock."

I shook my head. "No, that was just a nightmare."

"How I wish it were," she said.

I felt my lips trembling. "It was," I insisted.

She patted my hand gently. "You'll get stronger, Sasha. I used to sit with Alena in the early days of her illness and tell her that, and she would agree. It was because she had that attitude that she lasted as long as she did."

"Alena died," I said.

"Yes, she did, but she made sure she gave me as much as she could before going."

"Ryder's not dead." I shook my head, hoping to see her shake hers as well, but she didn't.

"I don't care who they are," she said. "They're suffering. If anyone knows how deeply that suffering is, it's Donald and I."

"No," I said.

"Now, we don't want you to blame yourself for this in any way. Donald is very insistent about that. He wants me to set up therapy for you to make sure that doesn't happen. He says the seeds for this were planted long before you met Ryder Garfield. There's a lot of history you don't know about, I don't know about, and no one on the outside knows about. This incident recently just set off a tragedy that was bound to happen. If it hadn't been you there at the time, it would have been some other girl. Donald's right."

I turned my back on her.

She put her hand on my shoulder. "I want you to know I'm here for you, Sasha. You can cry on my shoulder, talk to me, ask for anything you want or need, and I'll get it for you."

I didn't say anything. I closed my eyes so hard that my forehead ached.

"Mrs. Duval will bring you something soft to eat, some eggs, maybe, or hot cereal, okay?"

*If I don't talk,* I told myself, *this will all go away. It will be just a dream.*

"You need something in you. I don't want to have to send you to the hospital or something. Please eat something," she said, and stood up. "You poor dear."

I thought she had left, but when I turned around, she was still standing there looking at me.

"When I see you like this, I see Alena again. It breaks my heart."

"Alena didn't lose someone she loved," I said. Maybe that was a terribly cruel thing to say to her, but I was suffering too much to care. Anyway, she didn't look angry about it. She smiled, in fact.

"Of course she did," Jordan said. "She lost us. But you still have us. You still have me. Make sure you eat something," she said in the tone of a warning, and then she left.

I lay there for a moment, and then I heard a *ping* on my computer and sat up slowly. I didn't remember turning it on, but I had probably forgotten to turn it off when I had left to meet Kiera. I was sure all of my school friends were writing to me. It amazed me that my phone hadn't been ringing continually, but when I looked at it, I saw that it had been unplugged. *That's good,* I thought. I didn't want to speak to any of them, ever.

I got out of bed. I felt wobbly but flopped into the seat at the computer. The e-mail list was full, but there was one that caught my attention.

Kiera's.

I opened it. For a moment, the words looked fuzzy, but then I leaned closer and read it.

*Thanks for ruining my weekend.*

# 17
## Grief

*J*  didn't respond to Kiera, and she didn't call me. Mrs.
      Duval tried to get me to eat something. I refused. She
brought it anyway, but I didn't eat any of it, even though
I didn't leave my room. Jordan visited me twice before
she went to sleep. I never saw Donald. I didn't turn on
the television or reattach my phone. Later, I did go on
the Internet to read the news stories about the Garfields.
Everything being told to the press was being told by their
publicist. The story given out to the public was that both
Bradley and Beverly were too overcome with grief to speak
to anyone. Details were sketchy, but the publicist revealed
that Ryder had been in therapy and a troubled young
person for some time. The implication was that all of his
problems were the result of chemical imbalances. There
were no details about his death except the revelation that it
had occurred at home and was a suicide.

Reading the words on the Internet didn't make it all
less unreal for me. I continued to cling to the hope that this

was all a celebrity publicity event and soon there would be retractions. Ryder was still alive but perhaps in some rehab. I had no factual reason to have the hope. I knew I was behaving like someone who simply refused to believe the truth even though it was staring her in the face. I walked about the suite, talking to myself as if there were a therapist in the room.

*He wouldn't do this; he couldn't do this. Mama taught me always to be skeptical.*

*Yes, but not delusional.*

I was thrown back to when I was in the hospital after the accident Kiera had caused and I was told that my mother had died. No matter what anyone said, I wouldn't believe it until Jordan arranged for me to see my mother in the hospital morgue, and even then I tried to convince myself that it wasn't my mother.

When the truth is so horrible, you squirm and twist like someone chained to a wall watching the room fill up with water. Do what you can, you can't escape. You nearly drown in reality, and when you come up for air, the world you knew is changed forever and ever. You almost wish you were back in the room, even if it meant you'd die.

I was chained to that wall. I screamed and screamed inside. No one but me could hear it.

Later that morning, Jessica and Sydney made an attempt to visit me. Jordan came to my room to tell me they were at the gate, but I told her I didn't want to see them.

"It might do you some good to talk to your friends, dear. This is a hard thing to bear alone."

"They just want gossip to spread. I don't want to see them," I said firmly. "I don't!"

She winced, nodded, and left. I spent the rest of the day locked away, sleeping as much as I could. I wouldn't go down to dinner and hardly ate anything that was brought up to me. When Jordan looked in on me later, I pretended to be asleep. She stood there for the longest time but finally gave up and left. She was there even before Mrs. Duval the following morning. I was still in bed, of course.

"You have to come out of here, Sasha, and you have to eat more today. You're only going to make yourself sick."

I turned over so she would be looking at my back, and then she left. She was in and out constantly, looking to do something for me, but finally, she gave up after lunch.

Late in the afternoon, I went outside. Mrs. Duval had threatened to have me dragged out of the room if I didn't. I still had not seen Donald, nor did I care to. Jordan didn't hear me leave my room and go down the stairs. I was happy she hadn't seen me leave the house. I still wanted to be alone, and a walk to the lake seemed the most soothing thing to do.

Of course, what really drew me was the recent memory of being there with Ryder. The beauty of the lake calmed whatever demons were swirling around in him. I knew we both saw ourselves together there in the future, spending a quiet afternoon just drifting in a rowboat and talking softly. I would sprawl out on the floor of the rowboat and lean against him. Perhaps we would have stayed out until twilight and enjoyed the sight of the first star. Our kisses, our embraces, would have been extra special there. There was so much for us to do together. Why wasn't that enough to overcome anything that had depressed him? Why didn't that give him enough hope?

I hated to admit it, but Donald was probably right when he had begun that long preamble to telling me about Ryder's death. We really hadn't known each other, especially people our age who hadn't been with each other long enough to see behind the words as well as the walls. I had no doubt that Ryder had been honest about his past, but there were surely things he had not revealed, perhaps because he thought they would drive me away.

Still, it was impossible not to wonder what it might have been like if we had successfully enjoyed the weekend. Perhaps we would both have been restored enough and strengthened enough to overcome any difficulties. We would have outlasted them because we would have shared too much to forget.

I had no way of knowing exactly what had occurred when the police returned him to his home. When did they take off the handcuffs? What threats and punishments did his parents give him? Did they tell him they were surely going to send him to that military-type school he feared? How come they didn't know their own son well enough to anticipate that he might do something so drastic? How were they going to live with it?

And what about Summer? Did she feel bad about it? Did she really hate him as much as she pretended she did? Maybe she was the one who first discovered that he had left school and had run to her parents with the information. If so, she would live with the guilt and be marred for the rest of her life. It pleased me to think so, but then again, perhaps I was asking myself these questions to avoid feeling any guilt myself.

It wasn't hard to see why or how that could be. Was there any doubt that if I hadn't asked him to join me with Kiera, he wouldn't be dead? Should I have gotten into my car quickly and followed the police car back to his house to make sure he didn't think I was in any way to blame? Surely there was something more I could have done instead of spending the time worrying about myself and how Donald and Jordan were going to react to my lying about where I was going and why I was going there.

I stood by the bench and hugged myself. The terns were back, only this time they were circling the lake, not simply exploring and leaving. They looked as if they thought they had found a private place and were taking pleasure in their discovery. The ocean was too common. Here, they were special. It brought a smile to my face, and my face welcomed it.

"Hey," I heard, and turned to see Donald coming toward me. Whatever softness had come back into my body fled like the terns, which shot up and away at the sound of his voice echoing over the water.

He slowed down, paused, and looked out at the lake. "Look at this lake. I don't appreciate what I have here enough. Jordan's right about that," he said. "I was talking to someone who might get it stocked with some fish." He looked at me. "Glad you're out for some fresh air. How are you doing?"

"Okay," I said, and sat on the bench. He stepped up to it, but he didn't sit beside me.

"Look. I want you to know I never wished for something as terrible as this to happen. Maybe I didn't make that clear enough. I was just looking out for your best interests. I hope you believe me."

I nodded.

"Although I do blame myself for what's happened to you."

I looked up at him. "Why?"

"As I've been saying, I should devote more time to you. People think that when girls get to be your age, they don't want much to do with anyone older than twenty-five, but I know you're different. You've been matured by hardships, and as a consequence, you're mentally older than most other girls your age."

I didn't say anything. He stood there, waiting for me to say something nice in return perhaps, but I wasn't in the mood to hear compliments or say anything I didn't wholeheartedly believe.

"You don't think so now or believe it's possible, I'm sure, but this will pass. You have a wonderful future ahead of you, Sasha."

I sensed that my continued silence was making him uncomfortable. He fidgeted for a few moments, and then he walked over to the dock, checked something on one of the rowboats, and looked at me as if he had just thought of a brilliant solution to everything.

"How about I take you and Jordan out to dinner

tonight? Nothing fancy. Maybe we take a short drive up the coast and have some seafood. Okay?"

"I don't have much of an appetite."

"Well, you might in a while."

"I don't think so," I said. "You two go."

"I'm not worried about us," he said a little sharply. "If you change your mind, let me know. I was hoping to do something for you before I left. I have a trip I must make," he added, and started back to the house.

Was I being unreasonable, unfair? Should I give credence to the idea that after having been burnt so badly by Kiera's actions, he was sort of parent-battle-fatigued and justifiably overly concerned about what I did and whom I knew? If I were in his or Jordan's shoes, would I be the same way?

I glanced back at the house and up at my room, Alena's room. Considering their loss and the scars they bore because of it, as well as all of the embarrassing and nasty things Kiera had done, wasn't it unreasonable to blame either of them for any of this? Was I the impulsive and foolish one, after all? If I hadn't accepted Kiera's invitation with an air of defiance and had simply waited out the restriction concerning Ryder Garfield, wouldn't this all have turned out differently? In time, Jordan and Donald probably would have understood and become more sympathetic. Ryder might have come to trust them, and instead of plans being laid for his funeral, plans might have been made for our senior prom date.

The girls in my school, even most of the guys, looked

for every possible excuse whenever they did anything wrong or failed at something. I supposed that in that way, they weren't all that different from kids with far less. It was simply easier for them to get away with it. Their parents were more egocentric. They were all so worried about their image in the social community, so they were quicker to back up their children, to support their lame excuses and look for some other place, some other person or idea, on which to lay the blame.

The Garfields were already doing it in their first publicity attempts to explain their own family tragedy. Some chemicals in Ryder were unbalanced. How conveniently that would get them off the hook. So many other parents hid behind that socially acceptable excuse. Surely, there were some who had a legitimate claim to it, but I felt confident that this wasn't the case with Ryder Garfield. How much clearer did it have to be made to me that his parents neglected both him and his sister when it came to promoting and pursuing their own show-business careers?

If they did lay such heavy guilt on him for his mother's miscarriage in Italy, then shame on them for not realizing how deep and painful that would be for a child his age. I welcomed the anger I felt toward them. It helped me contain my sorrow.

Maybe I was no better than those I was criticizing, however. Maybe I was simply looking for something, someone else, to blame. Guilt and sorrow were too difficult to manage simultaneously.

These thoughts and feelings clung to me like leeches,

sucking out my energy. When I turned to head back to the house, I plodded along like someone carrying twice her own weight on her shoulders. It shortened my breath and made me ache all over. People were working on the grounds as usual, but I heard nothing. It was as if I had gone deaf. When I raised my head, I saw Mrs. Duval waiting for me. She waved, but I didn't respond. Drawing closer, I saw the look of terrible concern on her face.

"You have to eat more than you have, Sasha," she said. "It's why everyone everywhere serves food after funerals. It restores us. Please come to the kitchen. Mrs. Caro has made you a nice sandwich with poached chicken, just the way you like it. Come," she urged.

She put her arm around my shoulders. Maybe it was the tender touch of someone who I knew sincerely cared about me. Or maybe it was my body fighting to survive and remain healthy and strong, but I let her lead me into the house and to the kitchen, where Mrs. Caro waited. She hugged me, too, and then put the sandwich on the kitchen nook table. Neither of them said anything. They were probably afraid that one syllable might set me back and I wouldn't eat. Jordan realized that I was there, however, and came quickly.

"Oh, you got her to put something substantial in her stomach. That's good, Mrs. Duval. Thank you, Mrs. Caro."

From the look on her face when she sat at the table, I knew she had something to tell me. I waited, terrified of what else there might be.

"Dr. Steiner has arranged for every single student in your class to visit with a therapist this week," she said. "In other schools, when someone young is . . . dies, they usually do the same thing. It's much more difficult for young people to accept and understand."

"That's just a big publicity gimmick she's doing," I said, chewing harder and faster.

"What? No. I mean, why would you say such a thing?"

"Few, if any, students in my class got to know Ryder Garfield even well enough to say hello to him, Jordan. I doubt there'll be an iota of emotional stress. Some of the girls who went gaga over him might moan dramatically about the great loss to their fantasies, but there will be little more than that, believe me. It will be like he came to our school one day and then transferred out, nothing more."

"That's so uncharacteristically cold of you, Sasha."

"Not cold, just realistic, Jordan."

"Well, I hope you don't say something like that about the boy's funeral. It's being kept very private, which is understandable under the circumstances."

"What does that mean?"

"No one who isn't on their list can attend it at the church. You can understand how people would come just to gawk at them, and don't forget all the paparazzi who would haunt them. It would be so disrespectful."

"Then I won't be able to go?"

"Would that be wise anyway? I mean, under the circumstances?" she asked softly.

The food caught in my throat. She was saying that Ryder's parents might hold me somewhat responsible. I drank some water, glanced at Mrs. Duval and Mrs. Caro, both of whom looked as if they would break into tears, and then I finished the last bite of the sandwich and stood up. Everyone was watching me. I started to turn away to walk out, and then I stopped and looked down at Jordan.

"Would it be wise for the only person here who cared about him to be at his funeral? I don't know. You figure it out," I said, and left the kitchen. It was like walking out of a funeral, anyway. That's how deep and dark the silence was in my wake.

When I was back in my room, I thought about all Jordan had said. I didn't like doing it, but I realized that the only way to find out what was happening was to call Jessica. Yes, she could be the biggest gossip and very annoying at times, but she did look up to me, and she did have the fastest route to the best entertainment sources.

"Oh, Sasha," she said when she knew I was on the phone, "I was so worried about you. All of us were, especially when you wouldn't let us visit. Who could have possibly imagined that someone like that would commit—"

"What do you know about his funeral, Jessica?" I asked quickly.

"His funeral?"

"Don't pretend you haven't asked Claire about it all."

"No, I did. I was hoping that maybe you would call me and I would have information you might want."

"I do want."

"The church service is at St. Luke's on Monday, but their publicist is preparing a limited guest list. They'll actually have someone at the door at a desk checking off names, and they've hired private security to enforce it. No one from any newspaper, except a few of their friends in the entertainment press, will get into the service. What they can't stop is people going to the cemetery."

"What cemetery?"

"Cypress Park, near Ojai. Everyone's surprised at the choice. There are no famous Hollywood people buried there and—"

"Tell me the truth. Are any of you leaving school to go to the cemetery?"

Jessica was quiet for a moment. "Well, we thought that since we did know him, even for a little while, we might."

"You just want to see movie stars, right?"

"Oh, no, no. Well, some of the others might go there for that reason, but you know I won't. Do you want to go with me?"

"No, thanks," I said. "I'm not sure I'll return to school on Monday."

"I'll pick you up at home, and we can go to the cemetery together."

"No, I don't think I'll do that."

"Oh? Can you tell me what happened? I mean, where did you go, and what did you do? I heard rumors, but no one seems to know exactly what happened."

"Even Claire?"

"It's like top secret."

"Then we had better keep it that way. We don't want to endanger the country," I said. "Thanks for the information."

"Sasha—" she started, but I hung up. She sent me an e-mail soon after to offer again to take me to the cemetery, but I didn't respond.

Later, Jordan came by to ask me the same thing Donald had: would I like to go to dinner?

"He's leaving tomorrow, and he would like to do something more for you," she said.

Was Donald really feeling guilty about all of this? I wondered.

"I appreciate it, but I don't feel up to it, Jordan. I'll eat whatever Mrs. Caro makes for me."

"Well, I'm not going without you," she said. "If you change your mind, let me know."

I thanked her again, and she left. Not ten minutes later, the call I most dreaded came. It was Kiera. She began by telling me that she had checked out of the motel and returned to the college dorm. For a moment, I thought she knew nothing about Ryder Garfield, but then she said, "Boy, I guess there was a lot more wrong with him than you first thought."

"No, there was a lot more wrong with his parents than I first thought," I said. "That wasn't a very nice thing you wrote in your e-mail."

"Well, I didn't know it was going to turn out to be that dramatic an ending."

"It wasn't dramatic. It was tragic."

"Same thing."

"Did you confront your roommate about it?"

She was quiet a moment. "Oh," she said, as if she had just realized what I was referring to. "That blabbering idiot? I told her about Ryder just to make her feel guilty and terrible. She ran out of here in tears. I'm going to see about changing my room. Maybe I can get a single and not deal with any of these pathetic airheads. I'm beginning to hate this place."

"Why didn't you just come home for a few days?"

"I'm not that desperate yet," she said.

I wanted to ask why she felt that way now, especially considering how big this property was and how much there was to do on it. What had happened to all of her high school friends? Why wasn't she ever talking about any of them, and why didn't she want to meet any of them here again?

But I had no patience for Kiera March right now. Her problems looked trivial and selfish to me.

"So what did you learn about his suicide?" she asked.

"Nothing more. It's all too painful to talk about, Kiera. I'm tired."

"You should have stayed with me," she said. "You're probably just moping about there, and my mother is probably behaving like a worried hen or something."

I didn't say anything.

"What new wonderful thing is my father doing for you?"

"I think he feels bad. He wants to take us out to dinner, but I'm not up to it."

"You'll break his heart," she said.

"I've got to go, Kiera. I'm not feeling well," I said to cut off her sarcasm.

"So go. Send me an e-mail when you're up to it," she said, and hung up.

Since we weren't going out for dinner, Donald decided

to leave on his trip that night. Jordan told me that he had told her the faster he went, the sooner he could return. I didn't ask her where he had gone or why. Right now, none of that really mattered to me. So many things I had once thought important looked insignificant.

Dinner, with only Jordan and myself, reminded me of the earlier days when everyone was feeling uncomfortable being together. Conversation was forced, as were smiles. Donald was so formal, and Kiera was usually sulking or just sullen. Sometimes I had no appetite because of them but forced myself to eat so no one would notice. I thought Donald would think I was unappreciative and Kiera would be pleased.

"Donald thought it would be better for you if you did as originally planned and didn't attend school on Monday," Jordan said. "That way, you'll have until Wednesday."

I nodded. I ate as much as I could and then excused myself and went up to my room. Somehow, no matter what I thought to do, it seemed wrong. How could I distract myself with watching television? How could I read or do homework? It was even hard to return to the Internet. Doing anything made me feel as if Ryder's death didn't matter if I could return to my normal life that quickly.

Of course, I couldn't. I did know from my own experience after my mother's death that time would bring me back into the world. Right now, I hated the thought of it. I tried sleeping but couldn't fall asleep for the longest time, and when I did, I woke frequently. A little before ten, Jordan knocked on my door and stepped in to see how I was.

"I was thinking," she said after a few quiet moments between us, "that maybe we could go looking for your new dress this coming weekend."

"I don't know," I said. The idea of attending the concert Donald was arranging seemed so far off. I couldn't imagine not thinking about Ryder every single silent moment in my life. How could I concentrate on doing anything?

"It's more for me than for you. Please," she added.

"Okay," I said.

That brought a smile to her face. She kissed me good night and left.

When I woke up in the morning, I knew I would go to the cemetery to see the last part of Ryder's funeral. I would keep far back and hope that none of the girls from school would see me there. Jessica called to see if I had changed my mind, but I didn't tell her my intentions.

"We heard they're not letting Summer remain at Pacifica," she told me.

"Lucky Pacifica," I said.

"I know you haven't been out and about, but they already have the story on the front pages of *Hollywood Whisper* magazine in the supermarket. There's no picture of Ryder, of course, but there's a whole spread on Bradley and Beverly. Someone shot photos of them from a distance with a super lens or something. Have you watched *Entertainment Tonight*? They did about ten minutes on them and Ryder."

"No. I haven't watched any television."

"You're better off," she said. "I'll call you after the funeral if you like."

"No, don't. I'll see you when I return to school."

"Okay," she said. "If you're sure . . ."

"Thanks. Good-bye, Jessica."

I hung up before she could say anything else that might disturb me.

I didn't tell Jordan what my intentions were on Monday. She had a luncheon to attend in Santa Barbara, which meant that she would leave early. She asked me all morning if I'd be all right.

"I could cancel," she said.

"I'm fine," I told her. To illustrate it and keep her from asking too many questions, I ate breakfast well and then went out with one of the books I had to read for English. I sat by the lake and really did try to read, although my gaze kept slipping off the page and to my watch.

As soon as Jordan drove off, I rose and went to my car. When I arrived at the church, I saw the crowd of gawkers and the paparazzi. The police were keeping everyone a good distance away. Apparently, Bradley, Beverly, and Summer had exited through a rear door. They were in a limousine with tinted windows. The line of cars followed the hearse out, and then the parade behind them joined. I stayed as far back as I could. I did see Jessica and the girls in one car but none of the boys from school. That didn't surprise me.

By the time I pulled into the cemetery, the service had begun. I parked as far away from the other vehicles as I could. I watched from a good distance. The crowd of close friends hovered about Bradley, Beverly, and Summer like subjects protecting their royalty, but I was sure the photographers were still able to edge their way close enough to capture them sufficiently for magazine and newspaper front pages.

After the service ended, I stepped back behind a large oak tree to watch people leaving. When the last car pulled away, I stepped out. Two cemetery employees remained to finish. I saw a small backhoe with the driver waiting to operate it. They were talking but stopped when they saw me approaching. Neither said anything. I guess I really surprised them.

I stood on the edge of the grave and looked down at the coffin. I had this sudden vision that was both horrifying and glorious. The lid of the coffin was thrown open, and Ryder sat up, smiling.

"Hey," he called up to me, "stop looking so sad. Remember, 'for there is nothing either good or bad but thinking makes it so.'"

"How is this good?" I asked.

"I've escaped. Think of that."

"But in escaping, you left me, too."

"You'll catch up with me later."

"Thanks a lot," I said.

"Think nothing of it."

He smiled and then started to lie back in the coffin and reach up to close the lid.

"No!" I screamed.

"Excuse me, Miss," one of the cemetery workers said. "But we think you should find your way home now."

"What?"

"We're finishing up here. The service is over."

I looked at the two of them. The other man had boarded the backhoe.

"You can't do that," I said. "He's not really dead. He's just . . . doing this to annoy his parents. Ryder!" I called down to the coffin.

"Holy crap," the cemetery worker on the backhoe said. He pulled out his cell phone.

"Now, just take it easy, Miss," the one near me said. He put his hand out, palm up. "You back up a little now, please."

I looked at him, down at the coffin, and then back at him.

"We've got a problem out here," I heard the man on the backhoe say to someone on his cell phone.

"Now, you just take it easy, Miss," the first worker said to me.

I backed away. Then I turned and ran to my car. As I was driving off, one of the police patrol cars that was at the funeral pulled in. In my rearview mirror, I saw the cemetery workers talking to the two patrolmen. I sped up, made a turn, and then pulled over to catch my breath. I sat there with my eyes closed. I was shaking so much that my teeth tapped. I hugged myself and rocked from side to side until I heard someone tap on my car window and saw both the patrolmen standing there. When I didn't respond, one tried to open the door, but it was locked. He knocked on the window again.

"Please unlock your door, Miss, and step out of the car."

"Leave him alone!" I screamed. "If you hadn't put those handcuffs on him and dragged him away . . ."

He knocked on the window again. "If you don't open the door, we'll have to break the window," he said. "Shut off your engine, Miss."

I took a deep breath and did as he asked. Then I unlocked the door, and he opened it quickly.

"Are you all right?"

"No, but there's nothing you can do about it, and there's nothing I can do about it," I said.

"Can you step out of the car, please? Please show us your license, too," he said.

"I don't have my license with me. I got into my car without taking anything," I said.

"Where's your car's registration?" he asked. I recalled Donald telling me that he had put it in the glove compartment. I reached in, found it, and handed it to the patrolman. I stepped out of the car.

"Sasha Porter?"

"Yes, that's who I am."

"What went on back there at the cemetery?" he asked.

"My boyfriend was buried," I said.

"Boyfriend?" the other patrolman said, more to his partner than to me.

"Yes, he was my boyfriend."

"Well, look, are you all right? Would it be better for us to take you home?"

"I'm okay," I said. "Thank you."

"We'll follow you home anyway," the patrolman with my registration said. He handed it back to me.

I nodded and got back into the car. I drove extra slowly and carefully, but they followed me all the way back and waited while the gate opened. Then they followed me up the driveway. Mrs. Duval came out onto the portico as I drove up. Someone, perhaps her husband, had alerted her to the police car.

The two patrolmen got out of their vehicle when I got out of mine.

"What's wrong?" Mrs. Duval asked me.

"I don't know where I would begin if I tried to answer that, Mrs. Duval," I said, and kept walking toward the front door.

"Is Mr. or Mrs. Porter in?" one of the patrolmen asked her.

"No, this is the home of Donald and Jordan March," she replied. "Miss Porter is their . . ."

I paused to hear what she would say.

"Foster child."

"Is either of them at home?" he asked.

"Not at the moment, no. Is something wrong?"

I didn't wait to hear what they would say. I went into the house and hurried up the stairs. The image of Ryder sitting up in his coffin was still so vivid. I was still so shaken by it.

I actually went up thinking that he might just phone.

# ❧18❧

## *Changes*

O nce I returned to my room, I didn't leave for the rest of the day and night. Mrs. Duval brought me dinner and threatened that if I didn't eat everything, she'd have Jordan take me to the hospital. I ate, mindlessly chewing and swallowing. Afterward, I tried to do something else— read, watch television, go on the Internet. I even tried to practice on the clarinet, but every time I started to do something, I stopped to remind myself that Ryder was gone from my life as quickly as he had entered it. I lost interest in anything I did and slipped back into my dark depression. Before I was forced to talk to anyone else, I went to sleep.

I didn't have to go to school the next day, of course. This was the Tuesday that Ryder and I had first planned to spend rowing on the lake, having our little picnic, and just enjoying each other's company. When Jordan saw me, she insisted that I remain home the following day as well.

"You look very tired, Sasha. I know how devastated you are. Emotional fatigue is always deeper than mere physical fatigue. I'll have the schoolwork you missed on Monday picked up for you," she said. "And we'll do the same tomorrow. You really need a little more rest before you return to your regular schedule at school."

She had been gone all day Monday and was not home until sometime in the evening. I knew that Mrs. Duval had told her what the policemen had said, of course, but she didn't mention it. She didn't ask if I had gone to the cemetery, either. I had the feeling that she was tiptoeing around me, afraid that she might light one of the fuses inside me.

Later that morning, Jessica called, hoping to give me a full, detailed account of the cemetery service, but I told her I didn't want to hear any of it. Of course, I didn't mention that I had been there, too.

"I understand," she said, her voice dripping with disappointment. "Everyone is so upset and confused. There's been so little information. Can I just ask you if you had any idea that this might happen?"

"No, you can't. Return to sender," I said.

"Huh?"

"When mail is undeliverable, the post office writes 'Return to sender.'"

She was quiet. I think I was frightening her. "You're coming to school tomorrow, right?"

"I believe I'll miss school again tomorrow."

"When are you returning to school?"

"I don't know. I could be there Thursday. I could be there Friday or maybe not until next week."

"You are coming back, though, right?"

"I'll be back," I said in my best Arnold Schwarzenegger voice. She was silent again. I sensed that she didn't know what to say.

"Sasha, are you all right? I mean, I know you have to be very upset and all, but—"

"Thanks for calling," I said, and hung up.

On Wednesday, as she had promised, Jordan sent Alberto to pick up my work at the end of the school day. It didn't occur to me until sometime that afternoon that Donald had still not returned from his trip, wherever that was and whatever it was for. I recalled that he had left on Friday because we weren't going out to eat, and that would enable him to come home sooner. It had been nearly a week. What did he mean by 'sooner'?

Although she didn't say anything about it, I could see that Jordan was disturbed by that or perhaps something even more serious. She wasn't making her usual daily attempts to cheer me up or get me to avoid thinking about Ryder Garfield. In fact, to me, she looked even more withdrawn than I had been. I saw the way her eyes drifted, realized the long silences between things she said, and watched her move through the house almost like someone who was sleepwalking. I also saw my concern echoed in both Mrs. Duval's and Mrs. Caro's faces after they had looked at her or heard her speak. If she was doing any of this to get me to think about something else, I thought, she was succeeding.

"I might not be home for dinner tonight," she told me later that afternoon. She stopped by the sitting room near the front entrance. I had been wandering about like a lost soul myself all day. My schoolwork was little or no challenge. I had finished it all quickly, but unlike what I usually did, I didn't read ahead in any textbook. I think I had ended up in the sitting room because it was a room in the house besides my own in which Ryder had been. I recalled how he had run the palm of his hand over the piano, his face full of appreciation. I sat there staring at the piano, envisioning him and smiling to myself.

"I hate leaving you to eat by yourself," Jordan added, "but it's unavoidable."

"What's going on?" I asked. I thought it was time I did. She was wearing a conservative beige business suit, but her makeup was quite understated for her.

At first, she didn't look as if she would say anything. She shook her head and started to turn away, but then she stopped, and her shoulders shook.

*She's crying,* I realized, and leaped up to go to her.

"What is it, Jordan?" I wanted to add, *Whatever it is, it can't be so terrible.* I was thinking only of Ryder. What could be more terrible? "What's happened to upset you? Did something happen to Donald? Is that why he's still away?"

She turned slowly, tears hanging off her lower lids as if they had been caught trying to escape. "No, nothing has happened to him yet."

"Yet?"

"I'm meeting with my attorney. She's a high-powered divorce attorney."

"You're getting a divorce?"

She nodded and took a step toward me. "When I had that conversation with you at the lake, I already knew there were very serious problems between Donald and me. I wasn't completely honest. We had been with our marriage counselor for a while, but that didn't help us. Donald always found an excuse to cancel. Besides, he wasn't being forthcoming at those sessions, anyway. Half the time, he was manipulating both me and the therapist, but I wasn't completely stupid. I wasn't meeting friends for lunch all those times he thought I was. I was meeting with a private detective."

"Why?"

"A few times, I had caught Donald lying to me about his trips. I didn't make a big deal of it. I realize now that I should have. Once, his office actually called here looking for him, and his office manager, Charlie Daniels, had to admit that Donald wasn't on any business for the firm. He didn't tell me where he was. He didn't have to. I suppose I always knew this day would come," she said. "I was in denial."

She looked as if she was struggling to breathe. I stepped back as she went to sit in the nearest chair. She dabbed her eyes with her handkerchief and pulled up her shoulders like someone who had just been insulted. I stood there waiting.

"However, I assure you I'm not going to be like most of my divorced girlfriends and pretend that my getting half of his assets wipes away the pain and suffering he has caused me. I'll find the money he's hidden overseas, too. I won't be civilized about any of it."

"Donald is definitely having an affair, then?"

"No, not an affair. Affairs," she said, looking up at me. "Although my friends will think it, I'm not some poor, naive woman taken by surprise. I suspected that his being around all those pretty very young women was too tempting for him to resist."

She sucked in her breath and looked at me again.

"I tried to keep all of this from you right now, pretending nothing was seriously wrong. Children are always the ones who suffer the most when this sort of thing occurs, and with what you're going through, Sasha, you don't need any more grief, especially someone else's." She reached for my hand. "I know you're very fragile at the moment. You have your own deep psychological and emotional pain. I'm sorry now that I brought you into all this, but I have never regretted having you here. In fact, you've been my joy and salvation."

"How long has Donald known that you're moving forward with a divorce?"

"He doesn't know it yet. That's why I'm meeting with my attorney today and tonight for dinner. She'll have the papers ready to file. I'm thinking of bringing them home and leaving them on his desk in his office here. It's a cold way for him to find out, but he'll know I'm not the fool he thinks I am," she said, standing.

"I'm sorry."

"You don't worry about any of this." She smiled. "My attorney has been working simultaneously on the paperwork I need to legally adopt you. It's better that I do the divorce procedure first, since we'd need Donald's agreement on everything, and I want him separated from it all first."

"Have you told Kiera any of this yet?" If she had, I thought, Kiera was certainly very good at hiding it.

The light in her eyes dimmed as her face tightened. "No. I don't trust her," she said, and started out again.

I followed her to the front door. She opened it but hesitated and then turned to me.

"This is going to sound strange to you, but in a way, I envy your mother for the way she lost her husband. She didn't have to go through all that I will have to go through out there with my friends, my family. Her husband was out of her life almost instantly. Of course, I realize what that did to the two of you. I'm thinking of it from a purely selfish viewpoint."

She smiled.

"Try to keep busy, Sasha. Maybe you should return to school tomorrow. It sounds a little heartless for me to say it, but that old adage about getting right back on your bike after you fall off is so true. Lose yourself in normal teenage-girl stuff. Go to dances, flirt, do some frivolous things. Borrow a little of Kiera's attitude." She smirked. "At least she is a survivor."

"But she's not happy," I said quickly.

"I know. That girl's gotten everything she wanted whenever she wanted it. Well, maybe that's why she's unhappy. I'll see you later."

"What if Donald comes home?" I asked before she closed the door behind her.

"Give him a little of his own treatment. Act as if nothing is wrong. The only satisfaction I have right now is the satisfaction I'll enjoy when he is taken by complete surprise."

She smiled again and closed the door behind her.

I stood there feeling more numb than sad or frightened by anything she had told me. It was as if I had run out of emotion, any emotion. When I glanced at myself in one of the wall mirrors, I thought I resembled a prisoner of war who had been so brainwashed she was almost lobotomized. She wouldn't even realize she had been rescued.

So many new questions occurred to me. How would this divorce really turn out? I couldn't imagine Donald giving up his estate, despite the fact that he was gone from it so much lately. I knew how proud he was of the house and the beautiful grounds. The Richardson Romanesque architecture had been his choice, not Jordan's. He had been the one who wanted to build the lake, too. Would their settlement involve Jordan getting a new home? How long would that take to do? Would Kiera refuse to live in any new home with her mother? Would I have to change schools? What would happen to Mrs. Duval and Mrs. Caro? With whom would they go?

This estate, with all of its employees, was such a big responsibility. I couldn't imagine Jordan wanting to bear it all herself. It was impossible to be uncomfortable here or to be unimpressed with all it had to offer anyone who lived here, but I wouldn't be particularly devastated about moving away.

What did occur to me was Jordan's emotional tie to Alena's room, my room. Would she really be able to leave that behind her? I was sure she would take many of Alena's things, but I still had the impression that whenever she was in the suite, she was standing in a shrine.

Even without this news, I realized that there were many more cloudy days to come for me. The gloom that had entered with news of Ryder's death would settle for some time in every nook and corner of this mansion. The silences I had known here would deepen. Shadows would be more secure. Even the sunlight would feel out of place and gladly flee from closed shades and curtains. Neither the size of this estate with all that it offered nor all of its opulence and beauty could stop the winds of melancholy from blowing in and over us all.

Mrs. Duval knew I'd be eating alone. She suggested that I have dinner in the kitchen nook. She and Mrs. Caro would join me if I liked. Of course, I said yes. They were really my family now. I didn't think they knew what was coming. I would say nothing about it, of course. Sitting with them, I had the first meal I'd enjoyed since Ryder's death. I listened to them talk about their own youth and some of the silly things they had done. They laughed and made fun of each other. I knew they were doing it mostly for my benefit, but I so enjoyed them.

Afterward, I took a short walk around the grounds. I went to the pool and sat. Commercial jet planes looked as if they were as high as the stars. I imagined that those heading west were heading for Hawaii, Australia, or Asia. People in them were settling down after their dinners, too. Some were watching television or reading. I envied them, so far above the problems of the world below. They were leaving their mundane, everyday life behind and looking forward to some wonderful new adventure. They'd sleep peacefully, dreaming of their arrivals.

Ryder would understand why I was thinking like this. When would I meet someone like him again, someone with whom I knew I could share my most intimate thoughts and feelings? Maybe I never would. Maybe I'd fall into a marriage or a relationship doomed to end the way my mother's had or the way Jordan's was going to end.

Sitting there and thinking these thoughts, I realized why it was that Mrs. Caro would never predict anything terribly important for me—or anyone else, for that matter. It wasn't a blessing to see your future. First, it could be tragic, and second, if it wasn't, you'd worry about the tomorrows to come that might bring unhappiness, an unhappiness that would be deeper and stronger because it came after so much pleasure. Life, no matter who you were or how much money you had, was never a straight and narrow line in either direction. It was full of ups and downs, smiles and tears, joy and sadness. True, some people had less of one or the other, but no one had only one. Surviving seemed to be the only point to living. It was as true for me as it was for that ant I saw moving with determination over the edge of the pool. Maybe it was lost and was finding its way home.

*That's what we all do, anyway,* I thought, *try to find our way home.*

I sat for quite a while until I saw the glow of a pair of headlights sweep the grounds and turned to see Jordan pull into the garage. Carrying a folder, she went quickly into the house. I rose and headed in myself. I was tired, and I thought I just might take her advice and return to school tomorrow, even though I dreaded what awaited me.

When I entered the house, Jordan was coming back from Donald's office.

"I was just going up to your room to see how you were," she said.

"I'm okay. I think I will go to school tomorrow."

"That's good, Sasha," she said, and put her arm around me. "We both have to get stronger and stand by each other now."

She kissed me on the forehead, holding her lips there a moment or two longer, and then we headed up the stairway in silence. When we paused at my room, I asked her if she knew when Donald would be home, since he still had not returned.

"He left word that he would be back tomorrow, but he would be going to his company office first. It's not going to be pretty," she said. "I left the papers in his office here, and with them are the pictures and the details my detective accumulated. Don't you worry about it, though. Nothing will change for you," she promised, kissed me again, and went to her bedroom.

*Nothing will change for me?*

I was young when my parents' marriage was coming apart, but the memories of those arguments, the horrid things that were said, the rage my mother felt and showed, all of those images were like sleeping rodents. Once one was nudged, they all woke and scurried through my mind, scratching and clawing at my resistance until each scene was once again vivid enough to make me shudder and cry as hard as I had cried back then. I knew what to expect here. What little laughter there had been in this house lately would surely evaporate.

It was difficult to fall asleep. I listened to every sound in the great mansion like someone waiting for the second shoe to drop. On top of all of this was the sorrow I was anticipating the moment I entered homeroom tomorrow and saw Ryder's empty desk. I was afraid my heart would simply tighten up, shrivel, and stop. I knew everyone would be watching me, too, perhaps expecting me to burst into tears or simply get up and run out of the building. They would try to talk about other things, but their eyes would be asking questions constantly, hoping I would just break down and tell them everything.

Mrs. Duval came by in the morning to check on me as usual, but by the time she did, I was already dressed and ready to go down to breakfast. Jordan was up, too, and already at the table.

"How are you feeling?" she asked the moment I entered.

"Okay," I said. I wasn't. I was trembling so hard inside myself already that I couldn't imagine getting out of the car in the school parking lot and managing to reach the entrance.

"Would you like me to drive you to school this morning? It's no problem for me."

"No. If I'm going to do this, I had better do it all," I replied. "Thank you."

She leaned over to pat my hand. "That's what I like to hear. We're both going to be all right," she said. "I'll be home for dinner, so don't worry if I'm not here when you return from school. There is still much for me to do."

"What about Kiera? When will she know?"

"After Donald returns and sees what's what, we'll discuss informing Kiera. When you and I first met in the hospital after that horrible, unnecessary tragedy, you'll remember I blamed Donald for Kiera's behavior. He defended her too much and used his influence to get her out of trouble too often. It's very true when they say you reap what you sow in this world. I'm not wholly without blame, but Kiera is more Donald's daughter than mine, I'm afraid. She's always been closer to him than to me."

Not lately, I thought. She hadn't been close to either of them. Maybe she sensed that her father was drifting away. Perhaps it never had occurred to her that he would be an adulterer, and that was why she blamed his attention to me for his diminished interest in her.

"I'll let Donald lead the charge when it comes to explaining this to Kiera. But please try not to think of it all right now. Concentrate on building yourself back up. You have a wonderful future ahead of you, especially with your school grades. You have to decide on a college soon, don't you?"

"Yes."

"There's lots to think about and lots for both of us to do. Keeping busy is the best cure for sadness and disappointment."

I looked at my watch. "I guess I had better get going," I said, and rose.

"Call me if you need anything or decide you'd rather be home today, too. If you don't feel like driving back . . ."

"I'll be all right," I said.

"Of course you will. Be careful," she said.

She kissed me, and I started out. I picked up the books I had left the night before on the bench the way I always did and went out to my car.

I had eaten more than I had thought I would at breakfast. My reason for that was Mrs. Duval's watchful eyes. The butterflies in my stomach flew up and into my throat, but I swallowed them back. Now that I was actually going, it was as if I hadn't eaten a thing. My stomach felt hollow and empty. My body was so light that I thought I might float off. I forced myself to focus on everything I had to do and actually recited aloud the steps to starting my car and driving away as if I were taking my driver's test again and there was a motor vehicle agent right beside me. I thought that if I kept saying everything aloud, I would keep myself from thinking about what lay ahead.

"Turn right. Turn left. Stop at the stop sign. Speed up. Slow down. Signal."

Anyone overhearing me would think I had truly gone crazy. I tried not to look at anyone when I pulled into the parking lot and into my space. I kept my head down and my gaze low as I walked to the entrance. I was hoping to make it to my locker and then to homeroom before anyone approached me, but word that I had come to school was already being transmitted with the speed of a cell-phone call, especially to my classmates. Sydney and Jessica were waiting at my locker.

"How are you?" Sydney asked with the exaggeration of an amateur actor.

"Fine," I said, not looking at her. I started to open my locker and stopped. I had nothing to take out and nothing to put in.

"We've all already met with the counselor Dr. Steiner brought in. Maybe they'll bring her back for you," Sydney said, clearly making the point that I was the one who would really need it.

"I'm glad you're here," Jessica said. "You just tell us if you need anything."

"I need to be left alone," I said, and walked to home-room. I tried not to look at anyone else. My memories of the first day I had entered this school came surging back. There I was, limping my way from class to class, my face a portrait of terror for sure. I had not been in a formal school setting for some time, and despite the fiction Jordan had created for my biography, I still believed that anyone who looked at me saw nothing more than a street urchin.

I sucked in my breath, pressed my lips tightly together, and entered the homeroom, unable not to glance at Ryder's empty desk. To my surprise, Shayne Peters was sitting at it. For a moment, the shock kept me from moving. He smiled at me. I glared at him and went to my desk. Jessica sat just across from me in homeroom.

"Why is Shayne in Ryder's seat?" I asked her. She looked ecstatic because I was talking to her.

"We all got together yesterday and talked about what happened and about you. Everyone wants to try to do whatever he or she can to help you forget," she said.

"Forget?"

She nodded.

I could just imagine what else they had planned. They wouldn't let me be anywhere alone. To me, it was like being attacked by killer bees.

"I don't want to forget him, Jessica. You don't want to forget people you like just because something terrible happens to them. You don't erase human beings as easily as you change songs on your iPod."

Her eyes widened. I didn't realize it, but I was raising my voice. It had stopped all conversations.

"That's what everyone here is used to doing," I continued. She had opened a door that had kept years of frustrations trapped. "Whenever something unpleasant happens, you buy something or something is bought for you."

"Well, who wants to be unhappy?"

"No one wants to be unhappy, but no one should want anything and everything to be written off as just another bad hair day," I snapped. I looked back at Shayne. "Tell everyone not to do me any favors."

Homeroom began with the day's announcements, and I stopped talking. My outburst had the desired effect. They all kept their distance. In a way, I was grateful that they had gathered to decide on this plan. It made me so angry that rage took the place of sorrow for most of the morning. I didn't participate in class discussions, but I took notes and paid more attention than I had thought I would.

The only one I did talk to was Gary Stevens, the one Ryder had been comfortable talking to. I had always thought of Gary as a gentle, modest boy.

"I wish I had gotten to know him better," he said. Then

he smiled. "But once he became friendlier with you, I knew my chances were slim."

That brought a smile to my face. "Save me a place at lunch," I said.

His face lit up. "Sure will."

Just before lunch, I went to my locker to put my morning-class textbooks away. I was feeling stronger and felt sure that I could not only get through the day but also get through the remainder of the school year. I would discuss my college choices with Dr. Steiner and, despite the turmoil that was soon to set in at the March household, concentrate on my future. I would never forget Ryder. I would never treat any of the loving moments we had had together as something I could easily replace.

I opened my locker and started to put my books on the top shelf, but there was something already there. I laid the books down on the floor of the locker and reached in to take out a shoe box. There was a note attached to the top of it. I tore it off, unfolded it, and read: "This one is for you."

I opened the box and lifted out a small bottle with a delicate-looking sailboat inside it.

He had put it there before he started out to meet me, I realized.

It was so beautiful.

The sight of it brought my sorrow and shock back in waves. I just managed to put the bottle back in the box and the box back on the shelf before something inside me seemed to snap. It was as if my heart had cracked in two. My legs softened, and my eyes rolled back. It seemed to take me forever to hit the floor, but before I did, I was unconscious.

# ∽19∾

# *An Unwelcome Visitor*

I awoke in the nurse's office. She and Dr. Steiner were at my side. Mr. Huntington, whose classroom was right across the hall, had rushed to me first, picked me up in his arms, and carried me to the nurse's office. Seeing them all standing there looking at me as our nurse, Mrs. Millstein, took my blood pressure confused me for a moment, because I didn't realize that I had fainted. When she was finished, she looked up at Dr. Steiner.

"It's fine," she said. "Her pulse is okay, too."

"What happened?" I asked. I felt the cold cloth on my forehead.

"Apparently, you fainted, Sasha. I tried to reach Mrs. March, but she wasn't at home and didn't answer her cell phone. I did, however, reach Mr. March, and he's on his way here."

"Donald?"

"Excuse me?"

I closed my eyes. It was all coming back to me quickly. "What happened to the ship in the bottle?"

"Ship in the bottle?" Dr. Steiner asked, and looked at Mr. Huntington.

"I think it might be something in her locker. Should I go look?"

"Yes," I said before Dr. Steiner could respond. "Please, Mr. Huntington."

He smiled and headed out.

"Do you remember if you banged your head?" Mrs. Millstein asked, inspecting it and looking for some blood. "Does anything hurt you?"

"No. I feel funny, but nothing hurts."

"Did you skip eating today? Yesterday?" she asked.

"I didn't eat that much yesterday, but I ate breakfast this morning. Mrs. Duval wouldn't let me out of the house otherwise," I said.

Mrs. Millstein looked at Dr. Steiner and shrugged.

"Mr. March will probably take her to be examined. Perhaps you returned to school too soon," she told me.

The expression on her face told me she knew all about Ryder Garfield and me.

"I think I'm all right," I said, sitting up. I took off the cold compress, but for a moment, I was dizzy.

"Take it easy," Mrs. Millstein said. "You're not completely aware of what's happening. It's better you rest and do get checked out further."

"There's nothing physically wrong with me. I just . . . I was just surprised by what I found in my locker."

"Surprises don't cause us to faint, usually," Mrs. Mill-stein said.

"This was different. This was ..." I paused when Donald entered right beside Mr. Huntington, who was holding the ship in the bottle that Ryder had given me.

"How's she doing?" Donald asked.

Mr. Huntington handed me the bottle. I clutched it tightly.

"Her blood pressure is good. So is her pulse, and she has no fever. I don't see any injuries on her," Mrs. Millstein said. "However, you should have her checked out further."

"Will do," Donald said. "As you know, she's had quite an emotional shock," he told Dr. Steiner. She nodded.

"I can take her out in the wheelchair," Mrs. Millstein said.

"I can walk," I said. I knew that would create quite a scene, just the sort of soap-opera drama the girls in my class fed on. My phone would be ringing off the hook again.

"Sure you can," Donald said. "But we'd better let the nurse do it, okay, Sasha?"

Mrs. Millstein brought the wheelchair up to me before I could say anything else. She helped guide me into it, and then she started me out. I kept my ship in the bottle in my lap. Donald remained behind for a few moments to talk to Dr. Steiner. He caught up with us at the door to the parking lot. I didn't look back or around, but I knew that many of the students were watching from classroom windows.

After I got into Donald's car, he said he would send Alberto for mine. He sat there for a moment without doing anything. I thought for sure that he had found the divorce papers and evidence of his adulterous affairs and wondered if I knew what was happening.

"Luckily, I wasn't far from the school when Dr. Steiner's call came. What is that you're holding?"

"Something Ryder Garfield made," I said. "He left it in my locker. I didn't know it was there until just now."

"Oh? And you fainted when you saw it?"

"Yes."

"That makes sense. I was surprised Jordan wasn't found first," he said. "I don't know where she is," he added, still not starting his engine. "But I was happy to be the one to come fetch you. I spoke to Dr. Battie on my way over here. We don't have to take you to be checked out. He said you should take the sedatives he gave you that day and get some more rest. You returned too soon."

"I'm all right," I said. "I don't need any pills."

"Jordan will bawl me out if you don't do what the doctor said."

He started the car. Apparently, he had not been home yet and knew nothing of what was awaiting him. It was far more than being bawled out.

"You just close your eyes and relax, Sasha," he told me as he pulled away. "Young people do take these things harder. I shouldn't expect that just because you've been through a great deal more than the average girl your age, you'd be as tough as nails."

I felt his hand on my thigh.

"You're as soft and delicate as anyone your age, if not more so."

He squeezed gently. I closed my eyes again and pretended to fall asleep. He was on the phone with his office during the trip most of the time, anyway. Apparently, he had called ahead to the house before he arrived at the school, because both Mrs. Duval and Mrs. Caro were waiting when we drove up, with very worried expressions on their faces.

"Is Jordan back yet?" he asked them immediately.

"No," Mrs. Duval said. "I didn't try to reach her. I thought you would. How is she?" she asked, nodding at me.

"She'll be all right. Just get her up to her room and in bed. I'll be there in a few minutes to give her the medicine our doctor prescribed for her," he said. "Where's Alberto?"

Mrs. Duval told him, and he went looking for him.

Mrs. Duval helped me up to my room and got me undressed and into bed. She brought me a glass of water, and I asked her to hand me the ship in the bottle.

"What is this?" she asked.

"It was a present from Ryder Garfield," I said. "He had left it in my locker."

She nodded. I didn't have to explain any further. If this house had ears, one pair of them were hers and another pair were Mrs. Caro's. I put it beside me in my bed. She left to look for Donald. He was up a few minutes later.

"Here are your pills," he said, handing two of them to me.

"Two?"

"It's what Dr. Battie prescribed after I explained what happened. Go on. You need to rest. Mrs. Duval will look in on you. I can't believe Jordan hasn't returned my call yet.

I've got to get back to my company office for a few hours, but Mrs. Duval will look in on you."

I took the pills, and then he stroked my hair and smiled down at me.

"Even like this, you look amazingly beautiful, Sasha. Just rest. You'll be fine," he said. "You sure you want to leave that bottle there? You might roll over on it or something."

"I'm sure," I said.

"Okay."

I watched him leave and then closed my eyes. The pills were taking effect quickly. After another ten minutes or so, I felt light and comfortable and imagined Ryder lying there beside me. Like a genie, he came out of the bottle.

*"Sorry about all this,"* he said.

*"It was a very selfish thing to do,"* I told him.

*"Yeah, well, I've been brought up by experts when it comes to that."*

*"That's no excuse, and you know it, Ryder. You're better than they are."*

*He was silent a moment. "Only when I'm with you,"* he said.

*"So?"*

*"They were sending me away. I wouldn't have been with you."*

*"We would have found a way."*

*"Naw. It would have been too difficult. You'd have lost interest and found someone else. Besides, I stopped wishful thinking some time ago."*

*"Well, I didn't."*

*He leaned over to look at me. "You're different from any girl I ever met," he said. "You deserve someone better than me, anyway. Don't you worry. You're going to be something."*

*"I'm not thinking about me. I'm thinking about us."*

*"There will still be us," he said. "Just not in the here and now but someplace where no one can reach us or hurt us anymore."*

*"Where?"*

*"In the bottle. I'm on that ship waiting for you."*

*He started to float back into the bottle.*

*"Stop it," I said. "Ryder! Don't!"*

I must have been shouting for a while at the top of my voice, because my throat was aching when Jordan shook me and I opened my eyes.

"Sasha. What happened? Why are you screaming?"

"What?" I looked at the bottle.

"I'm sorry. I was in a meeting and didn't pick up my messages until a half-hour ago. I came rushing home. What is it? What's wrong? What were you yelling about?"

"He's in the bottle," I said.

"What? Who's in the bottle?"

"Ryder."

I closed my eyes again. She put her hand on my cheek. It felt cool and comforting. I smiled, and then, when I woke the next time, it was dark outside. There was just a small lamp on in my room. I groaned, and Jordan appeared, seemingly forming out of the shadows. She had been sleeping in a chair near my bed.

"How are you?" she asked.

"I don't know." I ran my hands down the sides of my body to see if I was all there. That's how light and empty I felt.

"You have to eat something. I'll have Mrs. Caro make some oatmeal for you and some tea and toast with jam. Do you remember what happened to you?"

I sat up and wiped my eyes. Images began to return, but they were so vague and distant I wasn't sure when it all had occurred.

"How long have I been sleeping?" It felt as if it could have been days.

"Five or six hours, I think. Donald brought you home after you fainted at school, and apparently at Dr. Battie's orders, he gave you sedatives. I spoke with Dr. Battie, and I also spoke with Dr. Steiner. She told me what happened. It's all my fault. I should have insisted that you remain home longer."

"Yes, Donald brought me home," I said, more and more coming back to me.

She nodded. "He's been in his office downstairs with the door locked ever since he came home from work. I suppose he's been speaking with his attorney and trying to devise some sort of defense." She smiled gleefully. "I'd like to be a fly on the wall in that office."

I stared at her. It was sad the way people who were sup-posedly once so in love, who had shared so many happy moments and once cherished each other, got to a point where they could happily inflict pain and suffering on each other. Was love only one side of a coin, the other side being hate? Was it this easily flipped? It was something I had wondered about with my own parents, of course. I could understand why Jordan was so upset, so hurt, and why that fit snugly into anger. Like my mother, she had been betrayed. She had eagerly risked the most intimate and vulnerable part of herself, her heart, her faith in someone else, someone she believed would love and protect her forever, and now she was deeply wounded. How would she ever believe in anyone or anything again? This was really what Donald had taken from her and what my father had taken from my mother.

"I'll see to your food," she said. "And bring it up to you myself. Just keep resting." She paused. "What exactly is that in the bed with you?"

I looked at the ship in the bottle. "A gift Ryder had left secretly in my locker before he ran off to join me," I said. "This was one of the things he made, his hobby."

"How beautiful." She smiled. "At least he left you with a treasured memory," she said in the tone of someone who longed for one herself.

She headed out. I put my hand on the bottle and closed my eyes.

Jordan didn't return with my food. Mrs. Duval brought it up instead. I could see from the look on her face that all hell had broken loose downstairs. She didn't want to say anything about it to me, probably worried that I was too weak or fragile to take more tension.

"Are they fighting? You can tell me, Mrs. Duval. I know what's going on here."

"Like cats and dogs," she said. "I'm to prepare one of the guest rooms for him. Thank goodness this house is big enough for them to avoid each other until it's all settled."

"You and Mrs. Caro knew this was coming?"

She rolled her eyes. "You know Mrs. Caro's powers," she replied. "You want a nice piece of freshly baked apple pie, maybe with some ice cream?"

"No. I think this will do, thank you."

"Just ring if you want something else," she said, and left.

I ate almost all of it. I thought I would get up, even go downstairs, but I was still wobbly, maybe more from the sedatives than anything else. I drifted in and out until Jordan appeared again, looking quite flustered.

"You all right?" I asked.

"I'm fine. You don't worry about me. His bluster won't work this time. He'll avoid us both until everything is settled."

"And Kiera?"

"He says he'll speak with her tomorrow, but I have my doubts. How do you feel?"

"I'll be all right."

"Well, you're not going to school until next Monday. That's settled. I'll have your work brought home. Don't worry."

I didn't argue. She looked more exhausted than I was, and I didn't want to give her any more trouble.

"I'm going to go take something myself and get some sleep. I need my strength for what's to come," she said. She kissed my cheek and left.

The next two days were difficult for everyone at the March mansion. Donald took his anger out on the servants, complaining about work done on the grounds, the pools, anything and everything. He had no meals here, not even breakfast. Jordan's initial glee and satisfaction with her legal actions against him waned. I could see the depression seeping into her face. Every phone conversation with one of her friends, despite how they sympathized, seemed more like salt rubbed into a wound. At dinner, she told me how she could hear the joy underlying their words.

"Joy? How could they be happy about what's happened to you?"

"It makes them feel superior. Some of them actually came out and said they knew Donald was having affairs, making it seem as if I were the stupid one. Some claimed he even flirted with them, and one of my so-called friends told me he had propositioned her once. Everyone claimed she had kept it from me to avoid upsetting me. If that was true, if they really cared about how I felt and what the news would do to me, they would never have told me."

"Has Kiera called you?"

"No," she said, "and I'm not calling her. She'll only upset me more by making me feel like this was somehow my fault. How about you?"

"Nothing, not even an e-mail," I said. I did think that was odd.

"Well, you're better off, too. You look much stronger. I know what we'll do. You and I will go out to dinner tomorrow night. How's that sound?"

"Good," I said.

"Thank goodness I have you here," she told me. I saw how sincere she was and nearly cried myself.

Afterward, I went to my room to do my schoolwork and read. My phone rang a number of times, as it had for the last two days, but as before, I let it go to the answering service and never even checked to see who had called. I wanted to be away from it all for a while. I kept checking my computer, however, looking for something from Kiera, but nothing came, and I didn't want to contact her first. She was too indifferent and cold about Ryder's death. For a while before I went to bed, I thought I might need another one of those sedatives, but I calmed myself and had only a cup of warm milk that Mrs. Duval brought to me at Mrs. Caro's insistence.

"Is Mr. March home?" I asked out of curiosity.

"Not yet," she said.

I thought he might not come home, that maybe he had gone to spend the night or the next few days with one of his girlfriends, but he did come home very late. He woke me up when I heard him practically pounding the stairs and the hallway floors. He must have been drinking, because he shouted something nasty, too. I listened to see if Jordan was going to come out to confront him, but she must have taken one of her sedatives. I lay back again and closed my eyes. I really was looking forward to returning to school now. I needed to get back into the world out there, if only to escape from the turmoil here.

Hours later, I woke when I thought I heard my door open and close.

"Jordan?" I called. She didn't respond.

I started to sit up, and Donald suddenly appeared at the side of my bed. I was shocked. He was standing there dressed only in his underwear. In the light from a moon caught behind the haze of thin clouds coming through my windows, his eyes looked luminescent. He stared down at me with a crooked smile on his face. For a moment, he wobbled, and then he sat hard on my bed. It was more as if he collapsed on it.

"What's wrong?" I asked.

"Oh, don't you worry," he said. He looked back toward the doorway and then at me again. "You'll be fine no matter what she and her lawyer do. You're too precious to abandon."

"Why are you here?" I wanted to add, *and in your underwear,* but I didn't dare.

"I was thinking about you, just lying there above you, right above you, and thinking about how alone and frightened you must be down here."

"I'm okay," I said quickly, trying to dismiss him, but he acted as if he hadn't heard me. He leaned toward me, and I could smell the whiskey on his breath.

"You have had bad luck when it comes to men. You just haven't had the right guidance. Remember? Remember how I said I was going to take better care of you, spend more time with you, take you places, wonderful, beautiful, expensive places? I will," he said, and he put his hand on my shoulder and fingered my hair. "You're too precious to abandon or to leave with her."

"I'm all right, Donald," I said more insistently. "Please, just go to sleep."

"Sure, you'll be fine. Sure," he said. "Don't worry. I bet you've been full of worry about what would happen to you now since she created this Third World War. You don't worry," he muttered, and then brought his lips to my forehead so quickly I couldn't avoid him. His hand slipped down my arm to my waist as his lips went to my nose. I started to pull away, but his grip on my waist tightened, and then he practically fell forward on me, pressing his mouth against mine while his hand moved up and over my breast. I struggled, pushing up on his chest with all my might.

"Don't be frightened," he said. "I'll show you how you'll be cared for and loved. You'll know you need not worry. Let me show you."

"Stop!" I cried. He had moved my blanket back to slide his legs under.

"I'll keep you with me. You don't have to stay with her," he said, pressing his cheek against mine.

I continued to push and squirm, but he was so heavy, and the stink of his whiskey was turning my stomach. Then he suddenly licked my face as if I were an ice-cream cone, and that put me into more panic. When his hand started to pull at my nightgown, I turned my head and screamed as loudly as I could. I knew these walls were thick, and as I thought before, Jordan was putting herself to sleep every night now with a pill. No one would hear me and come to help me. I was crying harder and still pushing at him, even trying to dig my nails into his body, but nothing was working.

"Don't be afraid," he pleaded. "Shh, shh . . ."

His hands were groping me everywhere. I was growing exhausted with the effort to push him away. I felt myself slipping, and I was terrified that I would pass out. When I felt his hardness searching between my legs, I reached out to my right and grasped the neck of the bottle. I had been sleeping with it beside me. He was moaning and mumbling all sorts of promises when I swung the bottle and struck him in the back of his head. Miraculously, the bottle did not shatter, but Donald was stunned enough to stop. I was able to slip out from under him.

"Get away from me!" I shouted. "Leave me alone!" I held the bottle up like a club, shaking, gasping.

In his clumsy effort to lift himself, he fell off my bed. I sat back, turned on my nighttable lamp, and clutched my knees against my chest defensively. I watched him as he battled to get to his feet. He looked at me, realizing what he had done, I think, because his expression changed. He looked more like himself. He shook his head and turned and stumbled toward the door. Just as he reached it, it opened, and Jordan stood there in her bathrobe.

"What are you doing in here like that?" she shouted at him.

He stumbled past her and out. She flicked on more light and looked at me. I was sobbing hysterically.

"Oh, my God," she said, and rushed to me. She embraced me and rocked with me. "I'm so sorry," she said.

She didn't have to ask for any details. I was still gasping too hard to speak anyway.

"He won't come near you again. I'll make sure of that. I promise. Oh, you poor child, you poor child."

The tears rushed from my eyes so quickly that I thought I would never stop crying. Nasty and ugly images from the past came attached to every tear. I saw my nearly unrecognizable mother trekking along on the beach, dragging her bag of old clothes and tools for calligraphy. I saw us being hit by Kiera's car that rainy night, and I saw the images of my hospital stay. I saw Kiera and her friends tricking me into getting that painful tattoo, and I saw myself struggling to avoid being raped on the boat.

"I'm afraid," I finally said.

"Yes, you are, and you should be," Jordan said. "Don't worry. I'm staying with you. He'll be out of here in the morning or else," she promised, and she took off her slippers and robe and lay beside me.

It took quite a while for me to calm down. She spoke to me softly, held me, stroked my hair. When I looked at her, my mother seemed to slip in and out of her. Finally, I fell asleep again, this time with her hand in mine.

When I woke in the morning, Jordan was already up and gone. I heard footsteps in the hallway, and I heard Jordan shouting orders at someone. I rose slowly and went to my door to peer out. Alberto and two of his men were carrying suitcases and garment bags down the hallway. Mrs. Duval followed, and then I saw Jordan and opened the door wider.

"What's happening?"

She stopped in front of me. "I want him out of the house. After what he tried to do to you, he put up no resistance."

"Where's he going?"

"I don't care. If he wants to come back for anything after this, he has to call first to let us know. It's either this or I call the police and have you talk to them."

Of course, she was right to be in a rage. I was still more frightened than angry about it. Jordan looked at my face.

"Don't you get like some of these women who find a reason to blame themselves. You did nothing to encourage this, Sasha. I had a bad feeling about his attitude toward you when he bought you that expensive necklace and talked about taking you places. As it turns out, he was unable, if I'm to believe him, to get three tickets to the concert he wanted to take us to. Remember that? Turns out that there were only two tickets, and guess who would be left home?"

She looked toward the stairway.

"It's his way," she said. "He often cut me out of things after Alena's death. He was always taking Kiera here and there and coming up with reasons why I couldn't or shouldn't go along. He gave Kiera plenty of expensive presents, too."

What was she saying?

"But surely, you don't think . . ."

"I don't put anything past him," she said. "I'll send Mrs. Duval up with your breakfast."

"No. I'd rather get dressed and go down," I said.

"Good. Neither of us will be sickly, pathetic, and weak now."

She walked off with a determined gait, the anger, grit, and fortitude so evident that I thought I could see it floating down through her legs to strengthen each step she took. My mind was spinning because of the speed with which everything was happening. It was as if I was in a real California earthquake, only in this one, the trembling was coming out of my heart, where the fault line had always been.

I closed the door and hurried to shower and dress. Just before I went down to breakfast, I paused at my computer. Maybe I did have Mrs. Caro's sixth sense. I turned it on and waited for my e-mail to show. There were a number of messages from the girls at school, three from Jessica alone, of course, but there it was, Kiera's.

I highlighted it and went to it.

Like before, it was short and nasty.

*I bet you're happy now.*

# ❧ 20 ❧

## *Recovery*

One of the first things Jordan decided to do was literally take over Donald's office. She was in there first thing in the morning to begin her education. She wanted to be as intelligent as she could be whenever it came to any aspect of their fortune. I went in to watch her after breakfast. She had papers piled on the desk and was sorting them out in separate piles on one of the tables. As she worked, she mumbled to herself. Finally, she realized I was there, too.

"Oh. Did you have breakfast?"

"Yes."

She looked around. "I can tell you this, Sasha. I am not going to be one of those weak, pathetic women who look like terrified, injured kittens when the whole thing is over. And if one more of my so-called friends tells me how sorry she is for me, I'll scream so loudly in the phone that it will break her eardrum. Feel sorry for Donald, I'll tell her. He's the pathetic creature, not me."

She paused, seeing the look of shock on my face. I

had never seen her this intense. I hoped her anger wasn't making her so crazy that Donald would get the better of her.

"Sorry I'm shouting," she said, and sat hard in the desk chair. "You know, I actually found some names and numbers of the girls he was seeing in different parts of the country. They were right here in his top drawer. How's that for chutzpah? You know what that is?"

"Bold, nervy?"

She smiled and took a deep breath, finally calming herself a bit. "Seems like you're in the middle of a hurricane, I know. I am sorry about that," she said. "I really am."

"I don't see how you could be blamed for anything." I hesitated and then decided to say it. "Besides, Kiera is already blaming me."

"What do you mean?"

"She sent me a one-sentence e-mail this morning."

"Which was?"

" 'I bet you're happy now.' "

Jordan lowered her head to think a moment and then looked up. "I don't know what I'll do about her now. She's old enough to make her own decisions legally, and she has quite a trust fund that Donald insisted she be able to access when she was twenty-one, even though we knew she would not be finished with college, if she ever finishes. Now that I no longer want to be the obedient little rich wife and mother, I feel obligated to make her see how imperfect her supposedly perfect father is. I gave in too quickly on everything, and I felt sorry for Donald, too, after we lost Alena. I guess I let him get away with far too much. He took advantage of my sympathy.

"I am sorry now about the way he treated Ryder Garfield," she continued. "Perhaps if I had been more sympathetic to Ryder's problems, none of this might have happened."

"You did what you thought was right," I said. "Anyway, you shouldn't blame yourself."

I thought I knew what was bothering her. It was understandable.

"When you called Kiera and spoke to her roommate, you couldn't keep that information from Ryder's parents. It would have been irresponsible of you, maybe even illegal."

"Excuse me?" she said, pulling herself back in the chair. "Kiera's roommate? When did Kiera get a roommate? She had such trouble with the girls in her dorm ever since she was enrolled that I didn't think she would ever get another roommate."

"But she went to Europe with them last summer."

"No, she didn't go to Europe with them. She went on a group trip Donald arranged to match the one the school was doing. Did she tell you something different?"

"She has to have a roommate now," I insisted. "Whom did you speak with when you called looking for us?"

"I never called, Sasha. I don't understand what you're saying. I thought you knew what had happened."

I felt the blood draining from my face.

"Oh, my God," Jordan said, realizing. "Kiera told you I called?"

I nodded. "What did happen, then?" I asked.

"Kiera called Donald and told him she had just found out that Ryder Garfield was going to meet you at the motel. She claimed she knew nothing about it and didn't want him blaming her. She told him exactly where you were, room number and all, and said she was sorry she had planned this special outing. She had been expecting it to be only you and her.

"He called me immediately, raging about it. He said he called Dr. Steiner to see if Ryder had indeed left the school. She had just discovered that he had and had just called his parents. Donald told her exactly where Ryder was going, and Dr. Steiner called his parents with the information.

"Of course, I don't think any of us imagined that Ryder would be so distraught that he would take his own life. No matter what was going on in that family, no parent would want to lose a child that way."

I really thought for a moment that I had lost the ability to move, even to swallow.

"You knew how adamant Donald was about it all," she continued. "Of course, I wonder now what really motivated him, just as I wondered what truly motivated him to buy you that expensive necklace."

"I don't want it," I said. "Sell it, and give the money to some charity, to the homeless."

She did look different behind Donald's desk; she did look stronger, and that took the trembling out of my body.

"What are you going to do today?" she asked as I started out of the office.

I thought a moment. "Get off my knees. I'm not making and selling lanyards anymore."

I didn't elaborate to take the look of confusion off her face. That would have to come later, I thought, and went upstairs to get my things together.

I wrote a note for Jordan, explaining that I wouldn't be able to have dinner with her. I asked her not to worry about me and pinned the note to the outside of my door, and then I left the house quietly. Alberto had parked my car in the garage the day Donald had picked me up at school. As unobtrusively as I could, I got in, started it up, and drove away. A short time later, I was on the freeway heading north to Kiera's school.

There is an old saying Donald actually uses. *Fool me once, shame on you. Fool me twice, shame on me.*

In the back of my mind, I could hear my mother softly chastising me.

*"Remember the safety valve? Remember being skeptical? Remember me telling you that the world is divided into two kinds of people, the gullible and the deceptive? It's only good and sensible self-defense to be distrusting and a little deceptive yourself. This isn't paradise yet. We're always in one danger or another, no matter where we are. Remember all that?"*

*"Yes, Mama, I do,"* I said. *"I was a fool."*

After nearly two hours, my cell phone rang. I saw that it was Jordan, but I didn't answer it. She would only ask me to turn around and come home. I knew she would be angry and disappointed in me, but I was as determined to do what I had to do as she was determined to do what she had to do. I hoped she would understand.

It started to rain, which made driving more difficult on the freeway. When I was taking driving lessons, my instructor always groaned at the sight of rain and went into a tirade about how people here didn't know how to drive in the rain. They didn't slow down, and they could easily lose control because the roads could get as slippery as roads with ice.

"Stay farther back," he'd advise.

The one thing I didn't want to happen now was a car accident. I heard his warning and dropped my speed. It was dreary and slow for the next two hours, and then the rain stopped and the clouds began breaking up. Weather changes in this part of California could come quickly. When I reached dry road, I sped up. I wanted to get there before it was dark.

Kiera's college had a population that wasn't much larger than the student body at Pacifica. All her life, she had enjoyed special treatment in ideal places. Her college reeked of privilege and wealth. Set off the main road in a beautiful rustic area with Monterey pine trees and perfect manicured grounds of rich green grass and flower beds and fountains, the college had two main buildings for classrooms and administration. To the left and right of them were the dorms. All of them looked like real residences, with pretty shutters, arched windows, and soft, light blue siding. There were walkways and bicycle paths linking every structure. Right now, young men and women were walking and talking, riding their bikes, or just sitting on the benches to get the last warm rays of a retreating sun. I saw the parking spaces for guests and pulled into one.

When I stepped out, there were two women who looked more like teachers than students walking by. I asked for directions to Kiera's dorm and headed toward it quickly. When I walked in, there were four girls in the small lobby talking. It looked as if they had all just returned from classes. They still carried books. Everyone turned to look at me.

"Hi," I said. "I'm looking for Kiera March."

"Try any rock outside," a tall, dark-haired girl said. They all laughed.

"Excuse me?"

"She's usually under a rock," the girl next to the dark-haired girl said. Everyone smiled.

"Well, right now, she might be in her room," I said. "Which way, please?"

"Just take the stairway on your right," a girl with pretty light red hair and green eyes said. "Her room is the first on the left upstairs. You can't miss it. On the door, she has a sign that says 'Keep Out.'"

"Yeah, like anyone would want to go in," the tall girl said. They all widened their smiles.

"Really, do you know if she's here?"

"We don't keep track of her," the redhaired girl said softly.

I started to walk toward the stairway and stopped, turning back to them. "Why do you all dislike her so much?" I asked.

"Are you related?" the tall girl asked.

"No."

"What did she do, try to steal your boyfriend?" she asked.

I started to shake my head and stopped. "I guess in a way, she did," I said.

They all lost their smiles.

Something else occurred to me. "Did she always have a room upstairs? I mean, did she move recently?"

"No. It's one of the few single rooms," the redhead replied. "There are only four in this dorm, and they're all upstairs."

But she had written that she was on the first floor, I thought, and in one e-mail claimed that was why she was able to sneak Richard Nandi Chenik into her room. I took a step back toward them.

"I don't know why she would be stealing other girls' boyfriends. Doesn't she have a boyfriend, someone she's been seeing for quite a while? A boy who goes to school here?"

No one spoke.

"A boy from England? Maybe some of you know him. Richard Nandi Chenik?"

They all looked at one another.

"This is a pretty small school," the dark-haired girl said. "There's no one named Richard Nandi Chenik from England."

"Who are you?" the redhaired girl asked me, more interested now.

They all waited for my answer.

"Another victim," I said, and headed for the stairway.

I paused in front of her door. The sign was there. It was probably her way of convincing herself that she had to fight off friends. Things had obviously turned sour very quickly for Kiera at this school. I was surprised that she continued to attend, although if she hadn't, she would have risked everyone learning how unpopular she really was. She had been used to being a star at Pacifica and probably came on too strong here, where there were girls who were just as sophisticated and as self-confident, if not more so.

I knocked on the door. There was no response, so I tried the door handle, and it turned and opened.

The room was dark because the shades were drawn on the two windows, and there were no lights on. I saw her in her bed, lying on her stomach. I waited to see if she had heard me enter, but she was apparently asleep, dressed in jeans and a black sweatshirt. I looked for a light switch and then closed the door softly. She didn't wake even when I turned on the lights.

I picked up the chair at her desk and set it down where I could sit and look at her. For a moment, I wondered if she had taken some drugs and maybe overdosed again, but her eyelids fluttered and opened. She stared at me without speaking and slowly pushed herself up, the confusion twisting her face. She sat back against the headboard.

"What the hell are you doing here?" she asked.

"I came to ask you why you did it," I said. She started to speak, and I quickly added, "Don't say, 'Did what?'"

"So my father told you everything, is that it? I can't believe you drove up."

"I wanted to look at you when you answered, Kiera. I wanted to see what was in your face so I would know what was in your heart. Do you have a heart?"

"Oh, don't go into any of that," she said.

"What?"

"Analysis."

"I won't. Analysis implies wanting to help you. I don't want to help you. I was just curious. I remember all those nice things you said after you almost died taking that drug. I remember how you cried and how you apologized and told me about your nightmares. I remember how much you said you missed your little sister and regretted not spending more time with her and being kind to her. I remember your great desire to be my older sister, to be my pal. I remember it all, Kiera, down to every last syllable you spoke and every promise you made."

"Don't you talk to me like that. I did try to be a big sister to you, and what did you do? You tried to take my place."

"Take your place? Where?"

"In my house! In my father's eyes! You were the good one, the perfect new daughter, outstanding in school, playing Alena's clarinet so well, getting the best grades, charming him into buying you that car and jewelry, and when that wasn't enough, you tempted him to come to your bedroom."

"What? Is that what he said?"

"He didn't have to say it. I know."

"What did I ever do to make you think such a thing?"

"It's all right," she said, nodding. "I know."

"So this was why you called to tell him about Ryder? You were trying to make me look bad again? That didn't work the first time you tried. Why did you think it would work now?"

She didn't answer.

"You planned it all, didn't you? You talked me into getting Ryder to meet me at the motel, all along plotting to turn us in, right?"

"I was sick of hearing him tell me how smart you were, how talented, and how beautiful you were becoming," she admitted. "He never gave me credit for being smart. Yes, he told me I was beautiful, but not like he talked about you. You were exotically beautiful, special, a weed that became a rose. And my mother . . . I told myself that if she bragged one more time about you, I would curse her so badly that she wouldn't speak to me again. At least, it would stop."

"Don't you realize what you've done? What a terrible thing you caused to happen?"

"It probably would have happened anyway. If anything, you should be thanking me for getting you out of what would have been a big mess later."

"You can tell yourself that to make yourself feel better if you like, but you know it's a lie. Your whole life is built on lies. That's all you know. You're pathetic, even more pathetic than I first thought when I saw you after the accident."

I stood up.

"Don't go off feeling superior," she said. Her eyes were glassy, teary. "You aren't any different from me. You're just better at hiding it."

"If that were true, I'd follow Ryder into the bottle right now."

"Bottle? What bottle?"

"You wouldn't understand."

"You don't scare me with your weird talk," she said.

"I don't want to scare you. I came up here to bash your head in, but I see now that even that wouldn't make any difference."

"Ha. You'll call me again."

"Really? And where would I call, Kiera? Would I have to call England? Is Richard ever coming back, or has he left your imagination for good?"

Her lips trembled.

"You couldn't find anyone to love you in reality, so you made someone up."

"Liar!" she screamed.

"You told your mother all those fantasies and sent me those ridiculous e-mails. Remember? Remember how you snuck him into your room easily because it was on the first floor? Your dorm mates told me you've always been up here."

"They're lying. Everyone's lying because they're jealous. They're jealous!"

She was still screaming when I closed the door behind me.

I looked at her sign again.

*Keep out.*

Her tragedy was that she never let anyone in—not her mother, not her father, really, and maybe worst of all, not her little sister, who must have tried so hard to open the door.

## ❧ *Epilogue* ❧

I didn't see Kiera for the remainder of the school year. Not long after I left her dorm, she had what Jordan described to her friends as a nervous breakdown. She didn't want to get into the technical diagnosis involving an anxiety-depressive disorder. She couldn't remain at the college. Jordan made Donald handle the situation. He found a good clinic in Oregon, far enough away to help him pretend she was simply at another school.

I did graduate as the valedictorian. I didn't expect to see Donald there, but when I got up to speak, I saw him way in the back of the audience, standing as unobtrusively as he could. Since the night he had come into my bedroom drunk, we rarely saw each other, and when we did, his gaze always shifted quickly from mine. He fumbled with an awkward apology that I thought was more a demand of Jordan's than his own desire. I listened and just said, "Okay."

What else was there to say? Anything more would have led to more discussion and maybe his belief that I was forgiving enough for him really to reenter my life. I didn't want that.

He didn't put up any resistance to Jordan's legally adopting me, not that he could have. She went through the divorce, getting just about everything she wanted in the settlement. She didn't want to remain at the estate, but she made it seem as if that was her compromise. She found a beautiful home in Beverly Hills. Of course, it was far more modest, but almost anything else in California would be.

Her graduation gift to me was that she and I would travel to London for sightseeing and then on to Paris and the south of France. I had decided to remain in Los Angeles and chose to attend Occidental. I wanted to remain close to Mama's grave and visit it from time to time. I also overcame my aversion to the places on the beach where she and I had slept and sold our arts and crafts.

A few times, I went to the beach where Ryder and I had spent part of an afternoon. I sat about where I thought we had sat and just looked out at the ocean and watched the terns and pelicans. It reminded me of Mrs. Caro's description of the sweet silence. It took time, of course, time and all the distractions Jordan provided for me, but slowly, hope seeped back into me.

Maybe in that way, I was doing what I dreamed Ryder predicted.

Maybe I was going into his precious bottle.

And maybe, as he said, we were on his ship sailing to a place where no one could harm us again.

After all, wasn't that what we all dreamed we would find?

Pocket Star Books
Proudly Presents

# *INTO THE DARKNESS*

## V.C. Andrews®

Available in paperback
March 2012
from Pocket Star Books

Turn the page for a preview of
*Into the Darkness . . .*

# ❦ *Prologue* ❦

*H*e was looking at me from between the full evergreen hedges that separated our houses and properties. I don't know why he thought I wouldn't see him. Although, it was what Mom called a crown jewels day because there were no clouds and the bright sunshine made everything glimmer and glisten, even dull rocks and old cars with faded paint, scratches, nicks, and dents. The sun was behind me so I wasn't blinded by its brilliance. In fact, it was like a spotlight reflecting off his twenty-four-karat-gold hair.

Even from where I was standing on our front porch, I could see he had blue-sapphire eyes. He had a very fair complexion, close to South Sea pearl, in fact, so that his face seemed to have a hazy, soft glow, which contrasted dramatically with the rich, deep green leaves of the hedges.

My first thought was that there must be something mentally wrong with him. Who else would stand there gaping at someone unashamedly? When someone stares at you and doesn't care that you see him doing so, you're certainly ill at ease, even fearful. You might be angry, but nowadays, especially, you don't go picking fights with strangers. He wasn't a complete stranger, of course. I knew he was our new neighbor.

I had no idea whether he had been spying on me from the very first day that his family had moved into their house, but this was the first time I had caught him doing so. Because the hedges were easily five and a half feet high and he was crouching a little, I estimated that he was at least five feet ten inches tall. He was wearing dark blue jeans and a long-sleeve khaki shirt with epaulets, the sort of shirt you might find in a store selling military uniforms.

For a few moments, I pretended not to have noticed him. I looked away and then sat on the wide blue moonstone porch railing and leaned back against the post as if I were posing for a sexy dramatic shot in a film. I closed my eyes and took a deep breath like when the doctor tells you to breathe in and hold it while he moves his stethoscope over your back. My breasts lifted against my thin, light jade-green sweater and I held the air in my lungs for nearly thirty seconds. Then, as if some film director were telling me to look more relaxed and more seductive for the shot, I released my breath and brought my right hand up to fluff my thick black-opal shoulder-length hair.

For as long as I could remember, my family always described most colors in terms of jewels. My parents owned a jewelry store that had been established by my paternal grandparents in Echo Lake, Oregon, more than forty years ago. My grandfather taught my father how to make original jewelry, and most people who saw them said that he created beautiful pieces. My mother ran the business end of our store and was the main salesperson. Dad called her his personal CFO. I helped out from the day I could handle credit-card sales. Rings, necklaces, bracelets, earrings, and pendants found their way into almost any conversation at our dinner table. Nothing was just good in our world; it was as good as gold. Many things had a silver lining, and if something glittered, it glittered like diamonds.

Mom said my hair was truly opal because it was just as unique as the jewel. The color and the pattern of opals could change with the angle of view, and she claimed that the same was true for my hair.

"No one that I know has hair that changes color as subtly as yours does, Amber, especially in the sunlight." She took a deep breath and shook her head softly. "I swear, sweetheart, sometimes when I'm looking for you and see you from behind, I'm not sure it's you. Just as I am about to call out to you, your name gets caught in my mouth as if my tongue had second thoughts."

Dad wasn't as dramatic about it, but he didn't disagree. Mom was often histrionic. She had a bit of a Southern drawl and was a beautiful platinum brown-haired woman who had once gone for a screen test at Screen Gems Studios in Wilmington, North Carolina, when she was still in high school because a young assistant producer had convinced her she could be the next Natalie Wood. She didn't get hired, but it was her moment in the sun. Dad was proud of her head shots and kept four of them on his desk at home.

I wondered if the boy next door would notice how my

hair color subtly changed when I sat up and then walked slowly off the porch and into the sunlight. No one but my parents had ever mentioned it, although people did compliment me on the richness of my hair. I kept my arms folded just below my breasts and walked with my head down like someone in very deep thought, someone who was oblivious to anything and everything going on around her. I was barefoot and wore an ankle-length light blue cotton skirt and a gold ankle bracelet with tiny rubies. I was taking every step pensively as if the weight of a major decision were wrapped over my shoulders like a shawl full of great and desperate concerns. I guess I was always in some pose or another because I lived so much in my imagination. Dad always said I lived in my own movie.

"You're just like all you kids nowadays, always in one sort of performance or another," he said. "I watch the girls walking home from school. You could see everyone is glancing around to see 'Who is looking at me?' Those girls with green, blue, and orange hair and rings in their noses drive me nuts."

"Don't knock the nose rings, Gregory Taylor. We sell them," Mom told him.

"Whatever happened to the au naturel look, the Ingrid Bergman look?" Dad cried, throwing up his arms. He had an artist's long, muscular fingers and arms that would have no trouble grabbing the golden ring on a merry-go-round. He was six feet two, slim, with what Mom called a Clark Gable mustache and jet-black hair with thin smoky gray strands leaking along his temples. He was rarely out in the sunlight during the summer to get a tan, but he had a natural dark complexion that brought out the jade blue in his eyes.

"Ingrid who?" I asked. I knew who she was. Both Mom and I just liked teasing him and suggesting that he was showing his age.

At that point, he would shake his head and either sit and pout or leave the room, and Mom and I would laugh like two conspirators. He wasn't really that angry, but it was part of the game we all liked to play. Dad was always claiming to be outnumbered and outvoted in his own home, whether it was a discussion of new furniture, dishes, drapes, or even cars. That comment would bring smiles but inevitably remind us that four years after I was born, Mom had miscarried in her seventh month. I would have had a brother. They seemed to have given up after that.

It was great having my parents' full attention, but I would have liked to have had a brother or a sister. I told myself I wouldn't fight with either or be jealous or be anything like most of the girls I knew when it came to their siblings. Their stories made it sound as if their homes rocked with screams and wails about unfair treatment or one being favored over the other. I could only wail or complain about myself to myself. It was like living in an echo chamber.

From what I could tell, the boy next door probably was an only child, too. I was certainly not spying on him and his parents, but my bedroom window looked out over the hedges at his house, and I couldn't help but see the goings-on. Days before, I was in my bedroom reading one of the books on my summer requirement list when I heard the truck arrive and saw the men begin to unload cartons. I had never really been in the house since the last people living there had left, but I recalled Dad saying they had left furniture.

Seeing new neighbors suddenly move in was a great surprise. My parents had never mentioned the neighboring house being sold or rented. No one had, in fact, and news like that in a community as small as ours usually made headlines. There were just too many busybodies to let a tidbit like that go unrevealed.

At first, I didn't even see that the neighbors had a son. His parents appeared along with the truck and the men. I didn't get that good a look at them, but the woman looked tall and very thin. She kept her opened left hand over the left side of her face, like someone who didn't want to be recognized, and hurried into the house as if she were caught in a cold downpour of rain and hail. Her husband was about the same height, balding, and I thought a little chubby, with an agate-brown goatee and glasses with frames as thick as silver dollars that caught the sunlight. He walked more slowly, moving like someone in deep thought. I wondered when they had first come around to look at the house. It had to have been a very quick decision.

After the movers began to bring things into the house, the boy suddenly appeared, as if he had been pouting in the backseat like someone who had been forced to come along. I didn't get that good a look at him, either. He had his head down and also walked quickly, but my first thought was that he was probably a spoiled only child, pouting, angry about having to leave his school and friends. Of course, he could have an older sister who was either at a college summer session or perhaps studying abroad.

I watched on and off as the move-in continued, the men carrying in clothing and some small appliances. It didn't take them very long. I waited to see more of the neighbors. No one emerged, and I didn't see the boy again until this day. As a matter of fact, I didn't see any of them. It was as if they had been swallowed up by the house. The moving men came out and drove off only an hour or so later. Immediately, it grew as quiet as it had been. None of the windows was opened, and no lights were turned on. One might think they had gone in the front door and out the back, never to be seen or heard from again.

Right now, I knelt down on my bright green lawn pretending to look for a four-leaf clover, but out of the corner of my eye, I was watching to see whether he would move away from the hedges or continue to spy on me. He never changed expression or turned his head away for an instant. Finally, I stood up abruptly and, with my heart racing, said, "Can I help you?"

I remained far enough away that I could quickly retreat to my house and lock the door behind me if need be.

He smiled. "What did you have in mind?" he replied.

"I'm not the one peeping," I said. "Maybe I should say gawking."

"Maybe you're not at this moment, but I've seen you looking for minutes at a time in my direction out your bedroom window between the curtains."

"That's different," I said, smothering my embarrassment. I had thought I was inconspicuous about my curiosity. And when had he seen me? I never caught sight of him or any of them looking out a window toward our house.

"And that's different because?"

"I was just . . . interested in who was to be our new neighbors. Who wouldn't be?"

"And I'm just curious about you. Who wouldn't be once he saw how pretty you are?" he asked.

I felt myself blush. Dad always said I didn't blush red so much as a cross between the translucent golden yellow of a bangle and a touch of a pink coral bead. Mom said he was color-blind for a jeweler and that I had more of a classic deep red ruby tint in my cheeks when I blushed. Both agreed that I normally had a light pink Akoya pearl complexion with a face that was truly a cameo because of my perfect diminutive features, especially my slightly almond-shaped eyes and soft Cupid's bow lips, all of which I had inherited from Mom.

"Well, you don't have to spy on me through the hedges," I said in a less belligerent tone. "You could have just come by to say hello and introduce yourself properly."

Although my parents and their friends always lavished great compliments on me, I was never sure of myself when it came to responding to one. A simple "Thank you" seemed to be too little. Not saying anything seemed to be arrogant, as if I was thinking my beauty was obvious, or I was too stuck up to respond. And pretending to be surprised and falsely modest always came off as phony, at least when I saw other girls and even boys doing that. I didn't deny to myself that I was attractive. I just didn't know whether I should rejoice in my blessings or be concerned about the responsibilities they brought along with them.

I know none of my girlfriends at school would understand how being attractive brought responsibilities, but I always felt obligated to make sure that I didn't flaunt myself or take anything anyone said for granted. I also felt I had to be careful about whom I showed any interest in, even looked at twice. People, especially older men, were always telling me I would be a heartbreaker. To me, that didn't sound very nice. I envisioned a trail of men with shattered emotions threatening to commit suicide everywhere I went.

"You're absolutely right," the new boy said. He stepped between the hedges and approached. I was right about his height. He was at least five feet ten, if not eleven. With the palms of both hands and his fingers stiffly extended, he brushed back his hair. Uneven strands still fell over his forehead and his eyes. His hair was almost as long as mine and certainly looked as thick and as rich. He had perfectly shaped facial features like those of Greek and Roman statues. I thought he had a remarkable complexion, not a blemish, not a dark spot or anything to spoil the softness and smoothness. For a moment, I wondered if he wore makeup. He wasn't heavily built, but he looked athletic, like a swimmer or a tennis player.

"I apologize for, as you say, gawking at you. I didn't intend to make you feel uncomfortable. Although," he added with an impish smile, "you didn't quite look uncomfortable. Matter of fact, you looked like you were enjoying it."

Before I could respond, he performed a dramatic stage bow and added, "I'm Brayden Matthews." He extended his hand awkwardly, as if he wasn't sure it was something he should do.

"Amber Taylor. And I wasn't enjoying it. I was uncomfortable seeing someone staring at me like that. Actually, I tried to ignore you."

He kept holding his hand out.

"I'm glad you couldn't," he said.

I offered my hand. He closed his fingers around it very gently, watching his fingers fold around mine as if he was amazed that his could bend or he was afraid that he might break mine. Then he smiled like someone who had felt something very satisfying, as if shaking someone's hand was a significant accomplishment. He tightened his grip a little and didn't let go.

"Can I have my hand back?"

"So soon?" he replied. He let go and then looked up at our house. "Your house is one of the older houses on the street, right? Not that it looks rundown or anything. Matter of fact, it looks quite well cared for."

"It's the oldest on the street," I said as modestly as I could. My father was always bragging about it. "It's been in our family for a little more than eighty-five years," I said. "Of course, there have been many renovations, but the first fireplace still stands just the way it was. The floors are the same, as are the window casings. My father treats it more like a historical site."

"I bet. There was a time when things were built to last," he said.

"Really? How old are you, ninety, a hundred?"

He softly laughed, flashed me an amused look, and then

gazed at my house again, concentrating, I thought, on my bedroom windows. "I bet you can see the lake from your window." He turned to look at his own roof. "Your house looks to be about ten feet taller than ours."

"Yes, I can," I said. "At least the bay. This time of the year, the trees are so full they block out most of it."

The lake was only a little more than a half-mile from our street, but it was a privately owned lake, anyway. Because our homes weren't lake homes, we weren't shareholders in the Echo Lake Corporation. Most everyone who didn't belong thought the people who did were snobby about their property and their rights, but I thought these people were simply jealous. It was true that no one without lake rights could swim, row, or fish there. You had to be invited by a member, but what would be the point of having a private lake and expensive lakeside property otherwise? We had been invited from time to time. Most recently, the Mallens invited us for a picnic on the lake. George Mallen was president of the Echo Lake bank, and Dad always gave him good deals on the jewelry that he bought for his wife and two older daughters, both married and living in Portland.

"So I guess you've lived here all your life," he said.

"Yes, that's a safe conclusion to make."

He laughed again. I could see that he really enjoyed talking to me. It was like sparring with words.

"Where are you from?" I asked.

"Oh, somewhere out there," he replied, waving his right hand over his shoulder. "We've lived in so many different places that the U.S. Postal Service has declared us undesirables. They're still trying to deliver mail sent to us ten years ago."

"Very funny, but you had to be born somewhere, right?"

"I think it was on a jet crossing the Indian Ocean," he replied. "Luckily, we were in first class. I'm a sea baby, or more of an air baby. Yes, that's it. I'm from the international air above the Taj Mahal."

"Sure. Your parents are Americans, aren't they?" I asked, not so sure.

"Yes."

"Then you're an American."

"Very constitutional of you." He looked at my window again. "My bedroom faces yours, you know. Yours is about six inches higher but diametrically opposite."

"Thanks for the warning, now that I know you're a Peeping Tom."

He laughed.

"I wasn't peeping, really, as much as I was wondering if you would see me."

"I'd have to be either blind or terribly oblivious."

"Well, I'm glad you're not either."

"Why was it so important to test me about that?"

He looked stymied for an answer. "I'm sorry. You're right. It was juvenile and not the best way to make a new friend." He looked afraid that I would end the conversation or continue to take him to task.

"Apology accepted," I said.

"Whew." He wiped his forehead. I couldn't help but smile at his exaggerated action.

"Okay, we don't know where you're from, but what

made your parents decide to move here of all places?"

"Why? Is it that bad here? You make it sound like the last stop on the train or the edge of the world."

"No, it's far from bad here. I just wondered. We don't get that many new families these days."

"I think my father put a map on the wall, blindfolded himself, and threw a dart. It hit Echo Lake, Oregon."

"You're kidding, right?"

He nodded and smiled. "It's what he tells people. My father has a dry sense of humor."

"Brayden," we heard. It was a woman's voice, but she sounded very far-off. "Bray . . . den." In fact, it seemed she was calling from inside a tunnel, and she sounded a little desperate, almost in a panic.

His smile evaporated. "Gotta go," he said. "It's been nice talking to you, and I apologize again for being a Gawking Tom."

"I'll settle for Peeping Tom. Who's calling you?"

"My mother. We're still moving in. Lots to do. Help with unpacking, setting things up, rearranging and cleaning up the furniture that was there, and organizing the kitchen," he listed quickly. He leaned toward me to whisper, "My dad's not too handy around the house." He pointed to his temple. "Intellectual type, you know. Thinks a screwdriver is only a glass of orange juice and vodka."

"I'm sure he's not that bad. What does he do?"

"He's a member of a brain trust. Meets with other geniuses to discuss and solve world economic problems. All quite hush-hush, top-secret stuff, so secret that he doesn't know what he's talking about."

"What?"

He laughed again. "I wasn't kidding about our living in many places. Often we go on family trips to foreign countries and around the country, when he's going to be away for a prolonged time, that is."

"Do you have any brothers or sisters?"

"None that I know of," he replied with a sly smile. "You're an only child, too, I take it, and your parents own a jewelry store on Main Street, a jewelry store that has been in your family for decades."

"You did some homework?"

"I've scouted the neighborhood. A few interesting people live on this block, especially that elderly lady who hangs her clothes on a line at the side of her house, visible to anyone walking in the street."

"Mrs. Carden. What about her? What makes her so interesting? Many people like to hang out their clothes in the fresh air. Mrs. Carden's not unique."

Mrs. Carden was an eighty-something retired grade-school teacher who had lived for ten years as a widow and never had any children of her own. She would smile and nod at me when I walked by, but I didn't think I had spoken a dozen words to her in the past five years. I was curious about why someone new would find her interesting.

"Oh, I think she is quite unique," he insisted.

"Why?"

"She whispers to her clothes as if they were errant children, scolding a blouse for being too wrinkled or a skirt for shrinking. I think she put a pair of stockings in the corner, sort of a time-out for wearing too thin or something.

Maybe that's something a grade-school teacher would do, but I've always found people who hold discussions with inanimate objects unique, don't you?"

"Errant children?"

"Hang around with me. I'll build your vocabulary," he said, winking.

"If she was whispering, how did you hear her? Were you spying on her, too?"

"A little, but I have twenty-twenty hearing," he kidded. "So watch what you whisper about me."

"Bray . . . den," I heard again. It sounded the same, a strange, thin call, like a voice riding on the wind.

"Gotta go," he repeated, backing away as though something very strong was pulling him, despite his resistance. He spun around to slip home through the hedges and then paused and turned back to me. "Can you come out for a walk tonight?"

"A walk?" I smiled with a little incredulity. "A walk?"

"Too simple an invitation?" he asked, and looked around. "It's going to be a very pleasant evening. Haven't you ever read Thoreau? 'He who sits still in a house all the time may be the greatest vagrant of all.' Are you afraid of walking? I don't mean a trek of miles or anything. No backpacks required."

"I'm not afraid of walking," I shot back. "And I love Thoreau."

He lifted his arms to say, *So?* And then he waited for my response.

"Okay, I'll go for a walk. When?"

"Just come out. I'll know."

"Why? Are you going to hover between the hedges watching and waiting?"

He laughed. "Just come out. A walk might not sound like very much to you, but I've got to start somewhere," he said.

"Start? Start what?"

"Our romance. I can't ask you to marry me right away."

"What?"

He laughed again and then slipped through the bushes. I stepped up to them to look through and watch him go into his house, but he was gone so quickly I didn't even hear a door open and close.

How could he be gone so fast? I leaned in farther and looked at his house, a house that had been empty and uninteresting for so long it was as if it wasn't there. I felt silly doing what he had been doing, gawking between the hedges, studying his house, checking all the windows, listening for any conversations. It's the very thing I criticized him for doing, I thought, and I stepped away as if I had been caught just as I had caught him.

He was very good-looking, but there was something quirky about him. Nevertheless, it didn't put me off. In fact, it made him more appealing, a lot more alluring than the other boys my age that I knew. No matter how hard most of them tried, there was a commonality about them, about the way they dressed and talked. As Dad would say whenever the topic of young romance came up, "I guess no one has yet set the diamonds in your eyes glittering, Amber Light." That was his nickname for me, Amber Light.

No, none of the boys in my school had set the

diamonds in my eyes glittering, I thought, and which one of them even would think to mention Henry David Thoreau as a way of enticing me to do something with him?

Looking around, I agreed that it truly would be a beautiful late June night. I laughed to myself. Almost any other boy I knew would have asked me to go to the movies or go for a burger or pizza or simply hang out at the mall as a first date. But just go for a walk? I didn't think so.

I started back to my house. I thought I might finish some summer required reading and then help Mom with dinner. It was Friday night, and Dad kept the store open an hour or so later than usual.

I was almost to the porch steps when I stopped and looked around. There was something odd about the day. What was it?

It was too quiet, I realized. And there were no birds flying around or calling, just a strangely silent crow settled on the roof of Brayden's house.

We lived on a cul-de-sac, so not having any traffic wasn't unusual, and it wasn't unusual to see no people outside their homes for long periods of time. Yet the stillness felt different. I didn't even hear the sounds of far-off traffic or an airplane or anything. It was as if I had stepped out of the world for a few moments and was now working my way back in.

And despite the brilliant sunshine, I felt a chill surge through my body. I embraced myself and hurried up the stairs. I paused on the porch and looked at the house next door. Up in what I now knew was Brayden's bedroom window, the curtains parted.

But I didn't see him.

I didn't see anyone.

And then a large cloud blocked out the sun, dropping a shroud of darkness over the entire property. It happened so quickly it was as if someone had flipped a light switch. Under the shroud of shadows, the neighboring house looked even more tired and worn. The new residents hadn't done anything yet to turn it from a house into a home. It doesn't take all that long for a house to take on the personalities and identities of the people living in it, but this house looked just the way it had before I saw the Matthewses move into it.

It was as if the whole thing, including my conversation with Brayden, was another one of my fantasies, another movie Dad thought I lived in. I could hear him laughing about it and then doing his imitation of me walking like someone in a daze, oblivious but content.

All of this from a short conversation with a new neighbor who made me realize how different I was from any of the girls I knew. None would have agreed to go for a walk with a stranger so quickly, especially at night. Why had I? Where was my sensible fear of new boys, especially one who talked and behaved as he had? I could just hear my friends when and if I told them. *You agreed to go for a walk with a stranger who was spying on you like that? Crazy.*

Maybe I was.

But when I looked at my reflection in the window, I thought I saw diamonds glittering in my eyes.